Two wonderful Regencies at one wonderful price!

Isabella
The English Witch

Praise for the Novels
of Loretta Chase

"Poignant, beautifully written." —Mary Jo Putney

"Well-matched, appealing protagonists, a lively, witty writing style, and excellent dialogue . . . compelling."
—*Library Journal*

"One of the great voices in romance."
—*Romantic Times*

"Witty banter . . . terrific scenes . . . sparks fly . . . sensual." —*The Denver Post*

"The dialogue and witty writing are a delight and the characters are lovingly created."
—*The Atlanta Journal-Constitution*

"Great reading." —Pamela Morsi

Isabella

and

The English Witch

Loretta Chase

A SIGNET BOOK

SIGNET
Published by New American Library, a division of
Penguin Group (USA) Inc., 375 Hudson Street,
New York, New York 10014, U.S.A.
Penguin Books Ltd, 80 Strand,
London WC2R 0RL, England
Penguin Books Australia Ltd, 250 Camberwell Road,
Camberwell, Victoria 3124, Australia
Penguin Books Canada Ltd, 10 Alcorn Avenue,
Toronto, Ontario, Canada M4V 3B2
Penguin Books (N.Z.) Ltd, Cnr Rosedale and Airborne Roads,
Albany, Auckland 1310, New Zealand

Penguin Books Ltd, Registered Offices:
80 Strand, London WC2R 0RL, England

Published by Signet, an imprint of New American Library, a division of Penguin
Group (USA) Inc. *Isabella* and *The English Witch* were each originally published
by Avon Books, a division of HarperCollins Publishers.

First Signet Printing, November 2003
10 9 8 7 6 5 4 3 2 1

Isabella copyright © Loretta Chekani, 1987
The English Witch copyright © Loretta Chekani, 1988
All rights reserved

 REGISTERED TRADEMARK—MARCA REGISTRADA

Isabella

and

The English Witch

Isabella

1

"Disappeared!" the earl repeated, in a dangerously quiet voice. "What the devil do you mean, 'disappeared'? Seven-year-old girls don't just vanish."

The thin governess trembled. She had never heard *quite* that tone from her employer before, and would have preferred that he shout at her, for his suppressed fury was far more terrifying. Edward Trevelyan, seventh Earl of Hartleigh, was an extremely handsome man whose warm brown eyes had often set Miss Carter's forty-year-old heart aflutter. But at the moment, the brown eyes glittered down at her with barely contained rage. And though his voice was low, the temper he so carefully controlled showed in his long fingers, which now, as he questioned her, were angrily raking the thick dark curls at his forehead.

Stammering and tearful, Miss Carter tried to explain. She'd taken Lucy to the circulating library. They'd then decided to see if they could find a ribbon to match Lucy's newest and favourite dress. Miss Carter had stopped only a moment—to admire the cut of Lady Delmont's pelisse as that grand and rather scandalous personage entered the shop across the street. Apparently, the governess had let go of Lucy's hand. Not that she actually *remembered* letting go—she was so sure she hadn't—but she must have, for when she looked down beside her, Lucy was gone. She had searched all the nearby shops to no avail.

Turning away from the governess in disgust, Lord

Hartleigh began snapping orders to his household. He dispatched a dozen servants to comb the streets, then called for his carriage, his hat, and his cane. When the door finally closed behind him, the remaining inhabitants commenced to whispering among themselves; all but Miss Carter, who, teary-eyed and red-faced, scurried to her room.

It served him right, he thought as the carriage made its way down the street. This was what came of being so hasty to hire a governess for his young ward. Yet Miss Carter had not seemed the least bit flighty—and she had come highly recommended. Even Aunt Clem had agreed with his choice of governess for Lucy. Well, actually, she had said, "I suppose she'll do—but *it* won't do, you know, Edward." Whatever "it" was. Clem had a tendency to fix you with her eye in that all-knowing way of hers and then utter cryptic pronouncements in the tone of a sybil.

Life certainly had changed when one must go to Aunt Clementina for advice, he thought ruefully. There was a time when he'd made his way across the Continent, close to Napoleon's forces, in search of information which would save English lives. But twice he'd endangered his own. He would be dead now if it hadn't been for Robert Warriner. Instead, it was Robert who was gone. News of his death had been delivered a month ago by the house-keeper's husband, along with a letter . . . and a seven-year-old girl.

The letter was short, and he had read it often enough to know it by heart, especially the closing lines:

It is rather a great favour I ask, my friend. But the doctors have no hope for me, and Lucy will be left alone in the world. Our housekeeper and her husband have offered to take her in, but they are hard-pressed to care for themselves, and I cannot place such a burden on them. For old times' sake, then, will you watch over my daughter as though she were your own?

2

Watch over her. And now the child was lost in the middle of a busy and dangerous city. Oh, Robert, forgive me, he thought.

"Mademoiselle Latham, you must trust me. I do not cut the gowns simply *à la mode*. I cut *pour la femme*. But see, how can you judge?" Nudging her recalcitrant customer along to the dressing room, Madame Vernisse continued in that sing-song of hers. "First you must try it on, and then we shall see what we shall see."

Although she obediently followed the modiste into the dressing room, everything within Isabella cried out for escape, and she had the mad urge to dash back out of the room, the shop, and London altogether. Back to Westford and the home she and her widowed mother had made with quiet, sensible Uncle Henry Latham. Life in Westford might be dull at times, and Aunt Pamela's social climbing a source of embarrassment, but there at least Isabella was not the object of constant scrutiny and speculation. Why, Lady Delmont had stared at her quite rudely, and for no other reason than that Isabella was Maria Latham's daughter. Well, let her stare. Mama may have disgusted her family by marrying Matthew Latham—a mere cit—but she was Viscount Belcomb's sister, nonetheless. And unlike her brother Thomas, Maria Latham was quite plump in the pocket. Isabella raised her chin just a little as Madame Vernisse slipped the blue silk gown over her head. And when the modiste stepped back with a little smile to admire her handiwork, Miss Latham bravely looked into the mirror.

It was lovely. It was also a trifle . . . shocking. "Madame Vernisse, are you certain . . . ?" She motioned vaguely toward her bosom, an alarming expanse of which was in public view.

"It is perfection on you," the modiste replied. "Of course the fashion is much more *décolleté* than this—but as I tell you, I do not cut just for the fashion; I cut also for the *femme*."

It was amazing what a new frock could do. The

elegantly cut gown clung to her slim figure, calling attention to previously well-concealed curves. The rich blue deepened the blue of her eyes and made her complexion seem creamily luminous. Even her dingy blonde hair had taken on a golden luster. She looked, in fact, almost *pretty*. Not that it signified how she looked. After all, this was her two cousins' first Season. Isabella need only look well enough to appear with them in public.

Thinking of the coming months, Isabella suddenly felt weary. She would have much preferred to stay quietly in the country with Uncle Henry and Aunt Pamela Latham, her late father's brother and his wife. It was, as Mama had said, a great bore to go where one was not welcome. But Aunt Pamela wanted her eldest daughter, Isabella's cousin Alicia, to have a London Season; it was hoped the girl would find herself a titled husband. And so Mama had been persuaded to write to her estranged brother, the viscount, with a simple proposal: The Lathams would be pleased to finance a Season for the viscount's daughter, Veronica Belcomb, if, in return, Alicia Latham was also provided entrée into Society. It was a bitter pill for the Belcombs to swallow, but they had little choice, as Aunt Pamela well knew. "Barely a feather to fly with," she'd said. "Veronica's dowry is nothing to speak of—and what good is even that, I ask you, when they can't afford a Season for her?"

The blue gown was gently removed, and an emerald-green gown took its place, to be in turn replaced by a series of walking dresses, and a deep forest-green riding habit.

"You see?" said Madame Vernisse. "The colours of the sea, and of the cool forest. And so your hair glows and your eyes sparkle. Was I not correct?"

Isabella nodded agreement, but her mind was on her family and its problems. And when her ever-restless abigail, Polly, offered to run some errands while the fittings continued, Isabella dismissed her with an absent nod.

4

To soften the blow to the Belcomb pride, Maria Latham had proposed herself as chaperone. This would save Lady Belcomb the embarrassment of being seen too much in public with a girl whose father was engaged in *trade*. And, of course, it would save her ladyship the expense of a new wardrobe—for it was one thing to take advantage of her only chance to see her daughter properly launched; it was quite another to be beholden to the Lathams for the very clothes on her own back. And so the offer was accepted, and Lady Belcomb had little to do but tolerate the three Lathams under her roof and smooth the way for her sister-in-law—whom society had not seen in twenty-seven years. The rest would be up to Maria.

It was unfortunate that Mama and Uncle Henry had both insisted on Isabella's coming to London as well. Of course, it was too much to expect her languid parent to be in constant attendance on a pair of "tiresomely energetic schoolroom misses," even though she had proposed herself as nominally their chaperone. The real task would fall to Isabella. And after all, they were under tremendous obligation to Uncle Henry, for had he not welcomed them into his home after Papa died, and helped them rebuild the fortune Matt Latham had speculated away? She came back to the present with a jolt when she heard the modiste's voice at her ear.

"So, mam'selle, I think we have done well for today. And by the end of the week, we shall have the others ready as well. *Bon*. It is a good day's work, I think." Nodding approval at her own artistry, Madame Vernisse was so pleased with herself that she even condescended to help Isabella back into her somber brown frock, although the modiste did frown as she fastened up the back and tactfully suggested that it be given—as soon as possible—to Polly. And then she hustled out of the dressing room, and promptly began scolding her assistants, who weren't looking busy enough to suit her.

Several pins had come loose from Isabella's hair, and she stopped to make repairs before leaving the dressing room. As she glanced in the mirror, she was a little disappointed to see a dowdy spinster again, and sighed. A tiny sigh echoed it, and she looked around quickly. No one in the room but herself. Then she heard it again. It seemed to be coming from a pile of discarded lining fabric that had fallen into a corner. Evidently it had been a busy day for the modiste; normally, the shop was scrupulously tidy.

Cautiously, Isabella stepped toward the fabric. It moved slightly, and emitted a whimper. As she moved closer, she saw a tiny hand clutching a red ribbon. She lifted a corner of the fabric to find a little girl, asleep. As Isabella gently smoothed the tousled brown curls away from her face, the child, who had somehow managed to sleep through the earlier chatter in the dressing room, awoke to the caress. "Mama?" she whispered. Then, when she realized that this was a stranger, the tears welled up in her eyes. "She's gone away," she told Isabella, and began sobbing as though her heart would break.

When Madame Vernisse reentered the dressing room to see what had become of her latest client, she was shocked to find that young lady seated on the floor, cradling a little girl in her arms.

"And so your name is Lucy, is it?" Isabella inquired, some minutes later, after the child had been comforted and her tears bribed away with sweets. "Is that all of your name?"

"Lucy Warriner," the girl answered.

"Oh, blessed heavens. It is Milord 'artleigh's ward," cried Madame Vernisse. "They will be frantic for her. I must send someone *immédiatement*. Michelle! Michelle! Where is that girl when you want her? Not here. Never here. Where does she go, I ask?"

"Polly will be back in a moment," Isabella replied, calmly. "We'll send her." Turning back to Lucy, she asked, "And how did you get lost in the dressing room?"

"Oh, I didn't get lost," the child replied. "I excaped."

"What did you escape from?"

6

"That lady. Miss Carter. My govermiss."

Suppressing a smile, Isabella continued, "I should think Miss Carter would be worried sick about you, Lucy. Don't you know it's wrong to escape from your governess? She's there to take care of you."

"Papa took care of me. He didn't get a govermiss. Even after Mama went to heaven, he took care of me himself. I don't need a govermiss. But I miss my papa." As tears threatened again, Isabella gave up her questioning and offered hugs instead.

When another quarter hour had passed and Polly had not yet returned, Isabella determined—despite Madame Vernisse's vociferous Gallic protests—to escort the child back to the earl's house herself. So it was that she emerged from the mantua-maker's shop with Lucy's hand in hers and nearly collided with a very tall, very well-dressed, and very angry gentleman.

"I beg your—" he began irritatedly. His eye then fell upon Lucy, who was attempting to hide in Isabella's skirts. "Lucy! What is this?" He glared down at Isabella from his more than six-foot height. "That child is my ward, miss," he growled. "I assume you have some explanation."

Stunned by this unexpected rudeness, and not a little cowed by his size, Isabella stared, speechless, at him. She felt Lucy's grip on her hand tighten. This was the girl's guardian? The poor child was terrified of him.

"Perhaps you would be kind enough to release her," Lord Hartleigh continued, reaching for Lucy's free hand. Lucy, however, backed off.

At this Isabella found her tongue. "I will be happy to—if in fact you are her guardian, and if you would calm yourself. You're frightening her."

Hearing the commotion, Madame Vernisse hurried to the entrance. "Ah, Milord 'artleigh. You have arrived at the *bon moment*. We have found your ward!" she cried triumphantly.

"So I see," he snapped. "Then perhaps you would be

7

kind enough to tell your assistant to let me take the girl home."

Madame Vernisse looked from one to the other in bewilderment. "But Milord—"

"Never mind," said Isabella. She was shaking with anger, but endeavoured to control her voice as she bent to speak to the little girl. "Now, Lucy, your guardian is here to take you back home."

"I don't want to," Lucy replied. "I excaped."

"Yes, and you have worried Lord Hartleigh terribly. You see? He is so distraught that he forgets his manners and blusters at ladies." This last caused the earl's ears to redden, but he held his tongue, sensing that he was at a disadvantage. "Now if you go nicely with him, he'll feel better and will not shout at the servants when you get home."

"You come, too," Lucy begged. "You can be my mama."

"No, dear. I must go back to my own family, or they'll worry about me, too."

"Then take me with you," the child persisted.

"No, dear. You must go back with your guardian. You don't want to worry him anymore, do you? Or hurt his feelings?"

The notion of this giant's having tender feelings which could be hurt was a bit overwhelming for the child, but she shook her head obediently.

Isabella stood up again. Reluctantly, the little hand slipped from her own, the brown curls emerged from their hiding place, and Lucy allowed her guardian to take her hand. "I'm sorry I worried you, Uncle Edward," she told him contritely. "I'm ready to go home now." As they began to walk to his carriage, she turned back briefly, to offer Isabella one sad little wave good-bye.

The missing Polly reappeared in time to see the earl lift Lucy into the carriage and then climb in himself. "Oh, miss," she gasped. "Do you see who that is?"

"Yes. It is Lord Hartleigh. And it is time we went home."

"A spy, you know, miss," Polly went on, hurrying to keep up with her mistress, who was clearly in a tizzy about something. "They say he was a spy against those wicked Frenchies. And they caught him, miss, you know, and threw him in prison, and he nearly died of the fever there, but he got away from them. And then came back half-dead. Laid up for months, he was. And all for his country. He's a real hero—as much as My Lord Wellington—but it's a secret, you know." She sighed. "Lor', such a handsome man. The shoulders on him—did you notice, miss?"

"Handsome is as handsome does," snapped her mistress. "Do hurry. I promised to be home for nuncheon."

Lord Hartleigh had ample time to consider his behaviour during the silent ride home. After all, one could not expect Lucy to speak. She was always sad and withdrawn, and speaking to her only made her sadder and more withdrawn. It was only at Aunt Clem's that the child had shown any sign of animation. But Lucy had not been the least shy with that strange woman at the dressmaker's. Good heavens, she'd even asked her to be her mama! As he recalled the scene, he was filled with self-loathing. What an overbearing bully he must have looked!

His behaviour that day had been abominable: Cold and impatient with Miss Carter, he had gone on to make a complete ass of himself at the modiste's. But he had been turned inside out by worry—and guilt. That hour he'd spent searching the shops had seemed like months. Robert had trusted his child to him. And after less than a month, this trusted guardian had proceeded to misplace her. I take better care of my horses, the earl thought miserably.

He glanced again at Lucy. She was the image of her father, with her hazel eyes and curling brown hair, but she had none of his spirit. Not that her recent losses

9

weren't enough to stifle the spirit of even the liveliest child. Pity for her welled up in him, and he felt again the same frustration he'd felt for weeks: He could not make her happy. Why had she run away? And what was so appealing about this dowdy young woman that Lucy wanted to go away and live with her?

Of course, that fair-haired young woman had *not* been the dressmaker's assistant; he should have known it as soon as she opened her mouth. He'd seen her somewhere before . . . at one of those dreary affairs to which Aunt Clem was forever sending him in search of a suitable wife? Or had it been somewhere else? No matter. He should have known by her dignity and poise that she was a lady. But he'd been too distraught to think clearly. He smiled ruefully. Distraught and blustering. Just as the young lady had explained so patiently to Lucy. He had simply reacted—out of fear for Lucy's safety and, it must be admitted, hurt pride. It was not agreeable for a man who'd taken responsibility for the safety of whole armies to discover that he could not adequately oversee the care of one little girl. Nor was it agreeable to see the way the child had clung to that woman, or the reluctance with which she had come to him.

But it was to be expected, was it not? Lucy wanted a mama; so badly that she would pick up strange women on the street. Well, if a mama was what was required, he would supply one. It was not pleasant to think of, but when before had he shunned a dangerous mission?

Dangerous. That was it. The woman he'd seen early the other morning, dashing across the meadow on that spirited brown mare. Good God! Lord Belcomb's niece.

Looking up timidly, Lucy saw that her guardian's face was turning red. Fearful of a scolding, she shrank farther into her corner.

2

"Do my eyes deceive me, Freddie? Or has a new face actually entered this redoubt of redundancy, this mansion of monotony?"

Young Lord Tuttlehope looked toward the doorway where Lord and Lady Belcomb had just entered, accompanied by a nondescript blonde young woman in a modish blue gown. Blinking away his friend's literary flourishes, he responded to the few words he understood. "Matt Latham's daughter. Belcomb's niece. Got a few thousand a year."

Basil Trevelyan lifted an eyebrow. "How few?"

"Ten or twenty. Maybe more. Matt blew up most of what he had in one scheme or another. But Henry took them in hand. Clever man, Henry. Shrewd investor."

Basil's interest increased. His topaz eyes half-closed in apparent boredom, he nonetheless watched the trio make their way through the room until they settled in a corner with Lady Stirewell and her daughter.

"Indeed. Charming girl, don't you think?"

Freddie blinked uncomprehendingly at his friend. The two had been at Oxford together and maintained a friendship ever since; yet it may safely be supposed that Lord Tuttlehope understood only a fraction of what his companion said or did. However, he made up for his slow wit with a strong loyalty. "Barely met the girl myself," he replied. "Introduced at the Fordhulls' dinner. Sat the other end of the table. Never said a word. Don't blame her. Meal was abominable. Fordhulls never could keep a good cook."

"My dear Freddie," Basil drawled, still watching the young woman, who had embarked upon a lively conversation with the youngest Stirewell daughter, "it does not require an intimate relationship to ascertain that a young woman with an income of more than ten or twenty thousand a year must perforce be charming. And to those already considerable charms, one must add the mystique of scandal. Didn't her mother up and run off a week after her come-out?"

"Heard something about it. Never said whom she'd run off with. Six months later sends word she's married the merchant—and breeding," Freddie added with a blush.

"I thought Belcomb had washed his hands of his regrettable sister and her more regrettable spouse and offspring. Or hath ready blunt the power to soothe even the savage Belcomb beast?"

His speech earning him two blinks, Basil translated, "Is his lordship so sadly out of pocket that he's reconciled with his sister?"

The light of comprehension dawned in Lord Tuttle-hope's eyes. "Thought you knew," he responded. "Bet at White's he'd be down to cook and butler by the end of the Season. Staff got restless—hadn't paid 'em in months. Then the Lathams turned up."

"I see." And certainly he did. No stranger to creditors himself, Basil easily understood the viscount's recent willingness to overlook his sister's unfortunate commercial attachment. Though he was barely thirty years old, Basil Trevelyan had managed to run up debts enough to wipe out a small country. Until two years ago, he'd relied on his uncle—then Earl of Hartleigh—to rescue him from his creditors. But those halcyon days were at an end. Edward Trevelyan, his cousin, was the new Earl of Hartleigh and had made it clear, not long after assuming the title, that there would be no further support from that quarter.

Basil had remained optimistic. Edward, after all, regularly engaged in extremely risky intelligence missions abroad, and one could reasonably expect him to be killed off one fine day soon—and, of course, to leave title and fortune to his more deserving cousin. Disappointingly, upon his father's death Edward had dutifully ceased risking his life on England's behalf, and had taken up his responsibilities as a Peer of the Realm.

"Not in the petticoat line myself, you know," Freddie remarked, "but she ain't much to look at. And past her prime. Closer to thirty than not."

His friend appeared, at first, not to hear him. Basil's attention was still fixed on the viscount's party. It was only after Lady Belcomb finally let her glance stray in his direction that he turned back to his companion, picking up the conversation as though several empty minutes had not passed.

"Yes, it is rather sad, Freddie, how the uncharming poor girls look like Aphrodite and the charming rich ones like Medusa."

Lord Tuttlehope, whose own attention had drifted longingly toward the refreshment room, recalled himself with a blink. After mentally reviewing the stables of his acquaintances and recollecting no horses which went by these names, he contented himself with what he believed was a knowing look. "Always the way, Basil, don't you know?"

"And I must marry a Medusa. It isn't fair, Freddie. Just consider my thoughtless cousin Edward. Title, fortune, thirty-five years old, still a bachelor. Should he die, I inherit all. But *will* he show a little family feeling and get on with it? No. Did he have the grace to pass on three years ago, when the surgeons, quite intelligently, all shook their heads and walked away? No. These risky missions of his have never been quite risky enough."

"A demmed shame, Trev. Never needed the money either. Demmed unfair."

Basil smiled appreciatively at his friend's loyal

13

sympathy. "And as if that weren't exasperating enough, along comes the orphan to help spend his money before I get to it. And to ice the cake, I now hear from Aunt Clem that he's thinking to set up his own nursery."

"Demmed shame," muttered his friend.

"Ah, but we must live in hope, my friend. Hope of, say, Miss Latham. Not unreasonably high an aspiration. Perhaps this once the Fates will look down on me favourably. At least she doesn't look like a cit—although she obviously doesn't take after her mother. Aunt Clem said Maria Belcomb was a beauty—and there was something odd in the story . . . oh well." Basil shrugged and turned his attention once more to the pale young lady in blue. Seeing that the viscount had abandoned his charges for the card room, he straightened and, lifting his chin, imagined himself a Bourbon about to be led to the guillotine. "Come, Freddie. You know Lady Belcomb. I wish to be introduced to her niece."

Miss Stirewell having been swept away by her mother to gladden the eyes and hearts of the unmarried gentlemen present (and, possibly, to avoid the two ne'er-do-wells who seemed to be moving in their direction), Isabella Latham tried to appear interested as her aunt condescended to identify the Duchess of Chilworth's guests. Her grace's entertainments were famous, her invitations desperately sought and savagely fought for, with the result that anyone of the ton worth knowing was bound to be there, barring mortal illness. "Even the Earl of Hartleigh," Lady Belcomb added. "For I understand he's given up those foreign affairs and is finally settling down."

Isabella's cheeks grew pink at the mention of the name. Though a week had passed since that scene at the dressmaker's shop, she still had not fully recovered her equanimity. True, the earl had called the day after the contretemps to make a very proper, though cool, apology—to which she had responded equally coolly and properly. Lady Belcomb had absented herself for a moment (to arrange for Veronica's "accidental" appearance), and Mama, as usual, was resting. Thus none of the family had been privy to their conversation. However, the footman who stood at the door guarding her reputation had heard every syllable, and Isabella wondered what exaggerated form the drama would have taken by the time it reached her aunt's ears.

"Indeed," that lady continued, "it was most astonishing, his coming to call. But he *is* rumoured to be seeking a wife. And Veronica was looking well Tuesday, was she not?"

"She is always lovely, Aunt," Isabella replied. She had not missed the increased warmth in the earl's manner when Veronica entered the room. Nor, when those haughty brown eyes had been turned upon herself, had she failed to notice how he'd sized her up, appraising her head to toe and, in seconds, tallying her value at zero. Not that it mattered. It was her cousin's Season to shine. At the advanced age of twenty-six, Isabella Latham need not trouble her head with the appraisals of bored Corinthians.

"It is a pity their come-out had to be put off so late," Isabella continued, forcing the handsome and haughty earl from her mind. "For Alicia and Veronica might have been here to enjoy this with us."

"Well, well. Alicia could not be presented to society in a wardrobe made by the village seamstress."

"That is true, Aunt."

"And after all," Lady Belcomb went on, not noticing the irony of her niece's tone, "there will be festivities enough. Although this is quite a brilliant assembly—did you notice Lady Delmont's emeralds? I was not aware her husband . . . but then, never mind." Reluctantly, she turned from contemplation of the jewels on Lady Delmont's bosom. "Veronica will have plenty of time to shine, along with your other little cousin. It is but two weeks until their little *fête*."

Her niece looked down to hide the smile quivering on

her lips. While the viscountess had accepted the exigen-
cies of fate and graciously agreed to oversee preparations
for the come-out ball, she was compelled to reduce the
situation to diminutives. Thus the come-out for Veronica
and Alicia, costing the Lathams many hundreds of
pounds, was a "little" party, and Alicia herself, though
three inches taller than Lady Belcomb, a "countrified little
thing."

"That reminds me; we must be certain Lord Hartleigh
has been sent an invitation. It would be mortifying, after
his thoughtful visit, to discover he had not been
included."

Isabella, who had, purely on her cousins' account,
resisted the temptation to hurl said invitation into the fire,
assured her aunt that all was well. With the coming ball,
Lady Belcomb's responsibilities would cease, according
to the agreement. It would then be up to Isabella to
accompany her cousins on their debutante rounds, for
Mama was bound to be too tired, or too bored. Idly,
Isabella wondered where she would fit in. Would she be
required to sit with the rest of the gossiping duennas and
attempt to converse with them? Did chaperones dance?
The music had just begun, and Isabella looked down to
see her white satin slippers tapping in time, as though
they had nothing to do with respectable chaperones. Were
chaperones allowed to tap their toes to the music? Smiling
at the thought, she looked up to meet a pair of glittering
topaz eyes gazing down at her.

"Lady Belcomb, Miss Latham, may I present Mr Basil
Trevelyan," Lord Tuttlehope announced, with the air of
one introducing Prinny himself. And she should count
herself lucky, Freddie thought. Mousy old thing for Basil
to be leg-shackled to, poor chap, with all his romantic
poetical nonsense.

But Mr Trevelyan was looking at the possible answer
to his prayers. Hadn't Aunt Clem warned him that few
parents would care to put their daughters' fortunes in his

hands? "Even I should not," she warned him, "though I do believe you'll outgrow it in time."

The Lathams, however, might be willing to trade some thousands of pounds to improve their position in society. Thus he had determined to find the unprepossessing Miss Latham charming, and to charm her in turn. After suitably flattering Lady Belcomb and hinting at the eagerness with which her daughter's entry into society was awaited, he left her to Freddie, and turned those strange amber cat eyes back to Isabella. "I understand, Miss Latham, that you are new to London."

"Quite new—unless you count my first visit, at the age of five."

"Ah, you were cruel to abandon us. Hard-hearted even at such a tender age. But we must be thankful that you have relented toward us at last, and must endeavour to correct your previously poor opinion."

Perhaps it was the penetrating gaze which unsettled her, as she conjured up the image of a five-year-old *femme fatale*. At any rate, her careful poise cracked for a moment, and laughter escaped. It was a low, husky laughter; a haunting, inviting sound, completely out of place in this large public gathering.

Her aunt cast a puzzled glance in her direction. Was Isabella flirting with Trevelyan? Lady Belcomb would have wagered half her stable (were it still hers to wager) that her niece had no more knowledge of flirtation that she had of flying. No matter. Trevelyan's expensive tastes were well known, and he was decidedly an unsuitable match for Veronica. This niece (and any of her Latham cousins, in the bargain) was welcome to him; at least *his* family was unexceptionable. That settled, the viscountess resumed her debate with Lord Tuttlehope over the merits of certain horses of their acquaintance.

For his part, Basil was pleasantly surprised: The Answer to His Prayers had a mind not quite so dull as her face. As he stared, puzzling, at her, Isabella, imagining that she had committed some sort of indiscretion by laughing at her interlocutor's extravagant comments, blushed. She did not know that the combination of heightened color and sparkling blue eyes transformed her face from nothing remarkable into something which, in a quiet way, was rather lovely. Nor did she have any inkling of why her laughter caused people to stare.

Indeed, she would have reddened to her fingertips had she known the thoughts it conjured up in the tawny-haired young man with the unsettling eyes. Basil found himself wondering what it would be like to hear that laughter rather closer to his ear, in more intimate circumstances. The thought cheered him enormously, as he studied her with increased enthusiasm—and curiosity. "Miss Latham," he continued, his voice dropping almost to a whisper, "I declare you are cruel still. Here am I so deadly serious, so monstrous earnest, and I succeed only in throwing you into fits of laughter. Perhaps, though, you suspect I am attempting to turn your head with flattery. Perhaps for some nefarious purpose?"

This time she controlled herself, and only a twitching at the corner of her mouth hinted at laughter. "I suspect," she replied, "only that you are talking arrant nonsense and that you do so to amuse yourself. Is London life so dull, then?"

"Dreary as an Irish bog—until now," he whispered, bending closer. Then, noticing that Lady Belcomb's attention had drifted back to them, he straightened and, in louder tones, requested the honour of a dance.

Stunned by the suggestiveness of his tone, Isabella could not think how to refuse him politely. She knew the relatively straightforward methods of business, but society and its ways were painfully indirect and convoluted. Certainly she could not tell him that he made her uncomfortable. There was something so . . . *feline* about him: the tawny hair and those strange amber eyes that slanted upward like a cat's. Eyes that were watchful, penetrating, even under their bored, sleepy lids.

"I promise I shan't bite," he said with a smile, leading her to the dancing area. "Although the ton may, if you have not been approved to waltz."

Although she privately felt that, considering her advanced age, such approval was rather irrelevant, Isabella assured him that she had been deemed worthy by the Almack's patronesses. And then she wished she had not, for while she had been taught, along with her cousins, to waltz, it had never before struck her as so perilous an enterprise. Dancing so close to him, her hand on his shoulder, she realised with some shock that he was more powerfully built than he seemed. He was only a few inches taller than herself, and slender, yet he had a supple strength which belied his slight appearance. The hand at her back was uncomfortably warm, despite his gloves, and it pressed her closer than seemed entirely necessary.

Apparently unaware of his partner's unease, Basil made light conversation (interspersed with generous doses of flattery), interrogating her about the sights she had seen thus far and her impressions of the city and its people. He was chagrined to learn that she had not yet been to Hyde Park, had not visited the Tower or the Mansion House or the Guildhall. *She* was chagrined to learn it was his intention to correct these oversights, personally. It was useless trying to explain that in attending to her two young cousins, she would have precious little time for sightseeing. "We'll take the little girls along with us, Miss Latham" was his rejoinder.

"They are not precisely little. . . ." she began uncomfortably.

"I daresay not. Nor am I—precisely—concerned with improving upon their education. I am not acting from purely altruistic motives; quite the contrary. But you see, society requires that we observe certain proprieties, and I believe I should prefer the superfluous company of your cousins to that of disapproving aunts."

Again she blushed. His tone seemed to lace every sentence with innuendo. "Mr Trevelyan," she protested,

19

"I wish you would recall that I am a mere naïve from the country and haven't the faintest notion what you are about. Did I somehow give you the impression that I am in the habit of roaming about strange cities in the company of strange men?"

The music stopped.

"I rather wish that you were," he murmured as he released her. "But at any rate, I would hope to become less of a stranger."

"So you have made abundantly clear. Are all London gentlemen as forward as you?" she asked as he escorted her back to her aunt.

"I daresay not. But I am rather a dreadful young man, as Aunt Clem is sure to tell you." He indicated a large woman of about sixty, who had just joined Lady Belcomb. Dressed in mauve, and wearing an ornate turban which made her appear to tower over the rest of the guests, the Countess Bertram was an awesome sight. Her height, her grand bearing, the slightly hawkish cast of her nose, all put one in mind of a warrior goddess. Indeed, she seemed to lack only armour and shield to complete the picture.

"Lady Bertram," said the viscountess, "I do not believe you have met my niece, Isabella Latham."

Both ladies pronouncing themselves delighted, Lady Bertram turned her sharp brown eyes to Basil. "So the prodigal returns," she drawled. "Miss Latham, I see you have already had the dubious honor of meeting my disreputable nephew."

"Aunt Clem! How very naughty of you. And here I have gone to heaps of trouble to present myself to these ladies in the most respectable light possible."

"A physical impossibility," the lady retorted. "I must warn you against him, Miss Latham. This disrespectful scapegrace has not deigned to call on his aunt in three weeks. And a woman of my age has not many weeks to waste." In punctuation, she tapped his arm with her fan and sat down.

"I am sure Mr Trevelyan cannot be as dreadful as you say," Lady Belcomb felt compelled to remark, though she firmly believed otherwise.

"Honourable chap, must say," added Lord Tuttlehope.

"And what do *you* say, Miss Latham? Or has he exercised his wicked charm upon you too?"

It occurred to Isabella that Lady Bertram had a pretty fair knowledge of her nephew—and possibly of the perils of dancing with him. As she turned to that lady to respond, she thought she glimpsed something sympathetic in the face beneath the mauve turban.

"I am afraid he has," Isabella answered. "But as he has just this moment himself assured me that he is perfectly dreadful, and as blood is thicker than water, I must submit to family opinion."

"Isabella!" her aunt exclaimed in disapproval. But Lady Bertram waved her away much as she would an annoying insect.

"Intelligent gel, Lady Belcomb. There's more sense in her than in both my nephews combined. Speaking of which, here comes the other one, to honour us with his company."

The turban nodded in the direction of Lord Hartleigh, who was disconcerted to find five sets of eyes fixed upon him. One pair in particular, sparkling like a matched set of aquamarines, unnerved him. His demeanour belied his discomfort, however, and only his aunt noted the minute crack in the calm social mask. He greeted the two elder women warmly, bowed courteously to Isabella, and coolly acknowledged his cousin and the young baron.

The next quarter hour was not the most agreeable of his life. Lord Hartleigh had intended only to stop for a minute, primarily to greet his aunt, but upon discovering that Basil had planted himself among the party and refused to depart, the earl stubbornly stood his ground. He was not certain why. Basil always irritated him, and he knew his own continued existence was an irritation to Basil. In addition, he was uneasy attempting to make

21

conversation with Miss Latham, who had seen him at his worst—he, the Earl of Hartleigh, known for his unerring courtesy.

But there was Basil, hovering over the young lady like one of those jungle cats hovering over its prey. Nonsense. His mind was working like some silly romance. But somehow she had aroused the earl's protective instincts, and he hesitated to leave her with no sentinel in attendance but his unpredictable aunt, since it was clear that Lady Belcomb either didn't know or didn't care that Basil was a fortune hunter.

Why he should concern himself, he didn't know. All he knew was that he wanted his cousin as far away from Miss Latham as possible. And since Basil appeared to have no intention of budging, Lord Hartleigh determined to remove the young lady. Therefore, to both their surprise, he asked her to dance.

Although the earl had done nothing to endear himself to her, she accepted his offer with an enormous sense of relief, as a means of escaping his cousin's overpowering presence. She was dismayed to find herself attracted to the . . . creature. Never in her life had she been so showered with poetic compliments, and she had begun to think that his "wicked charm" might indeed turn her head, for there was something so tempting about wickedness, wasn't there? Rakish young men were rather like forbidden sweets: You knew they weren't good for you and you'd suffer for trying them, but they were so very . . . seductive. What a monstrous improper train of thought! Gladly, she put it aside as Lord Hartleigh's arm encircled her waist.

This, too, was a waltz, but her response to this cousin was very different. Wasn't it odd that the one who had responded so warmly to her had frightened her, while this one, towering over her, who had insulted her and then dismissed her with cool arrogance, did not intimidate her in the least?

They were alike in some ways. There was a family

22

resemblance in the high cheekbones, the clear strong angles of the face, the long aristocratic nose. But there was nothing feline about Lord Hartleigh. His deep brown eyes, though betraying no emotion, appeared to gaze frankly at the world. His was not the catlike grace of his cousin but, instead, the assertive grace of the athlete. And the strong arm around her waist made her feel protected, rather than threatened.

Stiffly, they conversed about the weather, the temperature of the room, the attractive decorations. Then, quite abruptly (and to his own surprise), the earl changed the subject. "Miss Latham," he observed, "I do believe we got off on the wrong foot." Her startled eyes met his for a second, then looked away—into his neckcloth. However had he managed the perfect creases of that complicated arrangement? "I was rude to you once," he went on, "and compounded it with an equally rude apology. May we close the curtain on that unfortunate scene and begin fresh? My behaviour was inexcusable, but I ask that you dismiss it—as an unaccountable aberration."

"You were concerned about your ward," she replied.

"That is no excuse—"

"It is forgotten," she interrupted, smiling up at him.

It was Lord Hartleigh's turn to feel relieved, but his feelings were complicated by a new sensation: As he watched her face change with that smile, he felt a rather uncomfortable constriction in the general vicinity of his chest. Her eyes had softened to a deeper, smokier blue, and the curve of her lips was deliciously sensual. Several mute seconds passed as he gazed down into this suddenly very appealing face; seconds in which some unexpected notions drifted into his head. But he managed to recall himself in time. Clearing his throat, he told her that she was very . . . *kind*.

"And how *is* Lucy?" she asked.

This led to a discussion of various domestic details which Hartleigh had never previously considered. His bewilderment was plain—though he seemed to speak of it with humour—and when he quoted Aunt Clem's declaration that "the poor child was bored to tears in that stuffy house," Isabella laughed. The notion of this handsome, sophisticated, perfectly mannered, perfectly dressed Peer rendered helpless by a seven-year-old was highly diverting. As soon as she had shown her amusement, however, she regretted it; he would not like to be laughed at. Several couples dancing nearby were staring at them, and her face flushed crimson.

"I beg your pardon, Lord Hartleigh," she apologised hastily. "I am not used to being in such fine company, and fear I have a case of the nervous giggles."

He barely heard her, having become preoccupied with the constriction that was making it so difficult to breathe. Surely that deliciously wicked sound had not come from *her*. A host of even odder notions crowded into his brain, and he was very hard put to squash them. At length he managed to mutter something about a "perfectly absurd situation," and the dance, mercifully, ended.

It was a greatly unsettled Earl of Hartleigh who returned to his home that evening. He had gone to Lady Chilworth's ball specifically for the purpose of finding a mama for Lucy. Aunt Clem had provided a list of eligible females, and he had attempted to dance with all of them. He was determined to perceive this search for a mama as a mission: dangerous, yes, but critical to his ward's wellbeing. And to some extent he had begun to feel a bit of the excitement his political missions had engendered. But tonight he found himself unable to attend to his partners' conversation. He would gaze into their faces, expecting that each in turn would trigger some special response, and then would feel unaccountably irritated that they did not. He heard other laughter, and it irked him. Thus, as he guided one after another eligible young beauty through one after another dance, his attention would stray to a not-especially-pretty young lady in blue. And it was most provoking that Basil did not leave her side the entire evening.

3

The following day, the Belcomb home, already in chaos with preparations for the ball, was further disrupted by a parade of elegant gentlemen. Word of Isabella's material charms had long since made the rounds, but the attentions of the Trevelyan cousins the night before had considerably raised her market value among impoverished younger sons. Her dance card had rapidly filled from the moment that her dance with Lord Hartleigh ended. Basil, who had hoped for a relatively clear field, had not been pleased, but contented himself with hovering nearby and ingratiating himself with her aunt.

Today, then, all those who'd been privileged to dance with her made their courtesy calls. Lady Belcomb was not altogether happy at first with Isabella's sudden popularity, for it would appear to decrease her own daughters' prospects proportionally. But then, as she noted that the callers—*with one unfortunate exception*—were of straitened financial circumstances, her equanimity was restored, and she greeted them, if not graciously, then at least with forbearance. Unfortunately for the earlier callers, she was the only one to greet them. 'Isabella's customary morning ride (an exercise she took primarily to escape the quarrelling servants) had been later than usual, and she hadn't yet changed. Thus, Lord Hartleigh, among the early arrivals—and the *one unfortunate exception*—was disappointed.

Fortune smiled on Basil, however. He arrived shortly

after Isabella joined her aunt. All the other callers had left or were compelled to leave (the proper half hour having expired), and he and Freddie had the field to themselves. Having paid his courteous compliments to Lady Belcomb, Basil had just settled himself comfortably to flattering an uncomfortable Isabella when there was a tumult at the door.

Sounds of merriment drifted into the room, to be followed in another moment by Alicia Latham, who was trailed by an anxious abigail. Laughingly, the girl scolded her maid. "No, no, Mary. It is quite all right. We can see to that later, but first I must see Isabella—" She stopped short as she saw the two gentlemen in the room.

Lord Tuttlehope, who had been detailing the merits of a pair of greys seen the previous day at Tattersall's, stopped midsentence, and his jaw dropped at the vision before him.

Alicia's windblown straw-coloured curls tumbled recklessly from her bonnet. Her green eyes sparkled; her cherry-pink lips were moist and parted slightly in surprise. Blushing at the sight of the two elegant gentlemen, she was, all in all, so pretty and innocent and fresh that even the most jaded rakehell could not fail to be charmed.

But where women were concerned, Lord Tuttlehope could hardly be termed *jaded*. An excruciating shyness had resulted in a virtually complete ignorance of the other sex. But, shy as he was, he couldn't help staring. The green eyes met his for a moment, then quickly lowered in confusion. In that moment, his heart gave a great leap and abandoned him.

Basil quickly rose and bowed, then found he had to nudge his friend to attention. After a second's paralysis, Lord Tuttlehope remembered what his limbs were expected to do.

"I'm so sorry. I didn't know—oh dear," Alicia stammered.

"Don't be silly, love," her cousin replied as she rose

from her seat to lead the hesitating girl into the room. "You've finished your shopping early, I see."

"Yes. Oh dear. I did not mean. . . ." She glanced quickly at the gentlemen and blushed again.

Since Lady Belcomb simply sat there gazing at the girl with disapproval, Isabella made the introductions. Basil pronounced himself charmed, Lord Tuttlehope stammered something incomprehensible, and Isabella, with polite apologies, excused herself, and took her cousin away.

Had Basil not been quite so irritated at Isabella's casual leavetaking and a little stunned by her cousin's good looks, he might have noticed his friend's condition sooner. As it was, the viscountess made several attempts to return to discussion of the greys, and several times elicited only stuttering and confused replies from Freddie, before Basil noted anything amiss. He then calmly took over the conversation, brought it to a graceful close, and took his friend and himself away.

"It really is too bad of you, I must say," Basil remarked as they made their way to their club.

"Eh?" Lord Tuttlehope awoke from his stupor with a start.

"I said, it really is too bad of you."

"What is? Were you speaking, Trev?" Freddie shook his head. "Must have been woolgathering. Too bad— what?"

Basil clapped his friend on the shoulder and laughed. Freddie endured this for a moment, then responded, with some annoyance, "I say, Trev, fellow deserves to know what the joke is."

"Ah, my friend, I fear the joke is on me. I had new hopes. For a vision entered my life, complete with fortune, but younger, prettier, and, I think, far more susceptible than the icy Miss Latham. But what do you think? I look over and see that my bosom bow is struck on the spot, instantly besotted. Did you ever hear of worse luck?"

* * *

"Oh, Bella, what lovely gentlemen. I've never seen such cravats. Are they in love with you?"

"The gentlemen or the cravats?" Isabella asked, laughing.

Alicia's wardrobe for the Season covered every stick of furniture in her room: walking dresses, pelisses, gowns, slippers, shawls. All had been inspected, tried on, exclaimed over, and the two women now sat on the bed, resting from their exertions.

"But are they? They're so handsome." Alicia sighed. "And so beautifully dressed."

"Yes, they're impeccable," replied her cousin. "And not, you goose, in love with me. Why, I'm quite an elderly lady. Your ancient companion, remember."

"Fah." The blonde curls shook a negative. "The only reason you're not married is that you've been buried in the country all this time taking care of us and helping Papa. I knew the minute you came to London you'd have dozens of *beaux*. Even Papa said so—when Mama was not about. Polly said at least a dozen came today. Even the Earl of Hartleigh." She pronounced this last with some awe.

Isabella's heart gave a little flutter, but she took a deep breath and told her cousin, "That is only etiquette, my dear."

This was not sufficient explanation, for her cousin must hear all the particulars of the Duchess of Chilworth's ball.

"And the dark-haired one, who looked so shy?" Alicia asked, shyly enough herself, when her cousin had finished detailing the previous evening.

"Where Mr Trevelyan goes, there goes Lord Tuttlehope. I assure you he hasn't the remotest interest in me."

"Oh." Alicia became thoughtful. If Lord Tuttlehope could have seen the tiny wrinkle between her brows or the charming way she chewed delicately on her lower lip, his fate would have been sealed.

But fortunately for that bewildered lord, there was only

Isabella to see. She was curious about this interest in Basil's loyal companion, but had no opportunity to question her cousin, for Veronica entered then, demanding to see all the new finery. The wardrobe was displayed again, and Isabella soon left the two girls to their fantasies.

As the younger girls waited in happy anticipation of their special day—practising the most killing ways of plying their fans, inventing witty retorts to imagined compliments, investigating the festive arrangements, and generally getting in the way of the servants, by whom they were frequently in danger of being trodden underfoot—Isabella continued to make the rounds with her aunt.

She went again to Almack's, where she found herself at the center of a small but enthusiastic circle of admirers. This was in marked contrast to her previous experience within those hallowed halls, when only the patronesses' benevolent tyranny had saved her from sitting out the entire evening. Then she had been matched up with bored but polite gentlemen who did their duty, suppressed their yawns, and then went on to more attractive game. Now, however, she was stalked not only by the persistent Basil, but also by a select group of other gentlemen with pockets to let.

In the course of her engagements, she had regularly found Lord Hartleigh gazing down at her in that tight, courteous, yet somehow disapproving way of his. He would never spend more than a few minutes with her—perhaps a single dance, or some polite social chatter. And then he would be gone. She noticed that he divided his attention among half a dozen young ladies, all of whom had similar credentials: good looks and breeding. Their bloodlines were no doubt as impeccable as those of his horses, and she wondered sardonically if he were evaluating them in the same way he would his cattle. So far, Lady Honoria Crofton-Ash seemed to have the advantage of her competitors, for he had danced twice with her this evening and brought her a lemonade. Isabella shrugged.

The Marriage Mart was no different from Tattersall's. She only hoped that this cold and calculating business would not hurt Alicia. More than once she'd pictured her young cousin being snubbed by some overly fastidious member of the ton. More than once she had shook her head over her Aunt Pamela's obsession with status.

Well, it was too late now. Alicia would be thrust into Society, whether Society liked it or not, and she would have to endure the snubs and the slights. But Alicia was resilient. And intelligent. Perhaps less naïve than she seemed—for she had an uncanny knack of knowing when Lord Tuttlehope was visiting, and would manage to be seen. Perhaps she would simply pass by the door, conversing with her cousin or her abigail. Or perhaps she would stop in for a moment with an innocent question. These glimpses of the young lady seemed to leave Lord Tuttlehope in a state of stupefaction. He was inevitably tongue-tied if Alicia spoke one word to him.

Isabella smiled. There was evidence of mutual interest. If only Lord Tuttlehope's presence did not automatically signal that of his ever-present companion. Isabella awoke from her musings as Basil's shadow fell upon her. He had come to claim his dance. Ah, well. One must make the best of it, for Alicia's sake. If Basil persisted in trailing herself, then Lord Tuttlehope would not be far behind.

"Is it as dull as all that?" Basil asked as they took their places in the set.

"I beg your pardon?"

"Dull, Miss Latham. Though all at Almack's must *feel* it—at least those of any sensibility—you are the only woman here who clearly appears to wish she were elsewhere. In fact, so determined are you to be elsewhere that you travel there in spirit. It must be very dull indeed."

Firmly, Isabella brought her mind back from Alicia and *her* future to the present moment. "I assure you, sir, that this is all highly entertaining, and I was only tucking some observations into the back of my mind for later contemplation."

"Fortunate woman. I must do my contemplating now, and make the best of too few, too short hours," he murmured, as the requirements of the dance separated them.

She felt his eyes follow her as she moved away, and when, once or twice, she caught the intensity of his glance, she was forced to look away, suddenly feeling hot and angry. He had no business to stare after her in that way. It was most improper, and made her conspicuous.

When she rejoined him, she spoke out bluntly. "Mr Trevelyan, it is most inconsiderate of you to stare at me in that hungry fashion. Lady Jersey is watching you and is bound to make a story of it."

"*Hungry*, Miss Latham?" he queried, raising an eyebrow. "Your language is certainly most . . . most refreshing," he added with a chuckle.

"I have an unhappy habit of saying what I think—"

"And I an unhappy habit of showing what I feel." The topaz eyes narrowed, looking more catlike than ever. "But I beg your pardon. I did not wish to embarrass you."

Although she somehow suspected that he *did* wish to embarrass her—or at least to make her uncomfortable— she dared not contradict. She was afraid that he was only too eager to explain his motives. Abruptly, she changed the subject, asking after his aunt.

"Oh, Aunt Clem's quite well—in her element, in fact— busy at finding a suitable wife for my cousin." Another would not have noticed the way her smile froze on her face, but Basil was watching her closely. He noted her reactions as carefully as he would those of his opponents in a card game.

"Is it so massive an undertaking?" she asked, wondering why she suddenly felt unwell.

"She's been after him to marry since he returned to England. Responsibility, you know. Carry on the title and all that. But it's only since Lucy came into his care that he's shown any signs of enthusiasm." He glanced in the direction of a handsome young woman in ivory silk with whom Lord Hartleigh was conversing. "Though it may be too early to tell, I'd wager that Lady Honoria will be the lucky bride."

Reluctantly, Isabella followed the direction of his gaze. Yes, the earl *was* paying rather special attention to Lady Honoria. But then, what concern was it of hers?

Basil did not like what he was discovering, but persisted, nonetheless. For one, her discomfort compensated somewhat for his; and for another, well, he preferred to know exactly how the land lay. Thus she was relieved of hearing about Lord Hartleigh's matrimonial prospects and the wagers at White's on Lady Honoria's chances only when the dance separated them. When it finally ended, she urgently longed to be home again.

Unfortunately, the viscountess was enjoying a comfortable cose with Lady Cowper and clearly had no thoughts of departing. And then, as Basil brought Isabella back to her aunt, Lord Hartleigh appeared. This time Isabella was struck by the animosity between the two men. Oh, they were impeccably polite to each other, but the air fairly crackled with the tension between them. And when Lord Hartleigh led her away to dance, she knew that an angry pair of cat eyes followed them, watching every move.

Lord Hartleigh was not happy. He'd found himself walking toward her in spite of every intention of going in the opposite direction. For to speak with her meant enduring the presence of his insufferable cousin. Each and every time he'd seen her, he'd vowed to stay away. Yet each and every time, there she'd be, with Basil hovering nearby or stalking her with his eyes—and she looked so . . . so . . . in need of rescue, confound it! So the earl, relinquishing Lady Honoria to his rivals, would rescue Miss Latham, only to meet with, not gratitude, but an uneasy acquiescence. As though she mistrusted him as well. In fact, it was much the way in which Lucy looked at him. . . . Isabella's voice called him from his meditations. "I beg your pardon?" he responded.

"I was asking after your ward. I trust she's well?" Why did he ask her to dance if he was going to be so inattentive? Really, it was too bad. One cousin making her conspicuous by trailing her like a shadow and staring her out of countenance, and the other barely aware that she was alive—even when he danced with her.

"Quite well," he assured her. "At least in health," he added, after a moment. She was nonplussed to find him gazing down seriously at her, and wondered at the flicker of pain in his dark eyes. "I have little experience of children, yet it's clear to me she's unhappy." *Lonely*, he wanted to say. But to admit that the child was lonely, when everyone from the butler to the lowest scullery maid doted upon her, implied something wanting in himself.

"I think it's to be expected. The child still misses her parents, and her world now is vastly different from the world she knew. It will take time."

As she smiled up at him reassuringly, his throat tightened. "I hope that is all it is. . . ." His voice trailed off as he forced himself to look elsewhere—anywhere else—and thus met Lady Honoria's quizzical glance. He didn't mention that Lucy had asked for "Missbella" several times. Or that she had taken to none of the doting staff as she had taken to Miss Latham. Or that he had berated himself a thousand times for his behaviour that day at the dressmaker's—for had he been kinder and more patient, he might have learned Miss Latham's secret, and would not have this sad little ghost wandering aimlessly among her new toys and frocks. He mentioned none of these things, but they gnawed at him as he asked after Miss Latham's family and sought her impressions of London, now that she'd spent some weeks in town.

He was surprised to discover that her view of London had little to do with the balls and routs, the dinner parties and assemblies, the fashions and latest *on-dits* that occupied the minds of the women on his aunt's "list."

Isabella Latham was a different species, who spoke intelligently of books and art and even—gracious heavens!—politics; who could not for the life of her remember Brummel's latest witticism or Caro Lamb's most recent misbehaviour.

As he led her back to her aunt (and the infernal Basil), he puzzled over this odd young lady. Clearly, she had no thought of herself as a belated debutante—in marked contrast to Miss Elderbridge, now in her seventh Season. To Isabella Latham, this London visit was a practical matter of overseeing her cousins' first Season: no more, no less. Apparently, her small crowd of admirers was, to her, a puzzling nuisance, and (except for Basil) about as troublesome to her equanimity as ants at a picnic. A curious, clear-headed, competent female, he thought . . . so why did she look so devilish unhappy and vulnerable as Basil bent to whisper in her ear?

4

"Well, my love, it seems you have decided to take the shine out of your cousins' debut by snatching up all their *beaux* beforehand."

Isabella looked up in surprise from the neat hem she was stitching. She had thought her mother was asleep on the sofa among her many pillows. "Mama, whatever are you talking about?"

Maria sighed. "It wants less than a week until our grand ball, and the house has been so overrun with your suitors that one hardly knows where to turn. I have not had a moment to myself to think."

What her mother possibly needed to think about, Isabella could not fathom. Lady Belcomb and Isabella had shared all the labour of preparing for the ball and making peace among the staff, while Mama's sole contribution had been an opinion of the colour of Alicia's gown.

"I do not recollect our being overrun by anything but servants, Mama. They are always so dreadfully in the way."

"Don't be coy with your mother, Isabella. Here is Mr Trevelyan stopping by nearly every single day with his friend—the one who prates so interminably of horses." Another sigh. "Your father never showed the least interest in horses, Isabella, I am relieved to inform you."

Nor had he ever evidenced much interest in anything else, thought Isabella. Not his business, nor his daughter; and barely his wife—though (she glanced at the still-beautiful woman reclining languidly among the pillows) Mama may not have been the most stimulating of companions.

"At any rate," her mother went on, "as if that were not fatiguing enough, they are soon followed by a host of dandies and other fine gentlemen. And then comes that tall young man—Lord Hartleigh, is it?"

Isabella nodded, and bent quickly again to her sewing.

"And he was here again today, asking after you. I'm afraid your Aunt Charlotte is quite vexed."

A quick scan of her parent's features showed no evidence of distress at this state of affairs.

"He stayed only a few minutes, you know. And Charlotte was very cross with me after. You must not run about London breaking hearts, my love. It is very tiresome for your cousins." A throaty chuckle accompanied this last. It was a sound very much like that which had not long ago so overset the Earl of Hartleigh—who might have been relieved to learn that it was merely a family trait (like hair colour), and not some cruel siren trick.

"I'm sorry, Mama. I shall try to restrain myself in the future."

"Do, love. You have no idea how your aunt frets about these poor gentlemen. And I do sympathise. One can become quite suffocated with all these *beaux* sighing about the house." In illustration, she sighed once again.

"Mama," said Isabella firmly, "for one, if anyone is to suffocate us, it is the servants. For another, you know as well as I do that nobody is sighing, and certainly not on my account. And for a third—"

"I pray you will not indulge in higher mathematics, Isabella—"

"For a third," her daughter went on, "this is a light spring shower compared to the deluge we may expect after Veronica and Alicia come out. And for a fourth— Mama, you are the most dreadful tease!"

"Yes, I know, darling. I can't help it." Mrs Latham

pulled herself up to a sitting position and invited her daughter to join her on the sofa. As soon as they were settled, she said, patting Isabella's hand, "We must speak seriously, my dear. About two matters. First, you were very naughty not to tell your aunt about your first meeting with Lord Hartleigh. She has got wind of it from the servants and told me that when he came today she did not know where to look, she was so moritifed." A low chuckle indicated the extent to which Maria sympathised with her sister-in-law.

"Oh dear, Mama. I'm sorry I didn't tell you, but I was sure there would be a fuss and I just wanted to forget the whole episode." Isabella flushed. "I do hope Aunt Charlotte said nothing to Lord Hartleigh about it. . . ."

"No, my love, she said all she had to say to me; at considerable length, I might add. But no matter. Apparently Lord Hartleigh bears no grudges." She gave her daughter a sidelong glance. "As I am sure you do not, Isabella—for it is quite wicked, you know, to bear a grudge."

"Yes, Mama."

"But to the other matter. What of his charming cousin? From what I have heard, he suffers from an excess of creditors. Not that there is anything so unusual in that." Maria paused, apparently distracted by another thought. "And if there is affection, of course—"

"I believe he is simply after my money," Isabella responded softly.

"In that case, perhaps you might send him about his business?"

"Perhaps."

"Unless you are fond of him," Maria added, as though she had not heard her daughter's reply.

"No."

"At any rate, you do not lack *other* suitors."

"Mama, they are *all* in love with my income," Isabella cried. "Every impoverished gentleman in London has put his name on my dance card and made his call. I have had so many offers to ride in the park that I could spend the next ninety years in curricles, with my feet never once touching the earth.'' Though she spoke ironically, her eyes began to glisten with tears, which she determinedly withheld.

"How peculiar that so many impoverished young men should have so many curricles,'' her mother noted abstractedly.

"I am sure the money lenders do not find it peculiar at all.''

"You are right, my dear. Money lenders understand everything, even the most inscrutable. But that was not my point; or was it? No. What I meant was that many of these young gentlemen are perfectly respectable—although, admittedly, unfortunate in having elder brothers. But Mr Trevelyan's reputation, from what I can gather—and that is mostly from the servants, for your aunt prefers to look smug—at any rate, his reputation is not entirely, shall I say, 'sunny'?''

Isabella gave a rueful little smile. "Perhaps that's why I find him the least abhorrent.''

"My love, you are not turning romantic, are you? You have not been reading *Childe Harold* again? For you know your aunt will not have Byron's works in the house.''

Isabella laughed in spite of herself. "No, Mama. It is just that if I must choose among fortune hunters, I would rather they be clever and charming—and wickedly attractive,'' she finished with a nervous giggle.

"I see.''

Isabella had the feeling that her mother saw rather more than what had been spoken, but could not read in her face what it was.

"Well, then, go back to your stitching, though how your eyes can bear it I shall never know. I hope you will not wrinkle up on me, darling. Ah well, I suppose there's no stopping you. At any rate, I shall not tease you for at least the next hour. I am fearfully tired and must have a nap."

The wickedly attractive gentleman in question was in the process of being scolded—exactly like a naughty child—by his only partially indulgent aunt. He lounged carelessly against the ornate mantelpiece as, for the eighteenth time in one hour, she stressed the necessity of his getting his affairs in hand. In vain did he protest, his face absurdly innocent, that this was exactly what he'd been doing.

"Attempting to entrap a well-bred lady worth twenty of you in intelligence and good sense is not quite what I had in mind, you horrid boy." Lady Bertram was glaring at him most ferociously, but he did not cower; instead, he managed (though it hardly seemed possible) to look even more innocent. He was imagining himself a persecuted Muslim facing the Spanish Inquisition.

"Aunt Clem," he told her patiently, "I have been so prodigiously proper that it fair makes my hair stand on end. I have not spent a minute with the young woman when there were not at least half a dozen others standing watch in the same room—if not her aunt or her mother or her giggling cousin, then the servants. Belcomb has more footmen than he has furniture, you know. If anyone should feel entrapped, it should be myself."

This was met with a derisive snort.

"And I do not see, dearest Aunt, why you are so concerned with Miss Latham. Why, you are quite maternal—a veritable lioness defending her cub. Frightfully disloyal of you, you know. After all, *I* am your cub, or rather, one of them."

"Stuff! I like the gel, and won't see her made miserable for life. Bad enough her mother made such a mull of things."

While Basil did not find this response especially flattering, he was too aware of his own failings to contradict. More than likely he *would* make a wife miserable, and her misery would increase in proportion to her intelligence. That promised Miss Latham a thoroughly wretched future. Unfortunately, Basil hadn't enough conscience to overcome his self-interest. While he knew of several wealthy—and vulgar—peageese who might look upon him with favour, he had already spent much precious time cultivating Miss Latham and couldn't afford to start afresh with someone else. He would have preferred, certainly, to see a bit more evidence that she was succumbing to his charm. The creditors were beginning to raise a nasty clamour; and the way she watched Edward when she thought no one was looking was not at all encouraging to their interests. Even less encouraging was that Edward watched her in the same manner. This made Basil anxious, a state of mind entirely foreign to his nature and, oddly enough, not the least bit refreshing.

He ran his fingers through his tawny hair, making its carefully arranged windblown appearance more genuinely tousled. He did wish Aunt Clem would leave off scolding. For here was a tailor's bill in his pocket which, if not paid up by tomorrow, would render his current wardrobe his final one. And in frayed collars, limp neckcloths, and threadbare waistcoats, one could not expect to charm wealthy young ladies or allay the fears of their relatives. He offered his aunt a lazy smile. "Ah, her mother. But you know, Aunt, I suspect she hadn't the energy to make a mull of things. They must have simply mulled themselves."

"You know nothing of it. She was quite a lively girl in her youth. But her life in later years wore her down. As it will, you know." Lady Bertram spared her nephew a meaningful look before returning to her reminiscences. "What a pity she and Harry Deverell couldn't have made a match of it. You know," she mused, partly to herself, "I never did understand what made her run off with Latham."

Basil was all curiosity, the tailor momentarily forgotten. "You mean there was something between Mrs Latham and the new viscount? The one everyone thought dead all these years?''

The sharp brown eyes considered him, and a sad, patient look passed briefly across the aristocratic features. ''No, that's not what I meant at all. They grew up together and were like brother and sister. And even if their feelings had been more romantic, it would have been impractical, of course. Neither family was well off.''

''You see, Aunt? Even you realise that one can't live on affection alone. The grocer must be paid. . . .''

''And the tailor, too, I suppose. Don't play the innocent with me, you villainous boy,'' she went on, in response to his upraised eyebrow. ''My sources tell me that Mr Stutts refuses to extend you any further credit.''

''Aunt Clem sees all, knows all,'' replied the villainous boy, with some relief.

''Of course I do, you young jackanapes. Well, then, what will it take to pacify him?''

Now *this* was interesting, Basil thought, as he strolled down Saint James's. Harry Deverell and the languid Mrs Latham had grown up together. And yet, when the story about the mysterious viscount had come up in conversation, she had barely attended. But then, whenever she did put in one of her rare appearances, she seldom seemed to attend to anything. And every time Basil saw her, he was hard put to connect her darker, striking beauty with her daughter's pale, nearly nondescript features. Must take after the father, he thought. And yet that side of the family, too—if Alicia was the rule, rather than the exception—certainly was more strikingly handsome. Well, one could not always rely on family resemblances. Although that had sealed the mysterious viscount's fate, hadn't it? Basil cast his mind back, trying to recall the story that had had London in such an uproar . . . when was it, a year ago?

Harry Deverell, youngest son of Andrew, Viscount Deverell, had gone to sea. Evidently, he was not the clerical type of younger son, for he had decided on a distinctly hazardous mode of getting his living. But his career was cut short when he fell overboard in a sudden storm off the Cornish coast, and he was presumed drowned.

It turned out, however, that he'd been able, by some miracle, to make his way to shore, where he was rescued by some folk or other—smugglers, no doubt, as they all were thereabouts. Severely weakened by his efforts, he'd fallen seriously ill, and when the fever and delirium finally left him, several weeks later, he could remember nothing, not even his name. Only his sailor's garb offered any clue, and he returned to his trade, hoping this would help him recall his lost past.

From then on, he'd travelled the globe as an obscure sailor, never crossing paths with any who might recognise him. It was only when he finally settled in India—some five years ago—that he had contact with any of his class. But by then, Harry Deverell had been so long thought dead that even those noting a family resemblance would not connect him with the retired Captain Williams.

And then it happened that one who had seen him commented on this resemblance to an acquaintance about to assume a post in the same Indian town. Upon arriving, Sir Philip Pomfret had promptly looked up Captain Williams, remarked the resemblance himself, and instituted an inquiry into the captain's history. The timing of the accident at sea, coupled with the physical evidence . . . All the evidence pointed to one conclusion. But when confronted with this information, Captain Williams joked it all away, saying that dozens of men had been lost off the Cornish coast in one endeavour or another, and he was as likely the son of a low smuggler as of the late viscount.

Yet there was nothing low or common about Captain Williams. And when word eventually reached Sir Philip that the two eldest Deverell sons had been killed in a carriage accident, he took the captain aside and made a passionate appeal to his sense of duty: "If you are *not*

Harry Deverell, then you have nothing to gain or lose. But if you are, it is your duty to see to the welfare of your brothers' widows and daughters, who have next to nothing to live on."

Thus Captain Williams was persuaded to write to the family solicitor. That dedicated old gentleman, struck by the familiar handwriting, promptly embarked on a long and grueling voyage to India. He recognised Harry immediately. And his persuasions, coupled with those of Sir Philip, at length convinced the captain to assume his rightful identity and the title. Commitments in India made it impossible for the new viscount to return home with the solicitor, but he was to follow in some months. And the Deverells—what was left of them—were expecting him back anytime now.

Handsome, dashing—so Aunt Clem had described Harry Deverell, dwelling at such length on his fair hair and captivating blue eyes, which darkened or lightened with his mood (not to mention his tall, slim, muscular physique), that Basil had to tease her about nursing a secret *tendre* for young Harry. But Aunt Clem had only smiled wickedly, and reminded her nephew that she'd had her own handsome devil to reform.

Yet this attractive fellow had never married. Too wily to be caught in the parson's mousetrap?

"Maybe too honourable," Aunt Clem had replied. "For how could he know he was not already wed?"

"In that case, he does not seem to have exerted himself to discover his supposed widow—or anything at all about his lost past."

Aunt Clem had shrugged, saying that one did not know all the circumstances.

No, thought Basil, one did not. But it would be amusing to find out about Mrs Latham's former playfellow. At the very least, it would be a diversion from this, so far, unsuccessful assault on Isabella Latham's heart. And after all, there may be other ways to win her golden guineas than by winning her heart.

5

About the time a certain Bond Street tailor's troubled
spirit was being soothed by an injection of guineas, Lord
Hartleigh (his own tailor in a permanently ecstatic state)
was strolling in the park with a most fetching unmarried
young lady. No groom or maid trailed behind the attractive couple, and one or two persons, who had ventured
into the park at this early hour for interesting purposes of
their own, stopped to stare.

Lord Hartleigh was feeling rather foolish, for his
companion did not seem to find him stimulating. Nor did
her new cherry frock, brilliant with ribbons and lace,
cheer her. Her dark curls tumbled about a most lachry-
mose visage, and she plodded sadly and silently along
beside him, looking up obediently from time to time as
he pointed out various sights.

"Are you tired, Lucy?" the earl at length inquired.

"No, Uncle Edward," she murmured.

"Perhaps you'd prefer to visit another place?"

"No, thank you, Uncle Edward."

Blast! There was no pleasing the child. In response to
Aunt Clem's scathing remarks regarding "that suffocating
house," he had begun trotting his ward from one London
sight to another. But nothing had lifted her spirits—not
the balloon ascension, not Astley's Circus, not even the
British Museum with its odd assortment of curiosities. In
every case, she accompanied her handsome guardian in
the same obedient but sad, limp manner.

44

"Perhaps you'd like to play with the other children," he suggested in desperation, gesturing toward a distant section of the park where several nurses stood guard over their small charges.

Lucy dutifully looked in the direction he indicated, and was about to utter another polite refusal when she spied a young woman sitting, sketching, beneath a tree. "It's Missbella!" she exclaimed, looking up eagerly at her guardian. She began tugging at his hand. "May we see her, please, Uncle Edward? It's *Missbella!*" With unexpected strength, the tiny hands were pulling him in the direction of the tree, and he found himself obediently following.

When they were yet several yards away, Lucy broke free of her guardian's grip and raced toward the young woman. She flung herself upon the startled Isabella, nearly knocking the wind out of her with the eagerness of her hugs as she cried, "I found you! I found you!"

"Why, Lucy," the lady gasped, "what a lovely surprise."

"Lucy, I'm afraid you are crushing Miss Latham."

Isabella looked up from the mass of tumbled curls and cherry ribbons to see the earl frowning down at her. Her pulse quickened, and she blushed. "Lord Hartleigh. Good morning."

In prompt response to her flushed cheeks came the odd sensation in his chest again. As if this affliction were not bad enough, it was now aggravated by the fierce tweak of Envy. Lucy's face glowed as she held on tenaciously to her friend. She loosed her embrace only enough to begin an animated cross-examination. She asked a hundred questions and answered them all herself. She demanded to know where Isabella had been and why she had not come to see her. And she repeated for Isabella's enlightenment all that the earl had taught her about the park and its environs. The child's sudden loquaciousness and uninhibited display of affection toward Miss Latham was most surprising—and not altogether flattering to Lord Hartleigh.

Isabella seemed to sense this. After responding as well as she could to this barrage, she suggested that Lucy release her so that she might converse with her guardian, who was, she noted, being rather impolitely ignored. Thus gently chastised, Lucy let go. As Isabella began to struggle to her feet, Lord Hartleigh waved her back.

"Pray do not rise on our account, Miss Latham. I see you had been working most comfortably until our somewhat precipitate arrival." That said, he gracefully dropped down to sit beside them, careless of the grass stains and dirt that would later torment his valet.

"I'm afraid it is not work, precisely," Isabella explained, greatly flustered by the proximity of his long, lean body. "Usually I ride in the morning. But my groom could not be spared today. So here I am, making ladylike little sketches. It offers a change." In response to his quizzical look, she went on, nervously, "We are in a turmoil with preparations for my cousins' debut, you see, and I occasionally must come away, to escape the servants and restore my sense of perspective."

"And no doubt to escape the press of morning callers," he added ironically, and then promptly regretted it. He *wished* she would not blush so easily. It had a mischievous effect on his breathing apparatus, which seemed to have suddenly shut down.

"I—I believe I mentioned that I am unused to fine company," she stammered. There was that stern gaze again. Why must he look so very disapproving?

"I beg your pardon, Miss Latham. I did not mean to imply. . . ." But he didn't know what he didn't mean, and found himself at a loss to continue.

Fortunately, Lucy was subject to no such hesitation. She was oblivious to the grown-ups' discomfort and had grown impatient for the lady's attention. "I missed you so much," she announced, once more flinging her arms around Isabella's neck. "Uncle Edward takes me to see

46

so many things." She went on, to her guardian's amazement, to list every sight and repeat, virtually word for word, all that he had told her. He never believed she'd been attending to his commentaries at all. Yet his face did not betray his surprise; it seemed only to grow more stern.

"And now you must come, too," the child insisted. "You will come, won't you?"

Since the earl did not appear nearly so eager as his ward, Isabella was puzzled how to respond. "Well, you see, Lucy," she began, hesitantly, "we are very busy at home just now, and I am not quite sure when it would be possible. Perhaps in a few weeks. . . ." Her voice trailed off, her cheeks pink again. At this, the child's eyes began to glisten dangerously, and Isabella hugged her closer. "And besides," she added softly, "you did not think perhaps that your guardian would like to have you all to himself?"

The hazel eyes looked out from beneath the curls to that gentleman's stern visage, and then turned back to gaze at Isabella in incredulity. Her expression did not escape her guardian, who managed to force out, past whatever inside was trying to strangle him, that he would be honoured if Miss Latham would consent to accompany them one day; and that if there were time in her busy schedule, perhaps she would join them in their visit to an exhibition of landscapes. "I thought the scenes would be more interesting to Lucy than fashionable portraits," he explained. "I—I know she misses the country." His expression softened as he regarded his ward, and Isabella glimpsed something in his eyes that made her feel a twinge of sympathy.

"I should be delighted."

"Is tomorrow too soon?" Lord Hartleigh ventured.

Tomorrow was not too soon. A time being settled upon, and arrangements made for the earl's carriage to stop for her, Lord Hartleigh endeavoured to dislodge his young companion. "Lucy, I am certain Miss Latham

47

cannot breathe when you clutch at her in that way.'' He
did not add that, Lucy having disarranged Miss Latham's
hair, various blond tendrils had escaped to tickle a delicate
pink ear in the most enticing fashion. . . . He collected
himself with a start. "We must leave her in peace now—
else she may not wish to see us again tomorrow."

Miss Latham was not destined to be left in peace,
however, for her Nemesis (so Basil had come to style
himself) was not far behind his cousin. He had come to
the park in response to an urgent message from an elegant
young woman with creditors of her own to soothe. When
Mr Trevelyan informed the lovely Celestine—with beautifully phrased regret—that the creditors simply had to wait,
this interesting meeting had come to an abrupt end. He
therefore decided to devote the remainder of a fine
morning to planning the next stage of his assault on the
Answer to His Prayers. A broken heart, he decided, was
best. He would simply commence to pine away, and let
guilt lead her to the altar. He had been staring at the
pond, wondering whether an attempted suicide by
drowning would be overly theatrical, when his eye caught
a flash of colour from the trees beyond. He made out—
at some distance—his cousin, engaged in a *tête-à-tête* with
Miss Latham. Now here was an unseemly state of affairs:
his Intended conversing with a fashionable gentleman and
no abigail in sight. Unless you counted as a chaperone
the moppet bouncing up and down on her bosom.
Thinking of that bosom, he gave a little sigh. Then,
realising there was no one about to hear it, he left off
sighing and backed away into a more sheltered spot from
which he might await his own turn.

He hadn't long to wait. Edward rose; the moppet
ceased bouncing and was led away. Livelier than she was
last time I saw her, Basil thought as he watched her skip
along next to her guardian.

As soon as they were out of sight, he sauntered
casually around the pond and, in no apparent hurry, made

his way to Isabella's side. A glance back told him that they were not in view of the diverse nurses and their charges.

Not having noticed his approach—no doubt preoccupied with the recent conversation and, in particular, the earl's warm brown eyes—Isabella looked up, bewildered, at his greeting.

"I see you, too, have decided to take advantage of this brilliant morning," Basil observed, peering down over her shoulder at the neglected sketch pad. "But you will make a long job of it without your pencil." And without waiting for an invitation, he flung himself down on the ground beside her.

She had not yet had the experience of being alone with Mr Trevelyan and, considering his disconcerting effect on her when others were about, did not intend to broaden her education. "I was just preparing to leave . . ." she began, turning away from the cat eyes to search for her pencil, which had rolled away into the grass.

"And leave me to my lonely meditations? Yet I fear it is no more than I deserve."

"It is not on your account, Mr Trevelyan," she snapped. It was exceedingly uncomfortable to find him so close. "I have stayed overlong as it is, only I do not know where Polly can have got to. She has been gone this half hour at least."

After amiably suggesting that Polly must have drowned herself, Basil added blandly, "But see, you have had Lord Hartleigh as sentinel, and now that he is gone, here am I to take my turn as your protector."

For what seemed the thousandth time that morning, Isabella felt her face grow hot, but she forced herself to meet his gaze. It was an unsettling experience. The topaz eyes studied her, waiting. He reminded her of a cat crouched, ready to spring. Only he wasn't crouching. He was sitting, leaning back against the tree. "Lord Hartleigh was only trying to please his ward. She has taken a sudden . . . liking to me," she said, faltering.

"That is not in the least surprising. But my cousin should beware. The condition is contagious." Considerate of the moppet to have a wrestle with Miss Latham, for that lady's coiffure was in a most appealing state of disarray. A stray cherry-coloured ribbon dangling from her sleeve caught his eye. Apparently without thinking, he lifted it away, but she started at his touch. "Why, Miss Latham," he drawled, "I believe the child has frazzled your nerves. I'm sure I told you I won't bite. I was merely relieving you of this . . . love token she left behind."

"I shall return it to her," said Isabella, reaching to take it. But he snatched his hand away and pocketed the ribbon.

"Although I am all curiosity as to *when* you would have the opportunity, I shall keep in mind what happens to curious cats, and content myself with retaining this—as *my* love token."

"Mr Trevelyan, you have a highly overactive imagination." Hurriedly, she began gathering up her belongings, preparing to rise. His hand on her arm stopped her. "I wish you would not leave," he said softly.

Her heart began to pound. The voice and eyes were hypnotic, tempting her in spite of herself. She had only to pull herself free of his grasp. Yet she couldn't, or wouldn't. She had only to say a word to send him about his business, as Mama had suggested, but the word would not come. She had the curious sensation of observing herself, as though in a dream, as the sleepy cat eyes grew larger and seemed to swallow her up, as his fingers touched her cheek, and as she felt his lips on her own. For a moment all thought left her and time hung suspended. The sketchbook dropped from her hands. She felt his arms around her, pulling her closer, his mouth insistent. She felt his heart thudding next to her own. And then, as though from a tremendous distance, she heard a child's cry, and abruptly, the spell was broken. With all her strength, she thrust him away from her and struggled to her feet. He scrambled up after her, catching her before she could run away.

"Let go of me," she gasped.

"I will," he answered, a little breathless himself, "but you must not hate me. Isabella—"

"How dare you?" Angry tears welled up, and she had to bite her lip to keep from sobbing.

"I'm sorry I upset you. You must forgive me, Isabella. Here." He offered his handkerchief, which she angrily thrust away.

"Your m-manners leave a great deal to be desired."

"But my darling Isabella, I warned you I was not to be trusted. I told you I was perfectly dreadful. Even my aunt told you. Therefore, it is entirely your fault—"

"My fault?" He made her head spin. "You must be mad, and I madder still to stand here listening to your nonsense. And I am certainly not your darling," she snapped. "You may address me as 'Miss Latham'—if there is any occasion in future when I should be so idiotic as to permit you to address me at all."

"What you permit me to say aloud has no bearing on what I say in my heart. You *are* my darling. And my darling Isabella, you must compose yourself, for here comes your unreliable Polly, who has not drowned in the pond after all, and you don't wish to scandalise her."

Suspecting that the embrace had left physical evidence, she hastily endeavoured to restore herself to rights, and hoped that Lucy's enthusiasm would satisfy the abigail's curiosity as explanation for Isabella's dishevelled appearance. As she gathered her belongings and began to move away, he stopped her once more.

"You must say you forgive me, Isabella—"

"You are mad—"

"—for if you do not, I shall kiss you again, in full view of Polly."

Worried that Polly may already have had the pair in her sights, Isabella nodded, and struggled to break free of his grasp. He smiled as he released her, and watched as she hurried away.

The perfidious Polly was subjected to a scolding which left her as red-eyed as her mistress by the time they reached home. Declaring that she would see to her own hooks and buttons, and had too frightful a headache to eat nuncheon, Isabella slammed the bedroom door on her maid, flung herself on the bed, and burst into tears.

What a horrid, horrid man! To leap upon her the moment they were alone—as though she were one of his ladybirds. Oh, she knew he had them. He had probably come direct from a tryst with one of them. And what had she been thinking of, to allow him to kiss her? Of course she knew it would be no polite peck on the cheek. What a perfect idiot she was! What if they had been seen?

Her face feeling as though it were in flames, she got up from the bed and went to the washstand to bathe her eyes and burning cheeks. The cool water helped calm her. As she forced herself to look into the mirror, she knew why she had not prevented his embrace. Madame Vernisse may have been a worker of miracles, but even her powers could not render Isabella Latham beautiful. Or even unusually pretty. There was nothing uncommon about her blue eyes. They were not violet, like those of the infamous Lady Delmont. And while the right light— or the right frock—might enhance their colour, they had no real depth, no real mystery. And it was highly improbable that they were "that deep blue of the Ionian sea, wherein a man might choose to drown himself," as Basil had recently assured her. If only he *would* drown himself, she thought crossly. But in doing so, he would drown the only romance that had ever or would ever enter her life. She stared critically at her reflexion as she angrily yanked the comb through her hair.

She was twenty-six years old. And until this poetically inclined fortune hunter had come along, no man had ever looked twice at her. Not, of course, that she'd had much contact with young men; first poverty, and then the work she was so happy to do for Uncle Henry, had kept her from socialising. Still, her own father had barely noticed when she was in the same room. And now, though a small army of men had besieged her, not one except Basil had so much as hinted, in look or word, that she (as opposed to her income) was desirable. Oh, they had flattered her, but not with hidden suggestion, as Basil had. And as to the flattery, one could not even enjoy it for what it was, knowing that their eyes lingered more lovingly—good heavens!—upon her *mother*.

Thus, though she knew it was foolish, Isabella had wanted not simply to be kissed, but for someone to *want* to kiss her. She had wanted to know what it was like. Only now she could hardly recollect what it was like, so overset was she with anger and shame. She took a deep breath and forced herself to remember. His hand had touched her cheek, bringing her face closer to his . . . and then his lips, soft on her own. And then? What had she felt? She closed her eyes, trying to recapture that moment. But all she could remember was his overwhelming physical presence and her own warring sensations of fear . . . and curiosity. It was not quite what she'd expected from an embrace. She hadn't even felt that rush of warmth she'd experienced when Lucy hugged her. And not . . . that tingle of excitement when Lord Hartleigh sat down beside her.

For that was what she'd been contemplating when Basil had come upon her. Lord Hartleigh. Oh, worse and worse. Lord Hartleigh, who only tolerated her to indulge his ward. Had Isabella actually believed one cousin might substitute for the other? The idea drove her tears away. "Isabella," she scolded her reflexion, "you are perfectly absurd."

And with that heartening thought to cheer her, she dried her tears, changed her clothes, and went down to join her family.

6

"Lord Hartleigh!" her aunt cried. "Taking you for a ride in his carriage? But that—"

"Is yet another one," Mama interjected, in an undertone.

It was at tea that Isabella had quietly announced her plans for the following day. Alicia had nearly knocked over the teapot in her excitement and had been about to bubble forth predictions concerning the earl's intentions when the viscountess's outraged response immediately subdued her.

"What is it that you are saying, Maria? You know one cannot understand you when you mumble."

"It was nothing, my dear sister. Arithmetic. Counting to myself."

"I cannot think why you should do figures when we are discussing this highly improper state of affairs."

The only indication of alarm Maria Latham gave at this pronouncement was a slight lifting of one eyebrow in disbelief. "I do not see what is so improper about Isabella being invited for a drive. You were not shocked when Mr Porter invited her—and I am sure that high-perched contrivance of his cannot be safe."

Isabella attempted to step into the crossfire. "We are not taking a drive through the park, Aunt Charlotte," she began to explain.

"What, have you rejected him too, my love?"

Now this was very naughty of Mama indeed. Lady

Belcomb had not at all objected to the penurious suitors who crowded her drawing room every day the family was "at home." It was a convenient means of separating the wheat from the chaff, since, with neither looks nor charm, the only attraction Isabella could boast was her fortune. Those who called were therefore not at all the sort whose attentions one would wish upon Veronica. But Lord Hartleigh was not of this ilk. What doubly provoked the viscountess was that the earl seemed somehow beholden to Isabella on account of that absurd business with the little orphan.

And now here was Maria implying—with that studied innocence of hers—that the Earl of Hartleigh had been reduced to a state which rendered him vulnerable to *rejection*, and by a tradesman's daughter! The idea filled the viscountess with rage and, consequently, turned her face purple. She relieved her feelings by venting some of her wrath on her daughter.

"Veronica, I do wish you'd stop that dreadful noise," Lady Belcomb commanded, scowling at her. Under her parent's glare, Veronica quickly stifled her giggles and bowed her head to stare into her cup. Alicia, subduing her own mirth, bent her head likewise and endeavoured to look serious.

"Please, Aunt," Isabella interjected. "It is all very easily explained—and not a bit what you think." This being met by no other rejoinder than a "harrumph," she went on, "I believe you are aware that Lord Hartleigh has been named as guardian to the daughter of his very dear friend, who passed away a short time ago—"

"Such a sad business," Mama sighed.

"This ward," Isabella went on, with a brief frown at her irrepressible parent, "has taken a fancy to me; I am sure I don't know why. . . ."

"But, my love, you were always so good with children—even the most tiresome—"

"Mama, it is very difficult to hold my train of thought when you keep interrupting."

"Yes, Maria, do let her get on with it."

Murmuring an apology, Maria looked off toward the clock with an abstracted air.

"At any rate, the child has taken a fancy to me, and Lord Hartleigh—who, you can well imagine, is much at a loss to amuse a seven-year-old girl—"

A quelling glance from the viscountess squelched another of her daughter's giggling fits.

"—has invited me to this exhibition of landscapes *solely* to please the child, who insisted I bear them company."

There were some signs that Lady Belcomb was beginning to be appeased: Her face, for instance, was beginning to recover its normal colour. She was not entirely satisfied, however. "It seems to me, Isabella," she asserted, "that Lord Hartleigh is overly indulgent of his ward's whims."

"I am sure, Aunt, that is because he has had no experience of children. As he becomes more accustomed to his role, I am quite convinced he will be less indulgent."

"I would expect so. Nonetheless, I do not think he would take it much amiss if you were to indicate—tactfully, of course—that it is not at all to his ward's benefit to spoil her."

"At the very first opportunity," Isabella solemnly assured her aunt, while feeling quite convinced that the earl would take it very much amiss indeed.

"Well, then, I suppose we must at least commend Lord Hartleigh for wishing to do his duty by this orphan; although I do feel he has been carried away by his enthusiasm. But no matter. And you will take your abigail with you, Isabella?"

"I do not see why Polly must go as well . . ." Maria began, but the viscountess's face began to darken again, and she lazily added, "but then I suppose a seven-year-old child cannot count as chaperone."

"Of course not, Mama."

"Then I suppose we must let her go, Maria," Lady Belcomb announced magnanimously.

"Oh, I suppose we must," her sister-in-law agreed with a sigh. "I only hope the child does not tire her overmuch."

And with the crisis resolved, the ladies returned to their tea and managed to make a tolerable meal, despite the disagreeable necessity of having to shoo away diverse servants who persisted in duplicating one another's efforts, bustling in and out for no apparent reason, adding to and subtracting from the meal at their own whims.

It was not long after tea that Maria Latham entered her daughter's room. She was not wont to visit much, preferring to spend most of her time in her sitting room, where she could recline comfortably. Thus she was struck anew by the room's small size and inelegant decor. Gracefully, she dropped into a chair close by the little desk where Isabella sat composing a letter to her Uncle Henry. As she glanced about her at the threadbare furnishings, Maria lamented, "I do wish your aunt had selected another room for you, my love. These yellow draperies do not suit your complexion."

Isabella swallowed a smile. "I don't know where else she might put me, Mama. Veronica cannot be expected to share her room with Alicia, and certainly one could not squeeze so much as a mouse into the servants' quarters."

"Yes, I'm certain you are right, darling—although I'm afraid I must quarrel with any attempt to put you among the servants. But it is so distressing. I do not know whether it is the colour of the draperies that makes you appear so fatigued. Although, come to think of it, you appeared fatigued at tea as well. But of course, there was Charlotte being so very tiresome. Not to mention this distressing surfeit of servants. They quite exhaust me. It is no wonder Thomas could not afford a proper Season for your cousin, when he requires an army to run even such a modest place as this. At any rate, you must promise me that you will not allow this little girl to treat you as her hobby-horse. Polly tells me that the child made you most untidy. 'Like a big wind had blowed her from one end of London to the other' were her exact words, I believe.''

Isabella could not meet her mother's eyes. "I'm sure Polly was exaggerating, Mama," she managed to reply after what seemed like a monstrous long silence. "Lucy is very affectionate, and I believe she is very lonely—"

"No doubt," her mother replied, apparently engrossed in contemplation of a particularly inept sketch that hung by the door. As she brought her gaze back to her daughter, she went on, softly, "Still, it would not do for your aunt to see you return home tomorrow in the frazzled state Polly so vividly described."

"You are quite right, Mama. But as we are merely going to look at some pictures, Lucy will not have the opportunity to 'frazzle' me."

"Yes, that is so. Well, I believe I shall go to my own room and take a nap. Your aunt's lectures weary one so, and I do not see why she must be so disagreeable at tea. It is not at all recommended for the digestion." She patted her daughter's hand and rose to leave. But a few steps from the door, she stopped and said, as an afterthought, "By the way, Isabella, I do not recollect your mentioning meeting up with Mr Trevelyan as well as his cousin. But then, perhaps I was not listening as closely as I ought." She frowned once again at the offending sketch. "No matter. I should develop a headache as well as indigestion attempting to keep count of your *beaux*." And on that enigmatic note, she exited, leaving Isabella staring open-mouthed after her.

Miss Latham's was not the only equanimity to be ruffled by the morning's Adventure. Upon returning to his lodgings, Mr Trevelyan found himself uncharacteristically out of sorts. It was not the pricks of conscience which disturbed him, however; nor was it the tone of impatience

58

which had crept into his landlady's heretofore respectful inquiry regarding several months' back rent. After all, Freddie could most likely be counted on to advance a small loan. But one could not much longer continue to exist on the good offices of friends and Aunt Clem, and the once extremely remote prospect of debtors' prison now loomed closer by the day. The prison walls cast a long cold shadow which seemed to draw the warmth from Basil's cramped rooms. What else had led him, on this beautiful spring afternoon, to build a fire near which he huddled, nursing a brandy?

His friends' experience had shown him that debtors' prison could be a tolerable place. There at least one was free of the harassments of creditors. Yet though it might be tolerable, he had no wish to avail himself of that species of liberty, and was just now wondering how his normally reliable instincts for survival had led him so far astray.

Patiently, he'd been insinuating himself, little by little, into Miss Latham's good graces. And the hints he'd dropped among his acquaintance had led many to believe that her virtue was teetering on the brink. But this morning he had risked it all—for what? A kiss. And now she would not only cease trusting him, but would more than likely refuse to have anything further to do with him. This could not improve his position with his creditors, who, like his gambling friends, had begun to believe he was on his way to a prosperous match.

As he absently turned the brandy glass in his hands, he realised that he might have mistaken his victim. Her plainness, her naïveté, and her idiotic relations had all led him to believe she was less well protected and would be more easily manipulated than other eligible young ladies. But she would only be led so far; she was still wary of him, still taken with Edward.

He gazed for a long time into the fire, watching the logs crackle and break, to send off bright, hot little sparks before they crumbled into ashes. Though Isabella was not an antidote, she certainly was not beautiful. Next to the sparkling good looks of her young cousins, she was a mouse. But there was something about her innocent, blunt way of reacting to him which was rather appealing.

There was an odd mixture of longing and defiance in the looks which accompanied her earnest scoldings, and these looks somehow tempted him. Today he had succumbed to temptation. The brief embrace showed that she was truly inexperienced, despite that insinuating laugh of hers. But tutoring her might be rather pleasant, for she was—though in the oddest way—*attractive*. He did not love her, but maybe in time might feel affection for her. And perhaps those attractions might even command his attention—at least now and then—over the interminable dreariness of marriage.

Yet one could hardly contemplate marriage when one's Intended refused to have anything further to do with one. What a fool he'd been. What would it be now? Go to Lord Belcomb, confess to compromising her, offer to repair the damage by marrying her? He paused, the glass halfway to his lips. Could he carry it off?

Not likely. True, her noble relations might agree to any nonsense he suggested. When Maria had run off with her cit, they'd coldly washed their hands of her. They'd do anything to prevent another scandal. After all, a second generation run amok would indicate something depraved in the blood. But Isabella was just as likely to pack up and return to her commercial uncle and bury herself in the country. Marry a scoundrel? On account of one stolen kiss in broad daylight? No. Something else must persuade her, and soon.

According to Freddie, Lord Hartleigh had called more than once for Isabella; and he *was* seeking a mama for Lucy. So either he was interested in Isabella on her own account or he was courting her on account of the moppet. Not that it made sense, for Edward could marry where he chose. And of course, if he chose Isabella, she'd have him. Then Basil would have to start afresh with another

Answer to His Prayers, and that would take time. But time was running out.

In this unusual state of self-doubt, Basil continued until the fire had long died down and Freddie appeared, seeking company for dinner. As he waited for his friend to dress, Lord Tuttlehope helped himself to a glass of brandy and settled himself in the chair Basil had vacated. When Basil reemerged, Freddie eyed him up and down. "See Stutts came up to snuff after all," he commented.

"The aunt, Freddie, whose generosity surpasseth understanding," Basil explained. "She has paid the tailor, in hopes that—in appearance, at least—her nephew will not disgrace her."

This led to a discussion of the cut of waistcoats and a review of their acquaintances' merits in this area.

"All in all," Freddie noted, "only one in the same race with you is Hartleigh. But all his valet's got to do is dress him." And thus casually discounting Lord Hartleigh's sartorial achievements, he went on. "By the way, heard he's taking Miss Latham to look at some pictures tomorrow. Never fancied art myself. Hunting scene's not a bit like the real thing, you know."

Basil, who had been regarding his reflexion in the glass with a certain degree of complacency, whirled around. At Lord Tuttlehope's blink, he turned back again, adjusted his neckcloth, and responded blandly, "Indeed? So you've been to see the Belcombs *et al.* on your own today."

"Well, yes. That is. . . . Well, you were engaged." Discomfited, Freddie blinked at his brandy glass several times.

"And were you rewarded, my friend? Did you catch a glimpse of the fair goddess?"

"What? Oh. Well, that is. . . ."

Basil was amused to see his companion's face turn red as a beet-root. He turned from the mirror and gave Freddie's shoulder a comforting pat. "Try to restrain your lyric tongue, my lad. At least to me. It will be better spent on the young lady." He poured himself another glass of brandy. "But I gather you heard something useful?"

"Didn't stay long. Ladyship was in a pet. Just saw Belcomb on the way to his club. Said she'd rung a peal over him. Asked me why his niece couldn't see Hartleigh if she liked. Free country."

And in this clipped fashion, with the help of patient questioning, Freddie told his friend what he wished to know.

"Deverell?" Lord Belcomb repeated, trying to put the name to a face he hadn't seen in over a quarter of a century. Absentminded, like his sister, Basil thought; yet quite different. Where Mrs Latham was languid, he was bluff and hearty. And where he was the bumbling sort who knew a great deal less than he thought he did, Mrs Latham seemed to understand rather more than she let on. Basil had more than once felt her considering gaze upon him, and looked up only to find her staring off at nothing in particular. Yes, of course all considered her perfectly harmless—perfectly useless, in fact—but somehow Basil's instincts warned him otherwise. And even now, as he pumped the viscount for information, he had the dim sensation of having strayed too far.

"Ah yes," Lord Belcomb recalled. "Young Harry. The fair-haired one. Fine lad. Pity he died so young. Or rather, not dead after all, eh?" He signalled for more brandy. Charlotte had been in one of her takings this evening, and he—as was his custom on such occasions—had beat a hasty retreat to his club. He'd not been exactly delighted to see Mr Trevelyan, for that young man was one of the subjects on which Charlotte dwelt at unmerciful length; as though it were the viscount's business to bring the man up to scratch. And why? Lord Belcomb wondered. For here was the Earl of Hartleigh coming along, slow but sure, and probably would offer for the girl in a month or two, simultaneously restoring sister and niece to respectability. But Charlotte had turned purple when he'd ventured his opinion, and he had wisely refrained from arguing with her.

Now here was the Trevelyan chap, just as amiable as you please, wanting to hear about the old days. So Belcomb went on at some length about his youth, and about the Deverell family, who had been near neighbours.

"Then you knew him well?" Basil pressed, after patiently enduring a long-winded account of a youthful escapade. "Harry, I mean," he responded to Belcomb's befuddled look. "The new viscount."

"Ah, yes, Harry. No. Knew Marcus. Harry was much younger. And it was Maria who was his great friend. In fact—" He hesitated, but the brandy had loosed his tongue, and having a listener was a rare experience. "Well, everyone knows what Maria did. But I maintain to this day that if Harry had been home, he'd have tracked her down and brought her back before she could disgrace herself. He knew her ways, you see."

I believe I do, thought Basil. But aloud he asked, "Do you mean that by this time he was thought dead?"

"No. That was some months after Harry had gone to sea. No choice, poor lad. Old Deverell never had much to begin with, then ruined himself in one speculation or another. Left Marcus a title and a pile of debts—and the old ruin they were living in." Not unfamiliar with such experiences, Lord Belcomb sighed. But it was not his nature to be dispirited, and he became hearty again in a moment. "But that was all before, eh? For they say Harry comes back quite the nabob." And what with contemplating Harry Deverell's new wealth, and the repairs he might make to the family ruin, the viscount whiled away another half hour in Mr Trevelyan's amiable company.

7

Lord Hartleigh, who had begun the day feeling inordinately pleased with himself, was now out of sorts and cross with the world in general. As he gazed down at his attractive companion, he wondered how this picture business had grown so dull and stupid. He barely managed to squelch a sigh of exasperation as Veronica returned his glance with a simpering smile. She was pleased to see that her new bonnet had rendered the earl quite wistful.

For you see, it had been found, at the very last minute, that no other suitable companion could be spared, all the servants being required at home and the rest of the family otherwise engaged. And though it wasn't quite proper for Veronica to be going about with a gentleman before she'd been introduced to society, it was determined by Lady Belcomb to be the lesser of two evils. Thus Lord Hartleigh found himself expounding the merits of landscape painting to an empty-headed young miss fresh out of the schoolroom, who understood not three words in twenty and insisted on interpreting it all as flirtation. Isabella, meanwhile, trailed behind with Lucy, whose joy was not to be described. To hold Missbella's hand as that wonderful lady pointed out the beauties of the paintings was to be in heaven.

Not to imply, of course, that the Earl of Hartleigh—who could have bought every last painting in the gallery and still have had enough left over to buy the building in which they were housed with as little concern for his finances as if it were a new neckcloth he were purchasing; whose simple elegance and individual style had been admired by even the great Beau himself; who, moreover, was as highly respected in the very highest political chambers of the kingdom as he was admired in some of the most elegant private chambers of its ladies—to repeat, this is not to imply that the elegant and sophisticated Earl of Hartleigh would have the same notions of paradise as a little girl of seven. Still, it must be owned that he had looked forward to having a certain rather mousy-looking spinster lady on his arm, and to sharing with her his own knowledgeable enthusiasm for these landscapes.

But in vain did the earl endeavour to slow his companion's pace so that Isabella and Lucy might catch up with them. Veronica, bored with the work, hurried him along. She declared that every scene reminded her of the Belcomb country estate, and cross-examined him on the features of his own country home, Hartleigh Hall. Thus Lucy and Isabella remained several pictures behind—too far away to join in the conversation—and the earl found himself brought in less than an hour to the limits of his endurance.

Fearing that in another ten minutes he would throttle his happily innocent interlocutress, he begged that they might wait for the others to catch up. "Lucy cannot walk as fast as we," he explained to a blankly smiling Veronica, "and I am sure by now she has quite exhausted your cousin with her questions."

"Oh, Isabella doesn't mind," Veronica replied with a giggle. "Your ward is ever so sweet; and look—we're just coming to the landscapes you spoke of."

He, however, was not to be rushed again. He stopped and turned round—in time to see his cousin walking quickly toward Isabella. Blast, he thought. Must the man be forever hovering about?

But Basil stopped only for a moment. He chucked Lucy under the chin, laughed at her grimace, then slipped a note into Isabella's hand . . . and continued in his cousin's direction. A polite greeting to Lord Hartleigh, a handsome bow to Veronica, and Basil was gone, as quickly and quietly as he had come. Isabella stared after him, dumbfounded, then, collecting herself, hastily crushed the note into her reticule and endeavoured to continue her slow progress with Lucy.

Veronica, who had not seen the note change hands, batted her eyelashes, fluttered and smiled and sighed in vain. Lord Hartleigh had seen all and burned with outrage. Not jealousy, certainly. Just the . . . the . . . *impropriety!* A note? What nature of communication was it that could not be done publicly, aloud? His thirty-five years of aristocratic breeding, his faultless courtesy ebbed away, and his mouth tightened into a fine line as Isabella and Lucy approached.

Hoping he had not seen, yet with the sinking suspicion that he had, Isabella met his eyes only for an instant before dropping her own. She glared down at her reticule and its criminal contents, and quickly looked away again—at nothing in particular. "I'm so sorry we've dawdled," she said, too brightly, "but I have as much to learn here as Lucy. I wish I had one hundredth the skill and sensibility evident in even the least of these. Ah," she added, as her nervous glance took in the next series of works, "and here are Mr Constable's landscapes. He sees," she noted, forcing herself to speak to the earl, "what others do not, I think."

"You must not underestimate your own abilities, Miss Latham," he replied coldly, "for most of these gentlemen must get their living by painting, and must concentrate *all* their energies upon refining their skills in the one task. You and I—and your cousin," he added as an after-thought, "are blessed by fortune. We may turn from one interest to the next, all the while knowing we'll be well fed and housed. We who are not forced to one vocation are subject to innumerable distractions. Even in a gallery, our attention is not solely given to *art*."

The emphasis of these last words left no doubt that he had indeed seen. Isabella felt that the note she carried was like a burning coal which any moment would set her reticule ablaze, proclaiming her disgrace to the world. What must he think of her? But for all her guilty embarrassment, she was angry with him. So quick to judge, so quick to disapprove. Just as he'd been that day at Madame Vernisse's.

"I declare you're right, My Lord," said Veronica, smiling sweetly up at him. "When I look at paintings, they always seem to put me in mind of something else." She turned to her cousin. "Isn't it so, Bella? Isn't that funny cloud just the exact shade of my favourite bonnet?"

"Why, so it is," Isabella replied, wishing her cheeks did not feel so hot. "But we must not say so before Lord Hartleigh, lest he judge us hopelessly frivolous." She felt a tiny hand press hers a little tighter, and looked down to meet Lucy's concerned gaze. The child had sensed her discomfort, had recognised the familiar disapproving look on her guardian's face. She squeezed Isabella's hand again, in sympathy, and Isabella returned the gesture with a smile.

This silent exchange did not go unnoticed by the earl, who muttered something inane about an unfrivolous world being a very dull place, then turned abruptly to continue his progress with Veronica.

It was damned irritating. Yesterday this had seemed a thoroughly reasonable way to spend the afternoon. He'd hoped that spending time with Miss Latham would bolster his ward's spirits. Perhaps it would help him penetrate the barrier between himself and the child. And at the same time, he would spend a few hours in the company of an intelligent young woman with whom he might have a rational discussion about art. But see what had happened. Miss Latham was exchanging secret messages with his disreputable cousin, and his ward had sided with Miss Latham against her guardian. And for consolation, he had a simpering young miss whose reaction to works of art was that they put her in mind of *bonnets*.

They had not gone more than a few paces when they met the youngest Miss Stirewell, whom Veronica greeted warmly. Her display of affection might have been attributed to a deep and abiding friendship, but since the two girls had met only once before, a few weeks ago, the young lady's warmth more likely had other sources. Miss Stirewell's brother, for instance. That worthy eldest son of a baronet was as yet unmarried, and possessed an independent income which would double at his father's decease. Thus, while Veronica would vastly prefer being a countess, she was level-headed enough not to put all her eggs in one basket. In short, when Miss Stirewell offered to introduce Veronica to her mama and brother, waiting in the hall beyond, that young lady agreed with alacrity, leaving Lord Hartleigh, Miss Latham, and Lucy to amuse themselves.

Isabella endeavoured to fill the awkward silence which followed by retying a ribbon that had come loose from Lucy's hair. As Miss Latham bent to the task, Lucy told her, "I hope Uncle Basil doesn't come back."

"No?" said Isabella, forcing a smile. "And why is that?"

"He teases me and calls me Moppet." The hazel eyes met hers. "And he makes Uncle Edward cross."

Uncle Edward was about to utter a mild rebuke when he caught the expression on Miss Latham's face, which exactly matched that of his ward. Both looked as though they were expecting a scolding. A smile cracked his stern features, and he bent down to lift Lucy into his arms.

"I'm certainly not cross with *you*, Lucy," he told her.

She placed her arm about his neck, but pulled back a bit to stare into his face. "You're not?"

"No."

She considered this a moment, glanced at Isabella, then back at her guardian, and asked, "Are you cross with Missbella?"

His ears reddened, and "Missbella's" cheeks, in sympathy, did likewise.

"No, I'm not," Lord Hartleigh replied, although that infernal constriction, which had suddenly seized his chest again, made it difficult to get the words out.

"Good." The little girl surprised him with a shy hug. "But you may be cross with Uncle Basil," she added magnanimously, "because he *does* tease me, and I don't like it."

"Well, then, we must tell him to stop," her guardian agreed.

Isabella was struck by the way the man's face softened as he held the little girl. She wondered if this was the first time the child had demonstrated any affection for him, for he seemed so surprised and pleased at that gentle little hug. It gave her a queer tiny ache to watch them.

"But here is Miss Latham waiting patiently through these family affairs. Shall we continue our tour?"

Miss Latham acquiescing, he put Lucy down. The child placed herself between them, taking each by the hand. "We'll go on this way," she announced. "It's much better."

They had nearly half an hour to themselves before Veronica reappeared, and despite still feeling piqued about the scrap of paper hidden in Miss Latham's reticule, Lord Hartleigh was beginning to enjoy himself. With the barrier between his ward and himself crumbling, he relaxed, and soon found himself telling of an episode from his childhood, a story called to mind by one of the landscapes.

He'd had a pet frog, which was kept hidden in a box under his bed. His parents had given a party, to which all the best families in the county had been invited. "At the height of the festivities, the frog escaped from its box, hopped along down the stairs and into the drawing room. The horror of the scene was not to be imagined—ladies screaming and fainting; footmen scurrying about, endeavouring to capture the poor creature, and stumbling over swooning ladies."

A giggle from his ward and a low chuckle from Miss Latham encouraged him to go on.

"I awoke, hearing the shrieks, and immediately knew what had happened. I rushed downstairs in my night-clothes, clutching the box to my chest and screaming, 'Eliot! Eliot!' "

Picturing the scene, Isabella could control herself no longer. She burst into laughter. "Eliot?" she choked. "That was its name?"

"*His* name," the earl gravely corrected. As he went on with his story, he found himself embellishing the tale, just to draw more of that delicious laughter. By the time he had done, she was gasping for breath.

"A true scene of Gothic horror," she told him when she finally regained control of herself.

"It was indeed," he agreed, chuckling. "I defy even Mrs Radcliffe to match it."

"Ah, Mrs Radcliffe!" said Isabella. "Now that is another matter. Do you know, I suspect—"

But he was not to learn her suspicions, for Veronica had returned to them, chattering effusively about dear Miss Stirewell and her charming mama. And as it was drawing near the time they'd promised to be home, they hurried through the rest of the exhibit and out to the earl's waiting carriage.

"By the way, Maria, heard anything from Deverell?" Lord Belcomb had wandered into the small saloon. The house was in its usual state of uproar, with servants scurrying to and fro, moving furniture and bric-a-brac, and he was seeking refuge as distant from his wife as possible. Fortunately, she was engaged in haranguing the chef, and only his sister occupied the room. He didn't hear Maria's quick intake of breath at his question, and when he took a chair opposite, the blue-green eyes met his composedly.

"Harry, you know. Back from the drowned. The new viscount," Lord Belcomb prodded, wondering how the deuce Maria had grown so slow over the years. She used to be such a clever girl.

"Oh. Harry. No. I can't think why I should," Maria drawled. "His own family has heard little enough." Absently picking a stray thread from her sleeve, she asked, in a very bored voice, "What's put you in mind of Harry?"

The viscount described meeting with Basil at his club, and then, having found another listener (although not nearly as *attentive* as Mr Trevelyan, Maria did listen, more or less—certainly she did not interrupt to harangue him), went on at some length, reminiscing about old times. It was only when he saw his sister yawn for the eighth time that Lord Belcomb left off.

"How very interesting" was her polite response. "And now, if you'll excuse me, Thomas, I believe I must have a nap."

"You're not ailing, are you, Maria? For now I look at you, you seem not quite . . . quite . . . in colour, if you know what I mean."

"Yes, my dear. My constitution hasn't yet adjusted to the stimulation of city life." And, giving him a wan smile, she got up and drifted wearily from the room.

8

Isabella was just removing Basil's note from her reticule when she heard a scratching at the door. Quickly, she replaced the note, and looked up to see Alicia gazing at her from the doorway. "Well, come in, dear," Isabella told her, a bit impatiently.

"Oh, Bella, the most dreadful thing has happened while you were gone." Alicia rushed forward, took her cousin's hand and squeezed it sympathetically.

"What? What?" her cousin returned, alarmed. "Is Mama ill?"

"No, not dreadful like that. But bad enough. Lady Belcomb was at your mama for an hour this afternoon."

"Well, she's always at somebody—"

"But your mama *raised her voice*" was the ominous reply.

"Mama?" Mama was not capable of raising her voice.

"It's true. And it was all because of that old cat, Lady Jersey, who wouldn't give me a voucher to Almack's because Mama's grandfather kept an inn."

"I do not understand what your great-grandfather—"

"Not him. Lady Jersey. She told your aunt that everyone believes you are having a love affair with Mr Trevelyan."

"Alicia!"

The girl had the decency to blush, but went on nonetheless, "Well, one does know of these things, so I don't know why I'm not to speak of them."

"Because it isn't ladylike" was Isabella's stern response. But in a moment she softened again, for her cousin looked at her with such concern. "But who or what has put such a scurrilous rumour abroad?"

"From what I could hear—and I did try not to eavesdrop, Isabella, but as I said, even your mama raised her voice . . . anyway, it is apparently because of the way he behaves toward you."

"But it is all play-acting!"

"Lady Jersey and her friends don't see it that way." Alicia went on to explain that added to everyone's observation of attentions considered over-warm even in one's betrothed, there was a tide of rumours of clandestine meetings and a series of bets at White's regarding "a certain cit's daughter." In short, the gossip cast grave doubts on Isabella's virtue.

When her cousin had finished speaking, Isabella did not immediately reply, but sat as one stunned. No wonder Lady Jersey had sent such sly glances her way. And here Isabella had thought it was all on account of that old scandal about Mama. She had not expected to find complete acceptance among the ton—certainly not by the highest sticklers—but to have her name blackened because of the theatrics of an insolvent rakeshame; it was too much! Looking up, she saw that Alicia's eyes were filled with tears. "But darling, it's just ugly gossip," Isabella told her, forcing her voice to be soothing when what she wanted to do was scream and break furniture.

"That's what your mother told Lady Belcomb, but she answered back that our position here was 'delicate enough.' And worse, she said that we would all be shunned on your account." The tears could be restrained no longer, and Isabella found herself spending the next half hour trying to calm her cousin, instead of thinking, which she desperately needed to do. For the first time in her life, Isabella wished she were a man, so that she could have called Mr Trevelyan out, and shot him through

73

the heart. But of course he most likely didn't have one. Well, any organ would do.

But the thought of herself, armed with pistol, meeting the villain at dawn—and the thorny question of who would have served as her second—restored Isabella's sense of humour. "There, there," she said soothingly. "Aunt Charlotte has a tendency to see the black side of everything. No one will be shunned. We will simply have to set Mr Trevelyan right."

"But she said he would have to marry you, even though your mama said she didn't think you cared to." The innocent green eyes gazed seriously into Isabella's.

"Yes, I can see how that would be convenient for several parties. But Mama is right. I am not in a marrying mood this week, cousin."

Pretending a confidence she did not feel, Isabella was eventually able to persuade her cousin to dry her tears and wash her face and go away and leave her to think.

As soon as Alicia had departed, Isabella retrieved Basil's note, carried it to her desk, and opened it.

My dear Miss Latham,

I will not say the other thing, for it so offends your sensibilities, and though I am dreadful, I am not so dreadful as all that.

I apologise for distressing you yesterday—and yet somehow I cannot bring myself to apologise for what I did. Temptation was put in my way, and, never having any pretensions to sainthood, I succumbed. And yet I truly meant you no dishonour; quite the opposite. I am fully prepared to confess my transgression to your uncle, and to offer for your hand. . . .

At this last, a great wave of anger flooded through her. She crumpled the note and hurled it across the room. Offer for her? The nerve of the man! Did he think she'd offer her fortune and person into his keeping to make amends for a mere kiss? Did he think she'd jump at the chance to salvage her reputation with a hasty marriage? Isabella's bosom heaved in righteous indignation. And when she thought of how he had embarrassed her in front of Lord Hartleigh. . . . No wonder the earl was wont to be so cool to her; he'd probably heard the gossip, too.

Anger carried her through the next few minutes, but it was soon displaced by anxiety. If what Alicia had said was true, Aunt Charlotte would be more than willing to promote the marriage. She could bring considerable pressure to bear—perhaps even through Aunt Pamela. And *she* would make Uncle Henry's life miserable, for he'd never force his niece to marry against her will. This could be quite a tangle, indeed. She retrieved the crumpled letter and carried it back to her desk.

. . . I dare not hope that your feelings toward me have changed. I fear, rather, that my behaviour has alienated you entirely. That is why I have not yet attempted to see your uncle. Though I believe that you might acquiesce to the dictates of your family (not to mention those of society), I would rather merit your hand on some warmer basis. . . .

Isabella felt her cheeks grow hot. Warm indeed—the odious man!

. . . It is with the latter hope, then, that I beg you to forgive me and agree to see me again; after all, it was not so grievous a sin I committed. I have some words to utter in my own defence—words which, in all fairness, you must consent at least to hear, and which do not fall easily to paper and ink.

I beg your pardon for the garbled way in which I have scratched down these few sentences. I write in haste, in the hopes of being able to deliver this to you at a time when you cannot refuse it.

I shall be riding in Hyde Park at nine tomorrow morning, and will look for you then.

She looked up from the flourish of his closing, uncertain whether to laugh or cry. This was the man her aunt wished her to marry. This fanciful schemer and dreamer who dared to threaten her with a kiss—to be reported dutifully to the head of the family, and paid for with marriage. *He* had transgressed, had set the rumour mills going. He had kissed her, and now he expected to be rewarded with her hand and her fortune.

Under the tutelage of her Uncle Henry Latham, Isabella had learned a great deal about business. He had explained the various ploys and promises which had led her father to near-ruin. Compared to the machinations of men of business, Mr Trevelyan's trick was a child's game. And it would take more than that and an outraged viscountess to bring Isabella Latham to the altar.

Well, I will meet you, you horrid creature, she thought, tearing the note into pieces; if for no other reason than to show how little I care for your pathetic threats—and to put an end to this nonsense, once and for all.

Although the earl was pleased to see his ward so animated, as she eagerly plied him with questions all the way home, he found himself unable to give her his full attention. Over and over, his mind replayed the visit to the gallery, calling up Miss Latham's image and the delectable sound of her laughter as he'd told his frog story. What had possessed him to relate that tale? For a few moments he'd felt young and carefree himself; the painful memories of war, the burden of his responsibilities had vanished briefly, and he was simply a man, entertaining a pleasant young woman. What was there in that? It was only her enticing laughter and its secret, intimate promise that unsettled him.

No, there was more. While somewhat absently replying to Lucy's questions, he found himself wondering if he would have told that story to Lady Honoria. And he wondered why, though that lady possessed every requisite for a satisfactory—nay, superior—wife, he was not drawn to her. She was beautiful, yet he gazed on her with no special pleasure. She was reputedly clever, yet he quickly wearied of her conversation. She was—even Aunt Clem agreed—the best of the lot, and yet, and yet. . . . He shook himself out of his reverie as Lucy's voice became insistent.

"Then *when*, Uncle Edward?"

"What was that, child?"

With an exasperated little sigh, Lucy repeated, "*When* may we see Missbella again?"

"I don't know." When indeed? "Her family is to give a ball in a few days and she'll be quite busy. Perhaps after that. *If* you remember the special task you were to perform for me."

"My special task?" The hazel eyes looked away from his as she concentrated, trying to remember.

"Now you see, Miss Latham has put it quite out of your head. The pony. You were to decide what colour pony we should have."

"Oh yes! I know!" She bounced up and down, excitedly. "A silver one. Like the one in the picture. With the white on his face."

"Ah, well, that's a difficult order—" Then, meeting her look of disappointment, he went on, "Indeed, it is a dangerous mission, you propose, madam, but I, Edward Trevelyan, seventh Earl of Hartleigh, shall undertake it."

Lucy giggled in delight, and rewarded him with a fierce hug.

"Lucy talks of nothing but Miss Latham," Lady Bertram remarked as she poured herself a cup of tea. "She seems almost as much taken with the gel as your cousin is."

The smile on Lord Hartleigh's lips tightened. "I doubt my cousin is taken with much else besides himself."

"You're very hard on Basil."

"He has done little to warrant my compassion."

"Your father was much like Basil, at the same age. Yet

he settled down and led a respectable life soon thereafter. Some men come by their sense of responsibility late.''

"My father did not manage to squander his entire inheritance in five years—''

"He did not have the opportunity, coming so late to the title, and by then he had a wise and affectionate wife to guide him. But I did not invite you here to quarrel with you, Edward.'' Lady Bertram, whose back was always straight, straightened it just a bit more, and assumed a dictatorial air. "I wish to know what progress you have made.''

The long, strong fingers gripped the wineglass just a bit more tightly. "Progress, Aunt?''

"Don't play the fool with me, Edward. You have narrowed down the field to half a dozen, and I hear Lady Honoria Crofton-Ash is leading by a nose. When do you plan to offer for her?''

"Really, Aunt Clem, you make it sound like a race at Ascot.''

"Well?''

Curious how, lately, women seemed so often to be putting him at a disadvantage. Aunt Clem, with her cross-examinations concerning his prospective brides; Lady Honoria, with her meaningful smiles and glances which he was quite incapable of returning; Miss Latham, with her intelligent blue eyes and insinuating laughter. . . . Oh no. Not that train of thought again.

The majestic bosom rose and fell as Lady Bertram exhaled a sigh of impatience. "Are you still there, Edward?''

"Sorry, Aunt. I was just considering how to phrase it—''

"It? What? Will you offer for her or not? If you do not plan to do so, then you must cease paying her such particular attention.'' Her nephew's blank look told her that Lady Honoria little occupied his thoughts, and inquiries regarding other prospective countesses had the same result. His obvious lack of interest in these eligibles, coupled with his unusually passionate hostility at the mention of Basil, led Lady Bertram to put two and two together. Thus, she ceased her cross-examination, and casually turned the topic to his ward. She enquired about the new pony Lucy had been in such a flurry about, and then easily went on to Lucy's infatuation with Miss Latham. Noting that merely mentioning the young lady's name wrought an interesting change in the earl's demeanour, she pressed on.

"I have conversed with her several times," Aunt Clem said innocently, "and have been much impressed with her good sense. She can also be most amusing—once you can get her away from that cat of an aunt of hers. It's no wonder Lucy likes her. In fact, I've thought of inviting her to tea; but it would be so awkward."

Lord Hartleigh raised an eyebrow. Awkwardness, he knew, was not in his aunt's repertoire. "How so, Aunt?"

"Well, if Lucy is to come, I must have you, I suppose, for I will not have that ninny Miss Carter. And then of course I can't have Basil. But if I don't invite Basil, he'll be horribly put out, for he is quite besotted with Miss Latham."

"The devil he is!" the earl burst out, and then, catching his aunt's inquisitive eye, settled back in his chair and drawled, "I told you, Basil is in love only with his expensive amusements—which, I assume," he went on, unable to help himself, "he would like Miss Latham to pay for. As my father did. As Basil expected me to do. Aunt, you know he has no consideration for anyone but himself, has no thought of responsibility to anyone or anything—"

"In that case, what would you have him do?" his aunt asked. "Unlike you, he has no choice but to marry a woman with a fortune. And if Miss Latham finds him suitable, and is content to have him—"

"What?" Lord Hartleigh sat bolt upright, nearly spilling his sherry in his agitation. "Surely he has not offered for her?"

"Not to my knowledge, but if he should—"

"Aunt, you cannot permit it."

"I have nothing to say in the matter." Calmly, she helped herself to a piece of cake. "I cannot dictate my nephew's behaviour."

"You cannot think to abandon her to his . . . his . . . machinations."

"Edward, I do believe you have a touch of your cousin in you. You are growing quite melodramatic. I am sure Miss Latham is sensible enough to avoid whatever 'machinations' you are imagining. I understand she assisted her uncle and has a surprisingly sophisticated understanding of business. I doubt she'll be taken in easily. And if she is, then we may assume it was because she was inclined to be. May we not?"

Having discovered what she wished to know, Lady Bertram gently turned the conversation to other channels. She noted, however, that Lord Hartleigh never did fully regain his equanimity, and she wondered if he was too much of a fool—as men so often were—to realise what he wanted.

9

Isabella had never sympathised much with her Aunt Pamela's social ambitions. After all, the Lathams were not slave-traders; their businesses were respectable. And certainly they were far better off financially than many of the nobility. The latter were often obliged to bring themselves to the brink of bankruptcy, just to keep up appearances. Look at her uncle, Lord Belcomb.

Had Aunt Pamela not been so ambitious, her four daughters might have had their pick of any number of respectable, though untitled, young men. And Isabella might have stayed quietly in Westford, making herself useful to her uncle, instead of having to spend her time dodging the various parties so eager to make use of her fortune.

But that same social ambition had also provided her current means of escape. Insisting that a proper young lady must be conservant with the art of managing a horse, Aunt Pamela had insisted on riding lessons for her girls. After many debates on the subject, Uncle Henry had finally agreed—on condition that Isabella be taught as well. "The poor child does not have sufficient exercise," he'd told his wife in his quiet but firm way. "She must be encouraged to spend more time out of doors." That his wife demanded too much of the girl within doors was an issue left unspoken, for he had no wish to hear the lengthy denials.

Thus Isabella had been afforded some refuge from the

chaos of the viscount's household. And in this one case, at least, the viscountess did not require detailed explanations. Lady Belcomb's passion for horses, like her need for battalions of servants, had contributed in part to her husband's current unhappy financial state. Isabella, then, had only to don her habit in the morning and take her groom with her, and she would have an hour or more of peace. For that, today, she was doubly thankful.

She had left well before time, both to actually exercise the horse and to clear her own head. She'd lain awake a long time the night before, trying to calculate the risks of flouting her aunt's demands, and had at length determined that if all else failed, she would turn to Uncle Henry. He had straightened out worse tangles. And so, clinging to this comforting thought, she'd fallen asleep at last.

She took a side trail, away from the park proper, where there would be room to run. As she urged her horse to a gallop, the groom, by now inured to her headlong pace, patiently waited. On their first excursion, he'd been convinced the horse had run away with her, and had earned a good-natured scolding for his attempts to rescue her. Today, as he had ever since, he gritted his teeth and fervently prayed that Miss would not be killed—at least not while in his keeping.

But Miss was made of sterner stuff than most people realised. She flew across the meadow, confident and secure. As she felt the fresh morning air and the graceful power of the animal beneath her, aunts and debutantes and suitors faded from her mind. Life made sense again; as it rarely had since she'd come to London. She wished she could continue galloping, on, out of the park, away from the city, and back to her uncle's comfortable home. But one could escape only for moments at a time.

Reluctantly, she made her way back, and was guiding her horse along the more travelled paths (although, at this hour, few travelled them) when she caught sight of Basil. He was still some distance away, and as she watched his approach, she wondered what quirk of fate had led him to her—rather than any one of a hundred other similarly well fixed young women; and why, like most of that hundred, she could not be content simply to purchase an attractive, well-born husband.

For, though she felt his were no match for the darker good looks of his cousin, there was no doubt he was handsome: slim and graceful, impeccably dressed, with that beautifully sculpted face and those unsettling amber eyes beneath that mane of tawny hair. He was clever and poetic and amusing; he was, in fact, exactly the kind of wickedly romantic hero one might conjure up in one's dreams. But such a hero would want her for herself, not for her fortune. Not, Isabella thought with regret, that a mousy-looking spinster was calculated to inspire passion in any hero's breast.

But Isabella did not realize how un-mousy she appeared at the moment. Her face was flushed with exercise, her eyes sparkled, and her fair silky hair had begun to come loose from its pins. She looked quite . . . fetching. Once again Mr Trevelyan noted that Miss Latham was a great deal more appealing when she was stimulated—whether by merriment, anger, or exercise. It would be a fascinating study to discover the diverse ways in which stimulation might be effected; and more than ever he was determined that such discoveries would not be left to his cousin.

Neither the groom's suspicious stare nor Isabella's cold reply to his greeting disconcerted him. He wished she would look a tad more worried, but there was no help for that. If his speech succeeded, she would no doubt have reason to fret.

"I pray you will be brief, Mr Trevelyan," she told him. "I do not usually ride more than an hour, and I do not wish to cause anxiety at home."

"Briefly, then," he agreed, as they moved on a few steps, out of the groom's earshot. "As I indicated in my note, it is no small matter that I attempted to compromise you—"

He was interrupted by her low chuckle, and an angry light shone briefly in the cat eyes as he asked her to share the joke.

"It will not do, Mr Trevelyan," she told him, her face quickly solemn again. "I am not so missish as to think that a stolen kiss in a public park in broad daylight will sink me entirely beneath reproach."

"I'm afraid you are innocent in the ways of society, Miss Latham."

"No, I've had more than a month's education. If you wish to tattle about that episode, there will be gossip—and it will fuel the gossip you've so carefully cultivated—"

"Cultivated!" For the moment he was taken aback by her blunt assertion.

"Please don't insult my intelligence by denying it. If you truly cared for my reputation, you would not have behaved in a way to excite suspicion. Already half the ton thinks I'm your mistress, for you've shown less discretion in your looks, gestures, and words"—she gave each a special emphasis—"than you would if they were directed to an opera dancer." This being rather a mouthful, she paused for breath, and was pleased to see him look discomfitted. "In short," she went on, "if you do tattle, then you are no gentleman."

Basil had to smile at this, for though it was not what he'd expected, it was an apt rebuttal. Was she nearly a match for him, then? How utterly fascinating. "But perhaps I am not" was his amiable rejoinder.

"That's your lookout," she snapped, "for though you tell tales into the next century, no one can make me marry against my will. And before you think to frighten me with threats of scandal, think on this: My Uncle Henry—not Lord Belcomb—manages my funds. And Henry Latham would never deliver me into the hands of a fortune hunter." Her hands tightened on the reins as she turned her horse, preparing to depart.

"Stay, Miss Latham," he urged, bringing his own

mount around to block her retreat. "Those are harsh words, indeed." As she opened her mouth to retort, he held up his hand and continued, "And I don't deny I deserve them. But before you reject me out of hand, there's one other matter I wish to lay before you."

"I cannot imagine any other—"

"My cousin, you know," he said quietly.

There was that odd flutter near her heart, but she kept her face stony as she met his gaze. "I don't see what Lord Hartleigh has to do with this."

"You don't?" The glitter in his eyes belied the innocence of his tone. "How strange, for *I* do. I see, for example, that you have developed a *tendre* for him—oh, don't trouble to deny it," he continued as he heard her quick intake of breath. "I may be a thoroughly disreputable creature, but I am not an idiot. Even your aunt can see it; and doesn't like it above half, I assure you."

"Your imagination is running away with you," she interjected, but weakly.

"I wish it were. But no, the Fates are all against me. For here is Edward, in love with the fair Lady Honoria, who would make a most suitable mama for Lucy. But Lucy can't abide her. No, Lucy wants Missbella for her mama, and no one else will do. I greatly fear, my darling, that Edward will offer for you, just to please his ward. That he will be spiting me in the bargain will, I assume, add some little zest to the venture."

Of course. Lady Honoria. Had it not been obvious? Yet he'd give her up, for his ward's sake? Isabella's momentary joy at the prospect of being Lord Hartleigh's wife was quickly swamped by a wave of despair. To marry her, out of a completely selfless sense of duty. . . . No, he was not so indulgent a guardian as all that.

Basil felt the tiniest tweak of conscience as he watched the play of emotions on her face. Her confidence was crumbling, and the colour had drained from her cheeks. He sighed. "I suppose it must all come about right in the end. I hope so, for your sake. Imagine what it must be like to be married to the man you love, knowing he gave up the one *he* loved, out of too-acute notions of responsibility. Wondering," he went on, as though talking to himself, "as Lucy grows into adulthood, marries, goes away—wondering whether he'll come to love you in time. Or whether he'll come more and more to resent you."

It was cruel of him to say it, it was cruel to paint that bleak picture—yet wasn't it *true?* She couldn't deny how precious Lucy was to her guardian, how much her happiness meant to him. Hadn't Isabella seen ample evidence, time and time again? She forced herself to respond. "You presume a great deal," she told Basil, her voice flat and tired. "That Duty would lead your cousin to such a step; or that I would accept. I have no wish, no need, to marry anyone."

"But your family?"

"What of them?"

"Let's be businesslike about this," he said briskly. "In marrying me—or my cousin—you're firmly established in society. With Edward or myself to smooth matters with his family, there will be no difficulties in Freddie's marrying Alicia—if she'll have him. And then, when your other little cousins are ready to join society. . . ." Rebellion gleamed in her eye; abruptly, he changed his tack. "Pray don't look at me as though I were an ogre. I was trying to be practical, pointing out the assets and liabilities—and it doesn't suit me, I'm afraid. But the fact is, I care deeply for you, Isabella—"

"In spite of my fortune," she noted sarcastically.

"I'm cursed with an extravagant nature and little income of my own. I have no choice but to marry a wealthy wife. But that doesn't mean I have no feeling for you. The truth is, I've never cared for anyone so much in my life; except myself," he finished, with a rueful smile.

"Surely you realise I don't return those feelings."

"Not now. But maybe in time. If you'd but give me the chance, I might earn your affection."

Looking down at her hands resting on her saddle, she heard the sincerity of his voice, but missed the flicker of amusement in his eyes. "My uncle has taught me to steer clear of speculation," she answered, softly.

"I promise it is no gamble. I can prove it, but you must give me the chance. Will you at least think on what I've said?"

Oh, indeed she would. No doubt through many long, sleepless nights. She nodded.

"And perhaps we will talk again—soon?"

"Yes."

"And perhaps you'll save me a dance at your cousins' ball?"

"Perhaps." She started to urge her mount away. "I must go home now."

As he watched her leave, Basil shook his head. Pity the girl took it so hard. Well, at least he hadn't needed to bring out the heavy artillery. His recent investigations were all beginning to point in the same direction, but he needed another few days to be sure. And desperate though he was, even he must shrink at blackmail. Fortunately, there *were* other forms of persuasion: It had been well worth losing half a night's sleep to rehearse and perfect his "sincere" speech. Tonight he would compensate for the exertion with a visit to the talented, and very expensive, Celestine.

Henry Latham folded up the letter he'd just finished reading. He removed his spectacles and, taking out a handkerchief, began polishing them, a thoughtful look on his genial countenance.

"News from Alicia?" asked his wife, entering his den with a cup of coffee. She tried to get a glimpse of the letter, which he casually slipped into his pocket.

"No, my love. Business. Appears I'll have to go into town."

Pamela Latham's plump features were eloquent with astonishment. In recent years, her husband had avoided the city at all costs, preferring to send a representative to handle any problems which arose there.

"This matter calls for more than the usual discretion," he explained. "And though I'd trust William with my life, I'll feel more comfortable seeing to it myself."

The cup was placed at his elbow with rather more noise than was absolutely necessary. "You'll not attempt to see Alicia, I hope." Her tone indicated that this was not so much a wish as a command.

"Of course not, my love. Wouldn't dream of it. I'll be there and back in a week—two at most—and they'll never know I stirred from here."

"I fervently hope not, for you know it was a condition—"

"Of course." There was a cold edge to his own voice which told her that the matter was not to be discussed further. So, though she wished for another glimpse of that handwriting, she held her tongue and, like the dutiful wife she was, offered to help her husband pack.

10

While Henry Latham was preparing for his pilgrimage, Lord Hartleigh was already embarked upon one of his own. Like a restless ghost, he wandered from Boodles to Brooks to White's; managed, despite his best efforts, to lose less than a hundred pounds; and failed utterly in his attempts to get drunk. Defeated, he returned to his house shortly after two in the morning, called for his favourite brandy, and retired to his library with a growled command that he was not to be disturbed unless the house caught fire.

Slumped in his favourite chair, without the distraction of his companions, it did not take him long to realise what was wrong. Aunt Clem's confident prediction that Basil would offer for Miss Latham had thrown him into a rage, the likes of which he had not experienced since the day Lucy had been misplaced. Curiously, he had the same feeling of being personally at fault.

At first he'd refused to take it seriously, assuming that if Basil was bold enough to ask, at least the lady was sensible enough to refuse. But the earl's perambulations through the clubs of London had disburdened him of these optimistic notions. A great deal of talk was circulating about the two, and even if only a quarter of it was based on any semblance of fact, Miss Latham's reputation was in an uncertain state. She might be forced to marry Basil, just to stop the wagging tongues.

Benumbed, Lord Hartleigh stared around him at his

book collection, at the few choice pictures which adorned the walls of this, his private sanctum. With his intelligence missions ended, he'd turned his energies back to his first loves: literature and art. Lucy's coming had been a further encouragement, for he wanted his ward to grow up with a genuine appreciation of what great minds could create. Lucy would not be like the rest of those white muslin-decked debutantes. She'd be able to talk of and understand something besides bonnets and slippers and shawls. She'd grow into a beautiful, bright young woman, and the man who eventually won her would be worthy of her; not some debt-ridden gallant like Basil, or inarticulate dandy like his friend, Tuttlehope.

Of course, she wasn't old enough yet to share with her guardian his appreciation of books and paintings. In fact, there was virtually no one with whom he could share this love. And from time to time he had wished for such a companion: one with whom he could talk—about Lucy and the many questions he had about raising and educating her and making her happy. About books. About art.

He poured more brandy into his glass. Certainly it was difficult to imagine such conversations with Lady Honoria, or with any of her equally eligible rivals. They preferred talk of fashions, when they weren't flirting or gossiping. As he stared morosely into his glass, his alcohol-laden brain betrayed him, and a pair of intelligent blue eyes seemed to stare back at him. As he remembered those eyes sparkling with suppressed laughter, and a generous mouth parted to deliver a witty sally to one of his remarks, there was a familiar tightening in his chest. Only now he noted that it wasn't an obstruction but an ache.

He remembered the day at the dressmaker's shop, and the way her few gentle words to the child had effectively put him in his place. He remembered his visit the next day, and the way she'd coolly accepted his apologies— and her ghost of a smile when she had remarked that children, unlike the rest of one's possessions, seldom remained where one had last left them. He remembered that first dance, and the way her laughter and good-natured teasing had eased his worry about his ward. And other dances, other conversations; those scattered moments in her company, each so unique, all pointed to a quality he hadn't recognised before. She had a way about her which seemed to put things right. And now, angry and depressed by turns, disoriented with alcohol, he wished she were here, to put it all right again.

At length, weary of these drink-sodden reveries, he stumbled from the library and made his way, slowly and painfully, to his bedroom. Exhausted, he collapsed, fully clothed, onto the bed. But oblivion would not come. He stared at the ceiling, willing himself to think.

It wasn't so bad, after all, as being in a French prison, dying by inches in the filth. And he'd survived that, had he not?—with Robert Warriner's help, of course. Indeed, if all that was worrying him was the prospect of Isabella's being thrown away on his cousin . . . well, he must stop it, then.

He'd been a fool to let matters go this far. But the task of bringing Lucy out of her shell, added to the rigours of attending on now one, then another eligible young lady, had blinded him to what was going on. Only tonight had he heard how Basil supposedly took Miss Latham, unescorted by chaperone, to Vauxhall Gardens . . . and how they'd been surprised in a *tête-à-tête* at one party or another. He'd also heard of the diverse assignations and clandestine meetings which managed to place Miss Latham in half a dozen different locations simultaneously—and of course there was that matter of the note exchanged at the exhibition. That, at least, he could vouch for; but it did not necessarily make Miss Latham guilty. He knew from long experience that Basil had a talent for manipulating circumstances to his own advantage.

Having insinuated himself into the household, it would be child's play for Basil to learn of her comings and goings, and arrange to be in the right place at the right time. Just as it would be easy enough for Basil to "refuse to betray a lady" if someone asked, "Was that not Miss Latham with you at such-and-such a place at such-and-such a time?" And then smile and look in such a way as to confirm the questioner's suspicions. Basil had no principles, no sense of honour—except perhaps at cards—and would have no trouble with his conscience as he wove his meshes about her. And from what Lord Hartleigh had heard, no one in the Belcomb household was looking out for her interests; quite the contrary. Apparently, Lady Belcomb was more eager for the marriage than even Basil was.

Yes, with his own dogged pursuit of a proper mama for Lucy, he'd betrayed Miss Latham to the enemy. He should have gone with his first instincts; that night, when he'd seen Basil hovering over her, he should have warned her—and then done everything in his power to frustrate his cousin of his prey.

Well, there was no undoing what was done. But he might snatch victory from Basil—if only she would cooperate. And therein lay the problem. He could warn her. He could bribe or threaten Basil. But it was very likely things had gone too far for that. To rescue her, he must offer for her himself.

His throat was raw, his head spun, and something furry seemed to have grown on his tongue. Fighting back the nausea, he forced himself to sit up, and poured a glass of water from the pitcher on the nightstand. Doing so, he caught a glimpse of himself in the cheval glass. His curly dark hair was dishevelled, having been cruelly and repeatedly raked with his fingers. His eyes were red, with dark rings around them. A dark shadow of beard had sprouted on his face. What a pretty prospect for a bride-groom, he told his reflexion. Miss Latham's bound to be bowled over at the sight of you; bound to throw herself into your warm—not to say humid—embrace. Must smell like a French dungeon. If that good.

But tomorrow he would be repaired and refreshed. And tomorrow he'd present himself to her languid mama. And then, to the lady herself. One way or another, by fair means or foul, he'd rescue her from his cousin.

He struggled with his garments and eventually managed to remove most of them before falling onto the bed once more. This time, sleep came to meet him, and as he drifted off, he fervently hoped the lady would consent to be rescued.

He'd been forced to repeat his request three times before the much-harassed butler had finally comprehended that it was *Mrs* Latham he wished to see. And now, as Lord Hartleigh surveyed that delicate creature, gracefully posed among her numerous cushions, he found himself wondering how she'd ever summoned up the energy to bring a child into the world. She seemed to have barely the strength to keep her own heart pumping.

"I assume, My Lord, that you have some matter to discuss? For I'm certain you realise that I never *entertain*." She made it sound as though she were referring to a rigourous calisthenic activity.

He quickly reassured her on that count, remembering to add some compliments as to her very presence being reward enough—or some such nonsense—and was alarmed to hear himself stammering.

"Yes. Quite so. And I trust it is not about horses?"

His Lordship, whose head was not of the best this morning, wondered for a moment if the alcohol had permanently damaged his brain.

She looked past him at the ormolu clock on the mantelpiece. "I find horses tiresome," she explained to the clock.

Dazed, he assured her that he would not mention horses. "It's about your daughter," he added, growing more uncomfortable by the second.

Slowly, her glance drifted back to his face. "Ah."

Now he rather wished she would stare at the clock

again, for it was difficult to maintain his poise under her gaze. Despite that vacant air of hers, he had the sensation that she was measuring him. Forcing himself to meet her eyes, he began his rehearsed speech. "I have come to ask your permission to pay my . . . my addresses to her," he said, faltering. The blue-green eyes continued fixed, almost absently, on his face. "I realise that ours is but a short acquaintance, but in that brief time I've come to regard her with the greatest admiration and esteem. She has a superior understanding—"

"My dear sir," Maria interrupted, "you needn't catalogue her virtues to me. I am her mother, after all, and know all about them. Besides which, I find it thoroughly exhausting to contemplate her accomplishments."

"I only wished to assure you—"

A delicate white hand waved away his protestations. "Pray do not exert yourself on that account. I rarely need to be assured."

He had no idea how to get on with this conversation, and his head was beginning to throb dreadfully. After what seemed like hours of silence (but were actually only seconds), while the lady thoughtfully examined the diamonds on her finger, he managed to ask whether, then, he might suppose he had her approval?

"Why, of course, My Lord," she replied, perfectly calm. "What possible objection could I have to so eminently suitable a young man as yourself?"

"It is very kind of you to say so." Confound the woman! What did she mean by that? He was overcome with a sudden urge to wrap his fingers around her throat and choke her when a soft, low chuckle escaped from that very throat. That sound! So like, and yet not the same at all.

Meeting his bewildered look, Maria chuckled again. "My dear Lord Hartleigh," she began, "pray excuse me. Isabella is right; I am an incorrigible tease. But you see, I cannot help it. And you look so solemn that one would think you were asking permission to commit some grievous crime. In my experience, lovers are wont to look rather more cheerful, perhaps even idiotically so.''

The earl turned away from those suddenly intelligent eyes, feeling somehow unmasked. "Perhaps," he replied quietly, "it is because I am not entirely sanguine concerning my prospects." He didn't know why he'd told her, but her soft "I see" reassured him.

"I *do* care for her," he confessed, as though the words were being pried from him, "a great deal. But I did not realise it until very recently."

"Yes. I understand how that can be. But I must tell you frankly, sir, that I wish you'd realised it somewhat sooner. Isabella has always been a clever, sensible girl, but in the past day or so. . . . Ah, well. Time is always the enemy." She looked at him—rather sadly, he thought—but did not enlighten him further. "Nonetheless, I shall wish you success."

As he rose to take his leave, she added, "I'm afraid you'll not find her at home this morning. But we shall see you tonight?"

He nodded.

"Good." And, giving him a graceful white hand, she bid him *adieu*.

11

After one last go-round, to see that all was as it should
be, Isabella slipped away to a temporarily isolated corner
of what a great deal of money and a great many servants
had turned into a ballroom. Her face ached with the effort
of smiling, but it was nothing to the aching of her head
and heart. Basil's words had done their poisonous task.
Yes, of course she'd been discontented at times in
London. And she'd been unhappy at times at home. But
there had been nothing in her life—not Papa's death,
certainly, for he was a stranger to her—to prepare her for
this utter misery of spirit.

And of course it was all her own fault. What business
had she becoming infatuated with an earl, for heaven's
sake? An earl who had—if one simply looked at what was
under one's very nose—already found himself an entirely
suitable countess, thank you. See, wasn't he smiling
appreciatively at one of Lady Honoria's witticisms? She
was reputed to be very clever. And certainly, she was the
most beautiful woman in the room.

Isabella gave a small sigh, manufactured a benevolent
smile, and gazed out over the multitude. For multitude it
was, despite Lady Belcomb's ominous predictions. Mrs
Drummond Burrell might scold about "carryings-on," and
refuse to honour the proceedings with her presence; but
the vast majority were not such high sticklers. And they
were curious to see for themselves Isabella and Basil in
action. For the sad truth was, a great deal more had been

talked about than had actually been seen, and London Society was eager to learn whether Isabella would outdo even Caro Lamb in making a public spectacle of herself. To society's disappointment, Miss Latham was the perfect lady, and Mr Trevelyan's behaviour was punctiliously correct.

But Isabella was far less concerned with the ton's interest in herself than with their utter lack of interest in Alicia. The dowagers were coldly polite when they weren't outright rude, and the debutantes ignored her altogether. That Alicia was wealthy and devastatingly beautiful made her crime—a cit's daughter trying to elbow her way into Society—all the more heinous. Thus the early part of the evening had been an agony for Isabella.

Few gentlemen asked Alicia to dance, and those few were the same indigent gentlemen who'd made up Isabella's admiring circle in recent weeks.

Lord Tuttlehope had arrived rather late, on account of changing his clothes fourteen times and ruining two dozen cravats. And when he finally did arrive, he was so mortified at his tardiness and so convinced of having sunk forever in Alicia's esteem on this account that he was afraid to speak to her. It thus took him some time to notice that Veronica was surrounded by admirers and Alicia was not. Gradually, it penetrated his wits that his golden-haired darling was being snubbed. This made him mightily indignant, and he forgot his imagined disgrace as he bravely strode up to her.

Somehow Alicia managed to comprehend and accept his incoherent request for a dance, her face becomingly suffused with blushes. These having effectively routed his embarrassment, though causing him the most exquisite pain, he was able to keep both from treading on his fair one's toes and from stumbling over his own.

The next dance was claimed by Lord Hartleigh, who, if truth must be told, would never have noticed Alicia's plight on his own. But more than once he'd noted the concern on Isabella's face and her worried glances toward her attractive cousin. When the dance was over, he lingered a moment longer than necessary, as though he found Alicia's conversation utterly fascinating. The moment was just enough, however, to raise a flutter in the fair Honoria's breast and to kindle the competitive spirit of all the fine gentlemen in the immediate vicinity. After all, Alicia Latham was beautiful and rich, and if the Earl of Hartleigh, with his immaculate breeding, did not object to this cit's daughter, why should they? Within a quarter hour, Alicia found herself forced to break at least a dozen hearts because there were not dances enough to go round or hours enough to go round in.

Lord Tuttlehope, however, for his astounding act of courage, earned the promise of a second dance, and was allowed the unlooked-for privilege of escorting Alicia in to supper. Emboldened by this honour, the baron declared that he personally would speak to Lady Cowper in the matter of obtaining Alicia a voucher for Almack's. "But Lady Jersey has already refused me," Alicia gently reminded him.

"Her own grandfather was a banker. Don't know where she gets her notions. But no one shall refuse *you*," her hero replied, and blinked so hard at his own audacity that his eyes watered.

Alicia had found a moment to hurriedly relate this interesting exchange to Isabella before an eager young major swept her back to the dance floor. So, Isabella thought, Lord Tuttlehope had a spine after all. But would his family accept his choice? Though they might not be able to influence the young man, they certainly might contrive to make Alicia miserable. Immersed in her own thoughts, Isabella did not hear the two young ladies approach, and as she caught the drift of their conversation, she backed away into the shadows.

"Well, I wondered at it myself, but Lord Hartleigh has unusually high notions of duty. And he has always been the most chivalrous of men. How can one be surprised at his acknowledging the little merchant princess when he's taken in that nameless orphan child?''

"That is true, Honoria. And he thinks the world of the little girl, does he not?''

"Yes" was the tart reply. The rest Isabella did not hear, for the ladies slowly moved on.

Of course. Basil wasn't the only one to see it. "Unusually high notions of duty." She'd wanted to think it was for her own sake he'd asked Alicia to dance, but it had been chivalry, plain and simple. Another maiden in distress, and there was the Earl of Hartleigh, to the rescue.

"Ah. So here you are. I feared you'd gone off with your sketchbook and pencil—for a change, you know.''

Still caught in her unhappy meditations, her gaze stuck at the intricate folds of his neckcloth for a moment before she looked up into Lord Hartleigh's face. He was smiling, but there was an intensity she'd never seen before in his dark eyes. Her heart beat a little faster as she forced a smile in return. "I . . . we . . . had not expected such a crush—''

"Yes. This affair is an obvious success. But all the same, the role of hostess can be wearisome.''

"You give me too much credit. My aunt is hostess, and more deserving of your sympathy—''

"Your aunt has assumed the rights of office, but it's clear you have its responsibilities; not that you need have any anxieties. Your cousins have obviously taken.''

. He spoke as though he understood her mind, as though he genuinely cared what she felt. And *he* had been responsible for Alicia's success. The ton respected him. "Yes, My Lord, I think you are right. And I believe I owe you some thanks—''

But he sensed what she was about and wouldn't let her finish. "Your cousins are lovely, and Alicia has a genuine warmth and good nature which is tremendously refreshing. But I did not come to talk of your cousins. I have come for a dance. To command you to dance, if need be, for here you have been having all the responsibility and none of the fun."

She took his proffered arm, wishing she had the willpower to gracefully decline. But of course she could not. The muscular arm was a comfort, as were those warm brown eyes, as was that low, calm voice. While he spoke to her, all the gossip and snobbery receded into a distant background. And now, as they danced, even the bleak picture Basil had painted seemed a little brighter. What if he did love Lady Honoria? Wasn't it better to take whatever crumbs he might offer than to go on suffering as she had since that morning in the park? Even if in time, after they were married (she flushed at the thought), he came to resent her, he would be too much the gentleman ever to show it. But his next words called her back.

"Miss Latham, I hope you're not drifting away to a more interesting place, just now when I most need your help; for Lucy insists that I describe your gown in exact detail to her tomorrow morning. And though I have scrutinised you carefully, and committed you to memory, I fear my ignorance of feminine *couture* will cause me to fall far short of my ward's expectations."

She was brought back to earth with a jolt. And suddenly the accumulated tensions of the last few days were too much for her. She was exhausted. Since that meeting with Basil, she had slept fitfully—when she had slept at all. The ball preparations had demanded her constant attention. Her aunt's nagging had been a constant strain. Alicia's difficulties at the start of the evening had stretched her nerves taut. And now this innocent reminder of why he sought her out, why he was so kind to her, undid her. She tried to inject humour into her voice as she began to explain Madame Vernisse's mysteries, but her voice faltered, and tears glistened in the corners of her eyes.

Lord Hartleigh, who had been more intent on watching her lips and eyes than on listening to her lecture, found himself in a turmoil. His instinct was to take her in his arms and comfort her. But this was a crowded dance floor, and she was the object of considerable speculation as it was, and, well, it just wasn't done, no matter how one longed to do it. He willed himself to speak calmly as he asked, "Miss Latham, have I said something to distress you?"

"No." She wouldn't meet his eyes. "No, of course not. But I believe that between the crush of the people and the heat of the candles—"

"Yes, of course," he interrupted. "We must find you a quiet spot and a cool drink." Calmly, he led her away from the dancing, gracefully discouraging the several guests who attempted to stop their progress with chatter. As they reached the doors to the hall, he asked, "Shall I send one of your cousins to you? Or your mother?"

She smiled up at him, grateful for his thoughtfulness, even though it made her ache all the more. Of course it wouldn't do to wander off alone with him. Not in the circumstances. "My mother, please. To the small parlour."

He nodded and was gone in search of Maria. But Mrs Latham was much too fatigued to leave her comfortable chair. "Pray, bring the child a glass of lemonade," she drawled. "Isabella has a frighteningly strong constitution, and I'm sure will recover completely in a very few minutes." Seeing his hesitation, she added, "It's obviously the heat of the room. I'm sure she can be safely entrusted to your care for *five or ten minutes*, Lord Hartleigh. And if she's not recovered by then, I shall send a servant to attend her to her room."

"Five or ten minutes?" Was she telling him to take advantage of the opportunity? It was absurd, yet he hurried to procure the glass of lemonade. His practised calm served him well as he hastened, without appearing to do so, from one room to another, seeking this mysterious "small parlour."

At length he saw the slender form in the gown of

sapphire-blue silk he'd studied so carefully. The room was crowded with the excess furniture and bric-a-brac which had been moved out of the rooms in which the festivities were taking place. She was standing by the window, her back to him. One silky blonde tendril had slipped from its pins to caress the soft white skin of her neck, and he found himself wanting to plant his lips on the spot. Instead, he gently touched her shoulder. She started, and when she turned, he saw the tears in her eyes. "My m-mother?" she gulped, looking past him to where there was . . . nobody. And then, hastily, she wiped her eyes.

There was that great treacherous ache again. He deposited the lemonade on the nearest horizontal surface and took her into his arms. It was instinctive. He meant only to hold her, comfort her, but when she raised her head to speak, he saw the slight tremor of her lips, and could not keep his own from touching them. And that, too, suddenly wasn't enough. Her mouth was so soft, so warm. A faint scent of lavender seemed to tease him closer. His arms, of their own accord, tightened around her, and his lips pressed hers, gently at first, and then, as he felt her hands creep up around his neck, with increasing urgency. His pulse raced at her touch, and for a few delicious moments, as she responded to his kiss, he gave himself up to desire. The warmth of her slim body, its surprisingly sensuous curves molding to the hard muscle of his own, sent his blood rushing through his veins. He could feel her heart beating in the same wild rhythm as his own, and his lips moved from hers to draw a trail of kisses along her neck . . . to her shoulders . . . to the creamy flesh swelling at the neckline of her gown . . . and then she began to pull away. He wanted to lift her in his arms and carry her away—to . . . to . . . good God, what was the matter with him?

Summoning all his willpower, while inwardly cursing the place, the circumstances, all the rules and duties that made it impossible to take her now and make love to her, he released her. "Forgive me," he whispered as she backed away.

"Yes. Yes, of course. These things . . . happen."

Her voice was calm, detached, yet her lips trembled, and he ached to kiss them again. But it wasn't right. And there was so little time. Twisted one way by guilt and the other by the passion she'd so quickly, so surprisingly aroused, he found it impossible to gather his wits, and his words came out in a confused rush. "It isn't what you think—that is, I don't know what you think—but I didn't mean to distress you. I couldn't help—Isabella, I want you to be my wife."

The blue eyes which met his for an instant were filled with longing—and sadness—but when she quickly looked away again, he wasn't sure that he hadn't imagined it.

"That really isn't necessary, My Lord. After all," she added ruefully, "I didn't offer much of a struggle. None, in fact. Which makes me equally to blame."

"Blame?" he repeated, taking her hand. "When you've given me a glimmer of hope?"

The colour deepened in her face. "Please—we must end this . . . this . . . conversation. My family will be looking for me." She tried to pull her hand free, but he clasped it tighter still.

"Only tell me that you'll consider—"

"I cannot."

"No. Don't say you cannot. I know this is not the right time or place. I know it's too sudden. But I spoke to your mother this morning."

Her head went up in surprise, but he went on, oblivious to all but his urgent need to hear just one hint of encouragement. "Isabella, surely you must realise—you must have recognised by now that I hold you in great regard." Oh, why would the words be so stiff? But it was either that or confess to a passion which he hadn't suspected until a moment ago. And he'd shocked her badly enough already. Blindly, he plunged on. "And though I can't expect you to return those feelings now, will you not at least allow me the hope of earning your affection? We share so many interests; we're not entirely unsuited. And Lucy, who adores you, would be the happiest girl in the world."

"Please," she begged, "no more."

"You will not let me hope? Have I so disgraced myself?"

"No. It isn't that. But I cannot consider your proposal."

The words chilled him, and he tried to keep the frustration from his voice as he asked. "Is there someone else?"

There was a rustling of silk at the door, and a bored voice enquired, "Are you here yet, Isabella?"

The earl immediately released her hand, and Isabella hurried to her mother's side. "I was just returning, Mama. Lord Hartleigh was kind enough to . . . to. . . ."

"Yes, of course. Well, your aunt is asking for you, my love, in the most insistent way." Maria Latham allowed her daughter to leave, then turned to the earl. "Time, my lord. It is always the enemy, is it not?" Then she, too, was gone.

Isabella retired briefly to her room to compose herself and rinse away the evidence of tears. "Regard." "Shared interests." "Not unsuited." And, of course, Lucy. If there had been but one word of love. No, affection would have been enough. And if he chose to press her, she'd settle for even less. For regard. For tolerance. And that was impossible. Because every one of her senses had responded to his kiss. His kiss. Even now she could not believe she hadn't dreamed that embrace, for it was so like the other dreams that had come to her, unbidden, so many nights.

Gracious God, what had she done? No protest, no faint pretence at distress or disapproval. He had touched her, and she had gone to him, unthinkingly, returned his kiss with a hungry passion which even now swept through her in waves, making her tremble—and making her ashamed. What had driven her to humiliate herself in that way? It was shameful enough that she wanted him so badly, but she, sunk to the very depths of immodesty, had *shown* him she wanted him. And he? He had only wanted a mama for Lucy. But instead he'd found himself with a love-crazed woman in his arms. What choice had he but to politely accept that love?

He'd felt sorry for her—Lucy's prospective stepmama—and sought only to comfort her. And then, when she had behaved in that shameless way, he'd gallantly blamed himself for her behaviour. It was unbearable. She loved him past all reason, and he . . . he "held her in great regard." To be his wife on those terms was unthinkable.

No, her course was plain. She would accept Basil this very night, for by tomorrow her resolve would weaken again.

She was left to cool her heels for some time, however, for when she returned to the ball, Basil was oblivious to her efforts to catch his eye. He had seen her exit the room and his cousin follow shortly after. He had seen her mother follow some minutes later. The mother had returned, and the cousin had returned, but there was no Isabella for a quarter hour. Things looked promising. If Edward had offered and been accepted, would not the two have returned together, happily? But Edward was looking like a thundercloud, and Isabella's company smile was frozen on her face.

Calmly, Mr Trevelyan returned his plump partner to her chaperone. He then danced with two more antidotes before leisurely making his way to Isabella's side. "Will you dance, Miss Latham?" he asked, his voice coolly formal for the benefit of the curious dowagers nearby, whose conversation had come to a halt at his approach.

Isabella's acceptance was equally cool. It was only after some minutes of Basil's inane chatter that she finally snapped, impatiently, "Enough. I have decided to accept your offer." He began to speak, but she stopped him. There were conditions, which she would discuss with him tomorrow, in private. Meanwhile, she would trust him to say nothing, hint nothing—to anyone. He solemnly assured her of his discretion, but as the dance ended and she rejoined her other company, it was all he could do to keep from shouting his victory to the entire room—and most loudly in the ears of his cousin.

12

It was very late when an exhausted Henry Latham emerged from the elegant town house close by Grosvenor Square. He was not an old man, but the trip to town had been an arduous one. The gentlemen with whom he needed to speak—like his recent host—were reluctant to have their neighbours see him entering or leaving their homes, and thus had set their appointments late into the night. Used to keeping country hours, the businessman found it difficult to keep his eyes open, and his weary feet could barely carry him down the steps. The two figures hovering in the shadows saw him stumble as he plodded down the street, and nudged each other in anticipation: another drunken nob, ripe for plucking.

Well, thought Henry as he made his painful way, it was no surprise that his clients were loath to admit their connexion to trade. He smiled to himself, thinking how many of his host's neighbours were so connected, all trying to hide their guilty secret.

Ah, but it was their way. And their many little hypocrisies had served him well. Honour, pride, the dictates of fashion—their social code was an expensive one. Land was not always profitable, gambling was risky. Thus, sooner or later, a number of society's shining lights found themselves connected with Henry Latham. Whether it was to avoid disgrace and debtors' prison, or merely for profit, these shining lights found themselves working for him. He'd profited from the information these well-placed sources provided, and his sources had shared the profits.

And tonight, he thought, as his weary eyes scanned the empty street for a hackney, his sources had served him well, though there was no profit in it. No, there never was profit in anything his brother had touched . . . but there was still much to do, and he had no way of knowing—yet—if there would be time enough in which to do it. He looked around quickly as he heard in the distance hoofbeats and the rattle of wheels, and then there was an explosion in the back of his head and all went black.

Lady Bertram pounded with her cane on the roof of the carriage, demanding to know why they had stopped. Her coachman's face appeared at the window. "A gennulmun, ma'am," he explained apologetically. "Lyin' in the road. Looks as he's hurt pretty bad."

"Drunk, rather," her ladyship grumbled.

"Beg pardon, ma'am, but 'e don't smell uv hit. 'E's had a hawful whack on the 'ed."

Eager as she was for her bed, she ordered the coachman to investigate. When he reported back that the man was indeed hurt, and that further, the footman had seen two figures scurry off when the carriage approached, she bade the two servants carry the man into the carriage. "We're nearly home," said the countess. "No point in waking up another household. We'll take him back with us and send for a doctor."

As they entered the house, she was surprised to see her nephew, who was just handing his hat and walking stick to a servant.

"Good evening, Edward," she said, then turned her back on him and began issuing commands to the sleepy household. One servant was sent for the physician. Two were sent out to assist in carrying the man into the house. Maids were ordered to fetch tea, brandy, towels, and hot water. Not until the entire house was abustle did she condescend to explain the situation to her bewildered relative.

Lady Bertram brushed aside her new houseguest's thanks. "I did not wish to disturb you," she told him, "but thought perhaps you'd like to have a message sent to your family."

"Thank you, My Lady, but it's unnecessary. My family is in Westford, and there's no one here in town expecting me at any particular time."

"Well then, as no one will be made anxious about your absence, we won't worry them needlessly. The doctor says you will recover nicely; all you want is rest and proper food. So I will start by leaving you to your rest, Mr. . . ."

"Latham, My Lady. Henry Latham." Seeing her start at the name, he asked, "Is anything wrong?"

Lady Bertram smiled, "Why, no, Mr Latham. Not in the least. But I believe we have some mutual friends." She advanced upon the bed to offer her hand to the astonished patient, and surprised him further by adding, with a chuckle, "And may I say how *very* pleased I am to make your acquaintance."

Not long afterward, she and her nephew sat sipping sherry before a comfortable fire. Lady Bertram did not see fit to enlighten him as to the visitor's identity. At any rate, Edward did not seem particularly interested; not that this came as any surprise. She had seen all that Basil had seen, and a little more. She had, for instance, seen the gloating triumph on Basil's face after he'd danced with Isabella Latham. Miss Latham had looked very unhappy, though she had made a valiant effort not to appear so. And Edward's face had been a mask—cold, correct. But, like Basil, she'd recognised the anger behind it.

Right now he looked as he had when he was a boy, come to Aunt Clem to confide an unhappiness—and, just as when he was a boy, angry with himself for needing to. She knew it was best not to question him but, rather, to let him take his own time and way of getting to it. Still, it was late, and she was no young deb, and she wished he'd get on with it.

In response to her soliciting his opinion of the two young ladies who'd this evening made their debut, he went on at some length about the little golden-haired one. Then, abruptly, he stopped midsentence to stare at the fire.

"Are you asleep, Edward?" his aunt prodded. "For if you are, I should prefer you continued it elsewhere."

The dark eyes flickered in her direction briefly, then returned to the fire. "No, Aunt, I was just wondering. How badly dipped do you think my cousin is?"

"What difference does it make? You've made it plain you're not in the least concerned for his welfare."

"It's not *his* welfare I'm thinking about. As you well know. Aunt Clem sees all, knows all."

"You make me sound like one of those swarthy gypsy women."

"Then tell me my fortune." His voice was quiet enough, calm enough, but the flickering firelight emphasised the lines of his face, underlining the effort with which he controlled himself. "She won't have me."

"I believe you mean Miss Latham," said his aunt. "She has refused you?"

He nodded, not trusting himself to speak for the moment, for his aunt's words recalled the cramped room and the small detached voice saying, "I cannot," and the frustration seemed about to choke him. He could still taste her lips, still feel the press of her body against his, and it still sent shock waves through him.

He had come to his aunt's house not knowing where else to go, unable to bear the thought of his own pillow, where the remembrance would, he knew, come to torment him. And tomorrow, how would he tell Lucy—for she must be told sometime—that Missbella would never be her new mama?

"You must tell me what happened." As he began to protest, she waved him away. "Don't tell me what a gentleman does and doesn't do, Edward. I know all about it—and you know I don't intend to make this the latest *on-dit*."

"I know all that, Aunt. But there's no point in discussing it. She made herself quite plain. And though she did not say so, I suspect you were right; she does mean to have Basil." He spat out the name as though it were a curse. The thought of Basil touching her, holding her—it did not bear thinking of—and yet it seemed he'd be doomed to think of it the rest of his natural life.

"You are quite maudlin," she replied, motioning for him to refill her glass. As he did so, she continued. "I cannot believe you are willing to give up so easily after one skirmish. You've been mooning after the gel since you first clapped eyes on her—"

" 'Mooning'!" In his indignation at this lowering assessment of a thirty-five-year-old Peer and former intelligence officer, the earl nearly spilled his drink. "Really, Aunt—"

"Yes, mooning. Ever since she gave you that set-down you so richly deserved, you've been making excuses to see her. Lucy has been a convenient excuse, but I'm tired of it. The sooner you admit that you're head over heels in love with Isabella Latham, the sooner we can talk sensibly. And perhaps find a way out of this coil. I shall never to my dying day understand how you managed to make such a mull of this, Edward. Even an idiot can see how well you suit. But then, men are such blockheads where women are concerned."

Being lumped together with every other male of the species did little to lighten the earl's mood, but he was forced to recognise the truth in his aunt's words. And somehow, even this scolding, though not at all agreeable to one's dignity, brought some small measure of relief, as Aunt Clem's scoldings always did.

And so he found himself telling her all that had

happened. When he referred to "forcing his attentions," he was further relieved to hear his aunt pooh-pooh the idea. "You are being melodramatic," she insisted. "She did not scream, or faint, or box your ears. She was even honest enough to admit her own willing participation. And you think she has taken you in disgust?"

"Whatever it was, she refused to even consider marrying me."

"She said she *could* not."

"Will not, cannot. What difference does it make?" he retorted, pacing the floor now. "The answer is still No. And she will marry Basil—"

"That is very likely, unless you prevent it."

He protested that this was exactly what he'd tried to do.

"From what you've told me," said his aunt, taking the tone one would with a particularly slow child, "you did make an attempt. But your strategy was not well considered. And I am very surprised. For though Basil is a clever fellow, he is not nearly as clever as that little Corsican soldier you outwitted—"

"With some small assistance from Robert Warriner—not to mention the combined allied armies—"

She ignored him. "You did not study your opponent, master his weaknesses, or make any attempt to understand his plans. I know Miss Latham has a good head on her shoulders, but I doubt she's come up against one of Basil's ilk before. Don't mistake me, Edward. I love Basil dearly, with all his faults, but even I must admit that he is a very adept liar. So adept that he convinces even himself. Well, after all, his survival has depended upon it. What a great pity he has not entered politics. *Will* you stop pacing, Edward. A body can't think."

Obediently, Lord Hartleigh stopped, and flung his long form into a chair. It was amazing, his aunt thought, that for all his internal distress, only his hair—raked into disordered curls—gave any evidence.

"You're telling me to try again?" he asked.

"Yes. But for heaven's sake, do use a little more guile. I can't believe that when she drew away from you, you didn't think to draw her back with soft words. Instead you make her a speech. One would think you a schoolboy fresh down from Oxford and still wet behind the ears." Lady Bertram gave an exasperated sigh. "What *is* this generation coming to?"

In spite of himself, he smiled. For his aunt was right. He'd been so busy protecting his pride—ashamed of the way his senses had betrayed him, ashamed of taking advantage of Isabella's distraught state—and so busy convincing himself he was protecting *her,* that he'd omitted the most important words; the "soft words" his aunt spoke of. *Regard, respect, suitability*—how cold and patronizing those terms seemed now, unaccompanied by any whisper of affection or love. To one of Isabella's intelligence, how pompous he must have sounded. What an ass he'd been! He looked up to find his aunt watching him, her own face a document of concern.

"Yes, Aunt," he admitted, "I've been a great blockhead. Your perspicacity will never cease to astound me." He lifted his glass in salute.

"I'm merely old," the lady replied, "and have had time to learn." But she lifted her glass in return.

Light was breaking as Lord Hartleigh left his aunt's house. He'd had little sleep in the past three days, but his step was lighter than it had been. He had some hope. Perhaps the odds were with Basil. Perhaps his cousin had won the skirmish and was now on his way to winning the war. But Edward Trevelyan, seventh Earl of Hartleigh, would not relinquish the battlefield just yet.

13

The other members of the Belcomb household were yet abed when the groggy servant showed Basil into the library where Isabella was waiting. Mr Trevelyan himself had slept quite soundly, thank you, happy anticipation serving in his case as a soporific. And though it was an inhumane hour of the morning, he had no complaints. One must expect to make some sacrifices, after all. He was thus at his most sprightly as he entered the room, exclaiming, "Miss Latham, how perfectly charming you look this morning. I would say green is your colour, but then last night I was convinced *blue* was your colour, for you put your cousins altogether in the shade and quite took my breath away. But this morning I am breathless again. I declare it is a privilege and an honour for that dress to be draped upon your delightful person. Exactly as I should like to be," he added, *sotto voce*.

"Gracious God," she cried, "was there ever such a chatterbox?"

"My love, if I don't talk, then I must *do* something. And at present, what it is in my mind to do would probably not meet with your approval." When he made as if to move toward her, she backed away behind the great desk. He smiled, perched himself on the edge of the desk, and folded his arms. "But I shall endeavour to restrain myself—for the moment."

"Yes," she faltered. "We . . . we have business to discuss."

"How cruel you are. Not business, darling. A wedding." The amber eyes were wide open and innocent—angelic, even. "We're going to be married. And I hardly slept a wink for thinking of it," he lied. Clearly, *she* had not slept. The dark shadows under her eyes emphasised her pallour.

"Yes," she repeated. "We're going to be married. But as I told you last night, there are some conditions." She looked at him, expecting some protest, but he sat quietly, waiting.

"I believe," she continued, "that I am entering into this . . . this—*business*—with my eyes wide open. However, there are some demonstrations of good faith I require. Not for myself, for I have no illusions about your feelings for me—"

"You know I adore you."

"Cut line, Basil," she snapped. "I wish at least you'd stop insulting my intelligence with this absurd pretence."

"It isn't a pretence . . ." he began, but, thinking better of it, subsided, contenting himself with looking more angelic than ever.

"The conditions are for my family's sake," she went on, in an odd, dry voice. "First, there is to be an end to the gossip about us—"

"But, my love—"

"You encouraged it. Now you can discourage it. The gossip and the wagers are to stop. Completely. Further, you are to behave toward me with respect. And with discretion. You were able to do so last night, and I'm sure you can continue to do so. At least for two weeks, which is the time limit I've set—though I'm sure you could stop the gossip in as many hours."

His eyes sparkled dangerously, but "Yes, dear" was all he said.

"The fortnight's time limit is as much for your sake as my own. I realise that some of your creditors must be satisfied soon. If at the end of this period you have kept your part of the bargain, I shall immediately set things in train to pay the most pressing of your debts. Most of your creditors, of course, will be more patient when our betrothal is announced.''

Her generosity astonished him. He'd expected far more difficult conditions. He'd even come prepared for some blows to his pride. But this wasn't what he expected. It was too simple. Puzzled, he asked if that was all.

"No. That is, yes. As soon as I've settled with your creditors, you may do as you wish: send the announcement to the papers, set the date. Whatever." She shrugged. "I shall marry you when and where you say."

"But for a fortnight," he said, slowly, "no one is to know?"

"I plan to tell my mother immediately, and let her decide when to tell my aunt and uncle. In any case, all will see the advantages of keeping silence meanwhile."

"But, my love, how can I be sure *you'll* not slip away from me between now and then, while I'm hard at work crushing gossip and behaving myself?"

"Slip away?" she echoed. "Where? How? Where you have not hemmed me in, my obligations have. You know as well as I that what I ask is a mere token. To undo the damage done to my reputation, to allow my cousins a fair chance. I ask you this for my family's sake—a small act of good faith. And besides," she added listlessly, "I give you my word that I shall not break this bargain."

He was torn between delight and suspicion. "You exact no other promises—no other conditions?"

She shook her head.

"Isabella, you've made me very happy, but you astonish me."

"Why?"

He slid from his perch and circled round the desk to where she stood. This time she held her ground, even as he placed his hands on her shoulders and gazed into her eyes. "Because you might have offered me a marriage of convenience," he replied.

"You may have that, if you wish."

116

"I *don't* wish it. But do you?"

She stared at him—or, rather, through him—for a long moment before she answered, softly, "There's enough pretence in this business as it is. Let us at least make an honest effort at this marriage of ours. I will try to be a good wife. I ask in return that you make an honest effort to be a good husband."

"But it's so very unfashionable, my dear."

"Yes. I know it's all the rage to be miserably married and happily unfaithful. Well," she said with a shrug, "you'll do what you like in the end. Only give me some peace of mind for the next fortnight. And now, will you please go away?"

He dropped a kiss on her cheek, and she winced. As he drew away, he found himself, quite unexpectedly, quite angry. But he did not shake her or utter any of the cruel remarks which so quickly leapt to mind. Instead, he manufactured an affectionate smile, and politely took his leave.

Telling Mama was considerably more difficult, for she was exasperatingly obtuse today. At length, when Isabella had outlined the advantages of the match for what seemed the thousandth time, Maria Latham looked down at the diamonds sparkling on her fingers and sighed.

"Will you not at least wish me happy, Mama?" her daughter pleaded, struggling to keep her voice even.

"I cannot wish you happy when you persist in telling me the most outrageous bouncers, my love."

Startled by this accusation, Isabella gave a guilty glance at her mother's face, but Maria went on as though she noticed nothing. "But then, darling, I am quite at your disposal, and prepared to wait all day, if need be, for you to tell me why you have so abruptly decided to marry Mr Trevelyan." In demonstration thereof, Maria leaned back comfortably against her cushions and gazed out the window.

"But, Mama, I've told you several times already."

"Then I suppose you must tell me again."

Minutes ticked by as Isabella considered whether to give up and leave the room. Yes, there was a great deal more she could tell, but she couldn't bring herself to confide in her lackadaisical parent. And perhaps, anyway, it wasn't confidences Mama sought. As it became clear that no guidance was to be volunteered, Isabella asked, "What exactly is it you wish to know? And why did you say just now that I had lied to you?"

"It is equally a lie to me when you leave things out as when you put the wrong things in." The sudden flush on her daughter's face indicating a direct hit, Maria went on, once again apparently taken with what was beyond the window. "You have gone on interminably about Mr Trevelyan, yet you have not even thought to mention why you've refused Lord Hartleigh."

"What has that to do with it?" Isabella burst out before she had time to wonder how her mother knew. Had she been eavesdropping last night?

"That's what I would like to know. For Lord Hartleigh *most properly* sought my permission to pay his addresses to you." (The fact that Mr Trevelyan had not done so was thus left disapprovingly implied.) "And since last night I provided him with a decent opportunity in which to make a start—"

"Mother!"

"—and came upon you gazing soulfully into each other's eyes—"

"Mother!"

"—I must confess myself at a complete loss as to why you are telling me of your engagement to his *cousin*. It is quite the most ridiculous thing I've ever heard—your aunt's daily conversation excepted, of course."

This was too much for Isabella, who dropped into a chair and promptly burst into tears. Her mother bore this demonstration with perfect equanimity, and at length, when Isabella had regained some measure of self-control, bade her come sit by her and tell the entire story.

This exercise occupied a full half hour and was punctuated with sobs, tears, and an occasional hiccough. When it was done, Maria calmly ordered tea as a restorative.

"My love," she said some time later as she thoughtfully stirred her tea, "this is a bewildering tangle indeed."

Isabella merely nodded. To speak, she thought, was to choke. For now that she'd confessed her infatuation with the earl, every memory she'd so ruthlessly crushed last night and this morning rose up to haunt and torment her, compounding the exhaustion which had already made her dizzy.

"You are quite convinced that Lord Hartleigh's offer was primarily motivated by his ward's desires, rather than his own?"

"Yes" was the dismal reply. "And even it if weren't—which I know it *is*—it's too late now. I've given my word to Basil."

"Yes. Well. You know, Isabella, I do believe my lifelong opposition to arranged marriages was ill considered. It is perfectly amazing what a mull of things the principals will make when left to themselves. And it seems, now I think of it, to run in the family."

Isabella was too caught up in her own misery to perceive the implications of her mother's admission. She simply nodded in agreement.

"Well, at the moment I cannot think what can be done to mend matters. All these complications and insinuations and declarations—I confess it's quite beyond me. At any rate, I don't think it necessary to mention your betrothal to any of the others just yet. For now, we must be content to hope for the best. I shall hope, for instance, that your Intended is struck and killed by a passing carriage. This afternoon, preferably," she murmured, half to herself, "just about teatime. Now *that* would be an aid to the digestion." She got up, absently patted her daughter on the head, and left the room.

A moment later she put her head back through the door. "Which reminds me, darling. I shall be joining Lady Bertram for tea today. She was kind enough to invite us this morning, but I think it would be better if you stayed home with a headache."

It had been an overcast, oppressive day, and the air's heaviness seemed to have cast its pall on the features of the three who sat, pretending to take tea. Mr Latham was embarrassed and uncomfortable. Lady Bertram was never embarrassed, but her dignified features were thoughtfully solemn. Even Maria, who rarely registered any expression but *ennui*, had a tightness about her face which, in her, was indicative of perturbation.

It was the countess who broke the silence, striving to put the usually genial Mr Latham at ease. "No," she told him firmly, "you were quite right in making your investigations. She is your niece, after all. Certainly, I should have done as much, in your place." She lifted a tiny sandwich from the tray, looked at it as though it were a venomous serpent, then dropped it onto her plate and forgot about it as she turned to Maria. "And given the horrifying state of Basil's finances . . . well, in your place, I would have no scruples in forbidding the match, regardless whether she is of age, regardless what foolish promise she made Basil. Unless, of course, you are persuaded that she has conceived a passion for him and will be thoroughly miserable without him. And somehow," she added, with a ghost of a smile, "though he is a devilishly charming wretch, I cannot believe he has managed to charm *her*."

"No, but he *has* persuaded her," Maria replied.

"But surely you are not prevented by this scandal he threatens you with. If I may be blunt, Maria, you've survived worse."

Maria's features tightened just a bit more as she pondered this for a moment. Then, after casting a swift glance at her brother-in-law—who reddened slightly—she turned to the countess. "The scandal you speak of is nothing. Isabella is naïve to take it so seriously—perhaps because others around her make so fatiguing a fuss about it. But no, that is not the matter. Certain facts have recently come to my brother-in-law's attention—"

"Maria!" her brother-in-law interposed in a low, warning voice.

"Do not trouble yourself, Henry. Lady Bertram is entitled to know. And it is my experience," Maria went on, meeting that lady's gaze unwaveringly, "that she is the soul of discretion."

In a quiet voice, she went on to tell her story, interrupted once or twice by Lady Bertram's expressions of sympathy and surprise. When Maria had finished, the trio sat in silence for several minutes. The tea had grown quite cold by this time, and the biscuits and tiny sandwiches seemed to have hardened into rocks.

"But this is infamous!" Lady Bertram finally exclaimed. "And your daughter knows nothing of it?"

"With Harry presumed dead, there was no reason to tell her. It would only have made her unhappy, needlessly, and forced her to carry my secret as a burden for the rest of her life."

"And now?"

"And now I feel I owe it to Harry to discover *his* wishes in the matter, first."

"He has been wronged enough," Mr Latham put in, "that we wished not—even inadvertently—to wrong him further."

"But why do you tell me this? Surely Harry will not want the tale bruised about, regardless what he wants Isabella to know or not to know—" Lady Bertram stopped suddenly, as a suspicion struck her. "Ah, now I see. Basil. He has somehow ferreted out the truth."

"He has questioned my brother quite closely about Harry Deverell."

"And just last night, My Lady, I learned that he is

likely in possession of a letter never intended for public consumption.''

Lady Bertram shook her head sadly. ''Poor Basil. What a dreadful boy he's turned out to be.''

''Not so much dreadful, I should think,'' Henry suggested tactfully, ''but careless, as so many young men are. And now, it seems, desperation has soured his better nature.''

''That is very generous of you, my good sir, but I know my nephew, and he has been devious since the day he was born. Well, there's no help for it, then. I will have to speak to my man of business—''

Mr Latham jumped up from his seat in agitation. ''Gracious Heaven, no, My Lady! It will never do. You'll pay the old debts and he'll go on making new ones. No, no. It is unthinkable.'' He was adamant, shaking his head even after he'd finished speaking.

''Henry is right,'' said Maria. ''And he has some ideas of his own on how we may proceed. Furthermore, you've forgotten about your other nephew, who—unless I am greatly mistaken—will not be content with Isabella's tiresome excuses.''

''He's been devilish slow and thickheaded so far'' was the muttered response. ''To stand there and take no for an answer when it was plain as the nose on his face . . . but then I told him what I thought.'' She turned to the gentleman. ''Well then, sir,'' she urged, with the air of a conspirator, ''tell us your plan.''

14

"Uncle Edward! Look! Look!" But this time, instead of indicating her own accomplishments in the saddle, the child on the silver-grey pony was pointing in the opposite direction, across the meadow where a familiar figure in a dark green riding habit had just emerged from one of the park's side trails. Though she was some distance away, neither Lord Hartleigh nor his ward had any difficulty in recognising Miss Latham.

"Oh, Uncle Edward, it's Missbella. May I show her my new pony?"

The earl was about to agree when he saw Miss Latham turn back angrily toward her groom, then set her spurs to her horse and dart away. "No, I don't think so," he said slowly, never taking his eyes from the slim figure on the brown mare. "She is going rather fast"—he noted with alarm that it was very fast indeed—"and we had better not distract her."

Blast her! John, the groom, cursed to himself, watching helplessly as his mistress galloped across the meadow. Warning him to keep away, she had shot far ahead of him, as if all the fiends of Hell were after her. Was ever a man so cursed to have such a one in his care? Her usual way was bad enough, but at least she was usually in control of herself and her animal. Today, though, she was in a temper, and urged her horse on to a pace that even in a man called for a cool head and complete concentration.

Oh, she was an odd one, no doubt. And not just in her unladylike riding practices. There was talk in the stables which matched the downstairs talk Polly had passed on to him. And though he made it a practice to believe only half of what he heard, the half that remained did not match what *he'd* seen. Oh, yes, she'd met the light-haired gentleman in the park, but you could look as hard as you liked and precious little sparking you'd see. For Miss Latham might be a plain girl from the country, but she had a will of her own. He swore to himself as her pace increased—for even were she a man, riding astride, it would be a dangerous pace, damn her. She was like that black Arabian his lordship had had to sell at such a loss: quiet on the outside and very obedient, but with a willful streak. Would just take it into his mind he wouldn't have a rider, and he'd just shy and rear up until he was free. Turned around and bit his lordship one day for no reason at all. Aye, the one Miss married—if she married at all— would get himself bit now and then, depend on it.

Lost in earthy fantasies about Miss Latham's relations with some anonymous husband, the groom was slow to react when he first saw the horse shy at a bird that darted past. As John watched in paralyzed horror, the horse abruptly stopped, its head dropped forward, and its rider slipped over its shoulder, tumbling to the ground. Cursing once more his ill luck in having so wrong-headed a female under his care, he whipped his own animal toward the still—too still—form lying in a heap next to the now quiet mare.

But he was beaten to the spot by the Earl of Hartleigh, who was out of the saddle and kneeling beside her while the groom was yet halfway across the meadow. The earl was tearing off his coat as the groom drew near. "Good God, man," he upbraided him, "could you not see that her horse had gotten away from her?"

"B-but, My Lord, that's how she always does—and she won't let me—" The groom stopped, for there was murder in his lordship's eye.

"What's the matter with you, you fool! Can't you see she's hurt? And you there talking? Go for help!"

Relieved to escape the scene of his crime, John dashed away. But even as he rode, tormented with the prospect of losing his place and the even worse prospect of never getting another, he found a moment to wonder why his lordship looked so desperate; sick, almost. It was an odd thing, for one who'd surely seen worse in France and Spain.

Desperate and sick at heart Lord Hartleigh was indeed, as he gently placed his rolled-up coat under her head. He chafed her cold hands, by turns murmuring unintelligible endearments, then muttering curses on himself and his stupidity. Hours seemed to pass thus, rather than the actual few minutes, before her eyes fluttered open to gaze blankly at him.

His heart, which seemed to have stopped from the moment he'd seen her galloping madly across the meadow, resumed some semblance of normal operation. But his voice shook as he spoke her name, and the hand which brushed her fair hair from her face trembled. "Are you all right, Isabella?" he asked softly. "Are you in pain?"

"I never fall," she responded. Her eyes gazed blankly at him.

"Yes, I'm sure you don't," he agreed.

"I never fall," she repeated, more emphatically. As if to prove it, she started to get up, then winced and fell back.

With dismay, he realised that she did not know him or understand what had happened. A sickening dread filled him as he continued to stroke her forehead gently, and tried to make her understand. "You mustn't move. Your groom has gone for help. You mustn't move until we can tell how badly you're hurt."

She insisted that she could not be hurt and that she never fell, and again tried to get up, with the same result. "Stop it," he whispered. "Stop it." He told her who he was, he told her that help was coming soon, but she continued to repeat her two claims, no matter what he said to her.

After what seemed a lifetime, John returned, along with a carriage, a brace of footmen, and a doctor. Reluctantly, the earl gave up his place to the medical man and, only by sheer force of will, restrained himself from throttling that professional as he poked and prodded at Isabella. Turning away in frustration, Lord Hartleigh suddenly remembered his ward. He had barked an order for her to stay where she was when he first took off after Isabella. Had she seen the accident? Or had Tom been clever enough to distract her? Well, there was no time to worry about it now. He called to one of the footmen gawking idly nearby, and sent him off with a message to Tom to take Lucy home. Explanations would have to wait until later.

At length, the physician rose and joined him. The lady, he said, was not seriously hurt, but she was bruised. When the earl hotly argued that she didn't know where she was, he was met with an indulgent smile. "Just a mild concussion, My Lord, but nothing to concern yourself about. A bit dazed right now, but she'll come around in a little while. At any rate, it will be all right to move her."

Rudely thrusting him aside, the earl returned to Isabella and was relieved to find that, though she still didn't seem to know him, she had at least stopped insisting that she never fell. Over the exclamations of the servants, he lifted her in his strong arms and carried her to the waiting carriage. When he took a place beside her and slipped his arm protectively around her shoulders, he met the physician's raised eyebrows. "I have no intention of leaving her to the ministrations of these idiots," the earl growled, his tone daring opposition. "And besides, she should not be jolted overmuch." Well, Dr Farquahar was not a daring man, and decided to keep his opinions to himself.

When they reached the house, Lord Hartleigh insisted

upon carrying her up to her room, despite Lady Belcomb's vehement protests that there were strong healthy servants to see to it—and it was most improper—

"Pray control your grief, Charlotte," Mrs Latham interrupted rather sharply. "Your hysteria will not make Isabella the least bit better, and it is very trying to Lord Hartleigh, who, after all, has taken quite good care of her thus far."

Thus silencing her indignant sister-in-law, Maria accompanied Lord Hartleigh and Dr Farquahar to her daughter's room. When the earl had deposited his burden on the bed, he was still unwilling to leave her, but stood instead watching as the doctor mixed a potion of some sort and gave it to his patient. Still apparently oblivious to all that was happening around her, Isabella obediently drank it. After giving further instructions, the doctor left, and Maria turned to her distraught visitor.

"My Lord," she said quietly, touching his arm, "you must come away now."

"I cannot leave her like this," he answered, unable to tear his eyes from the blue ones that looked back but didn't appear to see him at all.

"But you must. When she does come to her senses— and the doctor assures us she will, quite soon—she'll be distressed to find you here." Seeing that her words were having some effect, she teased him gently: "And besides, if you do not leave soon, we must put her to bed in her dirty riding habit—for how can Polly undress her with you there staring, My Lord? That would not be at all the thing, I assure you."

This quickly recalled his sense of propriety, and the earl backed away guiltily from the bed. "Good God," he exclaimed, "what am I thinking of? Madam, you must forgive me—"

"For rescuing my only child? Well, perhaps in time I can manage it. Now come, sir. Let me offer you a brandy, for I'm sure you need it. And you most certainly deserve it." And so saying, she led him from the room.

Basil learned of the accident from Freddie, who had gone to claim Alicia for a drive in the park that afternoon. Upon being informed that Miss Latham was neither dead nor likely to die, Basil coldly remarked that he had not thought she would take such drastic measures to escape him.

Considering that his own heart had been permanently reduced to mush, Lord Tuttlehope was somewhat stunned by his friend's callousness. "Must say, old boy," he chided, "not a joking matter. Didn't know her own mother. And babbled a lot of nonsense at poor Hartleigh—"

" 'Poor Hartleigh'!" Basil exploded. "What the devil has my cousin to do with it?"

"Why, didn't I tell you?"

"Tell me what? All you've told me is that her horse threw her and scattered her wits in the bargain. What has my cousin to do with it?"

"Quite sure I told you," the baron insisted, blinking at this uncharacteristic display of temper.

"You have got your mind stuck, as usual, on something else," Mr Trevelyan noted with some irritation. Then, as he saw the hurt in his friend's eyes, he regained his self-command and apologised. "Sorry, Freddie. I didn't mean to snarl at you that way—"

"Not at all. Not at all." Embarrassed, the baron brushed away the apology. "No need. Worried about the girl, Basil. Know how it is."

No, you don't know how it is, you fool, Basil thought; but he swallowed his exasperation and bore Lord Tuttlehope's inarticulate reassurances with heroic fortitude. Finally, as Freddie sputtered to a close, Basil assembled his features into an appropriately appreciative expression and thanked his friend for his solicitude. "For I know I'm an ungrateful wretch, Freddie. But come, let us have the whole miserable business. I can bear it now." Meeting with two uncomprehending blinks, he prodded, "I believe that, in your anxiety to spare my tender feelings, Lord T, you left out half the story.''

And to be sure, he had. When Basil learned the whole of it, he burst into a long and only partially intelligible diatribe on the perfidy of women and the treachery of relatives. Not understanding more than one word in twenty, Freddie listened patiently, but with growing concern. He was used to Basil's extravagant speech, but was not used to seeing him so impassioned. And when his friend had done, he agreed (as he thought) that yes, Basil was barking up the wrong tree. "Best to chuck it," he added, nodding wisely. "Other fish in the sea, Trev.''

"Not for me, my friend. Come, let me show you something." Leading his friend to the window, Basil indicated a small, sallow-looking man in the street below. "Solsman and his friends have been very generous, you know, but for a price. I have three annuity payments overdue already and two more in another month. They come by now and then to remind me of our 'little business,' as they put it. But they haven't sent the bailiff for me yet, Freddie. Do you know why?''

Very ill-at-ease, Lord Tuttlehope shook his head.

"Why, they don't want to spoil the wedding plans, my boy. They're really most considerate fellows," he went on as he turned away from the window.

"Didn't know it was so bad, Trev. Only too glad to help—''

"You've thrown enough good money after me, Freddie. But you needn't worry. It's as I just explained to my friend down there on the street. Miss Latham and I have an understanding. A bargain, if you will. And though I'm on my somewhat questionable honour not to disclose the details, I can assure you that it will all come out right. Soon. Quite soon.''

He patted his friend on the shoulder and smiled reassuringly at him, but Lord Tuttlehope was not reassured. Long after the baron left his friend's lodgings, he was still trying to understand what had happened, and was still wondering whether it was the moneylenders hovering about like vultures or something very different which had made Basil act so odd.

When he reached home, Lord Hartleigh was relieved to discover that Lucy had borne the suspense surprisingly well. True, she had refused to be coaxed away from the window where she watched for her guardian's return. But she had waited, dry-eyed and quiet; and, when offered reassurances, had surprised the concerned staff by asserting that of course Missbella was all right—after all, Uncle Edward was taking care of her.

"You're a very brave little woman," he told her as he lifted her in his arms and hugged her.

"Yes," she agreed complacently.

But after he had satisfied her with all the details of Missbella's rescue and happy prospects of recovery, he was a trifle disconcerted to hear his ward read him a lecture. Missbella's family, she maintained, did not take care of her properly, and anyway there were too many of them to look after her as they should. And so it would be best if Missbella came to live with them—for Uncle Edward was big and strong and had only herself to look after. And there was lots of room, wasn't there?

In vain did the earl try to explain that there were rules governing these matters. Lucy informed him that she knew all about it; Miss Carter had told her. Oblivious to her guardian's astonishment, she went on: "Missbella is grown up, and they'll let her go away if she gets married. So you can get married to her and bring her back here and she can be my mama and you can take care of us."

The earl admitted that this was a sensible idea. "However," he added, "it is a very serious decision, Lucy. Whoever Miss Latham marries she will be married to forever. So she must be very, very sure it's me she wishes to marry."

"Oh, she'll be sure," his ward told him confidently. "But you must ask her, mustn't you?"

I already have, he thought. And, recalling the brief conversation he'd had with Maria Latham that morning, he wondered whether it would not be better to discourage Lucy's hopes. "She tells me she has given your cousin her word," Mrs Latham had told him. "And to Isabella, that word is as sacred as it would be to any gentleman. She has had, you see, a rather unusual upbringing."

But Lord Hartleigh couldn't bring himself to disappoint the child, especially after the terrifying experience she'd had, and the courageous way in which she'd dealt with it. So all he told her was that he would speak to Miss Latham, but only after he was certain she was quite well. And though she was fully prepared to assist personally in moving Missbella to her new domicile this very afternoon, Lucy promised to be patient.

15

The doctor's potion had the desired effect, for when Isabella woke in the early evening, she was once again in command of her senses. Her mother, upon determining this, ordered in tea, and spent an hour with her. Because Isabella was still rather dim on what had happened versus what she had dreamed, Maria offered up the account she'd had from Lord Hartleigh. The tale was told in her usual languid fashion, but contained so many sly hints and ironic references to the lengths to which the earl had gone—"solely on his ward's account"—that Isabella was finally moved to plead with her mother, "Stop teasing and tell me plain what you're about, Mama."

"Why, plain then, if you'll have it so, my love," Maria replied, gazing into her teacup as though the story were written there. "A man does not call one *his* 'poor darling' in that anguished tone of voice without some personal concern in the matter." Isabella opened her mouth to argue, but her mother was still talking to the teacup. "Certainly one wouldn't expect him to have rehearsed such words of concern and affection as I heard him whisper at you—although I did try *not* to hear, for it was most improper of him, you know." The cup not deigning to reply, she bent her gaze upon her daughter. "But then, all he did was so monstrous improper that we were all about the ears and didn't know where to look or what to hear. Your aunt, needless to say, was quite beside herself, but oddly enough, she didn't seem to think you compromised by it.''

News that a Peer of the Realm has so far forgotten propriety on one's account cannot fail to be gratifying, especially if said Peer is eligible, elegant, and handsome; and, more especially, if one would rather like to forget proprieties on *his* account. But the information also made Isabella feel quite desperate, and for a moment she was sorely tempted to leap from the bed and hurl herself out the window. If Lord Hartleigh *did* care for her, then her life was entirely ruined. It was one thing to give up the man you loved when he didn't love you. It was altogether another to give him up when he *did*. It was idiotic, in fact.

As though reading her daughter's mind, Maria went on, "In light of his behaviour this morning, I find it perfectly absurd that you have engaged yourself to his *cousin*."

"Oh, Mama, it's not absurd," Isabella cried. "It's completely horrible. Oh, why didn't that horrible animal kick me in the head and be done with it? What am I going to do now?"

"Isabella, you are far too unwell to engage in theatrics. But it's what comes, I imagine, of spending so much time in Mr Trevelyan's company. Whatever is the matter with you, my love? You have only to cry off. It's done every day. Some young ladies do it twice in a morning, I understand. To keep in practice, no doubt." She gazed thoughtfully at the biscuits on the tray and calmly selected and nibbled at one while Isabella protested that she could not. For one, added to her already questionable reputation would be the label of "jilt." For another, and more important, she had given her *word*.

"Considering that you were deceived into giving that word," Maria answered, daintily brushing a crumb from her sleeve, "and considering that your Intended has behaved dishonourably toward you, I don't think you need feel obliged to abide by it."

"But, Mama, he's desperate. I know he is. And if I break my promise . . . I don't know what he'll do."

"You cannot allow your life to be ruled by fear of what he'll do. And what can he do, after all? Blacken your name? Do you think for a moment his cousin would permit it?"

"I don't know."

"Of course you do." Maria stood up. "I would have preferred to postpone this discussion until you were feeling more the thing, but that is not possible. I have often found that in precisely those cases requiring lengthy and calm consideration, circumstances permit neither, but demand instead prompt action. Life can be very trying in that way, Isabella."

It struck Isabella that there was something unusual in her mother's expression. There seemed to be a note of something like regret in her tone, not at all in keeping with her usual air of indifference. But there was nothing to be read in Maria's face. The blue-green eyes were, as usual, focussed elsewhere, and the still-beautiful features appeared untouched by any emotion. She was still Mama, still languid, still an enigma.

"What circumstances do you mean, Mama?"

Maria sighed. "Lord Hartleigh will be here tomorrow. I don't think we need pretend he comes simply to enquire after your health."

"But I can't speak to him yet!" Isabella cried, her pleasure at this message quickly swamped by panic. How could she face him?

"That is both ungrateful and cowardly of you. And if that's the best you can do, then perhaps you and Mr Trevelyan will suit after all." Maria did not wait for a reply, but, in her normal manner, drifted out of the room. Abnormally, however, she slammed the door behind her, making Isabella cringe at the throbbing it set up in her head.

That same evening, Lord Hartleigh made his way to his cousin's lodgings. He had not visited the place in some years, and the closeness and shabbiness of the apartments shocked him, especially in their marked contrast to Basil's elegant attire. Mr Trevelyan was just applying the finishing touches to his ensemble, preparatory to an evening on the town, and he seemed neither surprised nor disconcerted by his cousin's abrupt appearance. "Come in, cuz," he told him cooly. "This is indeed an honour—though not, I must say, unlooked for."

"You expected me?" the earl asked, no whit less coolly.

"Oh, yes, indeed. In fact, I have been on pins and needles the whole day. Even sent my man out for a bottle or two of your favourite. And considering that I had to send ready cash along with him—for neither the vintner nor my valet will advance me another penny—I hope you'll do me the honour to partake of it."

At Lord Hartleigh's nod, he drew out from a small cabinet two glasses. These he minutely inspected, holding them up to the light. He then subjected the wine to the same scrutiny, and, after leisurely satisfying himself on these two counts, served his cousin and himself, and bade the earl be seated. Basil took a chair opposite and launched into a long stream of social chatter in which the weather and Lord Byron's relations with Caro Lamb figured most prominently. The earl bore with him. He knew that his cousin wished to irritate him, and therefore refused to be irritated. Finally, after some twenty minutes of relentless jabber, Basil broke off abruptly: "But then, cuz, I forget that this can't be a social call. I believe you have come on"—he smiled, recalling Isabella's tone that morning a few days ago—"a matter of *business*."

At the earl's nod, he went on, "Then tell me your business—although I believe I can guess it. Do you come on Miss Latham's behalf? I suppose you must, though I confess I'd rather she came as her own emissary."

"I come on her behalf" was the curt reply, "but she has *not* sent me."

"Ah, then perhaps she is still unconscious. How unfortunate that your *ministrations* had so little effect."

Lord Hartleigh suppressed the urge to hurl his glass in his cousin's face, and, wishing to avoid possible future temptation, he gently put it down. "I believe I'll let that insinuation pass," he answered, his voice just a shade too quiet, "though it does you no credit. For I've known you all your life, Basil, and I do believe you can't help it."

"You needn't patronise me, My Lord—"

The earl went on, as though he hadn't heard, "In fact, it's precisely because you *can't* help yourself that I've come. You seem to have gotten yourself into a surprisingly bad scrape, especially considering the advantages with which you began."

"You don't mean to lecture at me? For if you do, let me warn you that I get a weekly sermon from Aunt Clem. And, uplifting as it may be, it quite adequately meets my needs for that sort of thing."

"I haven't come to lecture. I've come to offer a solution—"

"But, cousin, perhaps I have one already."

"I don't doubt that you do. But it isn't worthy of you, Basil."

Basil's face flushed as he snapped, "Enough of this sanctimony. Let's have the word with no bark on it. In return for something or other, you want me to give the lady up."

"Yes."

"Well, I simply can't imagine what you could offer to compensate. It isn't only that Miss Latham is the perfect solution to all my difficulties. No. I know it'll surprise you—it surprises me—but I've grown rather fond of her. Oh, I'll admit she isn't very pretty; certainly not in my usual style. And she is overly serious and so terribly *responsible*. But I like to hear her laugh, you see. And at close quarters, Edward," he went on in confidential tones, deliberately baiting his cousin, "she is surprisingly appealing. Why, if I were at all poetical, I should write an ode to those delicious lips of hers.''

The urge to strangle his cousin nearly overcame Lord Hartleigh, but with superhuman effort he controlled himself, and merely pointed out that in such a case, Basil must, of course, consider Miss Latham's happiness above all things.

"Dear Edward, I should like ever so much to think of nothing but Miss Latham's happiness. Unfortunately, I am forced to consider the feelings of certain other parties.''

"And I gather these 'other parties' require certain payments in gold to soothe their tender feelings.''

"Why, there you have it, Edward. They are quite tender about their guineas.''

"You are telling me you want the money . . . and the girl.''

"Yes, of course.''

"And you would not consider an offer—say, an annuity which would allow you to pay the more pressing of your debts while still leaving you something to live on.'' The earl went on to name an amount which nearly took Basil's breath away.

But Mr Trevelyan recovered quickly enough. "Tempting, cousin. But no, it won't do. I mean to have her, Edward. And I recommend you give it up.''

The menace in his tone made the earl look up in surprise.

"You mistake me, cousin, if you think to bribe or trick me out of this game. And I believe you know me well enough to understand that I do not speak idly when I warn you away. You have your title. You have your lavish inheritance, which you so casually toss in my face. Be content with those, and find another mama for Lucy. For you will *not* have Isabella Latham.''

Now this was odd indeed. Lord Hartleigh had expected a struggle. Basil needed money, and had enough spite to want Isabella just because Edward wanted her. But Edward had hoped that his cousin would eventually be content to escape marriage—as long as he could do so profitably. After all, he had no real hold on Miss Latham. Basil knew Edward wouldn't stand for any more scandal-mongering. So what was it that made the little beast so confident? Another quarter hour's argument made it clear that the little beast had no intention of telling. He just sat there, smiling and smug, unmoved by threats or appeals to his honour or any other of the pleas to which his cousin at length resorted.

"No, Edward," he said, finally. "It won't do. And don't think to try to steal her away, for you may force some matters which can only cause my darling—and her family—tremendous pain."

And that was as much as could be gotten out of him. Edward took his leave calmly enough, but inwardly he seethed with rage and frustration. For without knowing what new villainy his cousin was contemplating, he hardly dared press Isabella to abandon the wretch.

Yet Lord Hartleigh knew he could not keep away from her—not if his life depended upon it. It was all he could do to stay away until tomorrow; all he could do to keep from rushing to her house and carrying her away—now—in the middle of the night.

Basil, meanwhile, was not quite as sanguine as he had appeared to his cousin. Before him on the table, next to a half-empty wineglass, was a much-creased letter.

It had taken a great deal of investigating, not to mention associating with persons Basil preferred not to know, before he had discovered Captain Macomber. Recently arrived from India, and an old friend of Captain Williams (now better known as Viscount Deverell), the lonely widower had been pleased to make the acquaintance of Mademoiselle Celestine. And Celestine, of course, required payment for entertaining the Captain. For after all, she had not only discovered his mission but—unlooked-for prize—had relieved the retired seaman of the precious scrap of paper.

. . . to learn the truth after all these years—or at least, some part of the truth. I do not know what words he used to convince Maria, but if they were at all like those he wrote to me, the man must have had the very Devil at his ear, prompting him.

And yet you must think it was my own damned fault, do you not? That I made no effort, when opportunity finally came, to see Maria myself—or to enquire more closely into the circumstances of their marriage and the birth of the child. But I thought to spare her trouble. And in truth, my pride was hurt that she had not waited longer before remarrying.

I know this is sorry repayment for all you have done for me these many years—yet I pray you understand the circumstances which prevented my revealing myself even to you, my closest friend. And I hope you will find it in your great and generous heart to forgive me.

Though he would not admit it, the heartache of Deverell's letter moved him. Mired as he was in his debts and machinations, Basil wished, for a moment, that he had accepted Edward's offer. But no. Just to keep out of prison would take up the whole of the annuity. With nothing over to live on, there would be further debts. No, it wouldn't do. And after all he'd done and risked, he was not about to leave to Edward the promised pleasures of that delicious mouth, that slim and sensuous body . . . and that low, intoxicating laughter.

16

Mama certainly was energetic today, Isabella thought, as she sat with her book in the now-restored small parlour. Maria had begun by convincing Aunt Charlotte to visit with Lady Bertram. "She begs for word of Isabella," Maria had sighed, "and will not be content with my note." In response to Lady Belcomb's protests that the countess could come see for herself, Maria provided seven or eight contradictory reasons why she could not, finally adding that she believed one of those Stirewells—or all of them—were expected, and Lady Bertram could not stir from home. This last silenced Charlotte, who immediately called for her daughter, found fault with her dress, made her change twice, and at length left the house, dragging the confused Veronica behind her.

Alicia was dispatched with her maid on a shopping expedition, and several dozen servants were provided with suitable occupations to keep them at some distance from the room in which Isabella sat reading. Mrs Latham then had a confidential interview with the butler, who had very little trouble memorising the names of those whose visits would not be too fatiguing for her daughter.

And so, when Lord Hartleigh called, he found only Isabella and her mother at home. He had no sooner entered the room and presented Isabella with a bouquet (which she promptly dropped, in her agitation) than the indefatigable Maria suddenly recalled an urgent matter for the kitchen, and was gone before her daughter had time to object.

But Mama's treachery was forgotten in an instant, for the earl immediately lowered himself onto the sofa next to his darling, took her hand, and pressed it to his lips. This proving insufficient expression of his feelings, he took her in his arms and kissed her until she was dizzy.

Now *he* knew it wasn't right, and *she* knew it wasn't right, but several blissful minutes passed before either of them was remotely inclined to act upon what they knew. As it was, Isabella was the first to act, but she made such a poor attempt at indignation that Lord Hartleigh immediately forgot the abject apology he owed her and told her instead that he'd been frightened half to death on her account, that his life was not worth living without her, that he needed her, wanted her, and other such romantical nonsense, which he then summarised by telling her that he loved her. And when those intelligent blue eyes looked back so adoringly into his, he silently bade the proprieties—and his cousin—to the Devil, and kissed her again.

Now this was all so very pleasant that it quickly began to grow indecent, for Lord Hartleigh was not *quite* content to plant tender kisses on Isabella's lips. He remembered a trail he had blazed a few nights ago, and let his lips travel upon it once again—from the ticklish spot behind her ear down along her neck to her shoulders to the not-insurmountable barrier of her bodice. And Isabella, to her shame, had tangled his lordship's hair into disorderly curls and had even disarranged the perfect folds of his cravat; not, as one would expect, in the struggle to protect her virtue, but rather to bring it into immediate danger.

However, as his lordship's gentle hands began exploring new territories, the danger finally penetrated Isabella's brain, and in the midst of a startlingly warm and enthusiastic response, she suddenly remembered that she was supposed to be engaged to someone else altogether. "Oh, no. Stop," she gasped. "Please stop."

Now it is very true that Lord Hartleigh had "unusually

141

high notions of duty" and a powerful sense of honour and right. But at the moment, having already sent Propriety to the Devil, he was exceedingly loath to recall it. He was, moreover, extremely reluctant to leave off his highly satisfactory explorations of Isabella's person. For though he did truly esteem and admire Miss Latham, and had great respect for her intellect, he was driven, at the moment, by naked lust. Every taste and touch was so delicious that he thought only of having more, and had completely forgotten everything else.

But now, for some unaccountable reason, she was telling him to stop. He pretended not to hear, and when her pleas grew more urgent, he tried to stop them with kisses. But she now refused to cooperate and was pushing him away. "Please stop," she hissed. "Mama will be back any minute."

Mama? Heated and breathless, he drew back and looked at her. Her silky hair had come loose from its pins, and one strand tickled the corner of her mouth. Lovingly, he brushed it aside, letting his fingers linger on her soft cheek, which grew bright pink under his gaze. "I quite forgot your mother," he said softly. "I thought—I wished—we were just . . . we two."

Feeling herself melting again, Isabella moved a few inches away from him, and strove—rather ineffectually, for her hands were trembling—to restore herself to rights. "For some reason," she muttered, trying to gather together some shreds of dignity, "I seem to forget myself in your company, My Lord. However, I hope you will remember that I've recently had a concussion, and cannot be held completely accountable for my actions."

Despite his frustration—for Lord Hartleigh did truly feel like a starving man who'd been invited to inhale the fragrance of a great feast and then forbidden to partake of it—despite this agony, his lips twitched with suppressed laughter as he gravely replied, "I'm fully aware of that, Miss Latham, and can only offer you my abject apologies for taking advantage of your . . . your weakened condition."

"Yes," she agreed, rather absently. Then, noting that he was as dishevelled as herself, she added, "Perhaps you should repair your cravat, sir."

Solemnly, he assured her that this was impossible. "A cravat," he whispered wickedly, "is very much like a reputation, Miss Latham. Once damaged, it cannot be repaired." Ignoring her gasp, he went on: "Except perhaps by some other, higher power. My valet can easily replace the neckcloth, you see. But your reputation is a matter for the parson. You will have to marry me as soon as possible." He reached for her, but she quickly got up from the sofa and crossed to the other side of the room.

"I can't," she said.

"You've made some foolish promise to Basil—or, rather, he's tricked you into a foolish promise. Come, Isabella, you can't seriously believe you're obliged to him in any way—"

"I am. I gave my word."

"If you discover that a man has cheated at cards, you do not proceed to pay him the money he's cheated from you." Impatient, he rose and strode across the room. Grasping her shoulders, he said softly, "Look at me and tell me you don't care for me. Tell me that you love him instead and want to be his wife. Tell me that and I'll go away and never trouble you again."

She hesitated, then met his eyes and smiled. "You know I can tell you no such thing."

"Good," he replied, then added with a wicked smile that made her heart flutter, "Then I propose we continue where we left off some moments ago, so that your mother will find us in a suitably compromising position. I don't plan to allow you the opportunity to change your mind later—when I've gone, and your infernal conscience tweaks you." So saying, he lifted her in his arms and carried her back to the sofa. He was just commencing yet another loving assault on her person when there was a rustling at the door.

"Now isn't that a pretty picture," Basil drawled as he sauntered into the room.

Isabella bolted upright, nearly knocking the earl off the sofa in the process. "We could ignore him," Lord Hartleigh muttered, disentangling himself from her gown. "Perhaps he'd go away."

"Certainly not," said Basil. He dropped his elegant form into a chair opposite, then pulled out his glass and calmly surveyed the scene before him. "Good heavens, Edward, your cravat is a disgrace. I suspected my fiancée had a passionate nature, but I did not think she had no respect for a man's neckcloth."

"She is *not* your fiancée," Edward growled.

"Oh, but she is. Hasn't she thought to tell you, cuz? Carried away by the heat of the moment, no doubt. But really, Isabella, you might have at least waited until *after* we were wed. I declare, you haven't the faintest notion how to go on in Society, do you, my love? First you get married, *then* you're unfaithful. Not the other way around. It just isn't done."

"Isabella has always had an odd way of doing things, Mr Trevelyan. She has had an unusual upbringing, you see. All those ledgers. . . ." This last trailed off into a sigh, as Maria Latham stepped into the room. Her weary gaze drifted from one to the next to the next, and she sighed again. "I do hope Fredericks does not subject us to any more visitors today. I find dramatic entrances most fatiguing." Acknowledging the gentlemen's bows, she wandered toward the sofa and, having waved Lord Hartleigh to another chair, took her place beside her daughter. "Isabella," she said, "I think you have been naughty."

"She has had a concussion," the earl began, but a speaking look from Mrs Latham quelled him.

"A concussion is no excuse for bad manners. Pray apologise to Mr Trevelyan, Isabella—"

"Mama!" Isabella gasped.

"And tell him to go away. Under the circumstances, he cannot wish to marry you."

"Oh, but I do, Mrs Latham. I am a very forgiving sort of person."

"Are you indeed?" The blue-green eyes met his, and Basil reddened slightly, but he went on nonetheless. "Yes, quite forgiving. She has had a concussion and my wicked cousin has attempted to take advantage of her weakened condition—"

"He did not!" Isabella cried, irritated at being treated like somebody's senile aunt.

"Well then, my love, I forgive you anyhow. I'm sure you had a good reason," Basil replied, with a maddeningly patronising smile.

"Yes, I did," she snapped. "I love him—and I'm going to marry him—aren't I?" She faltered, looking at Lord Hartleigh.

"Of course you are," that gentleman reassured her.

"There you are, Mr Trevelyan," said Mrs Latham, in tones of exhausted yet patient forbearance. "She means to marry your cousin. And now you may go away."

"Well, she's not going to marry him for all she thinks so at the moment." The topaz eyes glittered under half-closed lids as Basil toyed with his cane. "For one thing, what will her father say?"

There was silence in the room. Two faces stared at him as though he had suddenly gone mad. But there was a tiny crease between Maria Latham's brows as she watched him, warily. Isabella was the first to speak. "What are you saying, Basil? Papa died five years ago."

"Matthew Latham died five years ago. Your papa is alive and well. If he is not already in London, he is on his way—from India."

The tale had been told, and Isabella sat in stunned silence as her two suitors were summarily dismissed. Viscount Deverell—her father—and Mama had never said a word; not all these years, no, and not even today, as Basil's strangely harsh voice had gone on and on.

Yes, Harry Deverell had gone to sea. And yes, when Maria had run away, it was long after he'd left home. But that had been part of the plan—so that none would connect Maria's disappearance with Harry. And according to plans made well in advance, the two had married in an obscure town on the Cornish coast. The young couple had a few months of bliss before Harry was called away. He had just left when Maria discovered she was pregnant. And then, in less than a week, there was the accident, and Harry was presumed drowned.

What came next brought an aching lump to Isabella's throat, but she couldn't cry. What would she have done in her mother's place? Would she have waited, hoping against hope that it was all a terrible mistake? Would her pride have allowed her to present herself to her unsuspecting in-laws and demand that they care for her and the unborn child she claimed was Harry's?

Maria reentered the room, but she did not approach her daughter. Instead, she stood by the window, gazing out in her usual abstracted manner. It was only now that Isabella associated that look with the sailor's wife, gazing out to sea. As though she'd read her daughter's thoughts, Maria said, softly, "I did not know which way to turn. I had my marriage lines, but even so, it was more than likely we'd forfeited any claims to our families' support by going against their wishes. And even if they had determined it was their duty to help—they had little enough for themselves. When Matt Latham offered to marry me, it seemed the only solution. Harry was dead. I believed neither my nor Harry's family would take me in. And I had more than myself to consider. I did not want Harry's child to grow up in misery and want." Her voice never changed, never trembled. It was steady and detached throughout her recitation; and it did sound curiously like a recitation of a piece of fiction, rather than the true story of the ordeal she'd undergone.

Isabella got up and moved across the room to join her mother at the window. "In your place, Mama, I think I would have done the same. But why did you never tell me?"

"Neither when I thought Harry dead nor in recent months, when I knew him to be alive, did I feel it necessary to burden you with our secret."

"But surely when you learned—"

"No. I knew nothing of his life for all those years. I knew nothing of his wishes in the matter. I had rather even Mr Trevelyan be the first to tell you than that I do so without Harry's expressed consent."

Isabella took her mother's hand. "Poor Mama," she murmured.

"No," said Maria. "You must not pity me. Matt Latham did a terrible thing in driving your papa away. But he did love me. And except for betraying Harry, who had been his friend—Matt had even helped us plan our elopement, you know—well, apart from that, and those disastrous financial undertakings, Matthew Latham was a tolerable husband." The bored tone had crept back into her voice—and oddly enough, Isabella was relieved to hear it.

"But he knew my . . . my father was alive—and he never told you."

"Your father regained his memory almost a year later; he'd been struck in the head during some scuffle or other." Maria smiled, remembering Harry Deverell's quick temper. "He wrote to Matthew Latham—not his parents or brothers—first, asking him to break the news gently to me. But instead, my new husband wrote back, telling of the marriage, lying about the date of your birth, and, apparently, giving your father to understand that to reclaim me as his bride was to ruin me. I knew nothing of this. Nor did your uncle know of it, until a very short time ago. I had written to him that I suspected Mr Trevelyan knew something of the story. And Henry had that same day received a letter from a Captain Macomber, a friend of your father's, who related as much of the story as your father had finally confided to him. Apparently, once Harry received Matt's letter, he had determined to leave the past in darkness forever, and never to return to England. It was only the death of his older brothers that persuaded him otherwise. And in the course of corresponding with his family, he learned a bit more about us, and soon realized that Matthew Latham had lied about your birth."

Maria gently led her daughter away from the window, back to the sofa. Gazing earnestly at her, she went on, "Isabella, perhaps now you'll understand my reluctance to abandon you to the tender mercies of Mr Trevelyan. Matt Latham did a terrible thing, but he did it because he loved me. And because he loved me, I was able to have a tolerable life, though I was only moderately fond of him. I do not say that you may not have some mild affection for Mr Trevelyan. It is not difficult to see that there is a decent sort of heart there, somewhere underneath his poses and machinations. But he cannot truly love you. How could he, and wave the family's dirty linen in your face? To marry him would be to march merrily off to your own perdition."

"But he has threatened to spread your story—"

"Good heavens, Isabella. Caro Lamb stalks Byron everywhere he goes and he makes sport of her to his friends. I'm sorry to disillusion you, but their antics will quite take the shine out of this Gothic ancient history of ours. And as to a little accidental bigamy that happened more than a quarter century ago—why, has not our Regent made bigamy quite fashionable? No, society will buzz about us for a day or two, and then Caro will commit another outrageous act, and they will quite forget all about us. And you seem to forget—as Mr Trevelyan has—that at some point he will have to answer to Harry Deverell, if he does not first have to answer to Lord Hartleigh. No, my love. I do not think we need trouble ourselves overmuch with your nefarious so-called fiancé."

17

"There," said the lovely Celestine as she sealed the note and handed it to her visitor. "That'll fetch him. But I want you to know I'd never play him such a sorry trick if I wasn't about to get the toss myself, and need the money so badly."

"He won't suffer long for it," Henry Latham assured her. "Not if he's sensible."

"Ah, but he isn't," the young woman sighed. "Or he wouldn't be in such a fix, now would he?"

The middle-aged gentleman merely shrugged, and with a courtly bow of which she somehow wished she were worthy, he handed her a bulky envelope and left.

"You think," the earl snarled, as the two cousins made their ignominious exit from the house, "that because you are my cousin, I shall not call you out. Well, you are sadly mistaken—"

"I had rather thought to call *you* out," Basil retorted, "considering that she is *my* betrothed. If anyone has been insulted, it is I."

"Why, you wretched little slug!" the earl cried, grasping his cousin by the throat.

"My neckcloth, Edward. You're forgetting yourself." This last came out in a gasp, for the Earl of Hartleigh was, in fact, to the considerable interest of several passers-by, attempting to throttle his cousin. Words having no effect, Basil gave his lordship a sharp kick in the shin. The sudden pain made the earl loosen his grip, so that Basil was able to wrench his cousin's fingers from his neck. "Now," he croaked, "you are making a spectacle of yourself, and unless you desire to cause a riot on your darling's doorstep, I advise you to mind your manners."

Thus recalled to his surroundings, the still-furious Lord Hartleigh stepped away. "You have the effrontery to babble of manners. How dare you subject that girl to that villainous tale?"

"I did not make it up" was the tart rejoinder. But Basil's ears reddened—evidence that it was not only attempted strangulation which worked on him at present.

"True or not, it was infamous to tell it. It was obvious from the start that the poor girl had no idea—"

"That is her mother's fault." Basil attempted to adjust his neckcloth, but quickly gave it up and turned to face his cousin. "If you truly do wish to protect your precious Isabella, I advise you to keep your hands to yourself—not only in my case, but in hers as well. Good day, cousin." And he quickly took himself away.

For a moment, the earl debated whether to pursue him, but reason prevailed, and he took himself in the opposite direction, trying to collect his disordered thoughts.

Ever since the day when Lucy had been misplaced, it seemed that the Earl of Hartleigh was doomed to travel the streets of London in one state of fit or another. He did not understand why he, as well as his cousin, had been so cavalierly dismissed by Mrs Latham. Yes, Isabella needed comforting, but who better than himself to minister to her needs? And he had not been given opportunity to assure her that no matter what Basil knew or threatened to tell, she would be Countess of Hartleigh, and scandal would not be allowed to touch her.

Oh, scandal there would be, no doubt. But it was ancient history, and would soon be washed away as a new tide of gossip swept in. Why, by the time Harry Deverell made his way to London, it would all be forgotten . . .

wouldn't it? But if it were not forgotten, could he truly protect her from the pain? And if he could not, could he bear to watch it, and know he was the cause of it? For Basil had been adamant: The betrothal would be honoured, or he'd go directly to Sally Jersey with the whole sorry tale. That Basil should have sunk so low. . . . He hadn't used to be cruel—only selfish and irresponsible.

As he walked slowly in the direction of his aunt's house, Lord Hartleigh contemplated the twisted tale he had just heard. What had Matt written to Harry Deverell to drive him away, to discourage him so completely from attempting to see Maria himself, to drive him from England forever? Some appeal to Harry's honour, no doubt. And if Harry had loved Maria enough to run off with her secretly, to risk being cut off forever from his family, then he would be unable to bear living on the same island, knowing she belonged to another. At least, if Lord Hartleigh compared it to his own state of mind, then this must be the case. No, as Harry had reasoned it, he could not come back to life. He could not reclaim his wife. And should any discover the early marriage, his being alive would make her guilty of bigamy. Gossip would not take into account the circumstances. Her youth and her naïveté would be held against her, particularly by the spiteful old cats who resented her beauty. For she had been a beauty; was still.

And now Isabella? Even if she escaped relatively unscathed from the scandal, her Latham cousins' prospects would be ruined. And though their mother might be a social climber, the daughters—or Alicia, at least—seemed well-bred enough to move into a higher social strata.

But with no blood claim on Isabella, their fragile hold on Society would be cut away. Alicia would be forced to retire to Westford; no, she would not. The Countess of Hartleigh could take under her wing whomever she chose, and all but the very highest sticklers would be happy to recognize her protégées.

No, Isabella would not suffer her mother's fate. She would not be forced to sacrifice her future happiness on the simple threat of scandal. Basil was a fool, a desperate fool, and he would not have his way.

Abruptly, Lord Hartleigh turned and made his way back to Lord Belcomb's residence.

"Lord Hartleigh, you do tax my patience," said Mrs Latham as he was shown into the room. "Did I not just half an hour ago tell you and your cousin to go away until further notice?"

The earl maintained that he would *not* go away, that he intended to marry Isabella, and that he intended to do so immediately.

"Gracious God!" Isabella cried. "Are you mad? Didn't you hear what Basil said?"

"Yes. And that's why time is of the essence. I'm going now to procure a special licence. While I'm gone, your maid can help you pack."

"Pack?" she echoed blankly. "What are you saying?" She turned to her mother. "What is he saying?"

Maria Latham dropped gracefully onto the sofa. "You are excessively slow today, Isabella. It must be the concussion. Lord Hartleigh wishes to carry you off somewhere to be married. Under the circumstances, it would be best to begin packing immediately. I expect you'll be going some distance?" She lifted an enquiring gaze to Lord Hartleigh.

"To Hartleigh Hall. We'll stop for Aunt Clem, first, of course," he added. "Unless you wish to chaperone us, madam?"

"No, thank you. I find all this display of energy excessively fatiguing. And someone must remain to explain the situation to dear Charlotte. She'll be dreadfully cross." A low chuckle expressed the degree of concern Maria felt for her sister-in-law's delicate sensibilities.

"Then please make haste, my love," said Lord Hartleigh. He dropped a gentle kiss on Isabella's forehead, bowed to Mrs. Latham, and was gone, leaving his intended bride to gaze wonderingly after him.

"I still cannot decide whether he or his cousin is more handsome, but on the whole, I think he will make a better husband. Well, Isabella? Are you going to stand there gaping all day?"

"But, Mama, Basil just said—"

"Yes, and if you don't make haste, you will not have the pleasant opportunity of thwarting Mr Trevelyan. Why, what scandal do you think he'll dare provoke once you are married?"

"But, Mama—"

"Isabella, you're exhausting me. Please go away and pack."

Although he'd taken a calm leave of his cousin, Mr Trevelyan was an exceedingly uncomfortable man at the moment. He cringed at the greetings of acquaintances as he strode down the street, and may have been perceived to slink into the privacy of his club. But there was no privacy for him, really, for he must bear *himself* company, and that self had, in the last hour, turned into a decidedly unpleasant fellow—one whom, in fact, he'd prefer not to know.

First, of course, there was the shock and the blow to his vanity of coming upon Miss Latham in the embrace of his cousin. That she returned the embrace enthusiastically was obvious, even to an imbecile. And Basil greatly feared that this was exactly what he had become. He politely declined the various invitations to join his cronies, and found instead a quiet corner, where he sulked behind a newspaper. Hating himself, he was yet most angry with Isabella, for it was she who had reduced him to this state—reduced him to the level of a slug, as his cousin had so aptly labelled him.

Perhaps he was unfair to Isabella in this; yet it must

be known that for all his sophistication, Basil lacked a certain important experience: He had never in his thirty years been rejected in favour of another by a female.

True, his aim had not been high. Married ladies and members of the *demimonde* had always been his targets. And those young virgins with whom he had occasionally flirted had all been so naïve—and astoundingly stupid— that he had never been tempted to more than flirtation. In fact, it was Isabella's intelligence which was her undoing, for she didn't immediately bore him. Had she done, he might have more easily torn himself away. No, the matter was that from his doting mother to the complaisant matrons and eager Cyprians, women had always been captivated by him. And thus, never having experienced rejection, he had not philosophy to guide him. He had no idea how to shrug it off.

Perhaps he'd known in his heart that, in the end, Isabella would not have him. Perhaps he'd known even before that morning when she'd so stiffly outlined her "conditions" and promised herself to him—then winced at his kiss. Certainly he'd known it this afternoon, when he'd made his unwelcome entrance.

But the knowing was of no use to him, since it didn't show him how to salvage his wounded vanity. And of course, added to wounded vanity was the harsh reality of an army of creditors, lying in wait.

It was not surprising, then, that he'd revealed what he knew of Maria Latham's history; nor was it surprising that he'd stooped to blackmail. But he found it strange, and definitely unpleasant, to realise the whole while (indeed, even as the first words were out of his mouth) that in doing so, he had abandoned the ranks of civilised human beings and sunk to the level of vermin.

And now what would he do? Common sense told him to give it up as a bad job and make immediate arrangements for a flight to the Continent. Freddie would loan him the money. Good God, even Edward would help him, would do anything to see the back of him. And then there were friends he could join, for Napoleon had not the entire continent in his grasp, after all. But what would he live on?

One moment Basil was determined on flight; he would live somehow. The next, flight was impossible. And so he went, back and forth, until Celestine's note arrived, and then he thought he need not make so critical a decision at this very minute. First, he would see what the beautiful lady wanted.

No, Mr Trevelyan was not at his lodgings. No, the servant at the club told him, Mr Trevelyan had left hours before. No, none of the club members knew where he'd gone. But Sir Eliot gave a knowing wink as he remarked. that he believed Basil had had an urgent message from one of his ladybirds.

Lord Tuttlehope blushed as he knocked on the door. The little French maid's seductive smile only compounded his embarrassment as he stammeringly asked for Mademoiselle Celestine. The maid was so sorry, but mam'selle was engaged with a visitor. He was about to leave then, but screwed up his courage even as the door was closing in his face. "It's demmed urgent," he whispered hoarsely. "A message. Would you be kind enough—"

"But of course," the girl simpered.

"Then please tell Mr Trevelyan—"

"Oh, no, monsieur. Mr Trevelyan is not here." Perhaps monsieur was afflicted with a facial tick, for he blinked so. "It is another gentleman," she explained in a conspiratorial whisper.

Well, he had done his best. And to tell the truth, Freddie breathed a sigh of relief as he reached the street. For had he found Basil and told him what was in the wind, it was certain that his darling Alicia would never speak to him again.

18

It was nearly dawn when Basil opened his eyes. Only a faint grey light filtered through the drapes, but to him it was a blinding explosion which set off a sympathetic thundering in his brain. The wench must have drugged him, he thought, but had no time to consider more before blessed unconsciousness overtook him once again.

When he reawakened, the light was much stronger, but the thundering in his head had subsided to a dull throbbing, and he was able to look about him. It was not Celestine's bedroom; that much was certain. And it was not his own. He wasn't sure, but he thought he detected the faint smell of sea air. Perhaps that was what made his stomach rumble so. Where, then, was he?

As though in answer to his silent question, a plumpish, middle-aged gent who put Basil immediately in mind of a muffin, came to the doorway.

"Ah, you are awake, Mr Trevelyan," said the muffin in the kindliest of tones. "Then let us see what we can do about finding you some nourishment."

"Who the devil are you?" Basil snapped, as he hauled himself up, painfully, to a sitting position. But the gent had disappeared as quickly and silently as he had come, and Mr Trevelyan was left to simmer for a quarter hour before he reappeared. By that time, Basil had managed to crawl out of the bed and make some poor effort at dressing himself—a task rendered extraordinarily difficult by his trembling hands and weak, throbbing head. "Who the devil are you?" he repeated as the stranger placed a breakfast tray on the small table which stood in the darkest corner of the room.

"Latham," said the gent. "Henry Latham, at your service. And I do hope you'll consent to eat something, sir, for you look a bit peakish this morning."

The topaz eyes narrowed, although the effort cost some pain, as Basil asked hoarsely, "How do I know you haven't drugged that too?"

"Why, Mr Trevelyan, what would be the purpose in that?" Mr Latham replied mildly.

"It would be of a piece with the rest of it, wouldn't it?" But hunger gnawed at the young man. How long was it since he'd last eaten? How much time had passed since Celestine had put that glass of wine in his hand? He remembered—or maybe he'd only dreamed it—being jolted in a coach. And an inn. And more wine. And Celestine—or another woman. And apparently they were all in league with this kindly old muffin, who continued to smile innocently at him. The aroma of eggs, ham, toast, and coffee beckoned, however, and Basil determined to postpone further enquiries until he had recovered his strength.

But even as he fell to his meal, he wondered at it—at his sitting there eating a breakfast while Isabella's uncle sat benevolently watching him. It must be a dream, still. At length, as Basil was sipping his second cup of coffee, Henry Latham quietly remarked that he owed the young man an explanation.

"Ah," Basil murmured. "A dream with an explanation. So you mean to tell me you are not a figment of my overactive imagination?"

"No, Mr Trevelyan. But I would hope to play a beneficial role in your life."

Basil quirked an eyebrow. "You mean to *help* me?" At the other's nod, he went on, "Then you have a devilish odd way of going about it, my good man. I do not usually have to be drugged into accepting aid."

"Well, you see, sir, I was concerned that you'd create difficulties."

"I *never* stand in the way of charitable efforts on my behalf—"

"And I had to be sure," Henry continued, "that my niece was safely out of danger before I put my proposal to you."

The coffee cup clattered to its saucer. "The devil you did," Basil sputtered. "Where is she?"

"With your cousin, sir. Or I should say," he corrected with a gentle smile, "with her husband."

"That scheming—you conniving thief!" Basil shrieked, jumping up. "I'll have the law on you. Assault. Kidnapping." He went on with a list of various criminal complaints, punctuated at intervals with curses on his perfidious fiancée and cousin and their families, all of which Henry Latham bore patiently—benignly, in fact—as though it were an outpouring of good wishes.

"Yes," he responded, as Basil paused to catch his breath, "I can see how very disappointing it is for you, Mr Trevelyan. But you must see that Isabella's happiness must come first with all of us."

"Happiness," Basil snarled. "We'll see how much joy she has of her marriage. And the rest of your wretched, conniving family. What kind of a life do you think she'll have when all of London learns of her mother's hasty, bigamous marriage—and of your brother's part in Harry Deverell's disappearance?"

"Why, as to that," said Henry, calmly, "there's no telling how the wind will blow. Mayhap they'll make out Maria as the victim of my unscrupulous brother. And if so, 'tis only my family that must bear the shame. Alicia will simply have to come home with me and make the best of her prospects among her own kind."

"And give up her baron?" Basil sneered.

"She's no business with such. A plain 'Mrs' is all the title she needs."

"You think to convince me that the scandal doesn't matter?"

"No, Mr Trevelyan. For the plain fact is, much as I think my daughter was encouraged to look too high above herself—well, we'd all rather keep the shameful story quiet. And that is why I appeal to your better nature. Isabella has married your cousin. What's done is done."

"No, Mr Latham. It is not done. You've stolen my last chance from me, and I will not go down to destruction without some revenge. And if it is only the satisfaction of bringing misery and shame down on your whole miserable family, then I will have it." But even as he spoke, Basil knew he was defeated. What good would it do him? Driving Alicia from society would not pay his debts—and it *would* alienate Freddie. Dragging Isabella's family through the mire of scandal would not keep him from debtors' prison. The amber cat eyes were bleak with despair. Debtors' prison.

But as his gaze fell upon the open, kindly countenance before him, he realised that he had lost more than a fortune. Somewhere in the place where his heart was supposed to be had been a faint, unacknowledged hope: that Isabella would somehow make things right for him. Perhaps he'd even imagined she'd one day come to love him, and thereby prove that he'd done no wrong; had acted in her best interests, in fact. But he'd deluded himself. It was only now, as he contemplated his dismal future, as he thought of the friends who'd fall away when the prison walls closed around him, that he realised how completely alone he was. And if any suspected the level to which he had sunk . . . well, who *would* come to his aid?

But Henry Latham was speaking, and Basil forced himself to attend.

"You see, Mr Trevelyan," he was saying, "I do feel responsible, in a way. For I saw what you were about some time ago, when my sister-in-law wrote to me. You may not believe it, but none of us—excepting Matt—knew

159

the whole truth of the story. I learned of it myself the very day I'd heard from Maria. I was shocked then, but hesitated to act until I knew more—about *you,* especially. Maybe I should have been more forthright. Maybe I should have spoken with you directly, man to man, and we could have come to some agreeable arrangement.''

Basil gave a morose growl in reply.

"At any rate, I have a proposition for you.'' He went on to explain that he had bought up more than half of Basil's notes—"for there has not been time to locate all your creditors. It really is astonishing,'' Henry mumbled, half to himself, "the amount of credit a man in your position is extended; no wonder so many of you are ruined so young. But at any rate,'' he went on, more brightly, "I believe something can be done.''

"What the devil are you talking about? Bought up my notes? Why, there must be—''

Henry put up his hand. "Outrageous is what it is. Why, the interest alone could keep a family of six comfortably for several years. Well, what's done is done.''

"I am undone, is what it is. You are saying that if I don't consent to curb my tongue, you'll call in my markers and have me clapped into prison.''

"Why, that's the long and short of it. But it doesn't solve your problems, now does it, Mr Trevelyan? For how are you to get *out* of prison again?''

"I appreciate your concern, sir, but as I have no means of escaping to the Continent, and as prison most certainly won't agree with me, you can look forward to my early demise.'' Basil flung himself into a chair to contemplate this untimely end.

"Do you think India might be more agreeable?''

"India,'' Basil repeated dully.

"For I have some business there and could use a clever fellow.''

"Business. In India.'' Basil looked up from his mournful meditations to meet the kindly brown eyes.

"You are proposing I go into *trade?*" He said it as though he'd been asked to consider contracting a loathsome disease.

But Mr Latham explained that the young man would not be expected to dirty his hands with trade. Only to keep a lookout on things, to hobnob a bit with the local higherups. "It could be very profitable, sir, for both of us. A few choice pieces of information at the right time would pay handsomely. You might even be put in the way of information which would be of use to His Majesty's government."

Basil's eyes flew open at this.

"For to be quite frank with you, sir, I am rather in such a way myself. Business is inextricably tied to politics, you know. And even such as I have some concern in keeping our enemies at bay."

"You suggest that I take up the sort of endeavour my cousin was forced to give up?"

"In the way of business, no more. And as to business, why, I'd guess that with your talents, you'd earn enough to cover all your debts in two or three years—and come away with something handsome in the bargain. Are you game, sir?"

Basil thought quickly. He could try to convince Aunt Clem to hold off the creditors. But would she? And for how long? And if she would not or could not, he must leave England . . . with nothing to live on. No, there was nothing to be decided. It meant work; the very idea made his blood run cold. But it could mean adventure, of sorts. And maybe a bit of glory might drift his way and cling to him. A hero. He might even be a hero. In less than two minutes, in a very bored, very resigned voice, he replied, "Well, it seems I have no choice. Yes, Mr Latham, I am—as you say—game."

"Alone at last," murmured the earl, closing the bedroom door behind him. "No mama, no aunts, no cousins, no blasted servants—come to think of it, there *are* the servants, and with my luck . . . perhaps I'd better bar the door?''

"In your own home, My Lord?" Though her voice was playful, Isabella was suddenly nervous. For here she was, alone with her new husband in his—their—bedroom, and no officious relatives likely to burst in to protect her virtue. Good heavens. She was married to him and was not *supposed* to protect her virtue. Quite the opposite, in fact. She blushed and, seeing the dark eyes gazing at her with such intensity, backed away . . . and stumbled against the bedpost.

"Better safe than sorry," Lord Hartleigh muttered as he turned the key in the lock. A few quick strides and he was across the room, but to his amazement, his bride retreated. "Is something wrong, my love?" Then, noting the blush that spread from her cheeks to her throat, his lip quivered, and he whispered, "Surely you're not afraid of me, Isabella."

"No. Yes" was the subdued reply.

"Darling, you don't think I'm going to murder you."

"No."

"And after all, you've had some sample . . . or at least a prologue."

A faint smile began to curve her lips.

He held out his arms. "Then come to me . . . and let us complete what was so rudely interrupted a few days ago. As I recall, you have a most winning way with a neckcloth."

Taking a deep breath to slow her pounding heart, Isabella walked into his open arms and laid her head on his chest. She could hear his heart pounding, too. But then his arms closed around her, pulling her close. She felt his warm breath at her ear, and had only a moment to mutter something about a concussion before his lips were pressing softly on hers. Then love took over (and lust, too, it must be admitted), and the earl's cravat went bravely to its destruction.

* * *

Maria raised her world-weary eyes from her book. "Who?" she enquired of Lord Hartleigh's discomfitted butler.

Life in her brother's household had become increasingly uncomfortable after Isabella's departure. Although Charlotte had come rather quickly to accept Veronica's preference for the Stirewell heir, she could not forgive Maria the Earl of Hartleigh's defection. If Isabella and Maria had not conspired to entrap him, he would never have been enticed away from Veronica. That Lord Hartleigh had never evidenced the remotest interest in Veronica was all put down to the conspiracy. And then, of course, there was Lord Tuttlehope, who, out of the clear blue sky, up and offered for Alicia Latham. If that wasn't conspiracy, Lady Belcomb didn't know what it was—and she would not be surprised to learn that Napoleon was at the bottom of it.

It was the conspiracy theory that finally wore out Maria's patience. And despite her brother's pleadings, she accepted the Earl and Countess of Hartleigh's invitation to live with them.

Now it may be counted odd in a newly wed couple to invite a parent to come live with them. And certainly Isabella had wondered at her husband's proposing it, even before they learned how difficult life had become for Maria in London. But when questioned, the earl calmly replied that Maria was not the interfering sort, and that it was more than likely they would be unaware most of the time that she was even about.

In truth, the house and grounds of the Hartleigh estate were so vast that Maria could be lost for weeks before anyone noticed. And as it turned out, only Burgess, the earl's terrifying butler, who for thirty years had ruled his household with a rod of iron, was at all disturbed by the new resident. For from the first, when Maria had looked up at his immense height and stern demeanor with that faint indulgent smile—a smile one would give a great overgrown puppy, or a very small boy, as one patted him fondly on the head—the butler had been frightened of her. He lived in terror that one day this slender, lackadaisical, unpredictable woman *would* pat him on his head, and all his authority would crumble into dust. But for all that, he was fond of the lady, and very sharp with any staff member who so much as hinted a question of Mrs Latham's mental faculties.

Still, she was at it again. He had announced the visitor, and she acted as though he were saying it only to tease her. As she looked up at him, Burgess had the unaccountable sensation that he had done something *naughty.*

Nonetheless, his face was emotionless as he repeated, patiently, "Lord Deverell, madam. I have explained that you are not at home today, but—"

"Confound it, Maria, I've been up and down the whole blasted island looking for you, and this fellow has the effrontery to tell me you're not at home." A tall, fair-haired, quite handsome gentleman in his late forties pushed past the protective butler.

"Why, Harry," said Maria.

"Don't 'Harry' me, you unfaithful female. Where's Isabella?"

"Well, I'm sure I don't know," the female replied, sinking gracefully back onto her cushions. "Somewhere about. Perhaps Burgess can tell you."

"The Countess of Hartleigh," announced Burgess, with awful dignity, "is in the garden with Miss Lucy. Shall I inform her ladyship that Lord Deverell has arrived?"

"Whatever," said Maria, with a sigh.

Unperturbed by Burgess's dignified disapproval, the viscount plunked himself down, uninvited, in a nearby chair. As soon as the butler had departed, he said, "You might show a little interest, Maria. You haven't seen me in twenty-seven years."

"Well, of course I haven't, Harry. One doesn't *expect* to see a dead person. Unless one has a morbid turn of mind. Which I have not." And Mrs Latham fell to examining the diamonds on her fingers.

"Well, I'm not dead anymore," the viscount remarked, tapping his foot impatiently.

"No, you're not" was the unhelpful reply.

"In fact, I never was."

Another sigh. "How was I to know?"

Moments ticked by as the star-crossed lovers meditated. Then:

"Maria?"

"Yes."

"I missed you horribly."

"Well, I hope so, Harry," replied the lady. She considered for a minute, then raised herself to a sitting position and let her glance travel from the tips of his polished boots to his tanned face and his fair hair, so sun-bleached that it was impossible to be certain where the gold left off and the silver began. "I have missed you rather horribly myself." And for no apparent reason at all, she laughed.

The viscount sprang from his seat to take his long-lost bride in his arms.

"Why, Harry," she murmured as his lips met hers.

"Mama!" Isabella cried as she entered the room, to find her mother in the embrace of a stranger. It was quite the most shocking thing she'd ever seen; although her mother appeared to be participating most enthusiastically, and the stranger was, it must be confessed, a very handsome fellow.

Languidly, Maria drew away from Lord Deverell. "Ah, there you are, my love. What an unconscionable time you've been returning. Say hello to your papa, my dear."

Epilogue

Lord Hartleigh gently assisted his rather bulky wife into a comfortable chair on the terrace. Although he had, at the beginning, shown a rather alarming tendency to overprotectiveness, Isabella—with some help from her mother—managed to reassure the anxious father-to-be. He was at length convinced that it was not in his wife's best interest to be confined to her bed for nine months. After ascertaining that the walk from the garden had not caused her any irrevocable damage, he told her that she had a letter from his cousin.

"From Basil. Oh, thank heaven. I was so worried."

"I don't see why. Between his talent for gathering gossip and Henry Latham's talent for making money with it, he promises to do quite well for himself. Better than he deserves," the earl muttered, irritated anew as he remembered the trouble his cousin had caused him.

"Now, darling, he did write a very penitent letter before he left—"

"Maudlin, rather," the earl grumbled. But his wife reached for his cravat and pulled his head down so that she could plant a kiss on his forehead, and he remembered to be grateful to Basil for unintentionally thwarting those early plans to marry the fair Honoria. "Well then, let us see what he has to say."

" 'My darling Isabella,' " the countess read aloud.

"Not a promising start, the insinuating wretch."

" 'You will perhaps be pleased to hear that I have not

166

contracted any of the five hundred and eighty different varieties of foul disease that flourish in this abominable climate. That is because I am dying of a broken heart and haven't the strength to contract them.' "

"Broken heart, my foot."

" 'Nonetheless, even in my weakened state I have managed to be of some use to your uncle, who confesses himself astonished at the amount of helpful gossip I am able to relay to him. He informs me that my debt to him is now paid, and that whatever else I accomplish from now on is shared profit, my share being available to me for whatever wanton purposes I wish to pursue.

" 'Unfortunately, between the heat and the unending din of this vile city, I haven't the energy even to imagine any wanton purposes, nor would I have the strength to pursue such, could I imagine them. Therefore I am making a gift to your firstborn, care of your uncle, so that he or she might have at least one kind memory of the villainous Uncle Basil.

" 'Your uncle now talks of Greece, and suggests we might find something to our advantage there. No climate can be as vile as this one, and in the hopes that I might be set upon by marauding Turks, I have commenced packing my few miserable belongings, preparatory to leaving in the next week.

" 'Pray give my regards to my fortunate cousin, and you might pat Lucy on the head for me—if she'll stand for it. And if you can find it in your heart to forgive me . . . well, pray for me, Isabella—for I did love you as well as I could.

" 'Ever your affectionate and *humble* servant, B.' "

" 'Loved you as well as he could.' Well enough to spend your money and ruin your life—"

"He was desperate," Isabella reminded gently.

"And I was such a fool that without his interference, I wouldn't have realised how desperately in love with you I was."

"Was?" Isabella asked, tugging on his neckcloth again.

"Am. Will be. Always," Lord Hartleigh replied as he dropped to one knee to gaze lovingly into the intelligent blue eyes of his countess. "From the very first day I saw you and you scolded me."

His wife gave a low chuckle of satisfaction, and pulled him closer for a kiss.

"Poor Basil," the earl murmured a few minutes later. "I wonder what will become of him?"

"Something dramatic, no doubt" was the whispered reply. The letter slipped from her lap to the floor of the terrace, was picked up by a breeze, and slowly fluttered, forgotten, to the garden.

The English
Witch

Prologue

"Well, Maria, what do you think?"

Lady Deverell looked up from the letter she'd just finished reading, but her gaze went to the fire, rather than to her questioner. Though it was a bright, cozy fire, so comforting on this late winter evening, she sighed. "How cleverly she writes. But then, I daresay she inherited her scholarly Papa's intellect."

"Well, it wasn't from her Mama, that's for certain. Juliet, rest her soul, was a beautiful giddypate. A more ill-suited pair one could scarcely imagine. Juliet would never budge from London, and Charles was determined to be abroad. So, what happens but Alexandra is left with a governess and one or two servants in that lonely little place in the country. She was neglected shamefully, to my way of thinking—and now this. If only she had confided the matter sooner, I might have done something before she went away with her Papa. Wretched man." Lady Bertram nodded balefully at the letter, as though it were Sir Charles Ashmore himself.

Certainly, if it were—and if it had had any sensibilities at all—it would have crept away in mortification. A tall, full-figured woman of sixty or so, unbowed by age or infirmity, the Countess Bertram could, when she liked, make herself very intimidating to lesser mortals.

All the same, the letter lay, oblivious to the countess's scorn, in Lady Deverell's delicate hand. Nor was the languid owner of that hand intimidated. She, in fact, scarcely seemed to attend at all, so absentmindedly did she answer. "Yes, it is most tiresome. And yet they are so very far away. Albania. One can hardly think how to help her at this great distance."

"Nonetheless, one must. She's my goddaughter and requires my help. We must cudgel our brains, Maria."

"Oh, must we?" Lady Deverell sounded rather faint at the prospect, as though someone had proposed that she run from London to Brighton. "Oh, dear, I suppose we must. Well, let me see." She glanced down at the letter. "There is the money, of course. Though one cannot understand why Charles went to a wool merchant for financial backing."

"Because he is a proud, obstinate creature, who'd sooner shoot himself than 'toady to that bunch of aristocratic half-wits,' as he calls the Society of Dilettanti. So what does he do but put all his affairs into the hands of George Burnham—who was sly enough to toady to *him*."

"But it is only money, after all, and you have enough, certainly—"

"Yes, yes, I tried" was the impatient reply. "The day I received the letter, I dispatched a bank draft to Burnham. It came back with a curt note informing me that he could accept no funds on Ashmore's behalf without Ashmore's approval. Now Burnham has begun pressing for the marriage—and of course you see why."

Lady Deverell gave the letter another glance and sighed. "Ah, yes. The eldest daughter is nearly one-and-twenty and must make her comeout before she is obliged to wear caps."

"A pack of mushrooms, Maria. Why should the Burnhams care for my money when they might use Alexandra to introduce those ignorant, encroaching girls to society?"

Lady Deverell made vaguely sympathetic murmurs.

"I cannot think what to do next. For all her humourous comments, it's plain Alexandra is distressed. But if I write to her father, he'll resent my interference and, in one of his headstrong passions, is liable to haul them before one of those dervishes, to be married there. Really, he's the most vexing man."

Lady Bertram's companion, immovably unvexed, replied dreamily, "Yes. Matters seem to have reached a crisis. Your goddaughter has run out of strategems, and the Burnhams

2

press her Papa. Dear, dear. So he is determined to be back in England by summer.''

"Yes, and there's the devil of it. He'll pack her off to Yorkshire as soon as they set foot in the kingdom, and the poor girl will be married before she can blink.''

"How fatiguing to think of so much energy expended to such ill purpose. Yet that is exactly what he must do.'' Lady Deverell's preoccupied gaze wandered to the clock on the mantelpiece. "Unless, of course, some complication should intervene.''

"Yes.'' A faint smile softened the countess's patrician features.

Lady Deverell followed another bored sigh with a change of subject. "Dear me, what a dreary winter this has been with half the world in Brussels. But it is nearly over. I understand Basil Trevelyan plans to return from Greece by summer.''

"Yes. So he's written.''

"Well, that will be pleasant, will it not? After three years we shall all be glad to see him.''

"Oh, yes. Prodigious glad.''

"I wonder,'' Lady Deverell mused, her eyes still on the clock, "what he will think of Albania.''

"Albania, my dear? Is that where he means to go?'' the countess asked, very innocently.

"Why, yes, Clementina. Now I think of it, that must be *exactly* what he intends.''

1

It was called the "City of a Thousand Stairs." From a distance, the white stone houses with their elaborate red roofs appeared to be carved out of the mountainside itself. They were white fairy stairs, zigzagging their way up to the mediaeval citadel. Veiled by the early dawn mist, Gjirokastra seemed exactly the sort of place where evil sorcerers held fair princesses captive.

On closer view the houses—windowless on the first floor, bay-windowed and ornate on the upper stories—were miniature fortresses themselves, clustered about their majestic parent. And at this hour of morning there were no fairies, princesses, nor evil sorcerers. There were instead a few women, most of them dressed in black, soberly going about their chores.

The town was founded, according to folk legend, by a princess named Argjiro; but Sir Charles believed that its name came from the Illyrian tribe of Argyres that had settled nearby. Gjirokastra's recent history was less mysterious: like every other town and hamlet of Albania, it had known only rare intervals of peace since its founding. Just four years ago, in 1811, Ali Pasha Tepelena had bombarded the rebellious town with artillery.

In time, it could expect to be bombarded again by somebody, for some reason, but now in the misty dawn of what promised to be another sweltering June day, the place was quiet.

Occasionally the women of Gjirokastra spoke to one another, but mainly they attended to their work. Certainly they had better things to do than watch the departure of the small caravan. The English were leaving, they knew. They also knew why.

The women of Gjirokastra did not approve of "Skandara" Ashmore. Women were supposed to go about their back-breaking labour quietly, troubling nobody, but this English witch troubled everybody. Too many yearning songs had been composed in tribute to her green, sorceress eyes and gleaming dark curls. She made the young men restless, and that was bad.

Meanwhile, the small caravan descending to the valley was not quite so subdued as the sleepy town it had just left. Alexandra Ashmore had not given up trying to sidetrack her father. This endeavour had grown increasingly difficult, because he'd finally made up his mind to go home, and once he made up his mind to something, he tended to apply all the concentration he normally focussed on ancient inscriptions. At present his course was fixed. A certain Albanian family's apologetic warning the previous day had merely hastened a departure planned months before.

"But Papa," Alexandra was saying, as calmly as she could, "surely we cannot come so close to Butrint and not spend time there."

"I can go later, after you and Randolph are married."

"But think of the expense. To go all the way back to England and then return all the way here again."

"We've delayed long enough. You must be married. In a few more years, you'll be too old to have children. Randolph will want a family."

Glancing ahead at the young man who rode with their ragged guard, Stefan, and their slightly less ragged dragoman, Gjergi, Alexandra privately took leave to differ with her father. Randolph's beloved family existed already, in the remnants of ancient times. Her fiancé lusted for scraps of buildings and fragments of sculpture as another man might lust for women. He was blind even to her own charms. And she, while not vain, was not stupid either. She knew that most men found her very attractive.

Randolph had agreed to marry her because he was dimly

aware that he had to marry somebody. His father obligingly had found him a bride, thereby saving Randolph the trouble of looking for one, so he was content. Actually, oblivious was more like it. But aloud she said only, "Why, we can be married next year. Four-and-twenty is not the very brink of senility. And Randolph wouldn't mind. He, too, wishes to explore Butrint."

"No. There'll always be trouble until you're married. Today we leave Gjirokastra because Dhimitri Musolja's besotted with you. In another place, it'll be someone else. With these men chasing you and upsetting their families, we accomplish nothing."

That much was true. This was the fifth town they'd been forced to leave because of amourous young men. At any rate, it was futile to argue when those stubborn lines settled into Papa's forehead. Later she'd try again. She'd tempt him with Butrint once more.

Gjirokastra, nestled in the mountains of southern Albania, was mainly mediaeval, although pieces of ancient rubble formed part of the material of which the citadel was built, and there were traces of ancient settlements nearby. Butrint was another story. Marcus Tullius Cicero had written of it, and according to the *Aeneid,* it was founded by the Trojans on their way from Troy to Italy. Though Papa said that was mere legend, he was dying to explore the place, as was Randolph. Surely there must be some way to convince them to stay—just a while longer. And perhaps, while they investigated antiquities, she might have an answer to the letter she'd written so many months ago.

But what could Aunt Clem do, after all? Mama had adamantly objected to the match with Randolph; but as soon as she passed away, Papa had settled everything with George Burnham. While Papa had arranged the marriage as a means of paying off his long-standing debt to the wool merchant, he honestly believed he was looking out for his daughter's best interests. Her dowry was insignificant, and he had nothing to leave her after his death. Without a husband, her future would be a grim one.

Awake to the need for a husband, she'd convinced her parents to scrape together enough money for a Season. Unfortunately, though she attracted many suitors, her lack of fortune as well as her Papa's eccentricity had a dampening effect on Honourable Intentions. The few London bachelors whose sensibilities were not thus dampened were unendurable. Alexandra did not think herself, as Mama complained, excessively fastidious, but it was quite impossible to accept Mr. Courtland, who was sixty, or Sir Alfred, who was short and fat and practically illiterate, or Mr. Porter, a Pink of the Ton whose only real passion was his tailor.

In short, when, near the Season's end, her Mama had contracted a fever and died, Alexandra remained unclaimed. George Burnham was on the spot immediately, urging that the match go forward at once. Alexandra had responded by reminding her father that she was in mourning and convincing him to let her spend the time with him in Greece. Once they were abroad, it hadn't been difficult to stretch one year into another until six had passed. Papa forgot everything else when he was working.

Meanwhile, she'd occupied herself by helping him keep his sketches and notes in order. She had also learned how to say what was expected of her while her mind wandered elsewhere. Since the two men were generally unaware of her existence, this was no great feat. It was not the most stimulating existence, and she did not see how being married to Randolph would improve it. She would like one day to talk of something besides the Peloponnesian War. With Randolph Burnham, such a day would never come.

While she pondered her past and wondered sadly about her future, the group pressed on in relative silence, broken only by Gjergi's dropping into a soft song about the bravery of the Shqiptar—the Sons of Eagles. The mists that had enshrouded Gjirokastra were giving way to the bright morning sun, when the valley's peace was broken by the thundering of horses' hooves.

Good God. Bandits. Alexandra had scarcely formulated the thought when she saw Stefan and Gjergi reach for the long guns slung across their saddles. Even as they were taking aim, the marauders thundered into their midst, stirring

7

up a choking, blinding storm of dust. Her throat and eyes burning, Alexandra struggled to control her panicked horse with one hand while she fumbled with the other for the pistol tucked into her waistband. In the next instant, she was dragged from her mount and flung onto another. Strong arms gripped her, and she stared up into a laughing, triumphant face.

"Dhimitri!" she gasped.

Furious, she pounded and clawed, screaming at him to let her go. The huge Albanian only laughed and grasped her more tightly.

A single, curt command to his men, and Dhimitri Musolja galloped off with Sir Charles Ashmore's daughter.

Basil Trevelyan glared at the breathtaking prospect beyond the narrow window: green and yellow valley below and majestic peaks beyond. The faint, sweet mountain breeze that cooled the early evening air only made him wish desperately to be home again. After two interminable years in India and another, equally dreary, in Greece, he was as tired of picturesque views as he was tired of business and politics. Now, when he should be on a ship bound for England, he was in Albania, in a wretched mountain village, whose suspicious inhabitants would tell him nothing.

He turned angrily to the letters on the rough table before him. They'd come to him, one folded over the other, in Greece, and had plagued him ever since. His aunt, of course, habitually ordered him about. That was her character, just as it was his to ignore her. Since she was at least partially responsible for his three-year exile from England, it would have served her right had he torn the cursed things to bits. The trouble was, she knew what she was about. She'd enclosed Miss Ashmore's letter and let that do the business for her. Aunt Clem knew him too well—devious woman.

Basil Trevelyan enjoyed drama. He enjoyed intrigue. And he enjoyed women. He especially enjoyed women, partly for their own sake and partly because relations with them so often involved drama and intrigue—not to mention the obvious pleasures. Because he had excellent taste, he particularly enjoyed beautiful women.

Now here was a "good-looking gel," according to his usually critical aunt, who was attempting to conduct some sort of intrigue of her own. Alexandra Ashmore wrote coolly and humourously, yet movingly, of a typical maiden's plight: her Papa was making her marry a man she didn't love. The bridegroom had the Money. The bride had the Status—the usual trade.

He'd tried one like it himself, three years ago, and had even gone so far as to try to blackmail Isabella Latham into marrying him. He'd failed because not only her relatives but also his own had thwarted him. They'd even had him drugged and abducted to make absolutely certain he couldn't interfere with her marriage to his cousin Edward, Earl of Hartleigh.

Basil was still a bit ashamed of the way he'd behaved. He might not have been quite so ashamed, might even have nursed a grudge, had not Isabella, now Countess of Hartleigh, been the only one to write faithfully to him. Well, she'd always rather liked him. She just hadn't loved him.

How she'd laugh if she could see him now: dirty, unshaven, uncombed, his borrowed clothes ragged and filthy. He was a far cry from the elegant man-about-town she'd known. That sophisticated fellow had been deeply sunk in debt three years ago. Now, thanks to Henry Latham, Basil was rich and even rather a hero—business, as Henry liked to say, being inextricably tied to politics. Having persuaded Basil to work for him, Latham was bound to put the younger man's talent for intrigue to profitable use. Mr. Trevelyan succeeded where even skilled diplomats had failed. For his efforts, he received some modest rewards and generous praise from the Crown. Less modest rewards and fewer words had come from the divers British businessmen and Indian princes to whom Basil had proved himself equally invaluable.

Now when he returned to England, he'd be welcome everywhere. Proper Mamas would push their innocent daughters at him. All kinds of respectable young ladies—pretty ones and plain, poor and wealthy and every variety in between—would pursue him. He doubted whether their virginal charms could compete with the more practised arts of the Fashionable Impures he was accustomed to. Still, never loath to be the centre of attention, he looked forward to making the comparison firsthand.

One cleverly written letter had held him back from all that bliss. And why? He had a whim to meet the authoress. If her writing was any sample, she must be a very interesting young woman.

That was what had brought him to this wretched place. He'd had a hot, miserable journey ending in a miserable town whose sullen folk refused to understand his guide's northern dialect. The name Ashmore evoked nothing but stubborn incomprehension.

Basil ran his fingers through his tangled hair. The tawny, sun-bleached mane badly wanted cutting. His amber eyes were dull with exhaustion, and as he thought of more days wasted in search of the missing Ashmores, his head began throbbing horribly. Blast them! And blast his aunt as well. He wanted to be home in his own clothes and clean again. He wanted a familiar bed and familiar food. He thought longingly of London's cooling drizzles, forgetting that the city would soon be hot and odoriferous. He yearned for the quiet, cool comfort of his club. He even recalled wistfully the rustic peace of Hartleigh Hall.

While he was in the midst of tormenting himself with these reflexions, Gregor crept into the room. "Zotir Vasil," he whispered.

Basil awoke from his reverie and gazed stupidly at his dragoman. "What? What is it?"

"We have found Zotir Ashmore. A local boy, Dhimitri Musolja, has taken the girl."

"Taken her? Where?"

"Here, in the town, to his father's house. We must go quickly. There is big trouble now and soon, maybe worse."

Alexandra's Albanian was not very fluent, but then, it was a difficult language. Papa theorised that it was traceable to the ancient Illyrian tongue, preserved, despite repeated foreign conquests, out of sheer obstinacy. For instance, while the Turks had held the country in an undependable state of submission since the death of the great Albanian patriot Skanderbeg, in the fifteenth century, only a handful of Turkish words had been absorbed. Albanian was Albanian still, and its inflexions were Alexandra's despair. Nonetheless, though her speech could send her woman-servant, the jovial Lefka, into fits of laughter, Alexandra's understanding was quite good. Certainly she comprehended enough to follow the arguments going on in the room above.

The debate had continued all day, and their voices carried easily down to the shed where she waited, because they hadn't troubled to lower them. The father demanded that the English girl be returned to her father. The brothers shouted about shame and disgrace. Even the mother pleaded with her favourite, her youngest son, while the other women of the household complained that the English girl was a witch. Had she not been forced to leave Tepelena because she made the young men crazy?

So the battle had raged while the English witch sat on the dirt floor of a shed that smelled strongly of goats, and tried to understand why men were so pigheaded. There was her normally logical Papa forcing two incompatible and unenthusiastic persons into marriage. Here was Dhimitri trying to force her to marry *him*. How on earth had she imagined Aunt Clem could help her out of such a pickle?

Morning heated up into afternoon, and afternoon darkened into dusk while the family battled on. The odds were against Dhimitri, but he was spoiled and headstrong. A while ago, he'd raved that if his family would not accept Skandara as his wife, he'd go away with her to live among strangers. He'd go, he shouted, to Pogradeç, and make his living by fishing in the lake. His mother shrieked. His father screamed at him to go and be damned, and the others made a deafening chorus. Then, suddenly, everything was still. She heard new voices break the silence. Her spirits rose, only to sink again. They were not familiar voices.

What if Papa and Randolph had been hurt . . . or killed, all because of a young man she'd thought was content to gaze adoringly at her as he sang his mournful little love songs.

11

Who'd have guessed he'd dare abduct the daughter of Ali Pasha's honoured guest? Evidently he respected the great Pasha as little as he did the mourning Alexandra still wore. Lefka had promised that would keep the men at a respectful distance, but it hadn't.

Now nothing short of a miracle could save Alexandra from marrying the hotheaded youth. She'd be treated as a servant, a pack animal. She'd have to submit to his hot, eager embraces—and have his children! God help her, she'd kill herself first. She'd throw herself from a ledge. In Gjirokastra, after all, there were ledges aplenty.

A more delicate female than Alexandra Ashmore might have given way to tears. Certainly she had reason enough, but she refused to cry despite the horrible ache in her throat. She was wishing for her pistol—shooting herself was preferable to hurtling down from a precipice—when the door creaked open.

It was one of Dhimitri's brothers. She didn't know which, there being seven plus innumerable sisters, all of whom looked alike. Dhimitri stood out mainly because he was the giant of the family and understood a little English. This brother was ordering her to follow him.

He led her up into the house proper and on to the large, sparsely furnished room where the family was accustomed to gather and were all gathered now: parents, siblings, spouses, and divers aunts and uncles. There was, moreover, another Albanian she didn't know, speaking in the dialect of the north, and another man whose hair was sun-bleached gold. He must also come from the north, where so much of the population was fair, though his costume resembled nothing she'd seen before, north or south. For a moment, in the room's dim light, he seemed a golden Macedonian, like those who centuries ago had swept down from the mountains. As he turned his tanned, beautifully sculpted face towards her, she noted that his eyes were very unusual. Amber, with a slight upward slant, they reminded her of the eyes of a cat.

They were watchful, too, like a cat's eyes. As they lit upon her, the expression turned to one of joyful recognition, and she was astonished to hear him cry in cultured British accents, "Alexandra, my love, you are safe."

Before she had time to think how to react, he crossed the room, threw his arms around her, and crushed her to him. The suddenness of the onslaught made her gasp, but sensing quickly the role she was to play, she took her lead from him and returned his hug with feigned enthusiasm. His ironic smile made her blush as he drew away from her to gesture towards their suspicious audience.

"My darling, I have been trying to explain to these good people that I am your own Basil, your betrothed, come at last to take you home to be my wife. The trouble is Gregor cannot make himself understood, and that angry young man over there"—he indicated an enraged Dhimitri, now being held back by three brothers—"seems to think that you are *his* intended bride. Would you, my sweet, be kind enough to explain to them how it is with us?"

Though it was a tad daunting to have what seemed like a hundred pairs of suspicious eyes fixed upon her, she began, in Albanian even more halting than usual. She was not quite sure what she said—nor were the members of the clan, as they tried to puzzle out her bizarre grammatical constructions—but it was something about being promised to each other for years.

Though the others appeared satisfied with this incoherent babble, a red-faced Dhimitri demanded to know why her father claimed she was promised to that other one. He meant, of course, Mr. Burnham. In response, Alexandra promptly invented some nonsense about Basil's early poverty, and how he'd gone to seek his fortune. Basil smiled as his dragoman translated this with some difficulty, for she told the truth, all unwittingly. She went on to explain how she'd promised to wait for him. Her Papa wanted her to marry Mr. Burnham, but she didn't want Mr. Burnham. Now, she told them, as she gazed up at Basil with what she hoped was a look of adoration, her own true love had come for her as he'd promised. There was more murmuring, as the assembled audience struggled with her garbled prose, and then there were sounds of agreement.

Her would-be fiancé now turned to her with a look of such passionate longing that she was momentarily breathless. "I think, my love," he said softly, "that the parents are happy to believe in our star-crossed love. But Dhimitri wants convincing." As though unable to contain his feelings another moment, Basil wrapped his arms around her and kissed her.

It was not the make-believe kiss Alexandra was expecting, but a long, deep, dizzyingly thorough kiss that, when he'd finally done, left her stunned, overwarm, and breathing very hard.

Basil, meanwhile, was persuading himself that Dhimitri was still sceptical. Miss Ashmore was an uncommonly attractive young woman, surprisingly curvaceous under that shapeless black rag she wore. Though her chestnut curls were matted and her face was smudged with dirt and she did smell faintly of goats, he tightened his arms around her, preparatory to supplying more conclusive evidence.

Dhimitri's anguished cry stopped him. *"Mjaft!"* the young man wailed. *"Mjaft! Merre dhe largoju pref meje!"*

Basil looked at Alexandra questioningly.

"He says, 'Enough,' and tells you to take me and go."

"That's a mercy," was the muttered reply.

With one arm still about Miss Ashmore's lovely shoulders, Basil hurried her out of the house.

2

"I'm sorry I could not procure another horse on such short notice, Miss Ashmore. You'll have to ride with me. But I promise I won't fling you across the saddle."

Too emotionally drained to reply, she let him lift her onto the mount. They rode for some minutes with Gregor behind them, before she recovered sufficiently to ask where they were going.

"To meet up with your father. This business called for cool heads, and Gregor persuaded him to await us in the next village. I'm afraid that means we've a night's ride ahead of us. At any rate, they're all safe—including your horse. Not that I'd have any objections to continuing our present mode of travel the whole way to Prevesa."

His breath was warm at her neck, and his low, coaxing tone made her feel a little anxious. It was dark, and both these men were strangers. But she was too tired to be truly frightened.

"At this point, sir, I shouldn't care whether I was flung across the saddle or trudging behind. So long as I can get free of this horrid town." She turned to look at him. "Who are you, anyway?"

"Your fiancé, silly girl."

"Yes." She brushed this away. "That was very clever of you, but who are you really—and what brings you to Gjirokastra? The English rarely go beyond the coastal cities."

"Ah, yes. The country, according to Gibbon, 'within sight of Italy is less known than the interior of America.' "

"You've read Gibbon?" she asked, in some surprise.

"Yes, but I got my quote from *Childe Harold*. If it wasn't what Gibbon said or Gibbon who said it, we must blame

15

Byron for yet something else. But that is neither here nor there. My name—in answer to one question—is Basil Trevelyan. I am here—in answer to the other question—because Aunt Clem told me I must come and get you. And Aunt Clem, as you must know, is always to be obeyed."

"Aunt Clem? You mean Lady Bertram?"

"Yes."

"Good heavens! She sent you all the way here—but I never meant—" She bit her lip. She *had* meant—or hoped—after all, that Lady Bertram would perform a miracle. And here it—or he—was.

"It was not so great a distance, Miss Ashmore. I happened to be in Greece—or what one assumes is Greece, though you can hardly tell nowadays."

"So Lady Bertram wrote to you. Then you must know something of my story."

"Oh, yes." He didn't think it worth mentioning that her letter now reposed in the pocket of his worn cloak. "Of course, I was puzzled concerning what I could do to help you. My skills do not lie in coaxing parents out of marital arrangements for their offspring. But I have, as Aunt Clem knows, a weakness for intrigue, and the challenge appealed to me. So, here I am."

Though it was rather embarrassing that he knew of her plight, her sense of humour soon came to the fore. It was a ridiculous plight, was it not? With a rueful smile she said, "Still, you did not expect, I think, to have to rescue me from abductors."

"No, I hadn't anticipated adventures—but then, 'Fierce are Albania's children,' according to Byron. Shall I expect more adventures, Miss Ashmore? I wouldn't mind a little warning."

"Good heavens I should hope not. I can't think what possessed Dhimitri."

"You can't?" His voice grew softer. "How odd, for I can. Yet he gallantly gave you up to your own true love. One gathers that he did not think Mr. Burnham your own true love."

"I suppose you're right. Dhimitri did insist that he was rescuing me."

"Then bless his romantic heart. He believed the show we put on for him—and he's given me an idea."

Since it was most unlikely she'd fall off a horse proceeding at this slow pace, Miss Ashmore wondered why, as they conversed, he felt it necessary to press so close. Or why he must lower his voice to that insinuating timbre when there was only the dragoman to hear. She was unable at the moment to devise a polite way to put these questions to him, considering he'd just saved her from a Fate Worse Than Death. Instead, she asked what idea he had.

"I may have hit upon a way to confound your father's plans for your future. Was he in London during your one Season?"

"No, he came back only just before Mama passed away, at the end of June."

"Then he doesn't know I wasn't in London either. In that case, suppose you formed an attachment then, which you've kept secret all this time—for precisely the reasons we gave Dhimitri and his family."

"An attachment? But what—oh, I see. You think to convince Papa . . ." She trailed off, wondering why the idea made her uneasy.

"That your heart is otherwise engaged."

"I doubt it will make any difference. He's very set on Mr. Burnham."

"Ah, but he hasn't even met me yet, Miss Ashmore. Shall I tell you my credentials?" Without waiting for a reply, he began to enumerate his advantages in ringing tones that made Gregor sit up and take notice. While Basil himself had no title, his first cousin was the seventh Earl of Hartleigh. Furthermore, the Trevelyan family could be traced back to Norman times. His Aunt Clem, daughter of an earl, had maintained her status by marrying the Earl of Bertram, whose own line was equally ancient and honourable.

"Moreover," Basil went on, "in addition to being monstrous well connected, I am now quite plump in the pocket—which makes me a perfectly unexceptionable catch. Add to these my considerable charm and a reputed talent for making black appear white—and I cannot imagine any Papa saying me nay."

"But what of your character, sir?" Alexandra asked sternly, imitating her father at his stuffiest. "Mr. Burnham is honest as the day is long, a dedicated scholar and a gentleman, an earnest and honourable man."

"Deuce take it—you have me out there, madam. You see, my character is as black as black can be. I am an incorrigible liar, a wastrel, and—I beg your pardon, ma'am, but the truth must be told—a womaniser. Selfish and fickle, I am, as Aunt Clem will be quick to tell you, a perfectly dreadful boy."

Alexandra was able to suppress her gasp, but couldn't help turning to look at him in disbelief. The dreadful boy was smiling at her so angelically that she couldn't tell whether he was roasting her or not.

"Well then," she answered, careful to keep her voice light, "you'd better not tell Papa that."

"Of course not. I am a liar, after all. And a very good one, too, I might add."

Doubtless he was. He'd made such a good show of a passionate embrace that even now, thinking back on it, she felt a little dizzy. But then, what did she know of such things? One or two gentlemen had stolen kisses from her, but those were hasty affairs, easily halted by the simple expedient of stomping on a highly polished boot.

To have employed like measures in his case would have meant disaster. Consequently, his was the first full-length kiss she'd experienced. She wasn't sure whether she'd liked it or not. There had been a rush of sensation not altogether unpleasant. That sensation had made her feel powerless, and the loss of control frightened her. Though not nearly as large as Dhimitri—not even so very many inches taller than herself—Mr. Trevelyan was alarmingly strong. She was by no means a frail little thing, and yet it had seemed he might easily crush her to pieces if he liked. Now, as he held her too close, too tightly, she was acutely conscious of his lean, muscular form and of a tension between them that made her breath come and go more rapidly than usual.

"Well then, will I do?" His voice dropped to a whisper again, and his mouth seemed terribly close to her ear.

Fortunately, she'd had some experience with flirtatious

18

gentlemen, a species of which Basil Trevelyan appeared to be a member.

Taking herself firmly in hand, Alexandra answered with cool dignity. "I suppose you must, since there is no one else, Mr. Trevelyan. However, I am puzzled why you must hold me so tight. I assure you I am in no danger of falling off your horse. Unless you think to begin the performance already. But Papa is still miles away, so there really is no need."

"I was practising, Miss Ashmore," came the amused reply.

"I doubt you require any practice. You have quite convinced me of your aptitude for this sort of thing."

"Then perhaps *you* want practice," he persisted.

"I had much rather you trusted me to muddle along. I promise to follow your lead exactly."

He gave a forlorn sigh. "Which is all to say you don't trust me a bit. And after all we've been to each other. Cruel girl. I am yours to command." He loosened his hold on her. "There. Is that better?"

"Yes, thank you."

"Well, it seems a great deal worse to me. Let me know if you change your mind."

"There is very little likelihood of that. Now perhaps you'd be kind enough to change the subject."

"Heartless girl. You forbid me to hold you, and then you forbid me even to flirt with you. This is quite the worst engagement I've ever experienced."

"Ah, then you've been engaged before, Mr. Trevelyan?"

"Very briefly."

The terse reply and the tense silence that followed told her she'd inadvertently stumbled upon an interesting topic. He gave her only a moment to ponder this little mystery before he went on, in a more normal voice, to ask what had brought the Ashmores to Albania.

Alexandra explained that they'd come at the express invitation of Ali Pasha himself. Evidently, when Byron had visited, either he or Mr. Hobhouse had mentioned Sir Charles's work to the great Pasha of Egypt. Ali, being an Albanian and in a humour at the time to cultivate the English, had graciously invited the scholar to explore the little-known country.

"And Dhimitri dared to abduct the daughter of Ali Pasha's honoured guest?"

"The Albanians are afraid of nothing, Mr. Trevelyan. It is fortunate you were so inventive. Papa is no diplomat and might very well have threatened them with Ali. They would have promptly taken Dhimitri's part and laughed at the danger, because the Albanians are not only fearless, but proud and clannish as well. Once Ali got to hear of it—he hears of everything, you know, for all that he's in Egypt now—he'd send his men to kill everyone in the town just to set an example."

"Yes, I understand he roasts his friends on a spit if they annoy him. Well then, it only goes to show, as I've always maintained, that kisses are infinitely preferable to bloodshed."

She could hardly disagree with this pacifistic opinion, yet she dared not concur enthusiastically either. It was plain, even from the small sampling he'd provided of his talents, that his charm was, as he claimed, considerable, and she'd rather not have him exert any more of it upon her.

In other circumstances she might have enjoyed a lighthearted flirtation. But there were only the three of them on a dark road, and already his behaviour had been overly civil. He'd been very slow to release his hold on her and was only amused at her reproof. Besides, he'd admitted to being a liar and a womaniser and other dreadful things. While that, too, could be a lie, it was wiser to assume it was not and to be cautious.

She'd appraised Mr. Trevelyan accurately. Nonetheless, she was safer with him than she knew. His conscience, for instance, was an exceedingly feeble one that rarely troubled him. He was, as he'd told her, a womaniser. He was, moreover, feeling exceedingly amourous. He had not held a woman in his arms in many weeks. He had not held an Englishwoman in his arms in over a year. Here was a perfectly acceptable Englishwoman, who, despite the faint redolence of goats, was a perfectly delicious one as well. For all that, Miss Ashmore's virtue was as safe now as if she rode with her own Papa.

While his conscience was to all intents and purposes quite deaf, dumb, and blind, Basil's sense of self-preservation was strong. He wanted to hurry home and wreak havoc with the hearts of London's young ladies. He could not be free to destroy their peace if he were married to this particular young lady; and he knew perfectly well that if he didn't behave himself, he'd have to marry her. Even Basil knew better than to play fast and loose with Aunt Clèm's goddaughter. He'd learned, to his cost, what came of antagonising family members. No. The price of pleasure was, in this case, far too high.

These musings on self-preservation led Basil to another problem—one that struck him so forcibly that he abruptly drew back from Miss Ashmore, towards whom he had, rather naturally, been inclining as he meditated. Consequently, she very nearly did fall off the startled horse. Only an excellent sense of balance, nurtured by many long treks on narrow mountain paths, kept her in her place.

"Good heavens!" she cried. "Whatever is the matter?"

"I just thought of something."

"Well, it must be perfectly frightful. Are you trying to kill us both?"

He made no answer to this, being engaged for the moment in soothing his mount and then in soothing Gregor, who had also taken alarm. Only after these two were completely at their ease again did Basil apologise for startling Alexandra.

"I just realised, Miss Ashmore, that if we convince your father of our undying devotion, he'll expect us to marry."

The cold dread with which he uttered the words could not be construed as complimentary. Still, his voice was so chillingly sepulchral that she had to laugh.

She had a very nice laugh—low and husky, like her speaking voice—but Basil was too discomposed to fully appreciate it. Instead, he asked her, with some annoyance, what was so funny.

"You say that as though you expected to be buried alive. How high-strung you are, Mr. Trevelyan. And I wonder that you hadn't thought of it before. Of course Papa would expect us to marry, if he believes this folderol, which I rather doubt."

"Well, then?"

In answer she laughed again.

Basil's survival instincts appeared to have deserted him as he contemplated a few responses that would make her stop laughing—and rather abruptly, at that. He was, in fact, about to take steps towards that end when she spoke in more serious tones.

"Whatever Papa expects, I am not so hen-witted as to marry a perfect stranger simply to be rid of someone else."

"I will not be a perfect stranger by the time we're in England," was the huffy retort.

"Oh, so you mean to make me fall in love with you? That would be asking for trouble."

"That is not at all what I meant, wicked girl."

"Then what *do* you mean?"

He collected himself. Something had gotten in the way of his intellect. Lust, probably. "I meant, my love, only that this is a risky enterprise. I must trust you absolutely to jilt me once we are back, for I cannot, as a gentleman, jilt *you*. If I do, I will be driven away in disgrace—" He was about to say "again," but thought better of it. "My family would never forgive me."

"Yes, of course. There's an etiquette to these things." Her voice was a little tart, but recollecting that he was the only rescuer she had at the moment, she added hastily, "At any rate, I shall not lure you to the altar, Mr. Trevelyan. I solemnly promise to jilt you. In the meantime, if you don't want to give me the wrong idea, I suggest you save your 'my loves' for the appropriate audience."

He took her reproof with more of his natural composure and obediently turned the topic. They settled between them the story that would be told to Sir Charles. Then Mr. Trevelyan's curiosity had to be satisfied.

"How does it happen," he asked, "that we never met? Aunt Clem has godchildren over half England, it seems, and I'm forever stumbling over them. Why, I'm sure she's brought out half a dozen goddaughters at least."

"Yes. She wished to oversee my comeout as well. She wanted me to stay with her, from time to time, long before that. But Papa refused. He—well, he said he didn't believe in that foolishness." She hesitated.

"Foolishness? Oh. I see. Why put you on the Marriage Mart when he already had a husband for you?"

"Well, that was part of it." She felt a tad uncomfortable discussing family affairs with a stranger, even if he was Aunt Clem's nephew.

"And the other part?" he prodded.

"Really, you're the most inquisitive gentleman, Mr. Trevelyan."

"I want to know. I want to know what evil curse has kept us apart all these years."

She turned to look at him again, and he smiled. What a lovely, lazy smile, she thought. It made one feel so peaceful and relaxed, even while one's instincts warned one otherwise.

"No evil curse," she answered. "Only he hated Mama's friends, and has always believed London Society to be shallow, vain, stupid, and vicious. He did agree to a Season when I was eighteen, but until then, Mama lived in London, he was off travelling, and I stayed at our house in the country."

"Ah, I see. He didn't want you to turn out like the rest of Society's debs, so he kept you hidden away from evil influence."

She nodded.

"And what did you do in your rustic haven?"

"I read."

"I see."

Of course he didn't see. How could he? "My governess was rather a bluestocking," she explained. "Consequently, I do not handle my needle very well, and my watercolours are appalling, and—"

"Good heavens! You aren't about to tell me you don't play the pianoforte?"

This being uttered in horrified incredulity, she couldn't help but giggle, even as she admitted she could play *no* instrument—at least, not very well.

23

"You poor, benighted girl. What *can* you do?"

"I can, as Papa will tell you, talk a blue streak."

"Then talk, by all means, Miss Ashmore. It is, after all, the only *safe* thing one—or two, rather—can do upon a horse."

Deciding it was best to ignore his innuendoes, she invited him to choose a subject.

"Tell me of Albania. Tell me what you've discovered about Byron's 'rugged nurse of savage men.' "

She complied with his request, and he was a little surprised at what she said. She'd read neither Hobhouse's *Travels in Albania* nor Byron's *Childe Harold*, for those books had been published while she was travelling with her father. Thus, her perspective was all her own, with the focus on politics though she drew analogies from both literature and history. It wasn't a typical bluestocking speech—or at least, certainly not like that of any bluestocking he'd ever known. Her turn of mind was interesting, and her voice very pleasant to hear. Her letter, Basil supposed, had promised something, but this was more than he'd hoped for. He thought better of his aunt as a result, and the time passed more quickly than he'd expected, considering that it was not whiled away with dalliance.

They did not, as Basil had predicted, have to ride all night, though he guessed it was well past midnight when they reached the edge of the village to be met by Sir Charles, Mr. Burnham, and the Albanian servants. Alexandra, half-dead from exhaustion, gave herself over to Lefka's care and was lead away to a tiny cottage.

Meanwhile, Basil was set upon by the two Englishmen, who immediately began questioning him. Yes, he told them, Miss Ashmore was quite unharmed. No, he assured them, there would be no more trouble.

"But I must beg your pardon, gentlemen. It has been such an interesting day altogether that I am like to drop from fatigue. I assure you I cannot put another answer together tonight. We will talk more tomorrow. If you would be so kind as to point me in the direction of a comfortable mound of earth—or a stump or a rock—and topple me onto it, I should be very much obliged."

3

The following morning, after being ungently wakened by the faithful Gregor, Basil betook himself to a mountain stream for a rather chilly bath. Then, clean in body—though his travel-stained garments distressed his fastidious soul—he found Sir Charles and took him aside for private conversation.

Having upon awakening become painfully sensible of a fragrance of goat about her person, Alexandra was making her own morning ablutions about the time the two gentlemen were having their chat. Lefka, who stood guard nearby, persisted in making the most indecorous remarks regarding the beautiful young man who'd rescued her charge. As a result, Miss Ashmore was not only ravenously hungry but unrefreshingly hot and flustered by the time she joined the others for breakfast. One look at her father's face told her there was more aggravation to come.

"I'd like to have a word with you, Alexandra," he announced.

"Can't it wait until after breakfast, Papa? I haven't eaten a thing since yesterday morning—"

"Breakfast can wait."

She looked longingly at the table set under the grape arbour: thick slabs of bread, fruit, two kinds of highly aromatic cheese, and thick black coffee. But her father led her inexorably back into the little cottage.

"I've just had a startling conversation with Mr. Trevelyan, Alexandra."

Abruptly, one of Lefka's most lurid suggestions came back to her. She blushed furiously.

"Oh, my dear, your face tells me that it is true. But why did you never confide this thing to your Papa?" His words sounded sorrowful, but the creases were settling into his forehead.

She collected herself, speaking carefully. "Because I couldn't think you'd like it, Papa. He had nothing when I met him, and though I believed in him, I couldn't expect that you would."

"No, and I don't like it now." He then proceeded to remind her at interminable length about obligations, filial devotion, and the superior character of Mr. Burnham.

Since she'd heard all of this several hundred times before, there was no need to attend very closely. Instead, she concentrated on how best to manage her stubborn Papa. When he finally paused for breath, she answered as though she'd considered all he'd said very seriously. "Of course, that's all true, Papa. But you don't know Mr. Trevelyan yet, do you? Hasn't he made something of himself—starting with nothing—in only six years? And hasn't he been true to me all this while? With his background he might have had his pick of brides in England, but instead he's worked and sacrificed—all for me. Even if I did now have some doubt of my feelings—for I was only eighteen when I met him—I must esteem him for his courage and devotion."

This was doing it rather brown—especially the part about being true to her, when she strongly suspected that Mr. Trevelyan had about as much notion of fidelity as a tomcat. Nonetheless, Alexandra would have cheerfully committed any extravagance that promised freedom from the ghastly Burnhams.

Sir Charles, however, was not to be won over so easily. "Yes, dear, I daresay the young man has behaved admirably. But really, what choice had he, if he had, as you say, nothing? And what of Mr. Burnham's patience? He has waited several years, never complaining."

Well, of course he wouldn't complain. He didn't care one way or other about it. Summoning up all her patience, Alexandra dutifully endured her father's anxieties about the Burnhams, who even now must be preparing for the wedding.

"And what of Society?" he persisted. "Everyone knows you're promised to Randolph. No one knows anything of any attachment to Mr. Trevelyan. You'll be labelled 'jilt.' And everyone will think that the Ashmores have no sense of honour."

Bother your honour, Alexandra thought. And to talk of Society—as if he'd ever in his life cared what Society thought about anything, as if anyone in Society had ever heard of the Burnhams—was the height of absurdity.

Squelching a sigh of vexation, she answered ingenuously, "I don't understand, Papa, how it's less dishonourable to abandon a man who's sacrificed so much on my account and trusted me all these years to keep my promise to him."

The baronet was growing exasperated. He couldn't in all honesty claim that she had no obligation to Mr. Trevelyan. Sir Charles was beginning to feel cornered. "This is merely a childish infatuation, Alexandra. As I'm sure you and Mr. Trevelyan will soon find out. People change in six years. What seems romantic at eighteen looks very different at four-and-twenty."

She gazed at him as though struck by what he said. Then, in a slow, thoughtful voice, she answered. "Well, to tell the truth, I hadn't thought of that, Papa. I was so overjoyed to see him again—and as my gallant rescuer. I suppose it was very romantic."

Her father nodded, looking obnoxiously complacent. But his complacency began to fade as she went on.

"In that case, I don't see what you're alarmed about. For if it is, as you say, only infatuation, then we'll discover it soon enough, won't we? Very likely, by the time we're home again—or soon after, surely—Mr. Trevelyan and I will have taken each other in dislike. And everything will settle itself peaceably with neither dishonour nor hurt feelings. How perceptive you are, Papa."

Papa being, as they say, hoist with his own petard, could produce no answer for this. He had to content himself with grumbling about childish infatuations and wondering why he and Randolph should have to put up with such behaviour. However, as it turned out, he hadn't time to annoy himself or his daughter much more on that subject. They'd no sooner left the house and joined the others near the grape arbour when they heard in the distance a dull thundering.

This gradually resolved itself into the pounding of hooves, and then in turn became a lone figure on a brown stallion. The figure came to a halt some yards from where the group now stood, watching in alarm.

"Ah, the rejected swain," Basil murmured, moving quickly to Alexandra's side and putting a protective arm about her shoulders. Though the gesture filled Sir Charles with ineffable disgust, he had sense enough to hold his tongue.

The rejected swain was soon before them, looking so humble and abashed that Alexandra's heart, which had been pounding in concert with the horse's hooves, swiftly settled itself to a mere fluttering.

"Zotir Ashmore," said the young man quietly. "Zotir Tri—Tri—Vasil." He looked at Alexandra and heaved a great sigh. Then, raising himself very tall, very straight, he launched into a long, beautiful—nearly poetic—apology. While it was not nearly so poetic in English, the tone alone impressed his listeners. He had shamed his family and disgraced himself. His behaviour was madness and inexcusable. He despaired of obtaining their forgiveness.

The speech made Alexandra feel ashamed of having deceived him with her make-believe fiancé. Dhimitri was obviously sincere, and now, standing there so tall and sad and dignified, he was, she thought, noble.

Good heavens! now he was saying that he must go with them to Prevesa to make what small amends were in his power. He would personally see to their comfort and safety during their "perilous journey." He had friends and relatives in many of the villages along the way, who would make them all welcome.

"Would you tell him, Alexandra," Basil responded, when Dhimitri's offer had been translated, "that we accept his apology. His offer, however, is too generous. There's no need for him to accompany us."

Zotir Vasil was also generous, but the thing must be done. If Dhimitri could not bring his family assurances that the English had reached their destination safely, he could not go home at all.

It soon was plain that the offer must be accepted.

Sir Charles so counselled Basil in a low-spoken aside. "The boy comes of a good family, Mr. Trevelyan, and they're very proud. He must redeem his honour, and we could use the protection—though I must say it is deuced awkward, under the circumstances."

"Well, then, he must come, I suppose. Alexandra, my love"—she saw her father start at this—"I hope you have not too many other beaux between here and Prevesa. Otherwise, I fear we'll soon swell up into a great army and have Ali Pasha quaking in his slippers by the time we reach our destination."

"You see the difficulty."

"Ay, that I do, my lady." Mr. Henry Latham accepted a cup of tea from his hostess. "Burnham's a very close man with his affairs. My people have learned nothing that isn't plain and aboveboard. The situation may very well be as he says, you know. As the match means a step up in the world for them, it's worth a good deal more than the gold."

"Then you agree it's futile to attempt to communicate with him?" Lady Bertram asked.

"Oh, yes. A waste of pen and ink. And not only on account of this," he added. "George, you see, is preoccupied lately, due to problems with his labourers."

Lady Bertram smiled faintly. "Is he now?"

"Yes. And I expect it's going to get worse before it gets better. As things always do." Mr. Latham expressed this pessimistic opinion with the utmost amiability, as he carried a tea cake to his plate. "It's what comes of not paying an honest day's pay for an honest day's work. Your labouring classes like to get paid fair for what they do. It's a queer thing, but there it is. Human nature, my lady."

"You are a student of human nature, sir," the countess remarked drily.

"In my own modest way."

"Then what do you make of the other matter?"

Mr. Latham made it out, apparently, while he disposed of the tea cake. After it had vanished into the depths of his plump, genial countenance, he answered, "It's one thing to study human nature and another to predict it. I'm a businessman, not a prophet. But as a businessman—" He paused.

"I'm always eager to hear your views on business, sir."

"Well, then, as a man of business I can give you a fair idea of what ships are scheduled to cross the Mediterranean. Always allowing, of course, for the complications of this unfortunate unpleasantness on the continent. With good information and a little patience, I expect we can manage to be on the spot when that particular ship comes in."

"The information I leave, as always, to you. As to patience—only point me to the port, Henry, and I shall wait there, patiently as Job, though it take a twelvemonth."

Was it not enough that he'd done three years' penance in vile climates among villains whose treacheries made his own attempted "crime" a mere boyish prank by comparison? Was it not enough he'd been nearly murdered some dozen times? Apparently, the Furies were not done tormenting him. He must now spend all his waking hours with one of the most desirable women he'd ever met—and have to keep his hands to himself the whole blessed time.

The Devil himself must have fashioned her to make men demented. Small wonder that Dhimitri, perceiving Mr. Burnham's profound and incomprehensible want of interest, had tried to carry her off. Even the jaded Mr. Trevelyan would like to carry her off to some private place.

The Devil, surely, had designed her long-legged slenderness, so exquisitely curved, and woven her dark chestnut curls to glint copper in the bright sun. He'd sculpted the soft, full lips; and then, for Old Nick hadn't any conscience at all, he'd drawn those startling green eyes with their flecks of gold like speckled sunlight in a cool forest. Nor was that yet enough. She must move with sensuous, provocative grace and speak in that husky, intimate timbre. Even her unfashionably tanned skin must seem the palest golden silk, rising to a warm rose in her cheeks. All that, and Basil could do no more than look.

For one, she was the daughter of a gentleman. For another, she was obviously innocent; and for a third—and this carried by far the greatest weight—she was Aunt Clem's goddaughter. He wouldn't even have to compromise Miss Ashmore to be forced into marriage. She had only to become infatuated with him and confide it to Aunt Clem, and his bachelor days would be over. He needed to repeat this lecture to himself often as the days passed, for she made him very . . . restless.

Basil was not used to resisting temptation of any kind. When in his life had he lusted in vain? But then, when had he ever lusted after a gently bred virgin? Never. His problem was simply that he'd been too long without feminine companionship and wasn't used to controlling himself.

Still, they must keep up a show for the Argus-eyed Dhimitri. Therefore, Mr. Trevelyan was forced to sit very close to Miss Ashmore when they ate their modest meals. He must, certainly, engage her in conversation, though it only made him more restless. The more he talked to her, the more he wanted to talk to her.

It was partly because she was well educated and articulate. But there was something else, too, something he couldn't quite put his finger on. More than once he'd heard her render her intellectual Papa speechless with frustration after one of her exercises in twisted logic. What truly surprised Basil, however, was that he found himself, more often than he liked, at *point non plus*.

Though he didn't mean to flirt with her and knew it was dangerous, sometimes he'd forget about Aunt Clem and the life of idle dissipation awaiting him in England. He'd lapse into his coaxing ways, and she'd seem to respond as sweetly as he wished—until he realised that her tender glances and soft words were a precise imitation of his own. Every time, instead of taking offence, he'd end up laughing at himself and, in the next minute, making the most candid confessions.

Afterwards, when he thought about it, he felt uneasy. He wasn't used to being managed and objected to it on principle. Yet while it was happening it was, well, so *refreshing*. Any-

31

how, he reassured himself, it was a good idea to be candid with her. Knowing what he was, she'd be intelligent enough to keep on her guard against him.

Though it was only about forty miles or so from Gjirokastra to Saranda, the poor roads made it a journey of several days. As the time passed, Sir Charles grew more and more frustrated. The infatuation showed no signs of diminishing. On the contrary, his daughter and Trevelyan had too much to say to each other. They talked constantly, starting at breakfast and not leaving off until they retired for the night. Sir Charles would have preferred to keep them apart, but with Dhimitri present he didn't dare. Even Gjergi, who had spoken with the rejected swain at length, warned the baronet. Dhimitri had given the girl up only because he was convinced that she and Vasil were fated to be together. It was *kismet*.

Kismet, indeed. Well, they were a pair, those two, with their glib answers to everything. It would serve them right to be shackled to each other for the rest of their days. Looking now at Randolph—who rode along calmly, quite oblivious to the various tensions and countertensions of the party—the baronet remembered the debt he owed and decided to drop his assistant a hint.

In response, the conscientious Mr. Burnham, who'd rarely troubled to say more than two words a day to Miss Ashmore, began obediently to seek her out for conversation.

On the third afternoon of their journey, Mr. Trevelyan remarked to Miss Ashmore on this strange development as they sat, a little apart from the others, eating grapes.

She chuckled at this, and said, "He's courting me, Mr. Trevelyan. Can't you see? Papa must have told him to do it—and probably has hinted what to say, as well."

"You laugh, Miss Ashmore? I'm shocked. Still, with three men breaking their hearts over you, what else would a cruel girl like yourself do?"

"Three hearts? But you told me only yesterday you hadn't any heart at all."

"I never said any such thing."

"You implied it when you spoke of Almacks."

32

"I said only that I was looking forward to the experience."

"Yes, but you said it in such a self-satisfied way that I knew you were picturing all the lovely young ladies wanting you to notice them."

"You make me sound a perfect coxcomb. What a cruel construction to put on my innocent remarks."

"Then you mustn't let your eyes glitter so wickedly when you speak of such things, Mr. Trevelyan. I can quite read your mind."

For half an instant, he believed she could. He went on amiably to insist he *did* have a heart. "True, it's very small and very hard. Nonetheless, it exists and may, therefore, be broken."

"Well, I wish you wouldn't break it just yet, or between that and the other two you tease me of, we shall leave a deal of rubble behind us."

"Point taken, Miss Ashmore. I shall refrain from littering this lovely landscape. Still, I do worry that Mr. Burnham will steal you out from under my nose."

"Do you worry, poor man? But you're young and resilient. I daresay you could reconcile yourself to the loss quickly enough."

He immediately looked such a picture of wounded innocence that she nearly choked on the grape she'd popped into her mouth. She looked at him in wonder. "I declare you were meant for the stage. However do you manage those expressions?"

"Practise, my dear," he answered, with an odd little smile. "Practise."

According to Mr. Burnham, who was dutifully, if not altogether effectively, attempting to distract Alexandra from her Other Fiancé, Mr. Trevelyan also had considerable practise in deceit.

As they left Delvina and began their descent to the plain of Vurqu, Randolph had—in the politest way—replaced his rival at Miss Ashmore's side. A tad annoyed to see Basil give way so easily and go on so amicably to join her Papa—with whom he was now engaged in lively conversation—Alexandra gave Mr. Burnham a dazzling smile and asked him what he meant.

He was not in the habit of eliciting warm acknowledgement from Miss Ashmore. When she regarded him at all, and when he noticed, both of which were rare happenings, she did so mainly with profound weariness. So taken aback was he by this display of warmth that he smiled automatically in return.

It occurred to Alexandra that he wasn't a bad-looking man. Randolph's clear blue eyes, when not glazed over in their customary scholarly abstraction, were, at least, honest ones. You could believe what you saw there.

"I only hope he will not deceive *you,*" said Randolph, coloring slightly.

"What makes you think he will, Randolph? I thought you'd never met him before."

He hesitated briefly, then admitted that he hadn't.

"Then to what do you ascribe your concern?"

"I shouldn't have brought it up. I'd rather not speak ill of a man behind his back."

Well then, Alexandra thought, glancing at Mr. Trevelyan, who seemed to find Papa inordinately amusing today, let us by all means call him to us so you can speak ill to his face.

Aloud she said, "It isn't kind to drop such alarming hints to me, Randolph, and then say nothing more. Surely you must have some basis for what you claim."

As a scholar who prided himself on his logic, Mr. Burnham wasn't about to own he had no foundation for his remarks. On the other hand, it went against his gentlemanly grain to trade in gossip. The scholar won out.

"I was in London some two years after you left, as you know. While we did not travel in the same circles, I did hear of Mr. Trevelyan, and, I'm sorry to say, nothing to his credit. When I heard this story of six years' trying to make his fortune, I was astonished. Knowing what I did, I could not imagine that he had got his money any other way than by gambling."

Well, this was of a piece with everything else—and surely Randolph wouldn't say such a thing if he didn't have reasonable evidence. Gambling, too. Add that to the rest and it made a pretty sort of blackguard.

What of it, then? She certainly wasn't going to marry the fellow. Fortified by this comforting certainty, she rose—as she must—to Mr. Trevelyan's defence. "That would be very distressing news, indeed. But he *was* in low spirits when I last saw him," she lied, "and I understand that some men will turn to vice—temporarily—when they're in low spirits. Besides, he does say he's partners with Henry Latham, and we could always find out the truth of that."

Randolph nodded gravely. "Mr. Latham is a distant acquaintance of my father. It won't be difficult to ascertain the facts once we are home. Perhaps I wrong the man. I don't mean to. It is only that I cannot like to see you misled."

He was sincere, of course. Honest as the day is long: that was Randolph. He made her feel guilty. A little while in Mr. Trevelyan's company and she'd deceived her father, Randolph, and even Dhimitri. But when men persisted in being such blockheads, what else could one do? Still, maybe she'd been overhasty in rejecting Randolph. Charm and clever conversation weren't everything. Better to be a little bored occasionally than to be forever worrying what one's untrustworthy spouse might be up to.

Dear heavens! Whatever had led her into that train of thought? What unworthy spouse could she possibly be thinking of?

Randolph was still making apologetic murmurs. Alexandra collected her wandering thoughts and made him a soothing reply—exactly the sort of thing his wife would have to say every now and then when some bit of stone puzzled him or when he lost one of his sketches. Well, he was kind and sincere, but there were other men in the world. Nothing on earth—except perhaps her stubborn father—obliged her to choose between these two alone. Not that they were, she chided herself, willing to be chosen from. Had not one of them made that very clear the first night she met him?

4

Saranda now bore few traces of its origins as the ancient, thriving seaport of Onchesmus. It was a port, still, but a very minor one, and so a boat must be hired to take the group on to Prevesa. With luck—ill luck, as Alexandra saw it—they might speedily obtain places on one of the British vessels that regularly stopped there.

There was news in Saranda of Napoleon and contradictory tales of a great battle in France or Belgium. The outcome of that battle, unfortunately, was a matter of violent debate.

Basil was standing with Miss Ashmore, waiting for the dragomen to finish bullying the townsfolk as they loaded their belongings into the tiny boat.

"I suppose," he said, "we must wait until we get to Prevesa—or even Malta—to learn for certain. I should like to know, in the first place, how the Corsican eluded the British cruisers guarding his island. Then I should be curious to find out why he didn't attack Wellington in Brussels. He was still in Paris, last I heard—though it was all rumour and everyone contradicting everyone else, just as they do now. I couldn't stop to wait for news." He glanced at his companion.

Miss Ashmore seemed lost in reverie. She was gazing out across the narrow neck of the Ionian Sea towards the gloomy mass of Corfu's mountains.

"What do *you* think will be the outcome?" he asked.

She brought herself back, but her green eyes were still rather dreamy. "How difficult it is to contemplate war when one gazes upon such peaceful beauty. Yet this has never been a peaceful place. Ali Pasha and his soldiers have conquered, town by town, towns which had been conquered by others before. In time, someone will wrest his dominions from Ali. And he is so much more clever and efficient a manager than Buonaparte," she added, her eyes gleaming now with mischief.

"More Machiavellian, you mean?"

"Certainly that. Ali, I think, would never have been so careless as to alienate Talleyrand. Or if he had, he would have known enough to have the man killed, instead of leaving him to lick his wounds and plot revenge for five long years."

He wondered once again, looking into that heartbreakingly beautiful face, how she came by her opinions. As the daughter of Sir Charles Ashmore, she could hardly be expected to escape without some smattering of historical knowledge. But the baronet knew nothing of current events—beyond the dim awareness that there had been a war going on which occasionally interfered with his travel plans—and she seemed to know everything.

Much of Miss Ashmore's information, Basil had learned, came from divers diplomats the Ashmores had encountered in their travels, especially the many foreigners who paid court to Ali Pasha hoping to lure the sly Albanian to their side. Nonetheless, what Alexandra made of the facts and rumours she heard was her own and always interesting. To egg her on, therefore, he asked ingenuously what she meant. After all, Buonaparte couldn't help but alienate somebody and could hardly trouble himself about whose feelings he might hurt.

She shot him a look of incredulity. "To call the man a stockingful of excrement—and that before the whole court? He could not have helped that? And he reputed a brilliant strategist?"

Basil suppressed a grin. "Called him what?"

But she was already caught up in the drama of the moment she pictured. "Before the whole court," she repeated, shaking her head. "Talleyrand stood and bore the abuse, never saying a word. Yet, one suspects, from that day forth he must have plotted his revenge. Plotted, planned, biding his time for years." She shivered. "Such patience is frightening. I

37

should not care to have such a one about. I imagined him like Cassius, with his 'lean and hungry look.' "

Basil gave his own theatrical shudder. "That sounds exactly like Rogers, my valet. Left to his devices in Prevesa, heaven knows what he might be plotting. I hope, at least, he's guarding my trunks."

"If he's a proper British valet, Mr. Trevelyan, he'll be obliged to shoot himself as soon as he claps eyes on you."

Basil glanced down ruefully at his raffish attire: Turkish-style trousers, limp cotton shirt the Albanians called a *kamisha*, and travel-stained cloak. "Well, you see, my costume doesn't look like anything in particular, and so I can't be categorised, which makes men careful how they treat me. I may, you know, be mad."

Miss Ashmore assured him, with a little grin, of her certainty that he *was*.

"But sane enough to hope Rogers has kept my baggage safe from these rogues. I don't know why he shouldn't, as he's a worse rogue than any of them. At any rate, he'll not deign to notice my disgraceful appearance. He'll take me immediately in hand, and the next time you see me you won't recognise me."

"Ah, then I shan't be obliged to speak to you."

"In which case, I shall travel as I am," was the prompt retort. "But here we are, speaking of my sartorial tragedies, when I am on pins and needles to hear about this Cassius-Talleyrand of yours. And of Napoleon's Fatal Flaw. Is he a tragic figure, do you think?"

It wanted very little to coax her to talk. She led Basil on back through history, from Buonaparte and Talleyrand to Caesar to Alexander to Alexander's father, Philip of Macedon. Basil was content to go where she led, though he teased and questioned and tried to undermine her theories. He liked to listen to her, liked exploring with her the characters of those who'd made history, and those who'd made art and literature of history.

What had Dhimitri's relatives called her? The English witch. She wove spells, they claimed, entrapping young men with her beauty, but to Basil she was Sheherazade. He could have listened to her forever . . . and oh, how he wished she could keep him company through his long, restless nights.

They reached Prevesa by late afternoon—too soon—and he was jolted out of his trance as they prepared to disembark. Deaf to her protests and oblivious to Dhimitri's congratulatory smile, Basil lifted her out of the boat and waded to shore with her in his arms. No, he thought, he was under no spell. He only liked to hear her talk because he wanted her, and he wanted her because he'd been lonely too many months. There was no spell. Only Desire, and that must fade once they were home.

Lefka, Gjergi, and Stefan had stayed behind in Saranda, but Gregor and Dhimitri refused to part from their charges until those fragile English creatures were safely aboard their ship. A British merchant vessel lay in the harbour, awaiting the escort of a brig of war which was scheduled to arrive the next day and depart the day following.

While Mr. Trevelyan made arrangements for passage, Dhimitri saw to accommodations. The young Albanian had distant relatives in the town who were very well-to-do. Their spacious and well-furnished home was, he insisted, infinitely preferable to the Spartan lodgings of the English vice-consul. Too tired to argue, the travellers agreed to accept the hospitality.

After dinner, their hosts proposed that the Englishmen take a stroll through the town. Alexandra helped the womenfolk wash the simple dinner utensils and then decided to take her own quiet walk through the garden. She had, after all, a great deal to think about.

This make-believe betrothal to Mr. Trevelyan was not a satisfactory solution to her problems. They could not continue the charade after they reached England, which meant she was only postponing the inevitable. Her rakish co-conspirator would no doubt wish to recommence his raking immediately, thereby leaving no more stumbling blocks in Papa's—or rather, the Burnhams'—way. Mr. Trevelyan had turned out to be hardly any help at all, and he unsettled her. She was not used to being unsettled, and she didn't like it.

Well, actually, she *did* like it—and that, considering the man's character, was not a desirable state of mind.

Shrugging to shake off her thoughts of him she turned into the pathway leading to the terraced garden, lush with flowers. The air was sweet, but not cloyingly so. The sea breezes stirred and freshened, making it as deliciously fragrant, she thought, as the Garden of Eden must have been. From the distance came strains of the music she'd gradually come to appreciate, though it had sounded so odd and discordant at first. A tenor voice sang in a familiar, aching minor key accompanied by the wail of what sounded like an Eastern version of a clarinet. She couldn't make out the words, but imagined what they were: a tribute to native warriors and patriots or to the rugged beauty of the country. Sometimes there was a mournful song of love—but then, they all sounded rather mournful, even the triumphant tale of Ali Pasha's conquest of Prevesa. As she stopped to listen, she realised she wasn't alone.

Basil stepped away from the garden wall he'd been lounging against, and approached her. He was dressed now, as he'd promised, like a proper English gentleman, though he still seemed somehow a creature of her imagination. In the moonlight his sun-bleached hair was shot through with silver. Even his amber cat eyes seemed to glow as they settled on her in that watchful way.

"I was right," he said, in a low voice. "I was thinking this was almost—but not quite heaven. Now you are come to make it complete."

The words made her heart flutter, as they doubtless were intended to do, but she was determined not to blush. Nor would she be alarmed in the least at the way he so self-assuredly offered his arm. She'd stroll with him for a minute or two and then go back indoors.

"It is beautiful," she answered, deciding the honeyed words were best ignored. "For the six years we've been here, I find myself in one place after another, each time thinking it must be the loveliest scene in the world."

"I suppose then, you'll be sorry to leave?"

"Yes, of course. What other sea is as blue as the Ionian?"

"None. But I shall be deliriously happy to go home, nonetheless."

"You'd have been gone all the sooner if it hadn't been for me," she found herself saying, though that wasn't what she'd meant to say at all.

"Yes, but I wouldn't have been returning *with* you—and that, I think, more than makes up for the delay."

Naturally he'd say something like that. He probably thought she was fishing for compliments.

When she didn't answer, he went on. "Now, of course, all the advantage is with the later departure. Not only do I return with you, but I have managed by sheer perseverance to find you alone at last. It did take some doing, and I was wretchedly deceitful. However, I have my reward, and that's all that matters."

She stopped and looked at him. "What are you doing here, Mr. Trevelyan? I thought you'd gone with my father and Mr. Burnham and the others."

"Why do you never call me Basil? Is the name so disagreeable?"

"That wasn't what I asked, Mr. Trevelyan."

"But it was what *I* asked, Miss Ashmore, and I wish you would stop calling me Mr. Trevelyan. It puts such a monstrous distance between us and makes Dhimitri pity me, which is quite unbearable."

"You keep turning the subject, and yet you were the one to start it."

"Of course I did, and for nothing but the sheer delight of watching your green eyes flash at me. They are indeed flashing, Miss Ashmore, as they always do when I provoke you, and that should make me feel ashamed of myself if anything could. But nothing does, you know."

That was easy enough to believe. "In which case, sir, I think it best to take my leave of you."

She disengaged her arm from his and started to turn back to the house, but he stepped in front of her, blocking the way. He stood only a few inches from her. He was only teasing, of course. He was trying to make her nervous. He was succeeding. "You stand in my path, Mr. Trevelyan, which is very inconsiderate, because now I'll be obliged to trample on that lovely flowerbed.''

"I only wanted to kiss you," was the outrageous reply. "Here we are alone in paradise—the perfect moment—and you talk only of murdering these innocent plants.''

She was alarmed now, though something pleasantly anticipatory about that alarm brought warmth to her cheeks. He hadn't budged, and the glitter in those strange eyes forced her to look away.

She took a step backward. "I don't know what you're thinking of. What point is there in kissing me when there's no one nearby who needs to be convinced of our undying devotion?'' She took another step away from him. He stayed where he was, looking thoughtful.

"How logical you are. I think it's from spending too much time with Mr. Burnham. Randolph. You do call him Randolph. I've heard you. No use denying it.''

That was better. His tone was lighter now, and so hers became. "I've known him for years. But if it troubles you so much, then I'll call you Randolph, too.''

Her small grin made him even more restless than usual—or maybe reckless was more accurate a description, because in the very next moment he reached out and pulled her to him. He bent his face to hers, and then there was nothing left but to kiss her. He told himself it was that grin, provoking him.

Miss Ashmore certainly had not meant to let him kiss her in the first place or to kiss him back in the second. But his mouth was so unexpectedly gentle as it touched hers that it gentled her own response. Then there was a warmth, and it was so welcoming and tender and made her feel so very peaceful and cozy and safe in his arms, that she did respond. He'd pulled her closer until her heart was pounding, and the press of his lean, muscular body had kindled warmth into blazing heat, and everything familiar had been whirled away by the maelstrom into which he drew her.

She was, suddenly, very afraid of him, because he was drawing her into danger, and she was following too willingly. His fingers were in her hair. He kissed her forehead and her eyelids and her cheeks, and when his lips found her mouth again they were hungry, demanding, urgent. Because she did not want him to stop, tears—of frustration, anger, shame, she hardly knew—welled up in her eyes as she tried to push him away.

"No," he whispered, crushing her closer. "Not now."

"Yes, stop. Now," she gasped. "Please stop—you must stop. Please."

He barely seemed to notice her effort to push him away. "Alexandra." His voice was hoarse.

"Let go of me."

Very unwillingly he released her from his embrace; but he clasped her hand to keep her from fleeing. "This is a terrible time to stop, my love," he told her. He sounded rather breathless as though he'd been running hard.

"Oh, please. No 'my loves.' And will you let go of me? I must go back."

"You can't do that now, Alexandra. Look at you. Your wicked fiancé has disarranged your hair, and your eyes are wet. You look exactly as though—well, exactly as you should under the circumstances." Releasing her, he offered his handkerchief. "And you hate me, which is a great deal worse."

She dabbed absently at her eyes but made no other effort to restore herself to rights. Stunned and confused, she spoke without thinking. "It isn't that . . . I don't know what it is. I don't understand."

At the moment, there were a few things he didn't understand either. There was, for instance, the totally ungovernable desire. If she hadn't begged him to stop in that desperate voice, he wasn't sure what would have happened. Surely it must have stopped at some point. He refused to think beyond that.

She wasn't looking at him, but was staring off into the dark distance, as though some secret might be stored there. Somewhere in that distance there was music: a mournful, lonely voice calling to the heavens. Her face was like cool marble in the moonlight, so still did she stand, gazing off at nothing. He wanted to touch her, to make her warm again and yielding as she had been—but no, that was quite impossible. Firmly, he turned his mind away and became more charming. "I do hope you'll settle on hating yourself then, because you'll be kinder to me, and I do need a great deal of kindness now after being so cruelly rejected."

"Rejected?" She looked up in astonishment at those strange cat eyes, but they were blank and innocent.

"Isn't that what it was? 'No' and 'stop' to me mean rejection, especially when uttered in such anguish. Yet you needn't expect me to apologise. I'd gladly do the same again, even to be rejected again though that isn't the least bit pleasant, and you may certainly apologise if you like. I'm a very forgiving sort of person, you know."

Good heavens, but he was impossible. To chatter at her so when she was racked by emotions she could neither understand nor name. She stared at him. He stared back, his face still blank and innocent, as the silence lengthened between them. It was not a peaceful sort of silence. Something seemed to vibrate within it. That something finally drove Alexandra to regain her self-command and make a rather tart comment on his magnanimity.

"Yes, magnanimity is one of my failings. But come," he went on briskly, "your current state of dishevelment is unconscionably tempting, and I don't think I can contemplate you another minute without doing something perfectly dreadful."

Thus admonished, she attended to her hair—as best she could, with his helpful interference. He insisted the pins were in wrong and, looking very grave, pulled them out almost as quickly as she put them in. His touch, as he handed them back to her, made her tremble.

"Will you please stop helping me?" she snapped. "I'll be out here all night at this rate."

"You didn't think I intended to let you go back in so soon? However tedious my company seems to you, we've been here only a very few minutes."

"That's quite long enough to be alone in a dark garden with a gentleman, even in Albania. It's hardly proper."

"No, it isn't proper at all, and if I could think of some

beautiful lie to convince you to stay—well, obviously, you can't trust me to behave myself.''

"That's true. And it's very tiresome and unfair of you, Mr. Trevelyan—''

"Mr. Trevelyan, still.''

"Randolph, then.''

"Basil, you wretched girl. *Basil.*''

"Basil, then.'' Seeing the triumphant smile he wore, she smiled, too. He might have all the experience, but he needn't always have the upper hand. "Basil then, my love, my sweet,'' she went on in falsely ardent, breathless tones so like his own that she startled the smile off his face. "You are monstrous unfair. For you show me not only that I'm not safe in your company, but that you're unsafe in mine. I must look out not only for myself, but for you as well—since you seem bound and determined to compromise me.''

"Do I?'' he asked. He made no move to stop her when she stepped away. His smile was gone, and the bland innocence had turned to watchfulness again.

"Oh, yes. But I gave you my promise, and I mean to keep it, regardless how difficult you make it for me. I will save you from yourself, Basil, my love. So rest easy.''

She turned then and left him.

5

Although she found the voyage unspeakably tedious, Alexandra inwardly cursed the favourable winds that sped them on to England and the Burnhams. They learned along the way that the defeated Buonaparte had preceded them and, even now, was being ogled by curious mobs at Tor Bay. Their own vessel's captain, however, had no interest in twice-vanquished Corsicans and, furthermore, was in a tremendous hurry. He made directly for Portsmouth. There they were amazed to find both Henry Latham and Lady Bertram waiting for them, and in very short order these two contrived to separate Alexandra from her father.

Papa, it is true, did not leave his daughter willingly, but Lady Bertram swept all his objections away as though they were so many odd bits of scrap in her path.

"To Yorkshire?" she repeated, in magnificently disdainful, disbelieving tones. "At this time of year and after so arduous a journey? Unthinkable, my dear boy. I fear you must be near collapse yourself to harbour such a notion." To his stunned protests she answered severely, "You have cheated me of her company for six long years—and after dear Juliet had promised me I might give the girl a Season." This, of course, was a monstrous fib, but Papa didn't know that.

When he attempted to explain about betrothals and impatient Burnhams, Lady Bertram only gazed coldly down her patrician nose at him and demanded *what* he was thinking of to subject his daughter to the scandal that must arise if she were married so soon upon her return and in such a havey-cavey way.

Sir Charles was not easily cowed, but he was operating under certain disadvantages. He did not like being cast as the villain of the piece, especially when his solution was so reasonable. At once it settled both his debt to the Burnhams and the matter of finding his troublesome daughter a steady husband. Furthermore, there was nothing wrong with Randolph. His character was blameless, he was comfortably well-off, and he was good-looking enough to please any number of romantic females. If Alexandra would only cooperate, her father would not have to waste time dawdling in England when there was so much to be done in Albania. Still, Sir Charles considered himself a just man, and there was this business of Mr. Trevelyan's six years' toil. The tale appeared to be a great piece of nonsense concocted by his scheming daughter and Clementina's nephew, and yet it might be true.

Therefore, though he resented Lady Bertram's high-handed ways and mistrusted his daughter, he was somewhat relieved to have the problem taken off his hands temporarily. He'd like to have the leisure to think things over without being influenced by either Alexandra's sophistries or Mr. Trevelyan's treacly blandishments. To save face, however, he goaded Lady Bertram into delivering a few more ominous predictions and biting comments before giving himself up to be led away by the affable Mr. Latham.

Basil was led away as well, along with Randolph. Alexandra had time only to bid a hasty farewell to her two fiancés and kiss her father's cheek before she was whirled off in the countess's luxurious carriage.

"Well," the great lady said, "that went a deal easier than I expected. Your father was rather more fuddled than usual— I expect that accounts for his not being so obstinate as usual. I was anticipating quite a battle. What, I wonder, accounts for his fuddlement?"

"I think you have your nephew to thank for that, my lady."

"Aunt Clem, if you please. You never used to be so formal, Alexandra. Or is the wretched boy to blame for that, as well?"

The scrutiny of those sharp, brown eyes was a trifle disconcerting. Lady Bertram had such a way of ferreting out

47

secrets—almost as if she read your mind—and Alexandra did not like to have her mind read. Still, she made herself meet that gaze directly and answered, "No, that's my own doing. You were so majestic back there that I'm in awe of you myself."

"Well, your father is not easily awed normally. But tell me, how did Basil unsettle him so?"

Alexandra gave her a slightly abbreviated account of their make-believe romance. Actually, it was only abbreviated in two particulars, for though it was very easy to confide in dear Aunt Clem, one must draw the line at discussing her nephew's embraces. Broad-minded as the countess was, she might think Alexandra compromised, and that would never do.

Lady Bertram found the recitation highly amusing. "Leave it to Basil to find excuses for kissing a pretty gel."

"Oh, but he never—"

"Well, if he never then it most certainly cannot be my nephew we speak of. He is not in the habit of exerting himself on anyone else's account without making it as agreeable to himself as possible. I am disappointed, however, he could contrive no better scheme. It is not at all what I'd hoped for. Still, I daresay he found it immensely entertaining." Her tone, softened. "I hope he did not misbehave terribly, my dear."

Alexandra coloured slightly, though she replied calmly enough. "Oh no, of course not. It was all for show. He did have my father to convince and Dhimitri as well—at least until we were aboard ship. He was very successful. As you saw yourself, Papa was rather confused. The only push he made was to tell Randolph to stir himself."

"Nevertheless, in your father's eyes you're still betrothed to Randolph. It really makes me wonder at Basil."

"You speak as though he regularly accomplishes miracles, Aunt Clem."

"I know he's solved far more difficult and delicate matters for the Crown. It is usually a matter of pride with him to succeed completely at what he undertakes, particularly if it is something devious."

"Perhaps, then, the problem was beneath him."

"That would be a first," the countess muttered.

"Besides, Papa was suspicious of him. Add that to the problem of paying back Mr. Burnham. He did fund Papa's work generously and had those travel accounts published. He looks after all Papa's business now—though there's little enough profit in it for him."

"Yes, a philanthropist, I'm sure," was the dry observation. "How warm you are in defence of your tormentors, Alexandra."

"I've been trying to see it through Papa's eyes, Aunt Clem. After all, I've made so many difficulties for him. And I honestly wish I could care more for Randolph."

The fervour with which she expressed that wish made Lady Bertram raise an eyebrow ever so slightly, but lost in her own thoughts, Alexandra continued, "Papa says I'm only being obstinate—and maybe he's right."

The eyebrow elevated another fraction.

"After all," the young woman went on hurriedly, "Randolph is a kind and honest man. One could do a great deal worse, I suppose."

"Undoubtedly."

"Once he began taking the trouble to talk with me, I found him, well, not disagreeable company. He was most considerate throughout the voyage, certainly, and he *is* sincere and straightforward. One never wonders what he means, really—" She caught herself up in time and went on more matter-of-factly, "At any rate, I think better of him now than when I wrote you. Yet, if I hadn't written and your nephew hadn't come and shaken Randolph out of his complacency, I might never have seen his—Randolph's—better qualities."

Though the words were rational enough, there was an edge of despair in the tone. Nonetheless, Lady Bertram only nodded and remarked, "Basil comes out of the adventure quite a prodigy of virtue. How very distressing that must be for him, after devoting so much time and imagination to wickedness."

"Has he?" Alexandra couldn't help asking. "I mean, has he always been wicked?"

"My dear child—you don't mean to tell me he's pulled the wool over your eyes?"

"Of course not. I was only wondering if he was always so."

The countess hesitated, but only for a moment. Then, without mincing matters—yet without dwelling on them either—she gave her goddaughter a concise history of Basil's career from the time he entered Oxford.

When she had done, Miss Ashmore nodded as though the account was only confirmation of what she'd known all along. She smiled, very winningly indeed, and asked for news of Family and Society—in short, all the sorts of things a young lady who'd been out of England for six years would want to know.

A week later, as Alexandra reclined upon a chaise longue trying to read a book, she found herself wondering where Basil was and what wickedness he could be up to now. *Sense and Sensibility* lay neglected on her lap while she debated whether his new ladybird was an actress or an opera dancer and whether her eyes were blue or brown or even green like Alexandra's own.

But what concern was that of hers? She hadn't really expected him to visit her, had she? Still, she'd thought he might at least call on his own aunt. The days had passed, and there was no sign of him. Doubtless he was too busy with his dissipations.

She was a fool to wait and brood like Miss Austen's painfully passionate Marianne, pining in vain for her faithless Willoughby. At any rate, there were far better things in store for Alexandra Ashmore. Tonight she would dine with the Deverells and meet a young gentleman who'd been invited especially on her account.

"Randolph is all well and good, my dear," Lady Bertram had told her. "If you come to have a care for him, so much the better as you'll please yourself and your father all at once. But I'd rather you looked around a bit first. Marriage is usually a permanent arrangement, you know."

Tonight it was proposed that Alexandra look at one William Farrington, Marquess of Arden, heir to the Duke of Thorne, and "as handsome a devil as you're like to meet," according to Aunt Clem.

"He's all on pins and needles to meet you, my dear. He caught a glimpse of you the other afternoon as you left Madame Vernisse's and pestered Maria day and night for an introduction."

Alexandra closed Miss Austen's book with a resigned thump. Well then, she'd look at him, and he'd look at her. It would be pleasant if he was handsome and even more pleasant if he was also relatively intelligent—though that might be too much to hope for. Her experience of idle, upper-class English gentlemen had led her to conclude that they were exemplars of the evils of inbreeding and, in short, not very bright.

Mr. Trevelyan was bright, however. He did listen, too, and his answers were never patronising even if he did tease dreadfully. She missed his teasing, missed looking for the reality in his theatrical effusions and the bit of truth in his charming lies, just as much as she missed for once being treated by a man as an intellectual equal.

There had even been those rare occasions when she'd startled him out of his formidable composure. She'd certainly surprised him that last night in Prevesa. Apparently, he'd taken her words to heart, for he'd been scrupulously well behaved through the whole voyage. She didn't like to admit it, but she wished he'd been a little less well behaved.

That was the problem. She might have reasonably pleasant thoughts about him, except that the memory or his embrace kept intruding. Perhaps it wasn't terrible to enjoy being kissed—not when one was kissed so beautifully by so experienced a gentleman. With all that experience to inform it, perhaps a kiss *should* be enjoyable. Practise does make perfect after all. Still, the heat and breathlessness and sudden, frightening urgency of it—well, *that* wasn't proper. No, that part could not be proper.

Which was, of course, why respectable young women did not go off alone with gentlemen and get themselves kissed.

What started as a lovely kiss was bound to turn into something else, something that led to ruination.

It was humiliating to admit even to herself that she'd been—at least at the moment—willing to risk such ruin. She flushed at the memory. Pride, not regard for her virtue, had stopped her. She was afraid they'd be caught and forced to wed. Yes, Mr. Trevelyan did make her think wicked thoughts, and yes, he was very attractive, and yes, his kisses were lovely. But as a husband—one who'd resent and hate her for entrapping him, who'd humiliate her with his mistresses—he was out of the question.

How careless of him to begin it in the first place, to think only of amusing himself, and leave her to worry about the consequences. But why not? Hadn't she behaved like a common lightskirt? What was wrong with her anyhow? Was she wicked? Was she infatuated with him? Or was it only that he was so skilled a seducer?

Yes, that must be it. She was the innocent victim of his wiles.

While the innocent victim of Basil Trevelyan's wiles was staring obliviously at Miss Austen's book, Mr. Trevelyan himself had been having a highly agreeable conversation with Mr. Weston of Bond Street. Basil was just finishing his business with the tailor when Lord Arden sauntered in.

The marquess's enthusiastic greeting caused Basil to look at him suspiciously. While their families were intimate, and the two young men had grown up together and caroused and gambled together, they were rather too much alike to trust each other overmuch. Thus, no real intimacy had evolved between them despite many opportunities.

In a very few minutes, the mystery was solved. "I say, Trev," Lord Arden drawled as they left the tailor's shop and made their way to Watier's, "who is that perfectly stunning creature your aunt's taken in?"

Only a week and she'd called herself to Arden's attention. Naturally. Every rogue remaining in London must have sensed her presence in their midst, just as experienced hounds would sniff out a fox. Basil pretended to think very hard.

"Stunning creature?" he asked ingenuously.

"Why, you sly devil. Of course you know who I mean—is this some sort of family secret? Your aunt refuses to be at home to me, and Maria won't say a word, only tells me I might come to dinner tonight and perhaps the young lady will be there. You must tell me who the mysterious beauty is."

"If Lady Deverell is determined to tease you, then I certainly won't spoil her fun." To dinner. What the deuce did the woman mean by inviting one of London's most notorious rakeshames to dinner with Miss Ashmore? Arden's reputation was worse even than Basil's. The marquess had both enormous wealth and exalted rank and took full advantage of the privileges attached thereunto.

Not, certainly, that Basil could have expected an invitation. Lord Deverell, Isabella's father, was hardly likely to welcome into his home the young man who'd threatened his wife's reputation and his daughter's future.

"Then you *do* know," Lord Arden said, calling Basil back to the present. "Well, I must be content to look upon it as a delicious mystery. Obviously, I dare not describe her to anyone and invite rivals. Not, of course, that there's anyone in town at this time of year. Still, I expect she will be there tonight. Maria can't be as conscienceless as all that. Come now, you must give me a clue. Is she a relation? Part French, maybe? Lived abroad most of her life?"

"Possibly," was the unhelpful reply.

"What a closemouthed fellow you've got to be, Trev." There was a speculative gleam in Lord Arden's grey eyes. "But then I daresay you've got your eye on her yourself. Our tastes have always been remarkably like. Still, you must know she's not your type—not at all."

"And what, precisely, do you think is not my type?"

"Why, the price is too high, Trev. Marriage. Your aunt's standing guard, after all. No slip of the shoulder in this case, I'm afraid."

"Then why are you so eager to meet her?"

"Because I've taken it into my mind to marry. Actually, she's put it into my mind. You know that my Respected Parent has been growling at me the last decade at least to be married and get heirs. He's been throwing that insufferable Honoria Crofton-Ash at me this age. Fortunately, my mother believes that a young man must sow his wild oats.''

"And so you have, Will. You've sown them with a vengeance.''

"And here,'' Lord Arden rhapsodised, quite deaf to his companion, "is the most beautiful woman I've ever seen. Though she was across the street, stepping out of the dressmaker's, your aunt hurried her into the carriage as though all the demons of Hell were after them.''

"She only saw you coming, Will—''

"I could tell she was no schoolroom miss, and I had nearly resigned myself to one day being leg-shackled to some green girl fresh out of the nursery—and they're all so much alike, one Season after another, that you'd think Almack's baked them from a single mold. Well, I can only thank my lucky stars I obliged my sister by taking her into town. It's the greatest piece of good luck.''

The man was insufferable. He'd only glimpsed Miss Ashmore from across the street and promptly decided to take possession, as if she were a handsome stickpin he'd taken a fancy to at Rundell and Bridge's. What a coxcomb he was! Still, Basil only looked amused as he answered, "But you don't even know her yet, Will. I wouldn't count it good luck so soon. Suppose you find she's ill-natured?''

"She couldn't look like that and be ill-natured. It's completely impossible. And even if she is—why, I fancy I might find ways to put her in better temper.''

The smirk on Will's conceited face might have goaded a lesser man to violence. Basil, however, only answered amiably, "Pray, my lord, do not enlighten me on your methods. You must consider my delicate sensibilities.''

The smile broadened. "Delicate sensibilities, indeed. Oh, you are droll, Trev. Not changed a bit after all this time. And what have you been doing with yourself—what is it?—three years now? How time flies. But come. Though I can't take you to dinner—being so agreeably engaged elsewhere—I will have a glass or two with you, and you must tell me about these heroics of yours.''

6

"Ashmore? Not Sir Charles's daughter?" Lord Arden asked in some surprise. Surely that walking piece of antiquity had not produced this Incomparable? "I've read your father's accounts with the greatest pleasure, Miss Ashmore."

The melting look he bent on her belied entirely his private opinion that it was the most boring stuff he'd ever had the misfortune to come across and that even sermons were better by half.

Not having expected quite so sudden or so intense an assault, Alexandra was momentarily disarmed. However, having never been easily melted—well, perhaps with one exception—she was able, quickly enough, to school her features into a polite smile before turning to be introduced to someone else.

It was a small group. In addition to the Deverells and Lord Arden, there was Major Wells, an old friend of Lady Bertram, and Sir Philip Pomfret, an old friend of Lord Deverell, with his wife, and Lord and Lady Tuttlehope. The latter was Henry Latham's eldest daughter.

While civilities were being exchanged, Alexandra tried to sort out what Aunt Clem had told her about the Deverells and their affairs. Lady Deverell had been secretly married to Harry Deverell some thirty years ago. Not long after, Harry had drowned, and the then-pregnant Maria had married Matt Latham, Henry's brother. Only Harry hadn't drowned, after all. Three years ago, he'd resurrected himself and come back to England to claim his title and reclaim his wife and daughter.

Half of Society, according to Aunt Clem, had decided that Lady Deverell had been a bigamist. The other half, apparently, had decided that Harry was two people: the one who'd drowned nearly thirty years ago, and the one who was now a fair-haired, handsome man in his early fifties and very much alive. At any rate, regardless which half of the ton had decided what, virtually all its members somehow found themselves accepting the languid Maria into their midst, her scandalous history dismissed as little more than another one of her eccentricities. As to Isabella, she was not only Harry's legitimate daughter, but Countess of Hartleigh as well, and even the highest sticklers could not exclude her.

It was Isabella that Basil had schemed to marry. Alexandra wondered what she was like. She must be handsome since both her parents were. But was she languid and absentminded like her mother or energetic and blunt like her father?

While Miss Ashmore was at her wondering, she was also curious about Lord Tuttlehope. Obviously devoted to his lovely blond wife, obviously not a rogue of even the mildest sort, and so inarticulate and shy he could hardly put a whole sentence together—how could he be, as Aunt Clem had asserted, Basil's very best friend?

Alexandra had little opportunity for further speculation because the friendly, talkative Lady Tuttlehope pounced immediately upon her, drawing her away from the others.

"Oh, how pleased I am to meet you at last!" the baroness burst out. "What an exciting time you must have had. I haven't been abroad once, you know, because Freddie wouldn't stir from England while that dreadful Napoleon was about. I can't monopolise you now, I know," (though she showed every intention of doing so) "because that would be monstrous rude. But you must come to tea one day soon."

Not that her ladyship could wait for that happy time. Even as Alexandra smiled acquiescence, her companion went on chattering like an eager schoolgirl. Wasn't it an odd coincidence how they'd run into Basil so far away? And wasn't it amazing that Basil was a hero now and practically reformed—or so her Papa claimed, while Freddie maintained that Basil was quite the same as ever, and her ladyship must debate this with herself at length. "But here," she said, pausing to catch her breath, "I'm running on frightfully. What did *you* think?"

Alexandra didn't know what to think and was somewhat taken aback by both the barrage and the sudden question. Not that this incommoded her interlocutor in the least. Lady Tuttlehope went on about Basil and about how Harry Deverell had wanted to shoot him, but his wife had convinced him otherwise, saying that it was a very long way back to India, and Harry had only just gotten home, and it was bad enough that he had drowned, but then to get himself hanged for murder was too tedious for words. While Alexandra struggled to keep in countenance—her companion's imitation of Lady Deverell was uncanny—the baroness was telling her how terribly disappointed Freddie was that Basil would not be joining them for dinner.

"Oh. Then he was invited?" Alexandra asked in the most offhand way.

"Well, actually, I don't know. Aunt Maria made such a mystery of everything. She's so clever, you know, though one would never think it. They're *all* clever—at least they were clever enough for Basil," she added, meaningfully. "But then, you know about that. I'm sure Aunt Clem has told you." Without giving Alexandra a chance to reply, she artlessly confessed that *she* was not clever at all. "And it's a good thing, too, or Freddie would never know what to say to me."

As Lady Tuttlehope went on to tell what Freddie *did* say, Alexandra, feeling rather giddy, let her attention stray occasionally to the others in the company. She noted that Lord Arden had turned her way more than once, as though about to approach. Each time, Lady Deverell called his attention back to herself. Thus, when they sat down to dinner, Alexandra had still not formed any sort of opinion about him beyond the fact that he was a most attractive man whose attire could not be faulted.

Lord Arden, who found himself seated on the opposite side of the table from Miss Ashmore and down at the other end on Lady Deverell's right, was beginning to wish his languid hostess at the devil. Maria had placed him there deliberately to torment him. There was no way he could converse with Miss Ashmore at this great distance. He must perforce be content to hear Maria sigh at him now and then between sighs at Sir Philip, or to talk with Lady Pomfret, who only complained interminably of India when she wasn't complaining that there wasn't a cook in London who knew how to make a proper curry.

Well, if he couldn't talk, he could look, and there was feast enough for the eyes to make a man never eat again, although it must be admitted that Lord Arden did honour to his dinner, nonetheless. She was even more beautiful than he'd thought. What wicked chestnut curls, to tease themselves loose from their pins and make her look ever so slightly but oh so provocatively dishevelled. And those eyes. Quite emerald green—or darker even—with naughty gold specks that danced when she laughed. She was delicious. Though she hadn't said more than two words to him, he knew she was perfection, which obviously meant that she must be his wife.

This knowledge must console him as he lingered with the gentlemen over port—and they did linger, an unconscionably long time. When they'd finally done and moved on to the drawing room to join the ladies, Lord Tuttlehope drew him aside.

"I say, Will, odd thing, ain't it?"

"What is?" the marquess asked impatiently.

"Couldn't say a word back there—Harry, you know. But he ain't here, is he?"

"*Who* isn't here?" Really, Freddie could be the most exasperatingly slow fellow. A small crowd was forming around Miss Ashmore, and that made Lord Arden unhappy. Crowds were inimicable to private conversation, and besides, they blocked his view of her form, so tantalisingly outlined by the elegantly simple, sea-green gown she wore.

"Why, Trev." Lord Tuttlehope blinked in some surprise that Arden hadn't worked this out for himself. "Don't seem right when he went out of his way on her account. Could have come straight from Greece weeks ago. Least they could do is feed him, what?"

This was amazing eloquence from the inarticulate Freddie,

and it seemed to have a point. "On whose account was he delayed, Freddie?"

"Her. Ashmore's girl."

Lord Arden patiently questioned Freddie more closely and learned that Basil knew Miss Ashmore and had travelled with her all the way from Albania. The sly devil had never even hinted at it through all the bottles they'd shared this afternoon. But then, why should the man make anything of it? Even Trev wouldn't dare toy with his aunt's goddaughter. He'd said nothing about the matter because there was nothing to say. They'd travelled together with her Papa and others, and that was all there was to it.

Having thus reassured himself, the marquess proceeded to ease Freddie's troubled feelings. "As to Trev not being asked, what did you expect? Harry must still bear a grudge for that business three years ago."

Lord Tuttlehope blinked at him in surprise.

"Come now, Freddie. All Society knows Lady Hartleigh is Harry's daughter. They've made no secret of it, and any number of us know that Basil was up to some nasty business concerning her that got him packed off to India."

With several more blinks, Lord Tuttlehope stoutly denied that this was so and then in the next moment contradicted himself by insisting that Harry didn't bear a grudge. At least, so his beloved Alicia had assured him.

"Then," said Lord Arden, glancing at Lady Deverell, who was smiling lazily at something Miss Ashmore was saying, "it must be Maria."

Leaving Lord Tuttlehope to puzzle out for himself what the languid Lady Deverell had to do with the matter, Will made his way to Miss Ashmore's side.

At the moment she was explaining to the assembled group some of the pitfalls into which the subtleties of Albanian had led her. He had leisure, therefore, to admire—in addition to everything else he'd noted before—her low, husky voice. It thrilled him.

"And so," she was saying, "to pronounce it one way was to call him a boy—and yet to accent it only a bit differently was to call him a fiend. And the poor thing, who'd been so kind to find the goat for us, could not understand why I scolded him."

"But as it was a little boy, surely he could think of a reason for being scolded," Lady Tuttlehope responded. "They are always up to some mischief or other."

Lord Deverell added, with some pride, "Why, my grandson's only a year old, and already a prodigy at crawling into devilment."

Interesting as such conversation must be for doting Grandpapas, it eventually came to an end, and the party broke off into smaller groups. In time only Lord Arden, Lady Tuttlehope, and Lady Deverell remained with Miss Ashmore, and soon, to the marquess's unutterable relief, even this number dwindled. Maria, bored finally with standing between himself and Miss Ashmore, making conversation impossible with her sighs and lazy drawls, took herself languidly away to chat with Lady Bertram. That left only Lady Tuttlehope to thwart him.

The baroness, who had a romantic heart, was torn between leaving these two stunning creatures alone and wanting to hear what they'd say to each other. The choice was made for her when she saw her husband trapped into conversation with Lady Pomfret. She exclaimed softly, "Oh dear. Freddie is blinking terribly. Please excuse me." And off she went to his rescue.

Smiling a little at Lady Tuttlehope's ingenuous ways, Alexandra looked up to find herself the object of a very appreciative gaze. He was, just as Aunt Clem had promised, devilishly handsome. His hair was dark as a raven's wing, gleaming blue-black in the candlelight. The strong, rugged angles of his face were softened by grey eyes that managed to look boyish and innocent—though his manner was too polished to be boyish, his gaze too warmly appraising to be innocent. His manner, in fact, reminded her very much of someone else.

"I daresay, Miss Ashmore, that all of Society will be interrogating you about the mysterious country you visited. In a week you'll be sick to death of it and must swoon at the mere mention of the place."

The killing look he bent upon her would have invited a weaker-minded female to swoon in any case, but Alexandra was made of sterner stuff. "Surely there's no danger of that, my lord. My simple reports cannot compete with Lord Byron's romantic tales, and Society, I am sure, has got those by heart."

"You credit Society with longer memory than it possesses—at least on any matter not fraught with scandal. And even if people had got the stories by heart, they would prefer—at least the gentlemen would, I know—to hear of the place from the lips of a beautiful lady."

"Would they? How odd." She looked up at him in a puzzled way. "Oh," she said in soft surprise, as though she'd only then caught his meaning. "You meant that as a compliment."

"It's the simple truth, Miss Ashmore. Byron himself would second me. That cannot surprise you, surely. I daresay that even Basil required you to spin tales for him by the hour—and he likes nothing better than to hear *himself* talk."

She looked puzzled again, and he explained hastily, "I thought you and your father travelled with Mr. Trevelyan. Perhaps I misunderstood?"

"Oh. Why, yes, he did accompany us on our return." Lord Arden looked rather sly, she thought, and she wondered what Basil may have said about her. Surely he wouldn't have boasted of stolen kisses. And was the marquess another such? Did he mean to work his arts upon her, too? She looked away from him, seeking a polite means of escape from this suddenly depressing exchange. But the others were engrossed in their own conversations, and Lord Arden was talking again.

"Yes, well, I couldn't be sure. Basil never said a word. It was only Freddie who mentioned it just a moment ago. As a matter of fact, Miss Ashmore, no one would say a word. They've all contrived to make a mystery of you, as though you'd dropped from out of the heavens into London."

The slyly inquisitive look disappeared, and with it her discomfort. They could not all be Basil Trevelyans. Besides, Aunt Clem would never have specially arranged for her to meet a scoundrel. Smiling at her unwonted timidity and mistrust—although his lordship took the smile as intended for himself—she answered, "Well, I'm not at all mysterious. I was abroad for six years with my father—and not in the most civilised places. Most likely I was such a ragamuffin upon my return that no one wanted to admit my existence until I could be made to look respectable again."

Lord Arden opened his mouth to contradict, eagerly, this slight upon her charms but was prevented by the reappearance of Lady Deverell, who had drifted back to them.

"How tiresome of me," she announced, with inexpressible ennui. "I had quite forgotten what I meant to ask you before, Will. It was that recipe for curry Lady Pomfret explained at such length that distracted me, I'm sure. It was so absorbing, was it not?"

Lord Arden agreed soberly that it was most absorbing.

"And if I'd realised it troubled her so, I would have asked Auguste to make it—although it is likely Harry would have left the house. He declares he cannot abide to see another curried anything again for as long as he lives. My husband," she explained to Miss Ashmore, "spent many years in India. But what was I about?" She stared thoughtfully at her diamond bracelet and must have found the answer there, for in a moment she told them, very wearily indeed, "Oh, yes. Isabella. How tiresome she is, Will."

"Not a bit of it. She's perfectly delightful."

"Yes, that is what I meant. She is so determinedly delightful that it quite wears me out to contemplate it. But she insists that I come to Hartleigh Hall at last, and so I must go, I suppose. And she declares she must have you, too, Will, and Jess—for if you don't bring your sister, you can't come at all, poor dear. The children will never forgive you, such hardhearted creatures they are."

Lord Arden was delighted to accept and promised less delightedly to bring his sister.

"It will not be a very large party—such a pity your parents are in Scotland, though I daresay it's more comfortable for them. At any rate, Lady Bertram comes, of course, with Miss Ashmore." She did not appear to notice Miss Ashmore's little start. "And Freddie and Alicia. Oh, yes. Lady Bertram promises to write your Papa, Miss Ashmore—and that young man who assists him. She said he was very pleasant.''

Lord Arden's eyes might have been perceived to narrow ever so slightly.

"Though where to write them is the great question. If he has gone on to visit the Burnhams in Yorkshire, he will hardly wish to travel so far in this heat for a quiet house party among so many strangers. Yet I was positive Henry Latham meant to have him to Westford. At any rate, that is all, I suppose, though one cannot be certain with curry uppermost in one's thoughts."

The prospect of meeting her father at Hartleigh Hall with Randolph in tow was not pleasant to contemplate. Very sensibly, then, Alexandra put it out of her mind. It was not sensible, however, to feel so very disappointed that a certain name was conspicuously absent from the guest list. She forced a smile as she told her two companions she was looking forward to making so many new acquaintances.

"Well, I only hope we do not wear you out, Miss Ashmore. You have just got to London"—a perfectly heartbreaking sigh—"and now you must be dragged off again. You have only had a very little respite from Basil and now must be thrust into his company once more." Lady Deverell shook her head sadly over this, as one who could not account for the naughty behaviour of Providence.

"Then Basil is coming as well?" Lord Arden asked with a covert glance toward Miss Ashmore.

"Why yes. Didn't I say so? Well, perhaps I didn't. That curry plagues me so." And with another tragic sigh, the viscountess floated away.

7

"So," Basil was saying, as he played with the note he'd received that morning—nearly a week after the dinner to which he'd not been invited. "It isn't enough they bid me come and be roasted by all my relations at once, but they must have Will, too, and Jess. Well, we know what that's all about, don't we?"

Freddie didn't know, but he nodded sagely nonetheless.

"And if they mean to push her off on the first peer who comes along, it's not my trouble is it?"

Freddie shook his head.

"Arden's welcome to her. But I am not about to keep Jess amused while he woos Miss Ashmore. I'm not Hartleigh's court jester, after all."

Freddie was halfway into a nod but stopped suddenly and blinked instead. "Don't mean you're not coming?"

"I am not."

"But they ain't seen you in three years, and we're going."

"I'll be very sorry to lose your company, Freddie, but my family must learn that I am no longer to be ordered about, here and there, at their whim. Why, they make up some clap-trap about a young woman in dire straits and dispatch me off to rescue her. Dire straits. I'll tell you who's in dire straits—anyone who comes within a mile of her tongue, that's who."

"Seemed amiable enough to me. Alicia likes her."

"Freddie, your beautiful wife is so good-natured that she can discover no less in all those she meets."

Such praise could not fail to gratify one who saw his wife as the paragon of every sort of perfection and virtue. Even so, Freddie could not willingly forego his friend's company. He made a stammering attempt to change Basil's mind.

"No, Freddie, I can't do it. I'll see you in another month or so, no doubt, when you come back to town. I will not play the fool again, even to accommodate *you*. Besides, I have business to attend to."

"Business? This time of year?"

"Oh, yes. I must see about a house, of course, for I don't intend to live in a hotel forever. But more important, I've just met a perfectly charming barque of frailty, and if I go away now, there are half a dozen others ready to take my place in her mercenary affections. Such business cannot wait. Jess must contrive to entertain herself, and you must find consolation in the company of your beautiful wife."

Lord Tuttlehope returned home bluedevilled. He was the happiest of husbands, but he'd missed his clever friend dreadfully. Now to learn that he must endure that friend's absence until the Little Season at least . . . There was no understanding Basil lately. They'd only seen him twice in the two weeks since he'd returned. It was most disappointing, and so he told his wife.

"Oh, Freddie," she said, "whatever are you thinking? Of course Basil is coming."

"Not at all. Said he wasn't."

"Oh, he never means half what he says. You know that, dear. Maria says he'll be there, and so he will."

Lady Deverell, of course, knew everything. Quite like Lady Bertram in that respect. A couple of oracles they were. Nonetheless, Freddie stoutly maintained that Basil would not appear. *"She'll* be there, you know, and he can't abide her."

"Whom do you mean, darling?"

"Her. Ashmore's girl."

"Basil can't abide her?" Lady Tuttlehope's eyes opened wide with astonishment. "But she's so beautiful—and so clever and amiable."

"Hates her," her husband insisted. "Said so. Won't be made a fool of."

"So that's why he hasn't gone to see his aunt. Yet, what

kind of excuse is it, when he's been away three whole years? Then I hope he shan't come after all, the mean thing. For he's sure to be unpleasant to Miss Ashmore, and then I shall have to hate him. I think she's lovely, and I hope she marries Will. Did you see the way he looked at her the other night? It made my heart flutter.''

Lord Tuttlehope was a generous-minded man, but he did not like his wife's heart to flutter on anybody's account but his own. He blinked unhappily, and the tactful Alicia moved quickly to reassure him.

"Oh dear," she said, after a few very pleasant minutes had passed.

"What? What is it?"

"You came home looking so troubled, dear, that I forgot all about Marianne's letter."

"All well, I hope," her husband responded, though he really couldn't care less at the moment. He wanted more coddling.

"Quite well. Though she does say Mama has been very tiresome about her coming to us for a Season. Poor girl—she'd so much rather stay at home with her books.''

"Quiet, sensible girl." Lord Tuttlehope dimly remembered Marianne as the least terrifying of Alicia's three younger sisters.

"Yes. And she writes to say that Papa has brought guests with him. You'll never guess."

"Can't think who."

"Miss Ashmore's Papa. And a young man—a Mr. Burnham. Very agreeable, Marianne says. He knows heaps about old things—history, you know, dear—and must talk the livelong day about it, for she crossed an entire page telling me about the something wars. It begins with a 'p,' I think—something like 'Penelope'—but it's much too hard a word to remember.''

Her husband couldn't think what it was either and didn't especially want to know. He had much rather be assured again about Lord Arden and so found a way to stammer back to that subject and be comforted accordingly.

* * *

The post must have been doing a brisk business that day, for Alexandra also had a letter from Westford. It was not from Marianne Latham—Alexandra didn't know that young lady—but from Sir Charles. And, as was the case with most of the baronet's communications, it was annoying.

The long and the short of it was that he'd found out that Mr. Trevelyan was a perfectly dreadful young man. Sir Charles had found it out from Mrs. Latham, who, in the course of apprising him at unnecessary length of her dear daughter Alicia's highly satisfactory marriage to a baron, had also some choice words to bestow on the subject of the baron's good friend, Mr. Trevelyan.

"And it's no good," wrote Sir Charles in his crabbed script, "that Mr. Latham makes excuses for him. Nor can I think what excuse to make for *you*, Alexandra. Trevelyan is, and has been for all his adult life, one of London's most notorious libertines. I must believe you either the greatest fool or the most deceitful daughter there ever was. How, I ask, could the man be secretly engaged to you when three years ago he was so busy trying to get himself engaged to Mr. Latham's niece—or former niece—I cannot make out what the relations are in that family. Everywhere I turn, I hear nothing but scandal. If I were not kept here on important business, as Mr. Latham expresses interest in investing in my Albanian work, I would come and take you away immediately. Still, while I am here some matters can be put in train, and in a few more days I expect that Randolph and I can come to London for you."

There was more, a great deal more, and all of it unpleasant. Alexandra was scowling at the letter when Lady Bertram entered the room. "Good heavens, child, what dreadful news is it?"

The younger woman made no answer, but simply handed over the document so she might see for herself. Lady Bertram read it, glared, then crumpled the letter in a ball and tossed it into the cold fireplace. "Don't trouble yourself, my dear," she said. "No one is going to cart you off anywhere like so many bushels of corn. You're in England now, Alexandra, and among friends."

"But Papa—"

"—is only in bad humour because he hasn't any bits of ancient rubble to be poking at. This is nothing to distress yourself about. Go now. Will arrives shortly to take you for a drive, and you haven't even begun to dress. I will send Emmy up to you directly."

Smiling, Alexandra pointed out that it did not require two full hours to make herself ready.

"Then find something to do, there's a dear girl. I must write some letters."

Ordinarily, Lord Arden would not have taken his Intended to Hyde Park—certainly not at five o'clock—since this would announce her existence to every bachelor still in town. Fortunately, the party was scheduled to leave for Hartleigh Hall the following day. He trusted, therefore, that when she next appeared in the park, it would be as his wife. What a glorious marchioness she'd make! And when the Respected Parent finally stuck his spoon in the wall, she'd make an even more stupendous duchess.

Accordingly, Lord Arden set himself to being even more agreeable than usual, though it scarcely seemed possible, and suppressed his boredom when she firmly turned the conversation from gossip to politics. Nor did he patronise her (at least not very much) when she went on to talk so earnestly of literature, though he didn't listen either. He was too busy imagining what it would be like to have a beautiful bluestocking as his hostess. Fondly, he pictured her astonishing his aristocratic colleagues with her harangues. He even envisioned her teaching an assortment of handsome children—some green-eyed, some grey-eyed—to lisp Greek and Latin.

Yes, a beautiful wife who was slightly eccentric was even better than a beautiful wife who was much like everyone else. Thus, though he barely heard five words out of every twenty, he fancied he was quite in love with her mind as well as everything else about her.

In this state so closely approaching the platonic ideal, he felt generous towards his fellows. His heart went out to the elegant gentlemen who stopped to stare as they drove past.

He especially pitied his cronies who charged at them every few minutes, greeting him so warmly and begging to be made known to his attractive companion. It was only when Trevelyan appeared that this spirit of generosity ebbed away.

Trev was polite, certainly. But Lord Arden did not care for the way those devious cat eyes raked over Miss Ashmore, especially since that raking made the lady turn colour and lose her composure—and more especially since nothing his lordship had said or done had aroused so strong a reaction. It was, moreover, some time before she fully recovered. After Basil left, she seemed to have some trouble putting her sentences together—she who'd been so eloquent on the subject of Mr. Wordsworth only moments before.

His lordship was determined to help her along. "And so what do you think will become of Byron's poetry now that he's married?" he asked. "Do you think that wedded bliss will dull his sharp tongue?"

She appeared to shake herself out of a trance to answer him. "I haven't yet had an opportunity to read very much of his work. But from what I've heard recently, there's little bliss in that marriage."

"I fear you're right. But then, many of us maintain that he was bound to make a poor husband. Some are improved, even reformed, by marriage. Others, like Byron, are only made worse by it."

It occurred to her that perhaps it was not really Lord Byron he was speaking of, but someone else. Yet her features remained blank as she asked him to explain.

"Because it makes them feel 'cabin'd, cribb'd, confin'd.' And so they must run away to lose themselves in some desperate pursuit of pleasure."

"You speak so knowingly, my lord. Do you, too, view marriage as a prison?"

"Ah, you mean to trick me, Miss Ashmore. For if I say I do not, you'll throw my long bachelorhood in my face. And if I say I do—why, then, what will you conclude about my intentions towards yourself?"

Such a query was meant to be answered in one way only: with a coy claim of ignorance. His lordship then enlightening her in proper form—perhaps on bended knee, though it would be deuced awkward in the phaeton—the matter would be settled. Miss Ashmore might then turn her thoughts to her trousseau, and he—why, to any of those myriad subjects far too taxing for the minds of young ladies.

But Lord Arden received no claim of ignorance, coy or otherwise. Miss Ashmore stared at him for a moment as though he had asked whether he might stand on his head. Then, in the voice of a schoolmistress, she answered, "I would not presume to judge your lordship's behaviour or intentions, and most especially not on such *short acquaintance*. It was only your opinion I sought."

The emphasis she placed on the words told him plainly that he'd leapt ahead of himself and had better leap right back. He had not expected this setdown, but then he reminded himself that she was a tad eccentric after all, and that was one of her charms. And so, the obedient student gave it as his opinion that marriage improved partners who were well suited and worsened those who were not. In Byron's case, he went on, there was a moody, restless nature to begin with and too-early fame and adulation to compound the problem. In fact, he pointed out, if all those who shouldn't think of marrying didn't, it would be easier for better-suited persons to find each other.

"You think then," she asked, "that these ineligible individuals should be driven from Society? Or perhaps should be made to wear a badge of some sort to warn the unwary away?"

He chuckled. "That would be an extreme solution—and yet, perhaps it might conduce to greater happiness all around."

He dropped a deeply meaningful glance upon her, but she only appeared thoughtful as she added, "And thereby contribute to the greater prosperity of the British nation. What a novel idea, my lord. It does you credit, I am sure."

The prosperity of the nation was the very last thing on his mind, but he did not object to taking credit where it was not due. It was his aim, was it not, to win her admiration or respect or affection or whatever it might take to install her as quickly as possible as his marchioness. Therefore, despite the unexpected check to his impatient aspirations, his lordship passed the remainder of his time with her in remarkably good humour.

Mr. Trevelyan, lounging at his club, was not in good humour. He had a glass of very old brandy in his hand, and he glowered at it. His severe, black and white evening attire was perfect in every deceptively simple detail, and he scowled precisely as though these were the same filthy rags he'd worn in Gjirokastra. He had an appointment for dinner with a lovely blond barque of frailty, and he looked forward to it with the same cold composure with which he would, in earlier days, have awaited an interview with one of his creditors. Mr. Trevelyan, in short, was very cross.

Miss Ashmore had not, as any right-minded woman would—considering the trouble he'd taken on her account—greeted him with anything like enthusiasm. She'd turned rather pink, then rather white, and then had stared at him for an instant as though he were some great hulking monster. Then she'd turned to that snake beside her and let him do the talking for her, as though she belonged to him already. Clearly, Will seemed to think so. He had that proprietary air and that obnoxious, self-satisfied smirk on his arrogant face, and had even found it necessary—the great coxcomb—to lean close to speak to her as though the girl were quite deaf.

It was disgusting . . . and pathetic. The ridiculous chit had gone and put herself into the hands of one of the most—if not *the* most—untrustworthy, fickle, careless, selfish, and *depraved* men in England. Oh, yes, Will meant to marry her, but marriage meant nothing to him. He'd get his precious heirs on her and then be off about his usual lecheries.

Whatever was Aunt Clem thinking, to countenance the man? Surely she knew what he was. Aunt Clem sees all, knows all. Had she simply balanced off the brute's character against his material assets? It would, after all, be a great thing to marry off her goddaughter to a future duke. Single, good-looking dukes were rare, and single, good-looking dukes with vast fortunes were scarcer than hen's teeth. No, she could hardly do better than Will.

Still, Aunt Clem might have found an eligible *parti* with a better character. But then, what was it to him? Certainly he wasn't about to look out for a better husband for Miss Ashmore, and he most definitely was not about to go haring off to Hartleigh Hall just to make certain she didn't get into any trouble. Let her get herself out of trouble this time, the ungrateful wench.

He reached into his breast pocket and pulled out the letter he'd already read some five or six dozen times, and crumpled it angrily in his hand. Then, in the next moment, he just as angrily smoothed it out again, folded it, and tucked it back into his pocket. She might at least have smiled.

8

Alexandra sighed as she approached the breakfast room. She'd thought that the fresh country air would cure her sleeplessness, but the past five nights at Hartleigh Hall had been exactly like those preceding. When finally she did fall asleep, she had very troubling dreams. The gallant knights who rescued her from dragons that looked like the Burnham sisters kept turning out to have deceitful, amber eyes instead of adoring, grey ones.

Because she hadn't slept properly since she'd come to England, she was prey to headaches, one of which was now shooting sharp blasts of pain behind her dark eyebrows. The great racket coming from the breakfast room promised only to exacerbate it. Perhaps she'd better turn back and have breakfast sent up to her room.

Unfortunately, Burgess, Lord Hartleigh's terrifying butler, had already seen her approach. She was astonished to note faint creases, ominously hinting at a smile, at the corners of his mouth. And then—good heavens—he was actually opening the door for her himself.

She winced slightly at the Babel of voices, but in an instant her eyes flew wide open. There at the breakfast table, smiling with complete self-assurance at some sarcasm Lord Hartleigh directed at him, was the inconsiderate creature who haunted her dreams. He'd turned towards the door as it opened, and when his gaze locked with hers it carried all the impact of a physical blow. The other faces were dissolving into haze, the voices into a buzzing in the background, and all she saw was the slow smile that lit his wicked face. Then he spoke, and the familiar, insinuating sound shook her out of her daze.

"Thank heaven you've come, Miss Ashmore—and in the very nick of time. They're all lined up against me, and I want an ally badly."

"What's this?" Lord Deverell exclaimed. "Was India so taxing then? Are you so enfeebled that you require a woman's help to speak?"

"Ah, but I always require the ladies' assistance—"

"Oh, he hasn't changed a bit," someone murmured, but Alexandra barely noticed. He was still looking at her and talking.

"Luckily, Miss Ashmore has most kindly made it her business to look out for me."

She hadn't time to blush, being too busy thinking—and that wasn't the most agreeable exercise with her head throbbing so. How dare he say such things in front of these others? Lord Arden had leapt to help her to her chair, and she used the moment that gave her to collect her wits. His lordship placed her conveniently next to himself and inconveniently opposite Mr. Trevelyan. There was nothing for it then but to meet those glittering, feline eyes calmly. "I'm sorry, sir," she finally answered, "but I don't recollect undertaking any such formidable task. At any rate," she went on more briskly, "you can't expect one to do business of any sort before breakfast."

"Certainly not," Lord Deverell agreed. "Will, don't stand there gawking. Fill Miss Ashmore's plate for her."

It could not have been agreeable for Lord Arden to be ordered about by a mere viscount, as though he were an awkward schoolboy. On the other hand, it may have been the unwelcome addition to the company that made his lordship scowl so horribly as he stood at the sideboard selecting the choicest tidbits for his future wife and listening to the conversation.

"Well then, Miss Ashmore," Basil was saying. "I'll leave you to fortify yourself, though it means fending off this great company singlehanded."

Lady Hartleigh laughed. "Don't even think of fending us

off, Basil. Not when you've been so mean to tease and say you wouldn't come. But what is this great piece of nonsense you tell of Miss Ashmore?"

"It isn't a bit of nonsense," came the injured reply. "The whole while we travelled, Miss Ashmore was busy saving me from myself—and it was an uphill task, I assure you."

"And a thankless one, I make no doubt," his aunt put in.

The plate was set down before Miss Ashmore with an angry *thunk*.

"I wonder, Basil," said Lady Jessica, "how you came to need saving from yourself."

There was a deafening chorus of answers to this, most to the effect that Basil had needed to be saved from himself since the day he was born, that no one could do it, and that it must be given up as a bad job.

Alexandra was relieved that she wasn't left to deal with him all by herself, though their good humour surprised her. Hadn't he wronged at least four of these people? Still, his machinations had simply hurried Lady Hartleigh into her husband's arms and Lady Deverell back into those of her beloved Harry. It was rather, as Aunt Clem had claimed, a great joke. Basil's plots had succeeded only in getting him packed off to India.

"As to you, Miss Ashmore," Lady Jessica went on with studied innocence, "whatever possessed you to take on this monumental task?"

Alexandra very nearly choked on the fragment of toast she'd put in her mouth, but she managed to swallow it and answer calmly enough. "I daresay it must seem odd. But then, Albania has few amusements for an Englishwoman, and there's little enough to do on a long sea voyage. Papa and Mr. Burnham had their theories and writing to occupy them. I, on the other hand, had nothing. I suppose," she added, with a little shrug, "since Mr. Trevelyan is the very soul of honesty and he says I took on the job, then I must have—no doubt because I was so unspeakably bored."

Most of the company smiled appreciatively at this. At the other end of the table, Lady Deverell chuckled softly.

"Poor Basil," said Lord Hartleigh pityingly. "Only a diversion."

Lord Arden found the exchange a deal less amusing than the others and endeavoured to return Miss Ashmore's attention to himself. "Yet who would not delight to be Miss Ashmore's diversion?" he asked, sweetly.

"My lord," she chided, "you play into Mr. Trevelyan's hands."

"I?"

"Yes. You help him draw the fire to me and away from himself."

His disloyal sister joined in. "She's right, Will. We were all scolding him. Then you must say pretty things to Miss Ashmore and make everyone stare at her."

"When of course, dear sister, you'd rather they looked at you."

"Naturally—in good time. Now, however, it's Basil who must bear our stern scrutiny. He's been most unkind to his family." The look she directed at Basil would have been severe indeed, except that her eyes—amazingly like her brother's—twinkled with mischief. "Let's hear his excuse."

"Yes, you young jackanapes," Lady Bertram growled. "What can you have to say for yourself? Nearly a fortnight in London and not once do you call on your aunt."

"Dearest Aunt, if I called on you I might have stumbled upon Miss Ashmore as well, and she told me to keep away."

"Abominable creature!" Lady Hartleigh cried. "You blame Miss Ashmore for everything."

"But isn't that so, Miss Ashmore? Didn't you tell me to keep away until further notice? For my own good?"

Alexandra's green eyes flashed dangerously. He wanted to embarrass her, the beast. Spreading a dab of butter on her toast, she answered coolly, "How, I wonder, could I make it my business to look out for you on the one hand while I drove you off on the other? How could I look out for you when you were not about?"

"Why, I don't know. I really can't understand it. Usually, you're so logical. I'm sure I've mentioned that before—how logical you are."

Alexandra was seriously considering throwing the coffee urn, an ornate, silver monstrosity, at him—how dare he remind her of that conversation in Prevesa?—when Lady Deverell's bored voice was heard. "I cannot make it out at all, and it makes my head ache, Harry. After all, if—as he says—Miss Ashmore told him to keep away, then why is the tiresome boy here?"

Lord Deverell only shrugged and smiled while Lord Hartleigh turned to his cousin and gravely asked what answer he had for that?

"Why, cousin, it must be obvious." Basil stared at him in mock astonishment that he couldn't answer this simple riddle.

Alexandra's mind raced as she imagined a hundred different answers he might make—all of them disconcerting—and her own hundred possible setdowns.

"None of you can guess?" He turned that wondering, childlike look on all of them in turn. "But it's so simple." His gaze rested then on Alexandra, and something in his eyes made her heart skid to a stop. "Amnesia," he said softly.

In the din that greeted this she breathed a small sigh of relief. Though Lord Arden was looking at her rather strangely, he held his tongue, and she was able to finish her breakfast in relative peace.

There was peace after breakfast as well, for she went riding with Lady Jessica, Lord Arden, and the Deverells. The older couple rode well behind, but with Jess there to contradict and mock him, Lord Arden was forced to keep the conversation general. Alexandra could let her mind wander freely, the intense exchange between brother and sister precluding any real participation.

She'd thought Lord Arden the answer to her prayers. He was handsome and amiable, and he appeared to be intelligent, even if he did look at her in that unnervingly proprietary way. After all, he'd been brought up to believe the universe was basically his for the taking.

The Burnhams wanted a daughter-in-law who could help them claw their way into the ton, but if Papa paid his debt in gold they'd have to be content with that. Lord Arden could easily afford to settle matters with them, and even Papa couldn't object to a future duke as son-in-law. Yes, Lady Bertram had selected well of all the eligible gentlemen she might have invited to take notice of her goddaughter. Even his sister was delightful. Why then, had he suddenly become so irritating?

"How quiet you are, Miss Ashmore," said Lady Jessica. "But how can you help it? Neither of us lets you get a word in edgeways."

"Speak for yourself, Jess. It's you who monopolise the conversation."

"Because otherwise you tease her—and that's too unfair when she was teased unceasingly at breakfast."

"As, to your mortification, you were *not.*"

"I'm sure," Alexandra put in, "it'll be Lady Jessica's turn to be teased next. And as her performance is bound to be superior, I expect to learn a great deal from it."

"Miss Ashmore, you want no tutoring. I daresay you've had enough experience of Basil to know that he's immune to setdowns. Even if he were not, who could bear to stop him from talking so beautifully wickedly?"

"My sister," Lord Arden said with annoyance, "is and has been, since her debut, entirely lost to propriety."

"Well, you would know, my dear brother, so much experience you have of impropriety."

"She has the mind of an infant," he went on doggedly, "and exaggerates silly bits of gossip into great scandals—"

"On the contrary, I must reduce them to mere scandal in order to contemplate them—"

His lordship was growing exasperated. It had been vexing enough to find Trevelyan at the breakfast table this morning and to be forced to sit quietly as the man flirted outrageously with the future Marchioness of Arden. Now, here was one's own sister, holding up one's rather murky private life for Miss Ashmore's examination.

Still, Miss Ashmore did not seem horribly shocked. It occurred to him that he actually knew very little of his Intended—except that she was eminently desirable. She'd kept

78

him at arm's length, and he'd been patient knowing that these genteel virgins did like to be courted forever. Yet, Trevelyan's insinuations had not once elicited any of those cool, reproving looks his own more gentle hints customarily evoked. For all her cool composure, she'd seemed different somehow, as though she'd been lighted up from within, the moment she'd clapped eyes on the wretch.

As to the expression on Trevelyan's face—that predatory look so appropriate to those feline eyes—one knew that look all too well. It promised, at the very least, complications. Lord Arden wanted no complications. This courtship business was time-consuming enough as it was. And where the devil was her blasted father?

"Well, Maria," said Lord Deverell, "he's exactly as you described. I've never met a more ingratiating villain, though I can't understand what makes me like him in spite of my better judgement."

"Really, my dear? Then why, I wonder, did you look at him so thunderously?"

Her husband smiled. "It was too much temptation. When I saw him try to draw her aside after breakfast, I couldn't resist stepping in his way. After all, I was unable to do so three years ago."

"Well, you glowered at him sufficiently to make up for that oversight. How naughty of you, Harry."

Lord Deverell laughed. "He didn't seem in the least intimidated. What, I ask, is this scheming devil about?"

"The poor boy is starved for attention. And no wonder, after three years among foreigners in climates you yourself have pronounced fit only for vermin."

"Attention is it? I rather think it's something else he's starved for. Or someone else. He looked exactly as though—"

"Please, my love. No vivid analogies. It is too early in the day to tax my mind so."

"You needn't waste your die-away airs on me, my lady. I know better. And I wish *you* did as well, for I can see there's bound to be trouble."

Maria sighed. "There always is, I'm afraid."

"You and Clementina between you have put the cat among the pigeons."

"Yes, love. And who are the poor pigeons, I wonder?"

He'd come, Basil told himself, only because London was so stupefyingly dull at the moment. The blond barque of frailty he'd managed to entice away from her protector had proved to be, upon closer examination, both vulgar and witless, and he'd been obliged to entice her back into protection again. Anyhow, there was bound to be better sport watching Arden, who'd never had to woo anyone in his whole life, woo Miss Ashmore. It had been great fun to annoy him at breakfast and to see the difficulty with which he controlled his rage when he saw how easily Miss Ashmore's attention could be diverted.

And Miss Ashmore? For all her cool self-possession, there was murder in her eyes. Basil had hoped she'd rip up at him afterwards, but Harry Deverell had come in the way. Then Isabella was ordering him up to the nursery to admire little Gerald, and after that Basil had to visit the schoolroom because, her ladyship insisted, Lucy would never settle down to her studies otherwise.

Well, he went, and the Hartleighs' adopted daughter was nearly as excited about seeing him as she was about the lovely dark-haired doll he'd brought her. Unfortunately, he must then debate with the child whether it most closely resembled Lady Jessica or Miss Ashmore. Lucy pointed out that Miss Ashmore was even prettier than Lady Jess and that her stories were every bit as wonderful as Mama's. It was, therefore, Lucy's considered opinion that this paragon should marry Lord Arden since she was as beautiful as a princess and he was very nearly a prince.

"A duke, you know," she explained patiently, "is *almost* a prince, and Miss Ames says he will be a duke one day."

Miss Ames stepped in at this point to remind Lucy that she was gossiping, and gossip was better left to one's elders. Leaving the governess to explain why this was so, Basil exited the school room feeling inexplicably put-upon.

Nor did his mood lighten when he responded to a summons from Aunt Clem. No doubt his aunt meant her lecture to be uplifting, but as he stood there, enduring what appeared to be an interminable scold on virtually every subject under the sun, he only felt more ill-used.

What she lectured about, Basil hardly knew. He'd never attended before and saw no reason to start now. There was something about the Burnham business and some cryptic comments concerning one of those Latham chits and any number of blistering references to her nephew's incompetence. All that did matter was that she made it impossible for said nephew to catch up with Will and his riding companions. When he'd finally escaped his aunt, Basil found that everyone else, including the traitorous Freddie, had left the house as well.

He'd been completely abandoned. The only ones to show any interest in his reappearance were the children; and the baby had fallen asleep three minutes after meeting his cousin, while ten-year-old Lucy found him a deal less fascinating than household gossip.

A fine welcome, he thought, as he stomped into the library and threw himself upon a great leather sofa. Gone three years, and they couldn't keep their minds on him past breakfast. And *she* needn't have dashed off in such a hurry to ride with Will. Basil had risked his life to rescue her, and she couldn't even take the time to scold him for teasing her.

It was odd that a gentleman who'd wished his aunt at the devil for wasting time scolding him should now be equally irate that another lady declined to do the same. But then, journeying some fifty miles in the dead of night can render the most even-tempered of men out of sorts and, consequently, illogical. At any rate, after spending another hour or so alone in the library, unable to concentrate on a book and quite disinclined to betake himself elsewhere, his temper began to fray. Small wonder he sought to take his frustrations out on the very next person he saw.

His sense of ill usage had reached a perfect fever pitch when, some hours later, the door to the library opened and Miss Ashmore wandered in, looking for the book she'd left there the evening before. She didn't see him at first because the sofa was nestled close to the bookshelves at the other side of the room, and her glance went immediately to a small table not far from the door. When he greeted her, therefore, she started, and one mischievous chestnut curl bounced playfully against her eyebrow. This enraged him past endurance. Abruptly he sat up and asked, in a voice dripping with sarcasm, whether she'd enjoyed her little jaunter with the marquess.

"Well, yes, I did, rather," she answered stiffly. "He and his sister were very amusing."

"Yes, you couldn't ask for a better sister-in-law than Jess."

"I don't recall having asked for one, Mr. Trevelyan," came the cold retort.

"Hadn't you? Well, my mistake. But I was certain that was what you'd asked Aunt Clem for. Sister-in-law. Brother-in-law. Any sort of in-law. So long as the last name wasn't Burnham."

She'd picked up her book and was half a mind to throw it at him but made herself reply evenly, "That was uncalled-for, Mr. Trevelyan. As it is, however, entirely in keeping with your inconsiderate behaviour at breakfast, I must at least compliment you on your consistency."

"And I must compliment you on your alternative fiancé. Dear me, Will is a better catch than Randolph by a mile."

"Really?" she asked sweetly. "And even better than my *other* fiancé? Well, what a clever girl I am, to be sure." And she turned on her heel and left him.

He did not mean to let her have the last word, but the Fates conspired against him. After a light noonday meal, Edward insisted upon showing his cousin the divers improvements made to the estate. This occupied them until teatime. During that meal, Miss Ashmore was engrossed in conversation with Will. Immediately thereafter, Basil was again commandeered by his cousin, along with Freddie and Lord Deverell, who demanded a complete account of his adventures abroad. Nor was there a suitable opportunity to get the last word that evening, for he could hardly quarrel with her across the whole length of the dinner table. Shortly after, Miss Ashmore took to her room, pleading a headache.

"I daresay Will gave it to her," Jess confided, as she plunked herself down upon the settee next to Basil. "He's such a bore playing the decorous suitor. Hasn't the first idea of what he's doing. No wonder he made her head ache."

"What a disloyal sister you are, Jess."

"Well, he's such a pest. He wants her attention every minute. Though it is diverting to see him so monstrous well behaved, especially when I know for a fact he's keeping not one, but two high flyers—twins, Basil, if you'll credit it—in London. And he's hardly dared kiss Miss Ashmore's hand."

The thought of those polluted lips upon Miss Ashmore's slender, virginal fingers was more than Basil could stomach. Because that particular image promptly conjured up any number of far more ghastly ones, he soon found that his dinner did not agree with him and made a rather early bedtime himself.

Lord Hartleigh sat propped against the pillows, watching his wife brush her fair, silky hair. She was even lovelier now than when he first knew her. Actually, the first time he saw her she hadn't been lovely at all, with her hair so primly pulled back and her dress so dowdy. But later, the night he'd first danced with her, she'd been lovely indeed. Another thought came to him and he frowned. "I don't like it, Isabella," he said. "Basil and Will under the same roof with that dazzling creature. Whatever was your mother thinking of?"

Lady Hartleigh moved from the dressing table to his side of the bed where she stood, gazing fondly at him. "It would appear," she answered with a wry smile, "that Mama has matchmaking in mind."

Her husband retorted that Lord Arden didn't appear to require any encouragement. "Those killing looks he drops on her make me want to howl."

"Still, I've seen him look that way at a hundred other women. Probably Mama thinks a little healthy competition will hurry him to the point."

"My cousin, I need not remind you, is hardly healthy competition. Did you see the way *he* looked at her?"

"Oh, it's just as he always does. She handled it with aplomb, I must say. Gave as good as she got—and among so many strangers, too. In her place I should have been covered in confusion."

"I think," Lord Hartleigh remarked, "I'd rather see you covered with kisses." He pulled her towards him, causing her to topple onto the bed, and immediately set to making action suit word.

"After all" he murmured sometime later "it's not our problem, is it?"

"No, dear," came the faintly amused reply. "Not this time, thank heavens."

9

Though he did not, precisely, sleep the sleep of the just, Basil must have achieved sufficient repose to improve his humour. Certainly, when the neighbourly Osbornes visited the following morning, he was most agreeable.

Not all the Osbornes graced Hartleigh Hall with their company. Jane was in bed with a cold, and James and his Papa were in London. But Hetty and the twins, Sarah and Susan, had come with their mother to improve their acquaintance with the single gentlemen currently residing at Hartleigh Hall.

Hetty had sulked the whole way over because, as she complained to her Mama, Lord Arden would look at no one but Miss Ashmore, and everyone knew Basil Trevelyan was the wickedest man alive. Within a very few minutes of her arrival, however, her spirits improved markedly. As he greeted her, Basil swept such an appraising glance over her as to make her cheeks turn bright red and then stared so besottedly into her brown eyes that she nearly reeled from the impact. Fortunately, being a steady sort of girl if not a particularly intelligent one, she recovered sufficiently to reward him with a coquettish smile.

"Never say that this Incomparable is little Hetty," Basil exclaimed to Mrs. Osborne, who'd watched these proceedings with mistrust. "You must have required an armed guard for her comeout to prevent her being killed in the crush of suitors." Mama's censorious frown wavered. "And you, ma'am, could not have escaped unscathed. For how on earth could the poor gentlemen know which was the daughter?"

Alexandra, who hadn't yet had the opportunity of observing Mr. Trevelyan try his skills upon anyone other than herself, was here provided an admirable opportunity to broaden her horizons. Oddly enough, she did not find the experience quite as pleasantly instructive as one would expect. She watched in grim fascination as, one by one, he reduced each of the three Osborne girls to giggling imbeciles, while simultaneously showering upon the Mama such sickeningly sweet droplets of flattery that even that stout, formidable matron became, in a matter of minutes, another trembling blossom athirst for the nourishing rain of his admiration.

The lesson was not at all improving to Miss Ashmore's temper, which had gotten a bad start at breakfast when she'd learned, along with everyone else, that her Papa had finally decided to accept Lady Hartleigh's gracious invitation and was arriving tomorrow afternoon. He was, moreover, bringing Randolph with him. If Alexandra had thought to forestall her father with hints about the future Duke of Thorne, it looked as though she'd better think again. Even as she watched, that undependable gentleman began competing with Basil for the twins' attention.

Lord Arden had not meant to do so. He had, in fact, been wracking his brains since yesterday, trying to contrive some means of getting Basil out of the way so that the courtship of Miss Ashmore might proceed apace. He'd been pleased to note that his Intended had scarcely said a word to Trev at breakfast. She'd apparently taken him in intense dislike, for she'd met the wretch's pleasantries with cool politeness and reserved her warm smiles for himself.

All the same, the marquess considered it neither natural nor agreeable to be completely ignored by a set of pretty young ladies under any circumstances, least of all in favour of Trevelyan. To correct this inequity, he insinuated himself into the conversation, and the twins soon rewarded him with blushes and giggles.

He did not, however, intend to take the duo driving in the afternoon. Unfortunately, Basil said something provoking—then the marquess retorted—then the twins looked so sweetly pleading . . . and, in the next minute the marquess found himself trapped in an engagement that would not win him any credit with his Beloved. He vowed inwardly to make speedy amends. But after admiring the dimple on Sarah's chin and noting its perfect mate upon Susan's, then bidding gallant goodbyes to them all, he turned around and found that Miss Ashmore had vanished.

When he asked his hostess where the young lady had gone, he learned that Miss Ashmore had promised Lucy an hour of her exclusive company.

"And you know, Will," Isabella reminded, "that Jess and Miss Ashmore must take her by turns, for she made them promise, and it's no good my telling them they spoil her dreadfully. Everyone spoils her, and poor Miss Ames is left with the thankless task of repairing the damage."

Lord Arden promptly took Lucy in violent dislike. Being a courteous gentleman, he did not share his feelings with his hostess or anyone else, though he did, shortly thereafter, find fault with his valet and berate that villain accordingly.

"You engineered that," said Lady Jessica accusingly, as she followed Basil out to the stables.

He replied very sweetly that he hadn't the faintest idea what she was talking about.

"Lud, will you listen to the man? He believes I'm a chaw-bacon, I think. You trapped him into driving those cabbage-heads," she went on reproachfully. "I know you like to have your fun and show how clever you are, but this is not the time for it. What is Miss Ashmore to think?"

"That your brother's taste is faulty, perhaps?"

She shot him a shrewd look. "I think you want her for yourself."

"Of course I do. I want every lady for myself."

"And so you must make trouble for Will? Really, it's most unfair of you. This is the first time in his life he's ever shown the least bit of common sense."

"And a precious little bit it is when the first distraction that comes along is enough to knock it out of him. I don't know why you scold so, Jess. Why, you're the first to make sport or your brother. And now Miss Ashmore's seen him in his true colours, you're all in a fidge about it. Really, I'm surprised at you.''

Lady Jessica Farrington was nobody's fool, and most especially not Basil's. Knowing him as well as she did her own brother, she was not about to be shrugged off so easily. It was true she didn't want to mislead Miss Ashmore. On the other hand, she didn't want Miss Ashmore alienated.

Lady Jess lived in lively terror that her brother would one day marry some beautiful, shallow, self-centered aristocrat like her own mother, totally incapable of improving Will in any way. He needed a great deal of improvement—and soon, if his character was not to be irretrievably ruined.

She'd believed that Miss Ashmore was capable of effecting the desired changes, if only Will didn't make her despise him. Which, of course, she was bound to do when she saw, not that he was a rake, for rakes were rather appealing, but that he was such a fickle creature that he couldn't even manage a pretence of keeping his mind on the woman he was courting.

In a few sentences she laid the matter out for Basil. ''Don't you see?'' she pleaded. ''This may be his only chance to make something decent of himself.''

''As he isn't my brother, I really don't care two sticks about it,'' was the unsympathetic reply.

''I should think,'' said the lady, ''you'd enjoy seeing him taught a lesson—regardless your interest in his future.''

''You know as well as I there's no teaching him anything.''

They had reached the stables, but she drew him away, out of the grooms' hearing. ''He's never been so vulnerable before, Basil. He does want to marry her, you know. Unfortunately, he has no experience in the business and doesn't know how to go on. That is to say, he just goes on as he always does—or will, unless Miss Ashmore sets him straight.''

''Then what are you telling *me* for?''

''Because you must help her.''

''No!'' he snapped, with so much force that she was momentarily taken aback. ''That is to say,'' he corrected hastily, ''she wouldn't accept any help from me on any account. Nor do I think she'll take kindly to any advice from you on how to go on with your brother.''

"If she were agreeable, would you help?" Jessica coaxed.

Idly tapping his riding crop against his leg, he considered this for a moment or two. Finally he replied, "Well, it would be a bit of fun to see that self-satisfied smirk wiped off Will's face."

She'd won her point, and pressed the advantage without waiting to hear more. "Good. Now, you're not going riding yet."

He protested that he was.

"No. You'll ride with *her*, this afternoon, while Will is out with the twins. We'll make sure he knows about it as soon as he returns. That should make him think twice about taking her for granted."

Deaf to Basil's ironical comments regarding her powers of persuasion, Lady Jess stepped away briefly to tell the grooms to have horses ready for Mr. Trevelyan and Miss Ashmore directly after luncheon.

This done, she turned back to her victim. "Now you must go use all your wiles to persuade her to ride with you."

"I?" he asked indignantly. "I've only agreed to go along with the scheme, if you can effect it. Didn't I just tell you she won't—"

"If she won't, then you're not the man you were. Even if she hates you, you must know some way to get round her, Basil. Lud, Will could do it without thinking half a minute." Lady Jess knew her man, after all. It wanted only the one hint—that Will's powers of persuasion were superior to his own—to effect complete capitulation. Basil agreed to do as he was told.

Though he knew Miss Ashmore's citadel was not to be so easily stormed, he resolutely waylaid her after she'd left the schoolroom and was descending the stairs. He proceeded to offer such a variety of abject apologies, with every possible expression of penitence, as well as some quite impossible ones, that he soon had her laughing in spite of herself. Having obtained a rather choked pardon for his inexcusable misconduct of the previous day, he then went on to the trickier business of coaxing her to ride with him.

He'd intended to goad her into it. If she refused, he'd say she was afraid of him and incapable of keeping one mischievous gentleman in order. But those green eyes, sparkling with amusement, drove his planned scenario right out of his head.

"Will you ride with me then?" he asked. Seeing her face stiffen, he went on hurriedly, "Jess is furious that her brother's abandoned you for a pair of idiots, and she's determined that you're to teach him a lesson and I'm to be the means. And though I don't especially care to do him any favours, what choice have I when this is the only way I might have your company all to myself?"

Alexandra looked away and addressed her remarks to the bannister. "I believe," she told that gleaming object, "this gentleman attempts to play on my wounded vanity and my unwounded vanity simultaneously."

"Of course I do. You know I'm the sort of man who stops at nothing."

"In that case, a sensible woman must forego your company, I think."

"Then don't be sensible, Miss Ashmore. I'd like nothing better than to ride with you. I've missed you horribly."

The words were no sooner out of his mouth than he urgently wished them back again. He heard them for what they were—Truth—and that wouldn't do at all.

Of course, she didn't believe him. Her face attested to that plain enough though she was still looking at the bannister. Yet, her reaction changed nothing. He *had* missed her horribly. Why else would he have given in so easily to Jess? Even now, as Alexandra hesitated, he was wondering what he would do if she refused. He was unable to invent a satisfactory answer.

"Well, I suppose you can't help it," she said finally, with a teasing smile that rather surprised him. "Though you momentarily forgot to mention it, the sun does rise and set on my fair countenance, and you can't sleep for thinking of me, and—what else?"

"And," he answered steadily, "if you don't come riding

with me, I shall be the most miserable wretch that ever lived.''

''Oh, yes. I wonder how that slipped my mind.''

''Then you will ride with me?'' he persisted.

What was she to do? He claimed to be sorry. He'd apologised in every way his fertile mind could invent. If she was willing to ride with others, wouldn't it look odd that she wouldn't ride with him? After all, he did claim it was Jess's idea, and one could always ask Jess about that. In short, after a little more hesitation, and a little more persuasion, Miss Ashmore convinced her mind to agree with her heart and consented.

Jessica pounced on him after luncheon, as soon as he was alone. ''Well? Have you done it?''

''Yes.''

''Good. I knew you could. Now you must keep her out until teatime—later, if you can manage it. That'll have Will in a frenzy.''

''Until teatime! What do you expect me to do? Tie her to a tree?''

''Get lost. Have your horse throw a shoe. Have it throw you. Surely you can think of something.''

''I can think of a great many things,'' he answered, his face a perfect study in wickedness. ''However, I understood it was your brother you wanted shackled—not me.''

''Oh, stow it, Basil. If you keep her sufficiently amused, she won't notice the time passing.''

Without waiting for any more evil hints of the amusements he contemplated, Lady Jessica took herself off to her sitting room and the latest publication from the Minerva Press awaiting her therein.

''Going riding, are you?'' Lady Bertram enquired as she bestowed a look of approval upon her goddaughter's wine-coloured habit.

She'd been right to send the girl to Madame Vernisse. The modiste had settled upon simple, clinging lines in rich colours, ignoring the fussy furbelows currently in fashion, since they did not suit Miss Ashmore at all. Yes, Alexandra would do very well.

"Y-yes," came the nervous answer. "With Mr. Trevelyan."

"I see."

"Unless you think I shouldn't."

"Whyever not? Can't have Farrington thinking he's the only male in Creation, can we? You're quite right. Do him good. And Basil, too. The boy's so fidgety lately, he's bound to get into trouble out of sheer boredom. You'll be doing him a favour—not that he deserves it—but you know that. I don't need to tell you to box his ears if he misbehaves."

Alexandra, who'd been critically examining her gloves, looked up quickly. "Misbehaves?"

"I mean, child, if he behaves in any way you don't like. Which, as I said, I don't need to tell you."

Giving her goddaughter a kindly smile, the countess took herself away.

10

If Alexandra neither noticed the time passing nor felt obliged to box the gentleman's ears, that was probably because her companion was behaving so well. He was entertaining, as usual, but in such a friendly, nonthreatening way that she felt much in charity with him as they ambled in leisurely fashion about the enormous estate.

Estate was hardly the word. With its great expanses of field and meadow, its gently rolling hills and rich valleys, its little ponds and waterways, the Hartleigh property was more like a small kingdom. The estate even had its own forest, an extensive stand of wood left much as Nature had made it, though the clear trails showed that the same care was given to this wilderness as to the rest of Lord Hartleigh's beautifully groomed domain.

She had certainly admired the estate during other rides but Basil took her along paths she hadn't travelled before and talked of childhood escapades, sharing his associations with this stretch of meadow and that golden field and this little duck pond. The stories vividly conjured the childhood of this puzzling man and helped her, at least to some extent, to understand him better.

He had, naturally, been into mischief practically from the day he was born. He had, furthermore, been dreadfully spoiled by his parents, but especially by his indulgent Mama, who'd lost several babies before and after producing him. Under her doting tutelage, the precocious boy had learned early how to wheedle his way out of a scolding with a show of penitence. So, too, had he learned how sweet words could melt away anger and clever phrases turn disapproval into laughter. He'd begun early practising these and the hundred other arts of which he was now the consummate master.

Small wonder it was so difficult to resist him when he was determined not to be resisted. Nature had given him both a fiendishly quick mind and a handsome face and form. Nurture had showed him how to use these to his advantage, and somehow along the way, self-discipline had never come into the picture.

Not that it was so terribly helpful to understand him better. What she learned about him only made her heart warm towards him in a way that was not at all sensible.

She was a greater fool than any of the Osbornes, certainly. They at least had stupidity as an excuse. Still, it was impossible to be unhappy now when he seemed so determined to make the ride a pleasant one, free of teasing innuendoes. He'd actually provided her an escape of sorts. No worrying, as she always did when she was with Lord Arden, about whether she was behaving too warmly or too coldly. Nor was there the guilt she always felt about allowing the marquess to court her when she was promised to another, or about building a friendship with his sister under the same false pretences. What would they think of her if they learned the truth?

"You're thinking unhappy thoughts," Basil chided, breaking in on her meditations, "which is most inconsiderate when I'm confiding my deepest secrets to you. Or is it the secrets that make you frown?"

"Oh. Not at all. I was only envying you your playmates," she improvised hastily. "We lived very quietly, you know, and I hadn't any."

"Then you saved yourself and your household a deal of trouble."

He went on to give examples. The Farrington children habitually spent part of the summer at Hartleigh Hall, where Jessica had early cultivated the disagreeable habit of tagging after the boys.

"One day she annoyed Will so, he tied her to a tree, but not nearly well enough. The little thing—and she was barely six years old—got herself free, then proceeded to stumble into a ditch. Nothing daunted, the child stumbled her way out again and marched home, muddy and bruised. She swore up and down she'd been kidnapped by gypsies. Jess would never tattle, one must say that for her. Even so, Will earned himself a flogging, and I—at my advanced age—was kept indoors for a week and required to copy pages and pages of dreary sermons.''

"I daresay you copied them beautifully and learned a great deal from the experience.''

"And I can tell by the look on your face you think I'd have been better for a flogging. Yet it never did Will any good, did it? He tried, in fact, to drown her not long after. Shall I show you the melancholy scene of his attempted crime?''

Without waiting for an answer, he led her deeper into the wood through such a maze of paths that she lost her bearings completely. Not that she was capable of noting the direction they took. Basil kept up a stream of nonsense as they proceeded, making such a tragicomedy of his anecdote that all she could do was follow him blindly, laughing all the way, until they reached the famous stream.

"We'd better walk the rest of the way,'' he told her. "The going is treacherous on horseback. At any rate, the beasts deserve a respite, and I'm thirsty.''

He helped her dismount, and his touch at her waist sent a tremour through her. Rather unsteadily, she followed him to a curve of the bank where large rocks made a safe and comfortable sitting.

"A childhood paradise,'' he said, after they'd refreshed themselves and leaned back to relax upon the great, smooth stones.

"Or even an adult one,'' she agreed. "It's so beautiful and cool here.''

"Yes, it is. My cousin is a lucky man. There was a time I thought he'd never live to enjoy it, and it would all be mine. He was involved in some rather dangerous intelligence work during the war, you know,'' he explained.

"As were you. And you both survived.''

"Yes. What wonders we Trevelyans are.'' He appeared lost in thought, and not very pleasant thought at that. His features hardened slightly, and his amber eyes were shadowed.

"You didn't care for that work at all, did you?" she asked, after a bit.

"No. I hated it."

"Did your cousin feel the same?"

"He loved it—or at least the accomplishment. No one can like what he sees along the way. Of course, the accommodations are not always what they should be. He spent time in prison, and I soon learned to inspect my bed and boots before getting into them. When one is surrounded by unreliable allies, snakes and scorpions tend to turn up at the oddest times. At any rate, Edward knew what he was getting into and was prepared to make the necessary sacrifices. I'm not nearly so noble. I was sent away, you know, because—well, you must know that, too, by now. Ironic, isn't it? To be banished in disgrace, and then to find myself playing the hero. Hardly my style."

He'd never before discussed his exile, and the trace of bitterness in his tone surprised her. This wasn't the careless, complacent man she thought she knew.

"Yet you were—are—a hero," she answered carefully.

"In spite of myself." He tossed a pebble into the water. "I wonder," he said, after a moment, "what we'd become if we could do exactly as we wished."

"We should be in a sort of anarchy, of course. At least, that's what my governess always said."

"Why do I think, Alexandra, that you put little stock in what your governess said?" He tossed another pebble into the stream and turned to smile at her.

The smile was sunshine, breaking through the gloom that had clouded his handsome face. She smiled back, happy that she'd helped dispel his somber mood.

"Because," she answered lightly, "you've already discovered what an undutiful daughter I am."

"And if you could do as you wished? If there was no Randolph hovering like a tiresome ghost in the background?"

She closed her eyes briefly to shut out his smiling, sunlit face so that she could conjure up an acceptable response. "It would be pleasant to have a Season," she answered, opening them again. "I had one, but Mama was always nagging. Then she was so ill towards the end of it, and even back then, there was the Randolph ghost in the background. I'd like to be free to enjoy myself this time and make friends with aged debutantes like myself—"

"And flirt with all the gentlemen?"

She grinned. "Well, not *all*. That would be selfish, and then I shouldn't have any women friends, should I?"

"I'd like to see that," was the surprising answer. "I'd like to see you at all the balls and routs, leaving dozens of broken hearts strewn in your wake. Including Will's. For that I'd even volunteer my own. The one you say I haven't got. You know, the little hard one. Looks something like this." He held up a pebble in illustration, then flung it carelessly over his shoulder.

"And is that what you'd like me to do with it?"

"With Will's, rather. Mine—"

Basil broke off abruptly. His thoughts were tending in a rather disconcerting direction, as they had earlier, and he wondered at it. But then, just look at her. She was so beautiful that it took one's breath away to gaze at her. She was always beautiful, even in those black rags she'd worn in Albania, but now her beauty was more than flesh and blood could bear. The ruby habit seemed to shimmer in the sunlight with every graceful movement of that slim, provocative body. A glass of exquisite wine, he thought, from which he longed to sip. Fortunately, he had sufficient self-control not to say so aloud. To anyone else he *would* have said it. He couldn't understand what made her different, or why that difference made him hold his tongue. Perhaps, right now he'd rather not understand.

Looking into her eyes was like gazing into a quiet forest, a place of refuge, and her low, husky voice was a cool, soothing stream, murmuring beside him. Meanwhile, this actually was a cool, shaded place by a clear, sparkling stream; and it *was* a sort of refuge. She was close by with no Will, no Randolph, no irascible Papa, nor watchful relatives of his own to interfere.

He even wished, for one dreadful moment, that it could always be so, and that was the oddest thought of all. He wanted her. His desire hadn't abated in all this time. Nor was there any more prospect of that desire being assuaged than there'd ever been. In spite of all that, he felt peaceful and contented.

She'd shunned him, and he hadn't liked it. Now he was shunned no longer, and idiotically happy . . . So relieved, in fact, that though he wanted her no whit less than he'd ever done since he met her, he forebore to act. And that was something. That was rather an immense something. But he couldn't think about it now. Later, perhaps, when those cool green eyes didn't confuse him so. At the moment, they were gazing at him inquiringly. He wondered how long he'd been staring at her, speechless.

He gave her a rueful grin. "See? You've only to mention a Season, and I immediately begin cudgelling my brains how to get you one. In fact, I wonder what the matter is. Surely my aunt would pay your Papa's debt."

"She tried to pay Mr. Burnham directly, she told me. And he declined to accept. Most indignantly declined, she says. Not," she added hurriedly, "that she *ought*—"

"Aunt Clem is never troubled by 'ought' or 'ought not.' A trait that runs in the family, as you may have noticed. At any rate, she has no children of her own. Edward has always been a prodigy of virtue. Even I, despite every evidence to the contrary for over thirty years, have managed to get my own affairs in order. So you must be her offspring now. But it does puzzle me why there's only Will here courting you, instead of a few dozen competing for your attention."

Her face reddened. "You make me feel like the estate of a bankrupt to be auctioned off to the highest bidder."

"Why?"

"Because that's what I am." Though she spoke quietly there was suppressed emotion in her tone. He wasn't altogether surprised at what followed. "My father hasn't a farthing to call his own, and I'm his only asset. One way or another I'm to be used to pay his debt. If I'm not the commodity he offers in trade to the Burnhams, then I must be the means of getting them compensation." She shook her head then, as though to toss off what troubled her. "I'm sorry," she said. "I make it sound like a melodrama."

"You're stating the facts," he answered gently. "And the main fact is that whoever does pacify the Burnhams for your Papa will have a hold on you all the rest of your life, and the prospect appalls you."

She looked at him in astonishment.

"I understand you better than you think. And now," he went on, with a teasing smile, "you've as much as told me that Will hasn't won your heart, I'm more put out with my aunt than ever."

The faint rose of her cheeks deepened, telling him that she knew what she'd inadvertently confessed. Feeling absurdly relieved, he went on. "Since she's made such a mull of the business, perhaps I should step in and see what can be done to mend it."

"If you recall, you stepped in once already—"

"And must have accomplished something, for you aren't married to Randolph yet, are you?"

"No, I'm not, and it was very kind of you. If I didn't thank you before, I do thank you now. I do appreciate it," was her rather flustered reply.

"You needn't thank me. I might have done better, I suppose. Only I must confess I couldn't think of anything to improve upon our plan."

He could, of course, think of any number of improvements now, such as carrying her off somewhere out of Will's reach, out of everyone's reach. He could also . . . As the notion came to him, he crushed it. Momentary madness, brought on, no doubt, by the hope that flickered in her eyes.

"Well, it wants some thought, and I'm sure we've missed our tea. We'd better get back before they call in Bow Street."

He rose and offered his hand to help her up. He was alarmed to see that hand was shaking, but she didn't appear to notice as, rather absentmindedly, she let him help her to her feet.

He didn't let go, and she seemed oblivious to that as well, for her hand remained in his as he led her back to the horses. Though he'd much rather hold on to her in quite a different way, there was something so confiding in the simple gesture that he felt a rush of protectiveness towards her. Thus for the second—or perhaps hundredth—time that day, he forebore to act on his baser inclinations. If this set off any more alarm bells in his head, he decided to think about that later also.

The horses were now allowed to quench their thirst. He stood with her, quietly waiting as they did so. It was only when he'd helped her back upon her mount that he spoke again.

"How pleasant this has been. We haven't quarrelled once. I can't think how we've managed it."

"We've let our surroundings work their good upon us, I think. But I wouldn't worry overmuch about it. Once free of Nature's calming influence, I daresay we'll find something to dispute soon enough."

"I suspect you're right," he answered. It occurred to him that perhaps their relationship was a good deal safer when they *did* quarrel.

They returned to an anxious household. At Will's instigation, Edward had ordered horses saddled preparatory to searching for the missing pair. However, if he had it in mind to tax his cousin with keeping Miss Ashmore out so long, his wife's nudge must have distracted him. No one else scolded either, and Lord Arden could hardly make a scene. He had perforce to content himself with getting back into Miss Ashmore's good graces, while imagining divers hideous tortures to which Basil should be subjected if this were a more reasonable world—like that, for instance, in which the first Duke of Thorne had existed some centuries before.

Will soon found that he had best keep his mind entirely upon the former object, as Miss Ashmore's attention was not easily held. She was quite preoccupied and sometimes had to be asked the same question twice to be persuaded to answer at all. This circumstance was not encouraging. Lord Arden began to hate Basil desperately and the Osborne twins even more. Hadn't they sinned twice, after all: once in keeping him from Miss Ashmore, and again in boring him to distraction? Lord Arden began to consider the ugly possibility that he'd permanently alienated his Intended.

Fortunately for his lordship's spirits, which were sinking at an alarming rate, the group from Hartleigh Hall was engaged to dine that evening at Netherstone, home of Lord and Lady Dessing. In the course of that dinner, Miss Ashmore's behaviour gradually began to change.

She was less abstracted than she'd been. He had the good fortune to be seated at her left, a species of miracle, considering there were thirty at table. Will made the most of that advantage and he was soon rewarded with both smiles and humourous sallies from those sweetest of all lips.

He was also relieved to see that Trev was his usual self, flirting with all the females of the company by turns. He'd start on one and, as soon as that feminine heart was reduced to liquid state, would proceed on to the next. As there were at least half a dozen untried hearts to be worked upon, Basil was busy the entire evening.

When the gentlemen had consumed large quantities of port, they rejoined the ladies, and the marquess saw that Basil had reserved Lady Honoria Crofton-Ash, Dessing's daughter, for last. Well, if he could coax anything remotely resembling a natural smile onto the frigid countenance of that glacier-like creature, more power to him. Lord Arden did not believe Lady Honoria worth the effort. Priggish and haughty, entirely caught up in her own consequence, she held no charm for him, handsome as she was . . . and no charm, either, he suspected, for anyone else. After all, she'd be embarking upon her fifth Season in the spring, and for all her looks and all her Papa's money and consequence, she hadn't managed to find a husband.

At any rate, Basil's behaviour this evening showed that there was nothing to be concerned about there. He'd taken Miss Ashmore off this afternoon only to be provoking, and to prove what a prodigiously charming fellow he was—as he must demonstrate to every female in the county, apparently.

Let him be charming, the marquess thought as Miss Ashmore, who'd also glanced at the pair talking quietly in a corner of the room, turned back to him with a dazzling smile. Tonight Lord Arden did not envy the all-conquering Mr. Trevelyan his conquests. Not in the least.

11

Having, apparently, Learned His Lesson, the marquess was prompt to offer his services as driver the next morning when he learned that Miss Ashmore and Jess were going into the village.

His Intended did not seem to hear the offer, but Jess accepted readily, then went on to praise the local dressmaker who was taking in a gown for her. She complained about her London modiste whose careless work must now be repaired and ended by declaring she'd go to Madame Vernisse from now on. Look how beautifully she made Miss Ashmore's clothes.

Here Will interrupted with the avowal that whatever Miss Ashmore wore must be beautiful, since she adorned her attire, rather than the other way round.

Basil did not even look up from his plate, being busily engaged in creating a work of art therein. He moved a bit of egg here, a sliver of ham there, and was evidently so engrossed in this aesthetic endeavour that he forgot to put any of it in his mouth.

Doubtless he was fretting over his singular lack of success with Lady Honouria last night, for she'd been as stiff and proper with him at the end of the evening as she had at the start. Well, it was about time *somebody* found him resistible, Alexandra thought morosely. He'd tricked her into admitting she wasn't in love with Lord Arden, said he wanted to help her, then let the marquess monopolise her the entire evening. Mr. Trevelyan obviously couldn't be bothered with her problems when there was a roomful of ladies requiring his attention.

There was no help for her at all. It was either the marquess or Randolph, and no more delay, because Papa was coming—good grief!—this very afternoon. The recollection threw her into a panic, and she was so busy wracking her brains what to do next that she hardly noticed what she was doing now.

Which is to say she answered automatically what was said to her on the ride into the village and hadn't the presence of mind to think of a reasonable objection when Lord Arden insisted that Jess go on to the dressmaker by herself, to be met up with in another hour. Hardly had Jess been deposited at Mrs. Merrill's door and the horses put in motion again, when the marquess announced his intention of speaking to Sir Charles this very afternoon.

Alexandra's panic escalated. Stalling for time, she feigned bafflement about what the marquess might have to say to her father.

"Why, Miss Ashmore—Alexandra—surely it can come as no surprise to you," he said, with the tenderest of looks. "I'd thought I'd made my intentions perfectly plain. And I'd thought—or rather, *hoped*—that in some small way you might return those feelings."

She looked startled, and then she looked confused, and then she dropped her gaze to her hands which were tightly folded in her lap. She murmured that she had no business having feelings about anyone, as she was betrothed already. In halting sentences, she outlined the Burnham situation.

Lord Arden was, as she'd expected, speechless for a moment. She stole a glance at his face. His expression was composed, if rather tightly so, and the grey eyes seemed darker than usual, like cold slate, telling her he was angry. But whatever he felt, he held it in check, and only asked stiffly, "As to this betrothal—you say nothing of yourself, only of your Papa and this Mr. Burnham. Is it what you wish?"

With some hesitation, she admitted that it was not.

He seemed to relax a little. "Then dare I wonder whether there's any place for me in your wishes?"

She studied her hands again. She couldn't allow herself to

think about ... such things, she said. In fact—well, she'd been dishonest to keep this matter from others, and yet ... She couldn't continue, being covered in maidenly confusion, but not so much so that she couldn't manage another peek at his face. He was mulling it over, she could tell, and must have come to a satisfactory conclusion, for very soon he was smiling again, and the warm light was back in his eyes.

"It seems to me," he said, "that if you had told me from the first, you would have been saying there was no hope for me at all. But as you didn't—well, perhaps it was because you weren't wholly indifferent to me. Or do I presume too much?"

"It's quite impossible, my lord, to be indifferent to you—as no doubt scores of other ladies have demonstrated. Still, I suppose I should have told you. And yet," she looked up to meet his gaze—"it didn't seem so important. How could I think that I, or my family matters, were of any interest to you? That would be assuming that out of all the women you know, I would be anything special to you."

He was stymied. She barely hinted—though she did so tantalisingly enough—at caring for him, which implied that she'd been playing fast and loose with him all this time. Then, in the same breath, she claimed to be the one led on. Damn Jessica for telling all those tales of his romantic conquests. They had made Miss Ashmore think he was only amusing himself, and now, though he'd courted the woman all this time—two whole weeks, at least—it appeared he must begin all over again.

Meanwhile, she insisted she'd never believed his intentions were serious. She couldn't be expected to make up her mind on the spot whether she meant to have him, as she'd never permitted herself to think of him in that way. Besides which, she was already engaged, as she'd just told him, and she couldn't blame him in the least if he chose to forget this entire conversation. Certainly there were hundreds of women more deserving of the honour he so kindly offered.

The discussion went on for half an hour, until he finally convinced her that his suit was serious. As to speaking to her father, that—for now at least—was out of the question. Papa was sure to take alarm and ship her off to Yorkshire.

"He's very fixed on Randolph, and under great obligation to Mr. Burnham, and really—"

"And really," he interrupted impatiently, "his debts are the least of my concerns. The trivialities of the marriage settlement." He complained that she was bent on tormenting him.

She declared nothing could be farther from her mind, then looked as though she was about to weep. So he spoke more kindly, with a great deal of the sort of tender nonsense best calculated to soothe the tremulous flutterings of the fragile feminine heart.

Sir Charles arrived early in the afternoon in a state of high irritation. He had not liked to leave Westford so soon, as business with Henry Latham promised to be most satisfactory, but a letter from George Burnham had come to him there that drove everything else out of his head.

Nearly two days' journey in hot weather had only exacerbated his foul mood. Even Randolph had been provoking. The baronet had begun to speak of the Peloponnesian War, thinking to while away the weary hours with talk on Randolph's favorite subject, and got for his pains only a great, agonised groan.

The younger generation was going to the devil, and that was the long and short of it. His daughter was scheming with Clementina's nephew to foist this ridiculous secret betrothal nonsense upon her long-suffering Papa. Even Randolph—always such a steady chap—was in a fit of the dismals from the moment they left Westford. Well, Sir Charles would see about him, later. Right now, he had a few choice words for Clementina.

He could not say those words immediately, however, having only just arrived and been greeted by his host and hostess. Their warm welcome, along with the army of servants who appeared immediately to see to his comfort, the graciously appointed rooms allotted him, a hot bath, and a generous tray of refreshments provided for his delectation, helped control his impatience.

Nonetheless, he was determined to be in a temper, and when some hours later he was finally ushered into Lady Bertram's presence, he burst out without preamble, "I will not have it, Clementina!"

The countess sat perfectly straight in her chair and eyed him coldly as though he were a particularly hideous species of toad, then said with frigid composure, "Indeed?"

"How dare you?" he went on, undaunted by her haughty stare. "How dare you connive behind my back? How dare you attempt to bribe George Burnham?"

"Oh, do stop shouting, Charles. You'll have all the servants huddling by the door."

"I don't care a fiddle about the servants—"

"And *I* don't care to be shouted at. If you cannot behave yourself, you might as well leave." She gave him a dismissive wave.

"You needn't put on your high and mighty airs with me, Clementina," he retorted, but more quietly. "Though it's of a perfect piece with your interfering arrogance. You tried to bribe George Burnham. There's no use denying it."

"I," said Lady Bertram, with awful dignity, "deny nothing."

"Then you did try!"

"You understand nothing. I did not attempt to bribe George Burnham. I offered to pay your debt to him—"

"To prevent the marriage."

"To pay the debt. I do not see what marriage has to do with it. A financial debt is one thing; a marriage is another. You seem to confuse the two."

"Never mind what confuses me. You had no business."

The countess maintained that she had every sort of business since her goddaughter was somehow mixed into his business affairs. "As she did not create your financial difficulties, I do not see why she is required to solve them for you."

There was obvious truth in what Lady Bertram said, and that truth rather piqued his conscience than otherwise. Therefore, Sir Charles grew more enraged. "But you could see your way well enough to plotting against me, could you not? You and your scheming nephew."

"I collect you are referring to Basil."

"Of course I'm referring to Basil."

"Then why do you come and pick a quarrel with me? If Basil has offended you, it is Basil you should speak with."

Sir Charles's head was beginning to ache. The woman jumped about from one topic to the next with no logic whatsoever. Sir Charles hated illogic. He hated non sequiturs, and at the moment, he was so little fond of Lady Bertram that he would have liked to choke her. He wondered now why he had bothered to confront her in the first place. He should have known he'd get nowhere. Still, George Burnham's letter had wounded his pride, and Sir Charles wanted to take it out on somebody. He glared at the countess, but forced himself into some semblance of composure.

"That I will do—in good time—but first I wanted you to understand that I won't have you interfering in my affairs—"

"Where they concern my goddaughter, I cannot help but interfere. I hold it as a debt to Juliet."

"Was it part of that debt to send your nephew to connive with my daughter?"

"I cannot allow you to speak so when he is not here to defend himself." She gestured towards the bell rope. "Ring for a servant, Charles, and we shall send for Basil—and for Alexandra, too. If she has been conniving with him, then let her answer for herself."

Sir Charles rang, grumbling as he did so, and for several minutes after as they waited. Lady Bertram paid no heed to his ill-natured mutterings. She sat, straight as a ramrod, rigidly calm.

At last, the two connivers entered the room. Alexandra, who hadn't seen her Papa until now, gave him an affectionate peck on the cheek.

Angrily he waved her away. "None of your coaxing arts, Miss," he growled. "I've had enough of them."

He then launched into a tirade about make-believe fiancés, bribery of friends, and betrayal of Randolph, who was supposedly in the process of breaking his heart. No one but Lady Bertram noticed the flicker of interest in Basil's eyes as this last piece of information was communicated. Meanwhile, the baronet went on to his primary grievance—and here he took a letter out of his pocket—the very upsetting words he'd had from his friend, George Burnham.

"Well, Basil," said Lady Bertram when the baronet paused for breath. "What have you to say to that?"

"I hardly know what to say, Aunt. There's so much of it." He was leaning against the door frame, completely at his ease, wearing his most seraphic expression.

Miss Ashmore, he noticed, looked panicked, and well she should. It her Papa was not quickly brought under control, she'd be whisked off to Yorkshire and married to the wool merchant's son before the week was out.

It would be best if she were married and kept far away, beyond his reach. She was spoiling his fun. Hadn't she disrupted his entertainment last night? And he'd been so determined to find pleasure in other company, had so looked forward to it.

There was the Honourable Miss Sheldon, who'd refused to speak to him in the old days, and Miss Carstone. Even the haughty Honoria had endured a conversation, and her Mama had positively beamed upon him. Yet, they might have been a pack of murdering Hindoos for all the joy he had of them.

Not that he needed to wonder why there should be so little joy in it. The cause was here before him, artful creature that she was. Well then, if she was so artful, let her get herself out of this fix.

He glanced towards her then, their eyes met, and he found himself saying, "Of course, as to the fiancé part of your question, the answer is plain enough. She promised herself to me six years ago, and I mean to hold her to that promise."

"You *what?*" Sir Charles cried.

"I mean to—"

"What kind of fool do you take me for? I know as well as everyone else in this room that was a great piece of nonsense you concocted."

"Are you calling me a liar, sir?" Basil asked quietly.

Alexandra, who'd apparently been struck mute by the previous exchange, now found her tongue. "No, he isn't." She turned to her father. "You know you aren't saying any such thing, Papa."

"I most certainly am. And if this young blackguard wishes to name his seconds—"

"Oh, do be quiet, Charles. He wishes nothing of the sort. But you can hardly expect my nephew to stand quietly by as you denigrate his"—the countess appeared to have got something stuck in her throat, but she quickly recovered—"his tender feelings for your daughter."

"That's it precisely, Aunt. My tender feelings." He glanced again at Alexandra, expecting her to take the cue.

Instead, she crossed the room to Basil's side. "You can't get at me through my Papa, Basil," she said, with a look of deepest pity. "I told you it was a mistake." She turned to her father. "It's as you predicted, Papa."

"What is?" asked the now-bewildered baronet.

"Why, it was only romantic infatuation—as you said—and now—"

"And now," Basil interposed, beginning to grow very angry, "you're infatuated with someone else and mean to throw me over. I should have known I couldn't compete with a marquess."

"A what? What's going on here? Clementina, they're at it again, and I hold you responsible."

"On the contrary," the countess remarked serenely, "they are at each other. But really, Basil, you needn't sulk. After all, it is a compliment to be jilted in favour of a marquess. A future duke, actually."

"Will someone please speak rationally and logically? Because if they do not, I warn you, Alexandra, you'll be out of this house and on your way to Yorkshire in the next ten minutes."

"The situation is quite simple, Charles. Lord Arden, Thorne's heir, has evidently succeeded in engaging your daughter's affections."

"But the wretched girl is engaged already. Twice, it seems, if I am to believe all this faradiddle about tender feelings."

"That is neither here nor there. To expect her to marry a wool merchant's son or my black sheep of a nephew"—the nephew, at the moment, had a rather black look about him, indeed—"when the future Duke of Thorne wishes to make her his wife, is perfectly absurd. It is the most illogical thing I have ever heard."

Sir Charles, whose head was now spinning, dropped into a chair. "Thorne?" he uttered faintly. Then he remembered the letter still clutched in his hand. "But what of this? What reply am I to make to this?"

Casting a warning look at Basil, Alexandra took the letter from her father. She read it through, quickly, frowning as she did so. "Why, this is infamous, Papa!" she exclaimed, when she was done. "See how the man insults you. And to go on at such length about injured friendship and in the next breath talk of the money, when he as much as says the money is nothing to him. Oh, Papa, no wonder you were so overset." She spoke with such tender compassion that even Basil half-believed her—for a moment.

"Well, it was most distressing. Especially when he knows I fully intended—but what reply can I make him now?"

"Why, that I'm to be mar—"

Basil hastily interrupted, "If it's as your daughter says, sir, then perhaps you should make no answer—not immediately. You'll want to frame a suitable reply, will you not?" he added, ignoring Miss Ashmore's look of outrage.

"Basil is right, Charles. The man has no choice but to be patient. And in a week or so, perhaps, you may answer him as coolly and logically as you like."

"Yes, Papa. You'll know exactly how to put him in his place—but later, when you're calmer."

He gazed for a moment at the three faces surrounding him, but all looked perfectly sincere—all seemed, suddenly, prodigious concerned with his peace of mind. He didn't trust any of them, and yet what could he do? A dukedom was nothing to sneeze at. With Thorne's patronage, a man might explore the globe for the rest of his life with never a care in the world. And if there were no dukedom, then Alexandra would marry Randolph.

Defeated for the moment, the baronet shrugged and agreed that George Burnham could wait. Exhausted with trying to distinguish between truth and humbug, he struggled up from the chair and out of the room.

"Well, what are you glaring at each other for?" Lady Bertram asked when the door had closed behind him. "You fuddled him well enough, between the two of you, and I should be deeply ashamed of you both if it had not been so very amusing. Well, well. Run along now, Alexandra. I wish to have a word with my nephew."

Alexandra ran along readily enough, not liking the expression on Mr. Trevelyan's face. Whatever was the matter with him? Was this how he meant to help, with that old betrothal farce that Papa plainly didn't believe for a moment? Thank heavens she hadn't counted on help from that quarter. Now what was she to do?

The amount George Burnham referred to in his letter wasn't the "thousand pounds or so" she'd heard Papa mention over the years. She'd read the words again and again, disbelieving her eyes, and hardly noticing the rest of the insulting missive. She couldn't understand how the amount had grown so. But then, what did Papa know of finance? Annuities and percents were as unfathomable to him as his beloved ancient inscriptions were to others. That was why he'd put everything in Mr. Burnham's hands. And how he'd tied the noose about her neck.

She'd have to marry Arden now—if he'd have her. If he wouldn't, Papa would simply shrug and take her away. She could appeal to Aunt Clem—but both conscience and pride recoiled at the idea of begging more help from her indulgent godmother.

Alexandra went to her room and tried to think. So many lies—to everyone—and matters only grew more muddled and horrible. Arden hadn't turned a hair when she'd mentioned Papa's debt—but what would he think now?

Did he want her badly enough to pay this outrageous marriage settlement? She didn't believe he truly loved her. He struck her less as a man in love than as one pursuing a prize.

Was that what offended her so? Though he said all the right

words, she felt he could have been saying them to anybody. He didn't seem to know—or care—who she was.

Not, she reminded herself, that he'd necessarily *like* who she was: a manipulative, deceitful woman who was only using him to save herself from boring Randolph and his appalling sisters. She had no right to judge the marquess so harshly.

She'd have to think of some way to break the news about the money. That was sure to be awkward. She attempted to compose an appropriate speech, but her mind kept returning to one point in the previous conversation, when Basil had said he meant to have her. He'd sounded as though he *did* mean it, and her heart had thumped dreadfully, as it was thumping now. Oh, such a fool she was. What was the good of his saying it if he wasn't going to sound as though he meant it?

12

For the next two days, Basil kept well away from her, Aunt Clem having warned him, as she told Alexandra, "to keep his interfering self out of this business." It was most gratifying to see how well he obeyed his aunt, especially, Alexandra thought dismally, when Aunt Clem's orders so perfectly coincided with his own fickle inclinations.

Still, it was odd that he'd taken up with Randolph, of all people. Apparently determined to be Mr. Burnham's bosom bow, Basil stuck to the young scholar like glue, toured him about the estate, and spent hours talking with him. Randolph must have found these discussions uplifting, for he'd come to Hartleigh Hall in a state of tragic melancholy. Now, after only two days, he was actually grinning at the man he'd begged her to beware of.

Oh, well, Alexandra thought wearily, it was nothing to her. She had her hands full with Arden.

Today they were sharing a picnic lunch with the Osbornes and another group of neighbours. Determined to have her exclusive company, Lord Arden had borne her off to a spot a little distance from the others. There he treated her to such a series of compliments and affectionate hints and delicate renderings of life at Thornehill—as well as the rest of the Farrington estates, so numerous she couldn't keep them straight in her mind—that he gave her a splitting headache.

Remarking her pallor, he suggested a walk. The meal had been laid out in a cool, shady grove, and he pointed to a path that followed alongside a sparkling stream.

"Hadn't we better invite the others?" she asked, as he helped her to her feet and drew her arm though his.

"Whatever for?"

She cast a furtive glance towards Basil, whose head was now bent very close to Hetty's simpering face. Any excuse Alexandra might have made died on her lips. Gripping the marquess's arm more firmly, she manufactured a shy smile.

That was answer enough for Will. He smiled down at her in a protective, proprietary sort of way, patted the slim fingers that lay on his sleeve, and bore her off towards the path.

No one appeared to take any alarm at their departure. Not Sir Charles, certainly, to whom it was comforting proof of the marquess's interest in his daughter. As Alexandra's own Papa did not object to the business, no one else felt required to do so, either.

No one, that is, but Basil, who took great exception to this impropriety. He wondered, as his hooded gaze followed the departing pair, what the devil Ashmore was thinking of to countenance it. It would have been easy enough to persuade Hetty to stroll in the same direction, but that was risky. Her Mama was bound to expect certain news at the conclusion of the exercise. Nor could Basil look with equanimity upon the prospect of stumbling, with witnesses, upon what was bound to be a compromising situation.

As the minutes ticked away, the danger of there being a compromising situation to witness increased. Still, if no one else cared, why should he? Consequently, between tormenting himself with imagining what was happening between the pair, and assuring himself of his perfect indifference to the lurid scenes presenting themselves to his imagination, he did not at first notice the parasol that tapped his arm. It tapped again, and a weary sigh floated down from somewhere above his head. He looked up to see Lady Deverell gazing down at him in a very bored sort of way.

"Dear me, how tiresome I am, to be sure. You did not look to be asleep, Basil, and yet Harry is—" She pointed with her parasol to her husband, who appeared to be dozing, propped up against a tree. "And I had hoped to have your arm for a bit."

114

Basil, who'd been reclining upon a cushion Hetty had thoughtfully provided for him, scrambled to his feet, all gallantry. If he thought it odd that Maria, who considered sitting down upon her chaise longue a calisthenic exercise, wanted to take a walk, he was too polite to mention it.

"It would be an honour, my lady. I'm yours to be led wheresoever you wish."

Having been deserted by one swain, Hetty very sensibly turned her attention elsewhere. She had a riddle, she told Lady Tuttlehope, that she was sure even the clever Mr. Burnham couldn't solve. Lady Tuttlehope protested that this was impossible. Mr. Burnham made modest noises that it was not, and Lord Tuttlehope, greatly baffled, blinked in wonder as he watched his friend stroll away with Harry Deverell's wife.

"I felt so dull," was the viscountess's soft complaint. "And that little path by the stream seems pleasant, does it not?"

Agreeing that it seemed most pleasant, Basil bore her away in pursuit of the missing couple.

"It has rather more twists and turns than one would expect," she noted languidly, when they'd walked some moments in silence. "Why, here it branches off. Now I wonder—" She paused at a place where the trail divided into three narrow paths.

Although it was not one of the sites he'd shown Miss Ashmore, Basil knew the place well, having, in the past, coaxed more than one willing village maiden along the more private of these ways. Yet, strangely enough, it was in this very direction that he proposed they proceed.

"Oh, well, I suppose you know best, my dear. And yet how easy for one to become lost—it does grow rather a wilderness, does it not? I do hope that Will has not lost his way."

"Highly unlikely," was the stiff reply. "He knows the place as well as I do."

"Does he? Then I daresay he will not cause Miss Ashmore to overexert herself."

"I daresay."

It appeared that Lord Arden must have expected exertion

of some sort, for as the path turned and branched off once again they came upon a pretty, sheltered spot, and upon the marquess with his arms wrapped around Miss Ashmore, treating her to a very interesting sort of exercise, indeed.

Being fully occupied, the pair were unaware they were observed, though Basil was instantly prepared to bring that matter forcibly to their attention. He was, in fact, about to rush forward and knock his lordship to the ground when he felt a surprisingly firm grip on his arm, and found himself being tugged backwards, out of sight.

"Scenes," her ladyship whispered, as he opened his mouth to object, "are so very fatiguing." She went on, in more carrying tones than normal, to rhapsodise in her usual weary way about the attractiveness of the spot. "Yes, a charming place, my love. I daresay Mr. Wordsworth would be moved to compose any number of odes upon it—with a perfectly exhausting number of stanzas." As she spoke, she led Basil forward again. "But you know, these noisy brooks do grow rather wearisome to the head after a time."

He hardly knew what he answered—some incoherent inanity. For all his outward composure, Basil was in a murderous rage, a condition not conducive to clever repartee. He thought of another stream and another private spot, and of how careful he'd been not to offend Miss Ashmore by making improper advances. Now that designing female was locked in an embrace with a man she'd admitted she didn't love. With a man, for heaven's sake, who had a set of twins in his keeping in London. It would serve her right to be shackled all her days to that monster of depravity.

If he did not stop to recall that Will had done little worse in his lifetime than he had himself, it was perhaps because Basil was not quite himself at the moment. How else explain that he, who'd always thought it great sport to steal kisses as often as he could, should now be filled with moral outrage that another gentleman did so? But it was Miss Ashmore from whom the kiss was stolen, and that, somehow, turned everything upside down.

Not that he could tell, really, what was upside down or right side up, for he was nearly choked with fury. He was, in fact, vowing to himself that as soon as the ladies could be removed from the vicinity, he would tear the marquess limb from limb. And as to *her* . . . There was a warning pressure on his arm, and he tried to collect himself. They were once again in view of the couple, now walking innocently towards them.

Miss Ashmore, who'd apparently found it unnecessary to lean upon her escort's arm, hurried towards Lady Deverell, and greeted her with a rather set smile.

"It seems," she said, in a voice as tight as her smile, "that Lord Arden has lost his way—"

"Has he, my love? Well, that is what we thought, is it not, Basil?" Without waiting for his reply, the viscountess remarked what a confusing sort of maze it was, and how it was no wonder Will went astray. "Yes, very likely, my dear," she told Will as she absently let go of Basil's arm to take that of the marquess. "You confused the spot with that lovely little wood you told me of, at the edges of your place in Scotland."

The way his lordship leered at Miss Ashmore as he accepted this excuse could not be agreeable to certain of the company. Miss Ashmore, however, resolutely turned her head . . . only to confront a face that appeared to be carved in stone. Lady Deverell having laid claim to the marquess, Alexandra had no choice but to take the arm Basil stiffly proffered her.

She no sooner touched his sleeve than she was acutely aware of the taut strength beneath her fingers. A tear pricked her eye, and she struggled to fight it back. It was unfair. Will's kiss had left her profoundly unmoved, and now . . . oh, Lord, she had only to touch Basil's coatsleeve and she was all atremble inside. It was unfair and cruel.

And he was cruel as well, hurrying her along ahead of the other two and acting so cold and silent just when she most needed him to tease her out of her misery. If only he'd say something provoking to make her forget Will's embrace and the self-loathing she'd felt in permitting it. She'd felt like a Cyprian, selling herself to a man she didn't, *couldn't* love. When it had come to the point, when she'd heard the voices and known that she had only to stay in his arms a moment

117

longer, and all her problems would be solved . . . she couldn't do it. It had only wanted a moment. They'd have been caught, and Papa would have made her marry the man who'd compromised her. But what had she done? Jerked herself away—because all she could think of was Basil seeing her in another man's arms.

As if he cared. He was only in a hurry to get back to Hetty and her sisters. Well, who told him to leave them in the first place?

"My apologies," Basil said in a harsh undertone, "for interrupting your tête-à-tête."

He'd broken in upon what was rapidly becoming a most satisfying wallow in self-pity. She managed to invent a cold retort, but his accusing tone had made her throat ache and her eyes fill with tears. To her horror, she heard her voice quavering as she answered, "Pray don't tax yourself with it, sir. I daresay his lordship makes his own opportunities for private conversation."

The tremulous sound made Basil look at her sharply, just as one treacherous tear stole down her cheek. He'd been about to say something brutal, but now found that he couldn't. A tear. He'd tasted a tear once before, eons ago, it seemed. It hadn't then, as it did now—so hurriedly brushed away—aroused in him this frenzy of emotions: pain, rage, sorrow, shame, and he didn't know what else.

He wanted to pull her into his arms, pull her close to him, as though that would end the turmoil within him—or at least punish her for causing it. She'd driven him to this: made him mad with jealousy and then in the next instant broke his heart in a thousand pieces when she shed a tear.

Mad with jealousy? Heart in a thousand pieces? Good heavens! That was what one *said* to women. It wasn't what one *felt*.

Mr. Trevelyan was not a stupid man. He knew himself very well. He knew, therefore, that whatever his previous opinions regarding what one said and what one felt, Reality was presenting him with a very different state of affairs. He had better take his hint from Reality for now and work out his opinions on the matter later.

118

"I'm sorry," he said quickly. "I was only teasing, and had no business—oh, for heaven's sake, Alexandra." Another tear was trembling on her long, black lashes. "Please don't cry. Not about *him.*" He quickened his pace to draw her still further ahead of Will and Maria, then took out his handkerchief, which he surreptitiously gave her.

"I was not crying," she insisted, though she did wipe her eyes hurriedly before returning the linen square to him.

"No, of course you weren't," he agreed. Tearing the marquess limb from limb was too kind by half. If that clumsy brute had in any way abused her . . . but his voice was light enough as he went on. "And so, of course I needn't worry that the others might notice it and wonder what's been going on. Or if they do," he added, "they're bound to think it's my fault and naturally I'm quite used to being scolded. I daresay Edward will horsewhip me, but don't trouble yourself about it. Really, don't."

In this wise he got her to smile and compose herself, so that when the four wanderers rejoined the rest of the party, not a murmur was made regarding their wanderings.

Lord Hartleigh was a cultured man and had, in addition to an excellent art collection, a well-stocked library. It was to this place that Sir Charles would repair as soon as he'd discharged his little social duties. The earl had not only invited him to make himself at home there, but had considerately pointed out those parts of the collection in which his guest would have the greatest interest.

It was to this, his favourite refuge, that Alexandra accompanied her father after they returned from the picnic. He was so eager to get back to the old Stuart and Revett volume, *The Antiquities of Athens*, with its beautiful engravings, that he forgot to ask his daughter whether Lord Arden had shown any signs of coming to the point during their stroll.

Spared having to tell her Papa more lies, Alexandra breathed a sigh of relief as she stepped over the threshold. Closing the door behind her, she turned . . . and nearly collided with Mr. Trevelyan.

"Good heavens, I didn't know you were there. How quietly you come upon one." Like a cat, she thought. Backing away, she found herself flat up against the door.

He only stared at her in a considering sort of way that made her acutely uncomfortable. She took a step to the side to put a little distance between them. He copied her motion.

"Very funny," she muttered. "Now if you'd please get out of the way."

"And if I don't please?" His voice was soft and beckoning, and he was close, much too close. But with a grandfather clock a few inches away on one side, and a rather heavy table on the other, she couldn't continue to sidle against the wall. Besides, it wasn't dignified. She was about to push past him when his hands abruptly came to rest upon the wall on either side of her, blocking her escape. He was so very close that she could feel his breath on her face. Directly in her line of vision was his mouth. Feeling her cheeks grow exceedingly warm, she dropped her eyes to his neckcloth.

"Stop it!" she hissed.

He only bent closer, his mouth inches from hers. "Or what, my love? You'll scream for your Papa? I don't think so." His lips brushed hers softly, and her own parted helplessly. She found herself crushed between him and the wall—which was fortunate, for her knees immediately buckled, and it was most unlikely she could have stood up under her own power.

Even as he kissed her he knew it was exactly the wrong thing to do. He told himself, as he tasted her soft, sweet lips, that he must leave her—immediately. Then he felt her hands creep up to his chest, as though she'd push him away. Except that she didn't. Her hands rested there a moment—she must feel his heart hammering—before proceeding, hesitantly, up to his neck. The light touch upon his skin sent a tiny, delicious chill running down his spine to the very tips of his toes.

He shivered slightly and crushed her close to him, as he'd wanted to do all these long weeks. In a moment, he promised himself, he'd stop. At any rate, she'd *make* him stop, but she only gave a faint, surprised gasp, and melted against him. His mind grew very hazy, as though a thick fog was enveloping his brain. All that remained was sensation: her skin was like silk,

120

and the curves of her lithe body molded naturally to his own, as though she were a part of him long missing.

His lips brushed her ear, then moved to tickle the nape of her neck with soft kisses that made her tremble, but still she made no struggle. When his tongue invaded her mouth, her fingers only pressed his shoulders more tightly, as though she felt the same hunger he did. The fog thickened. It was such a warm, inviting sort of fog, and he was such a lazy, unreliable vessel that he gave himself up for lost, content to drown where he was because she was in his arms, and that was all that mattered.

The lost Trevelyan vessel might have drifted onto treacherous waters, but something awakened him to his peril. At the very edge of his consciousness, a warning bell seemed to go off. Not struggling. And where were they? In a hallway. A hallway!

He drew a ragged breath. "Alexandra, you must make me stop."

She pulled back from him a little to gaze into his eyes. In the next instant, she was smiling in the most provocative way, as her hands dropped to his coat, which she methodically began to unbutton.

"Alexandra," he gasped. "Stop it!"

She looked up at him innocently. "Or what? You'll scream for Papa? I don't think so."

Though he felt like screaming, he didn't. Instead, his hand closed firmly over hers. Damn! What on earth was wrong with him? He endeavoured to summon up some dignity. "What do you think you're doing, you wicked, wretched girl?"

She looked at his rumpled cravat and at his creased shirt and at his unbuttoned coat and answered, "Isn't that what I was supposed to do?"

"Good God, no—oh, damn it all—" He pulled her along, down the hallway and into the music room. When he'd shut the door, he burst out—though he kept his voice low—"Are you mad? In the *hall?* Where the servants—"

"Well, you seemed to think it all right—"

"It is not all right to undress me in public. Who ever

taught you such things? Don't tell me that sneaking Farrington—''

"No," she answered indignantly. "Nobody taught me. I
deduced it. From the general to the specific, you know.''

"From the what?"

The words made him feel warm, dangerously warm, again.
Her hand was still in his, and he wanted that slender, provocative body close again. Her curls, in great disorder now,
fell about her face, and he wanted, so much, to disorder her
a great deal more. That was insane. No, it wasn't. He was
lost, quite lost, and there was no point pretending that anything else—his freedom, the pleasures he'd fantasised about
for three years—mattered. There was no peace for him without her. But what could he say? What would she believe,
knowing him as she did?

While he struggled to collect his scattered wits, she'd evidently gathered hers. She was replying, and quite composedly, too, "Well, there you were, you know, set on amusing
yourself with me again. So I thought I'd use the opportunity.''

"Use the opportunity?" he echoed stupidly, wondering at
the icy chill that suddenly replaced all that cozy warmth.

"Why, yes. For practise." Smoothly she disengaged her
hand from his. She smiled—the same pitying smile she'd
given him a few days ago, when they'd put on that performance for her father. "For my husband," she explained.
Then she laughed . . . and left him.

As he stared after her at the empty doorway, a great clat-
tering started up in his brain. She could not mean, really—
not another man tasting those kisses, touching her. No, it
was impossible. It was wicked, and *cruel*. Practising for
her husband—on *him*—he'd kill her. No, he'd teach her a
lesson she wouldn't soon forget—but there was Randolph,
and Arden, and a thousand other men. She couldn't be so
stupid, to throw herself away—and yet she knew him too
well—amusing himself. But he wasn't. He *wasn't*. Through
it all, as his brain leapt from one half notion to the next, he
could still feel her touch, still feel the aching need that

122

had gripped him as her fingers tugged at the buttons of his coat.

He stood there, frozen, for what seemed like hours, his mind churning. Then, drawing a deep breath to steady himself, he rebuttoned his coat and left the room.

13

Alexandra was crouched down outside the library door when she heard footsteps. Hastily she rose, preparing a plausible explanation for crawling about on the carpet. Oh, Lord. It was him, again. Her pulse began to race. In answer to his quizzical look, she said, "I was looking for my hairpins."

He stared at her tousled curls, then down at the carpet and back at her hair. "I'll help you," he said quietly.

"No—"

But he'd already bent to search and was quickly gathering the stray pins. "It wouldn't do for the servants to find them." He straightened and dropped them into her outstretched palm.

"I'm leaving," he said.

"Oh."

"To London."

"Well."

"It's what I meant to tell you before—" He nodded towards her hand, in which the pins were clutched.

She hardly noticed that they were digging into her flesh, for she felt ill suddenly, and frightened. Going away . . . abandoning her . . . to Will. Oh, why hadn't she kept her spiteful mouth shut? Why had she tried to best him at his own game? That disgraceful scene a few minutes ago had been as much her fault as his. She should never have let it go so far—should have stopped it at the outset. But he had only to touch her, and she went to him, like one mesmerised. It was better this way, she told herself, fighting down the panic. Better he should go away.

"I see. Well, then, good-bye, Mr. Trevelyan."

"You might at least bid me to the devil by my given name, and it isn't Randolph."

She shifted the hairpins from her right hand to her left and put out the empty hand. "Good-bye, Basil."

Instead of shaking her hand, he raised it to his lips and dropped a kiss on her palm. "Good-bye, Miss Ashmore," he whispered. Then he was gone.

Mr. Trevelyan for once was as good as his word. He left Hartleigh Hall a little before dinnertime, despite his family's strenuous objections to his travelling at night. Alexandra did not raise any objections, having gone to her room with a headache.

It must have been an excessively painful one, because she wept half the night and only fell asleep when she was too tired to sob any more. The few hours' rest was sufficient, apparently, for no sooner did she open her eyes the next morning than her tears fell afresh. This would never do, she scolded herself. It was stupid to weep over him. She had, it appeared, fallen in love with him, as had, she was sure, hundreds of other women. She should, therefore, be thankful she hadn't got into worse trouble. If they'd been in a more private place yesterday, he might easily have seduced her. She had absolutely no self-control when it came to him, and she could hardly trust him to take care what he did.

Nor could she expect, if he did ruin her, that he'd marry her willingly, or attempt to change his behaviour thereafter. Because she did love him, his inevitable infidelities would humiliate and grieve her all the rest of her life. Will's infidelities, on the other hand, she could look upon with equanimity: his mistresses would only relieve her of his company.

Having disposed of matters of the heart to her morose and cynical satisfaction, she went on to matters of business, i.e., Papa's radically increased debt. She'd been reluctant to confide the news to her godmother. It had troubled her when Aunt Clem tried to pay George Burnham before—and look how it had infuriated Papa. Besides, no one should pay it. The amount was outrageous. Papa couldn't possibly have run up such a sum unless he kept a dozen mistresses and spent the remainder of his time in gambling halls. Someone should investigate. But if it were Aunt Clem, Papa was bound to resent the meddling in his affairs, take three temper fits at once, and hustle his daughter off to Yorkshire before she could blink.

The more she thought of it, the more obvious it became that the only person who could investigate without enraging Papa was her future husband. The Duke of Thorne's lawyers would insist on it, anyhow, and George Burnham would probably find himself swatted down like a pesky fly. Well, then. That was that.

Having mentally settled all that needed to be settled, Miss Ashmore gave up thinking for the duration. She passed through the first day of Basil's absence like an automaton, saying and doing what she was supposed to, without really knowing or caring what it was.

The next day was much the same. She agreed to drive with Lord Arden and let him say whatever it was he had to say without contributing any brilliant insights of her own. *He* must have got a brilliant insight though, for they'd not been driving twenty minutes when he stopped the horses, preparatory to giving physical expression to what was on his mind.

This did rouse her from her trance. As she looked up into his face, now bent so close to hers, everything within her recoiled. She did not want him to touch her—not now, not yet. Another embrace was too fresh in her memory. She turned away, covered her face with her hands, and began to weep.

Now Miss Ashmore was not, in the normal way of things, a watering pot, but philosophy had deserted her for the moment. Being miserable and not a little frantic, she found the tears came easily. She wept copiously, and nothing his alarmed lordship could say or do would calm her. Ten anguished minutes passed before she was finally persuaded to confide her trouble. By then, she'd made up her mind. Between hiccoughs, she told him what she'd learned, and what she suspected, and why she was afraid to confide the matter even to her godmother.

He looked puzzled at first, but in a very little while his

face brightened into an abominably smug expression. "Why, you poor child. Is that all? You should have told me of this sooner. No wonder you've seemed so distracted the past few days."

Relieved to find that it was only a trifling matter of money that troubled her so, the marquess became transformed. He patted her hand in an indulgent, husbandly sort of way, dabbed lovingly at her tear-streaked face with his handkerchief, and went on to reassure her. It was the merest nothing, he told her. The Duke of Thorne's man of business would see about the details. They must think only of their future happiness.

While this was more or less what she'd hoped for, his personality change was not. Before he'd been the adoring suitor, striving to win her affection. Now he had conquered. To his mind, everything was settled. She was his. She'd confided in him—and hadn't she told him she'd confided in no one else? Wasn't he one of the few men in creation to whom a debt like Papa's was a mere trifle? The cocksure look on his face made her want to slap him. Still, there was something to be thankful for: he was too caught up in his triumph to remember to do more than squeeze her hand.

"Elope?" Alexandra repeated incredulously.

"Yes. It's the only way, don't you see?"

He'd drawn her and Jess out to walk in the shrubbery the following afternoon. After summarily ordering his sister to make herself scarce, he'd come right to the point. Now, her insides churning, Alexandra stared stupidly at him. She hardly noticed that he'd taken both her hands in his, because that was only a minor detail of this nightmare. Telling herself she must wake up soon, she listened to him explain his Perfect Solution to their difficulties.

He'd decided that it was too risky to go about marrying in the normal, straightforward way. "An investigation will take time, and we can't risk it until after we're wed. Don't you see? I still can't go to your father and ask his consent, because he's obliged as a gentleman to refuse. As you said, it's a debt of honour to him. Moreover—if you'll excuse my saying so—he has struck me as being quite as obstinate as my own Respected Parent. If he denies me on the grounds of his obligation to Burnham, and I hint that Burnham is a bounder—well, what do *you* think will be the result?" He didn't wait to hear what she thought, only went on to reiterate that they must take matters into their own hands.

She'd brought it all on herself. If she'd let him speak to Papa in the proper way, in the first place, she might have had a great Society wedding, and crowds of people about. Now she must run away with him to Scotland, putting herself completely in his hands.

"B-but, my lord. You don't consider your family in this. To-to run off with the daughter of a mere baronet—and a penniless and eccentric one at that. They're bound to feel you've disgraced them—and they know nothing of me."

"Your father's family is an old and respected one. Your Mama was the grandniece of an earl. It's hardly as though I were running off with an opera dancer. Why do you torment me with these matters? Isn't it enough that I'm driven half-wild with fear that your father will any minute carry you away to Yorkshire? Do you realise that I dare not speak to him, for fear—*fear*, Alexandra—that it will drive him to do so?"

To expect the future Duke of Thorne to live in fear of anything was to expect the planets to hurtle out of their courses in the heavens. To expect him to care anything what his relatives thought (if, that is, they had the effrontery to think differently than he did) was to expect the sun to rise in the west or Great Britain to sink into the sea. In short, it was futile to argue with him.

There being nothing to say, she was silent, listening and nodding her head while fervently wishing she had thrown herself over a ledge in Gjirokastra when she'd had the chance.

They'd elope the evening of Lady Dessing's birthday gala, three nights hence. Alexandra would not attend, because of one of her headaches. It was unlikely, he condescended to point out, they'd call in a physician for that; equally important, the household would leave her in peace.

As soon as the others left, she'd escape from the house, dressed in clothes he'd provide. With the servants belowstairs

128

enjoying their leisure, she needn't fear detection. He'd slip away from the party to meet her, and they'd travel in disguise, using public conveyance for the first half of the journey. As to accommodations, as he tactfully put it, they'd travel as brother and sister.

Well, at least he didn't intend to deflower her before the wedding night. The technicality of marrying a virgin did, apparently, count with him—after all, the future Duke of Thorne was rather like a monarch, wasn't he? And like a monarch, he required from her only obedience. He would see to everything else.

14

Everything, to her regret, went as smoothly as Lord Arden had claimed it would, so that now—while the others were miles away, dancing at Lady Dessing's gala—Alexandra and the marquess were dining together in the Blue Swan coaching inn's only private parlour.

More strictly speaking, Alexandra was listlessly pushing her food around in circles on her plate. Interpreting her silence as prenuptial nerves, her considerate companion kept up an ongoing monologue between mouthfuls. The mail coach was due to arrive in an hour, he told her, and they had best fortify themselves. Given the eccentricities of public conveyance, the next few hours would be uncomfortable, but after that they'd travel in their own carriage. Though only a rented vehicle, it was, he assured her, comfortably sprung.

There was a light tap on the door, followed by the waiter. He was a surly fellow, with a great scarf wrapped about his head—for the toothache, he sulkily claimed—so that one could see little of his face but his nose. That was smudged with soot. He walked with a limp and with his head sunk to one side, as though he were in the habit of ducking, Alexandra thought with pity, the slings and arrows Life hurled at him. Will, having never been a victim of Life's cruel artillery, felt no such compassion. Majestically he gestured to the fellow to put the bottle down: "Mr. Fairstairs," as the marquess had chosen to style himself, would pour his own. Not that she could blame him. The waiter's hands were none too clean or too steady. Too bad, she reflected idly. Well-shaped and long-fingered, they might have been graceful hands, had Providence seen fit to give him the marquess's advantages.

Because Alexandra was greatly tempted to drink herself into insensibility, she confined herself to water. She took a sip, noted it was as bad as everything else, and forgot all about the waiter's existence.

Will hadn't forgotten, however. The door had hardly shut behind the fellow when Lord Arden wondered aloud what the landlord was thinking of to hire such a filthy, disgusting creature. He became very apologetic then about subjecting his Beloved to this shabby place. He said he hadn't expected it to be quite so bad, and he seemed to take it as a personal affront.

Well, of course. He was a Farrington, and the rest of God's creatures—with the possible exception of the Royal Family—were put on this earth for his comfort. Including herself. She'd come to suspect that the real reason he'd insisted on eloping was nothing more than the impatience of a spoiled, overgrown boy. What he wanted he wanted now, and without a lot of bother.

Not that he minded a little costume drama. The clerk's garb, for instance, that clashed ridiculously with his aristocratic mien. As she stopped glowering at her plate a moment to glance at him, Alexandra much doubted whether the landlord had been taken in. He'd "Yes, sir'd" and "If you please, sir'd" the marquess to death from the moment they'd stepped through the door. The whole business was absurd. They might have travelled in comfort in their own clothes. A few coins dropped here and there would have stilled eager tongues. But no, Will must make a whole production of it. It was obvious he thought it all most dashing and romantic.

Actually, it would have been romantic if he were someone else. If that were only another face across the table, and if those eyes had been amber instead of grey. If that voice droning on and on were a teasing mixture of ingenuousness and irony. But it was stupid to think of that, to think of *him*, when that only made her heart ache. She was wretched enough as it was. From the moment Will had proposed his scheme, it had never occurred to him to consult her wishes in anything.

Not that she had any wishes any more—except that the coach would overturn along the way, and she be crushed to death beneath it.

Which was mere histrionic self-indulgence. After all, she wasn't running off with an ogre. He was handsome, wasn't he? And immensely rich and important. So what if he was spoiled and selfish. Weren't most of his peers? She was dutifully removing the scowl from her face and struggling to replace it with an affectionate smile when the marquess's voice mumbled off into silence. Looking up, she discovered to her amazement that Lord Arden's head had slumped to his shoulder and he was sinking in his chair.

Good grief! Was the man drunk? Yet he'd consumed only two glasses of wine with his meal, and he'd seemed cold sober when he'd come for her. Bewildered, she sat staring helplessly at her unconscious husband-to-be and frantically wracked her sluggish brains. What on earth should she do?

"What a stimulating dinner companion you've got to be, Alexandra. You've talked the poor man unconscious."

She sprang from her chair to turn towards the door, whence the voice had come, then only stood there, frozen. It was a nightmare. She'd been dreaming all this time.

"Or have you poisoned him at last, my love?" Basil asked as he sauntered over to have a look at the comatose marquess.

"What—what are you doing here?" she gasped.

"Rescuing you, my darling. As I always do. Dear me." His face assumed a theatrical expression of horror as he lifted Lord Arden's limp wrist then let it drop back onto the table. "I hope you haven't killed him. It'll be a job to keep you from swinging for it, lovely as you are, and sympathetic as the judge is sure to be when you tell him how Will had bored you past all endurance. But a peer of the realm, my dear. Or peer-to-be, actually. Shocking."

His wit, in this case, was entirely wasted. The young lady scarcely heard a word of it, being in the process, for the first time in her twenty-four years, of fainting dead away.

Though she was inexperienced in the business, Basil, fortunately, was not. He caught her up in his arms before she sank to the floor and carried her out of the shabby parlour.

"Just as I suspected," he told the innkeeper, who was hovering anxiously a little distance from the door. "It is my sister. There'll be a reward for you, my good sir. Your sharp eye has helped preserve an innocent female from disgrace. Now do you keep that eye on that villain there while I restore this poor, foolish child to her senses."

She felt something damp at her forehead, opened her eyes, then closed them again. Surely she was dreaming, had dreamt everything, and must be still lying in her comfortable bed at Hartleigh Hall. She could not be in this dingy room, and that could not be Basil sitting on the edge of the lumpy mattress, bending over her.

"Come now, Alexandra. Time to rejoin the living."

It *was* something damp—a towel—and it was Basil and not a dream. She opened her eyes again.

"That's better. What a turn you gave me. I never took you to be the swooning type. But then, I never knew you were another Lucrezia Borgia either."

"Good heavens!" She pulled herself up to a sitting position. "Surely he isn't dead—"

"No, he isn't, unfortunately. I gave him only enough medicine for a long sleep—not an eternal one. Though the temptation was strong enough," he added with a twisted little smile.

"You *drugged* him?"

"It was the best I could do on the spur of the moment. Really, dear, I was never so shocked in my life—to see you enter this shabby place, dressed as—well, I could hardly tell what. The vicar's daughter, perhaps? Running off with her Papa's clerk? Was that it? Yet I'd never before heard a humble clerk order an innkeeper about in that imperious way. How fortunate for you I was here, my love. The story would have been all over the county in a matter of hours and sure to take all the shine out of Lady Dessing's birthday fête."

Shock was rapidly giving way to vexation. How could he chatter on so calmly—and Lord Arden lying somewhere unconscious. "What," she very nearly shrieked, "are you doing here?"

133

"Rescuing you, as I said."

"I didn't ask to be rescued."

"Didn't you? Yet I could have sworn when I saw you enter that you looked precisely as Marie Antoinette must have done when they led her to the guillotine."

"Never mind how I looked. Why are you here? You're supposed to be in London."

"Yes, I am. I'm such an unreliable fellow, you know. Never where I should be, doing what I should be." He still had the towel and was absently wrapping it around one hand, then disarranging it, then arranging it again as he spoke.

Dazedly she stared at the towel and at the hands playing with it. Light dawned. "It was you. *You* were the waiter," she cried accusingly.

"Yes, I was." His smile this time was so sweet and tender that her heart skipped a beat. "I couldn't, after all, trust Mine Host to so delicate a business, could I? Though he's most observant—calling my attention to the rum pair deigning to honour him with their patronage. I suspect he wants the subtle touch."

"But why? Why?" Even as she asked, she knew, or thought she knew, for one dizzying instant. But he looked away quickly, and she told herself she was overwrought and imagining things.

"Because the pair of you were about to spoil everything after I've been running myself ragged the past five days to make everything perfect." He tossed the towel onto a chair. "Now, though it complicates everything dreadfully, I'll have to take you both back. Did anyone see you on the road?"

"I don't know—but what are you saying? I can't go back now. Lord Arden and I—"

"Yes, my love. You were eloping, which is perfectly absurd."

"It isn't," she protested. "You don't know—"

"I know you're not going to Scotland with Will, as he can't go anywhere under his own power for the next several hours. I'm taking the two of you back. Now," he went on, consulting his pocket watch, "there are bound to be dilatory stragglers headed for Netherstone, so we'll have to keep off the main road. Fortunately, I know a shortcut—but then, so does half the world. Still, we can risk that if . . ." He nodded to himself. "Yes. That should do."

He got up from the bed and walked to a corner of the room, where he began rummaging in some bundles.

While he was thus engaged, she found her tongue again and set up a steady stream of objection, though, as he hadn't yet confided his plan, she wasn't sure what exactly she was objecting to. Nonetheless, she explained, albeit incoherently, about the increase in Papa's debt and how she'd had to confide in Will and how, if she didn't elope with the marquess, that left Randolph and his insufferable family. She might as well have saved her breath.

"Yes, dear," he patiently agreed. "I daresay it may be as you claim. If you'd only listened to me in the first place, you wouldn't be in such a predicament."

"L-listened to y-you?" she sputtered indignantly.

"Didn't I say I'd help you?"

"And then turned round and left for London," was the scornful rejoinder.

"Did you think I'd abandoned you, darling?" He approached the bed. In his hands was a pile of clothing which she barely looked at, being mesmerised by the sweet, fond look he bent upon her. Good grief—a few minutes alone with him and her mind turned completely to mush.

"I am not your darling," she snapped, rather savagely.

"As you like. Here." He dropped the garments into her lap. "Get into those."

She glared down at the little heap, and then blinked as she recognised what it was: his clothes. What on earth was he about? "Why?" she demanded. "Why must I go back?"

"Because I said so. Because you haven't any choice. Because anything you like, only do hurry up. We've got some hard riding ahead if you're to be back before the family is."

"I am not," she announced, folding her arms across her bosom in a very determined way, though, actually, it was to conceal its heaving, "going anywhere until I hear an explanation. It was bad enough having Will order me about all this

135

time, when at least I knew why. But you appear out of no-where and start dictating—"

"Darling, I'm only trying to help you," he said, sooth-ingly, sitting down upon the bed again. "There isn't time to explain everything. Can't you just trust me this once?"

"*Trust* you?" Her voice dripped sarcasm. "You've only just drugged the future Duke of Thorne. Not to mention the fact that you've never behaved properly in all the time I've known you. Or done anything but tease and mock and lie. Trust you, indeed. I don't know why," she went on, angrily, "I ask you to explain, when you're bound to lie about that as well."

"I have, I agree, lied to everyone else on the whole blessed planet. But, Alexandra, to you I've hardly lied at all. Why do you scold so?"

He looked so genuinely baffled that she began to wonder why herself. Oh, what was the use, anyhow? She dropped her gaze to her hands. "I'm tired," she said. "I'm tired and my head is spinning, and nothing makes sense. Now you tell me I must go back. Oh, Basil, how could you?"

"How could I what?"

"You left me," she blurted out. "You left me and let me think you were gone for good—" She stopped short, realising that she was on the brink of betraying herself.

"I'm sorry, my love. I shouldn't have." He took her hand in his. "But does it matter to you what I do?"

"No," she lied, snatching her hand away.

"No, of course it doesn't. It's too much to hope. No reason on earth you should trust me, is there?"

She shook her head.

"Not even when I'm only hours away from solving the Burnham problem once and for all?"

She looked up at him, suspicious still, though hope flut-tered faintly within her.

"Not even," he continued softly, "if I say I do it all for you because it matters to me what becomes of you?"

She shook her head again automatically.

He went on more lightly, "No, I suppose there's no help-ing *that*—not now, at least. Well, then, here is the situation.

136

We must get you and Will back for a hundred reasons I can't go into now. Except that I will have laboured in vain if you run off with him. I did understand—correct me if I'm wrong—you weren't really keen on doing so.''

It was useless to pretend otherwise. "I wasn't," she admitted. "I'm not."

"Then won't you please do as I ask? I can give you about half an hour to change while I deal with the innkeeper and see about horses. I promise you, it means the end of the Burnham business—without alternative fiancés and husbands. I give you my word, my love.''

Well, she hadn't any choice, had she, whatever his word was worth? Will was useless at present. And she could hardly go off by herself, even if she had anywhere to go. She acquiesced.

"Oh, you are wonderful." He dropped a light kiss on the top of her head, then left the room.

She stared at the door for a moment, her hand creeping up to touch the spot where his lips had been. Of everything that baffled her—how he came to be here, why he'd drugged Will, what this mysterious plan was to solve the Burnham problem—it was this that puzzled her most. All the usual endearments, the usual mix of melodrama and farce . . . then one small, affectionate gesture to upset all her conclusions.

It recalled that afternoon they'd ridden together, when he'd put aside his practised arts for a while and treated her like a friend. He'd promised to help her then. But if he'd meant it, why in heaven's name had he gone off without a word of explanation, letting her think he'd gone out of her life for good?

"Oh, Basil," she murmured to the empty room, "it's always 'why' with you."

The room making no suitable reply, she shook her head and turned to the business at hand.

It was a disconcerting and troublesome business. For one, there seemed to be at least nine thousand fastenings to unfasten before she could get out of her dress. For another, his clothes didn't fit. The shirt was too big, and his trousers, which were indecently snug about her hips, gaped even more

137

indecently at the waist. Frenziedly, she unbuttoned the trouser flap and stuffed her shawl inside, as padding. It felt stupid, and looked stupider, but at least it helped disguise her unmasculine curves. Having no idea how to deal with the neckcloth and afraid to crumple it, she ignored it, and jerked on waistcoat and coat. Apparently, since he'd not supplied her with his footwear, her own half-boots would do.

It was the oddest feeling to be wearing his clothes. Though they were fresh and clean, something of him pervaded them—something that made her feel uncomfortably warm and flustered. Nervously she pulled and tucked and pushed at the garments. Then, when she was certain nothing more could be done to improve her appearance, she sat down on the edge of the bed and waited.

In a few minutes there was a light tap on the door and Basil's voice asking if she were decent.

"If you can call it that," she answered, turning pink. She turned pinker still when he entered the room and, after studying her for a moment, broke into a smile.

"You needn't laugh," she snapped. "You could hardly expect a perfect fit—and I hadn't a valet to help me."

"I would have been thrilled to death to valet you, my dear, if you'd only asked. Now, if you'll pin your hair up, I shall tie your cravat. In that at least you shall not be faulted."

She did as he asked. But when he stood so close to wrap the linen about her neck, her knees grew shaky and weak, and her heart promptly commenced knocking in concert.

He was, she thought, an unconscionably long time about it. When, finally, she began to express impatience, he retorted that it was no simple business when the cloth was about his own neck; to have to work *backwards* was a feat of inexpressible difficulty.

"And it doesn't help—" But he thought better of it and held his tongue.

No, it didn't help at all that Alexandra in trousers—in *his* trousers—was provocation beyond all endurance. His hands were unsteady. They wanted to be everywhere else but at this dratted piece of linen. Her padding only invited removal, and the ill-fitting coat . . . oh, that was even worse. To look at it was to imagine her wearing nothing but. Being cursed with a fertile imagination, he was plagued with more disconcerting visions still, with the result that he didn't dare move a muscle beyond those required to tie the cravat, for fear he'd lose all control, drag her to the bed, and ravish her.

Finally, the job he'd been a fool to undertake was done, and he could step away from her. "There," he said, turning away. "You'll do. Just put on your—my—hat, and let's get out of here."

With the innkeeper's assistance, Will was carried out and flung unceremoniously over Basil's mount. After a brief, whispered conversation and the clinking of coins, Basil leapt up behind the marquess's prostrate form.

"It's going to be deuced uncomfortable," he told his companion. "Both the horse and I had much rather it was you. But leading another beast would only slow us more. Ah, well." He gave a forlorn sigh, and they were on their way.

They reached Hartleigh Hall a little before midnight and rode quietly round to the servants' entrance.

"Now do you go on ahead," he whispered. "My valet was supposed to leave the door unlatched—"

"You've been here already?"

"No, but I sent Rogers. You must slip upstairs and go to my room. He'll be waiting. Tell him there's been a slight change in plans and that he's to come down to me."

"You want me to go to him looking like this?"

"My dear, Rogers cannot be shocked. It's out of the question. Besides, he's the most close-mouthed fellow in creation. And I must have his help in getting Will dressed and back to the party. Come." He strode over to help her down from her mount.

If he took the opportunity to hold her a little closer than was absolutely necessary for rather longer than was absolutely necessary, and if his lips touched hers before he let her go, it must be blamed on the excitement of the moment. As must, of course, Miss Ashmore's delay in letting go of *him*. In any case, there was a brief embrace, at the conclusion of which Mr. Trevelyan gave it as his opinion that she'd better go in quickly. She retorted that it was he who kept her back, which led to another, longer embrace and Mr. Trevelyan's husky observation that if she didn't go in now he couldn't answer for the consequences.

"Then let go of me," she snapped with rather more ferocity than circumstances required, for he was not holding her so very tightly as all that, and she had suffered two kisses without giving any sort of battle.

At any rate, he did let go, and she fled, her face blazing with shame. She got upstairs undetected, found Rogers—who, as promised, never turned a hair at seeing her in his master's coat and trousers—and communicated her message. Then, red-faced again, she crept on to her own room, shut the door, and fell, shaking, onto the bed.

15

Emmy clucked with sympathy as she placed on her mistress's lap the tray containing a steaming cup of coffee. "Oh, Miss, is it still bad then? You look as if you never slept a wink—and it's no wonder, such a to-do as we had last night."

Lifting the cup with two trembling hands, Alexandra informed her abigail that she'd never heard a thing, having slept like the very dead she was sure. That was true enough.

Basil had come to her door last night just as she was preparing to climb into bed. Yanking her dressing gown tightly about her, she'd gone to answer the knock. With no thought of decorum, he'd pushed the door open and strolled in as assuredly as though he'd dropped into his own club. He'd looked so elegant and handsome—every hair in place, his evening costume perfectly pressed and spotless—that she'd begun to think she'd imagined the whole evening's adventure.

It was only after his eyes raked her insufficiently clad form and he'd made a rather indecorous proposal that she'd collected her wits and seized the washbasin as a weapon. After declaring her cruel and heartless, he'd said he'd only come to take his clothes back and to tell her she must pretend she'd never left her room that night—no matter what Will might be foolish enough to say when he recovered.

Basil had gone on to explain that he must be away for a few days, but he begged her to trust him in the meantime. "No one," he'd promised, "is going to drag you off to Yorkshire. So there's no need to fall in with any more of his lordship's schemes. Is that clear?" It wasn't clear, and she didn't like taking orders, but she'd nodded.

He'd then asked for a good-night kiss. Being threatened with the washbasin instead, he'd taken mournful leave of her, once more remarking on her want of feeling.

After he'd gone, she'd taken the laudanum her hostess had so thoughtfully provided earlier for her headache. It would have been impossible to sleep otherwise. She had, therefore, slept very soundly and never heard the others return. She did not mind that her tongue, at the moment, was thick and unpleasant-tasting in her mouth, or that her head felt as though it were in a vise. She'd had blessed oblivion for a few hours at least.

Emmy seemed about to burst with suppressed excitement.

"A to-do?" Alexandra asked, with admirable composure. "What sort of to-do?"

"Oh, Miss, every sort of thing. Mr. Burnham is gone off, no one knows where. His lordship—Lord Arden, that is—was carried up to his room, and I don't know what else. We were all at sixes and sevens and no one in their beds until sunup at least. That was only the ladies, as the gents was down in the library talking the longest time after."

As she took in her mistress's white, drawn face, Emmy was stricken with guilt, and began berating herself for upsetting the poor lady when it was plain she was still ill. She plumped up the pillows, straightened the coverlet, and left the room, still muttering at herself.

It was several hours before Alexandra heard the full story, as the rest of the family and guests remained in their beds until well into the afternoon. She dressed herself but, not caring to risk a confrontation with Lord Arden, kept to her room and tried to focus on Mr. Richardson's *Clarissa*. Though she'd read the old novel years ago in defiance of her governess, and though the interminable epistles did tax her patience dreadfully, Alexandra was determined to read the story through, "for the sentiment," as Dr. Johnson had recommended.

She would have preferred, certainly, that Lovelace did not so very much remind her of Mr. Trevelyan, and that Clarissa's parental difficulties did not make her own pale into insignificance. Nevertheless, she read on doggedly until Aunt Clem appeared to give her a full accounting of the night's events.

Lady Bertram told the tale in her usual blunt way. That rattle of a nephew of hers had put in a surprise appearance just as the party was going in to supper. He'd treated them all to some cockamamie tale about his horse stumbling into a ditch and the consequent several hours' delay which had prevented his arriving at Hartleigh Hall in time to accompany them to the gala.

Her ladyship communicated her private opinion that it was no four-footed creature that had delayed him but a barmaid, for he wore an insufferable cock-of-the-walk air that made his aunt want to slap him senseless.

At any rate, he'd exhausted himself during supper and a couple of sets after, cutting a swathe through all the debutante hearts in the vicinity. He'd gone out to the terrace for a breath of air. There he'd come upon Will who was sprawled out, unconscious, on one of the long stone benches.

"I'd wondered where he'd got to," her ladyship muttered. "Hadn't seen him for hours. Well, evidently he'd been fully occupied, drinking himself into stupefaction."

Lord Arden was bundled off to an unoccupied parlour while the festivities continued into the small hours of the morning. When it was time to depart, the servants carried him out to the carriage. Basil, who'd been supervising this procedure, was the one to find the note addressed to Sir Charles. It was lying on the seat of the vehicle in which the baronet had ridden to the gala.

At this point in the narrative, the countess's patrician features broke into a grin of unholy glee. "What do you think, my dear? Your Papa's scholarly companion—the steadiest chap in the world, according to Charles—has run away. Run away!"

"Good heavens," said Alexandra, rather faintly.

It was true. Mr. Burnham had, according to his note, decided to take control of his own life for once. Though he'd worded it diplomatically enough, it was plain—to Aunt Clem at least—why he'd gone.

"Is it not astonishing, my dear? The dutiful boy blankly refuses to marry you."

"Yes, it is astonishing, Aunt Clem. Randolph Burnham running away. Randolph flouting his Papa's commands. I can scarcely credit it," said the young lady. Her face was pale, but her voice was steady enough.

"Well, credit it, my dear. Even your father, shocked as he was, was forced to believe his own eyes. I am sure that if he had not feared for Randolph's safety—for, in truth, as Basil said, the young man's an innocent lamb and might easily stumble into difficulties, left to himself—well, if that were not his main concern, he'd have shrugged it off soon enough. At any rate, Basil offered to go look for Mr. Burnham to reassure us all that the young man was safe. Obliging fellow, my nephew, isn't he?"

Miss Ashmore nodded.

"But I'll tell you, my dear, your father was not so very distressed by that note—though of course he grumbled and carried on. I was most pleased, as you can imagine. For you see what this means. Now, at last, you may have a proper Season."

Miss Ashmore must not have appeared as delighted at this prospect as the countess had expected, for her ladyship went on reassuringly, "Well, of course you must, Alexandra. Will's behaviour last night does make one wonder whether he's settled and mature enough to make an acceptable husband. I recognise, of course, that the gentlemen must indulge, but it is very bad form to show the extent of the indulgence. A man who cannot hold his liquor had better not drink it in the first place. Most especially not when he is endeavouring to win the esteem of a gently bred woman."

In the event the implications of this breach of etiquette had not already occurred to his lordship, his sister was in the process of bringing the matter forcibly—and at altogether unnecessary volume, he thought—to his attention. She stood over his bed of pain delivering a scathing lecture of nearly an hour's duration. This he was forced to endure in relative silence, having learned at the outset that no one knew anything of the aborted elopement. All assumed that Miss Ashmore had been sleeping innocently in her own bed the entire night.

When his sister—with the parting declaration that she fervently hoped Miss Ashmore would give him his *congé*—finally took herself off, Lord Arden considered the facts as he had them. It was not easy or pleasant to do so. His head felt as though his horse had been dancing upon it, and twice he had to abandon his meditations in order to retch into the chamber pot. Nonetheless, sick as he was, he saw plainly enough the fine hand of Basil Trevelyan in this business. Trev's sudden appearance so late at the gala. Trev finding him on the terrace.

Damn the intriguing, interfering devil! He'd arranged matters very neatly, very neatly indeed. The marquess could hardly accuse him openly without admitting his own guilty secret—and if he did, he must implicate Miss Ashmore. His hands were tied. After his allegedly low behaviour of last night, he must count himself lucky if allowed within fifty miles of the young lady. And, for the moment at least, there wasn't one blessed thing he could do about it.

"Basil?" Lord Hartleigh repeated, looking at his guest as though the fellow had just escaped from Bedlam.

He had, it was true, expected an apology. But the gothic accusations that followed made the earl wonder whether the young man should be sent back to bed and a physician called in. In the next few minutes, however, as Will summed up the suspicious circumstances, Lord Hartleigh was forced to admit to himself that this tale was very much in Basil's style.

"You know me, Hartleigh," the marquess pleaded. "When have you ever seen me make such a cake of myself? Why, if you called all Dessing's servants together and questioned them, you'd find I had no more than three glasses of champagne altogether."

"So you suspect Basil somehow slipped something into one of those glasses?"

Though Lord Arden meant other glasses at another place, he nodded grimly.

"Why? What had he to gain by it?"

"I'm not sure," the marquess hedged. "Though I can make a good guess, and I mean to set him straight."

"Well, that's only natural. Though I might add it's also a

great waste of time. Basil can't be set straight. It's physically impossible. Besides, he's gone after Mr. Burnham.''

"Yes, and I'm going after him."

"Now, Will, don't make a mountain out of a molehill. Whatever you suspect—"

"It's no secret that I have been endeavouring to win the affection of the young lady under your roof," Lord Arden interrupted rather pompously. "Last night's events are not calculated to inspire her confidence. I intend to clear this matter up—and with it my character."

In vain did the earl attempt to pour oil on the troubled waters. Will was determined to find Basil and wring the truth out of him. That failing, he would, he hinted darkly, seek other satisfaction.

Well, if he must, he must. Lord Hartleigh shrugged. Basil could take care of himself. Fortunately, not having the remotest idea where his cousin had gone, the earl was spared the disagreeable necessity of offering Lord Arden any other assistance than a reluctant "Godspeed."

My Lord Hartleigh, as was his habit in all things, confided the matter to his wife and was a little surprised to see her intelligent blue eyes lit with vexation.

"Gone after him?" she repeated. "And you let him, Edward? Gracious God! What if he kills him?"

"Of course he won't kill him. They've been playing pranks on each other and vowing revenge since they were boys. Will isn't about to risk disgrace and exile on account of a mere female—regardless how much he thinks he wants her."

"I still don't like it. This whole business has gotten completely out of hand."

"Which is what I predicted in the first place. There's nothing you or I can do now. Except, perhaps, report to your mother—as if she doesn't know already."

"Gone after him?" Lady Deverell repeated, bored past all expression. "How very wearisome in this heat." She returned her attention to the book that lay in her lap.

"Mama!"

"Yes, my love." The viscountess did not look up.

"What are we to do?"

"I suppose," Lady Deverell answered vaguely, apparently preoccupied with the book, "we shall have to dress soon. We are promised to the Osbornes for dinner. How distressing for them. With the three gentlemen gone, the numbers at table will be sadly out. How tiresome for Mrs. Osborne when she goes to so much trouble."

"She won't be tired at all if there's gossip to be gotten out of it," Isabella retorted. "I daresay it's all over the county by now after that scene at Netherstone. Mr. Burnham runs away, and then Basil goes after him for no apparent reason, and then Will after *him*. I wonder who'll be next?" She cast a speaking glance at her mother. In answer she received a world-weary shrug followed by a world-weary sigh. "I suppose," she told her provoking parent, "I had better let Miss Ashmore know of it."

"Why on earth should you do that, my love?"

"Because," was the exasperated reply, "she's bound to remark Will's absence sooner or later, and though you like to tease and make secrets of everything, I do not."

"Why, Bella, my darling, what on earth are you in such a pother about?"

"You, Mama. You know exactly what is going on and you tell me nothing, only sit there like the Sphinx. As though it were the most natural thing in the world that a quiet, studious gentleman like Mr. Burnham should take it into his head to run away. Or that Will Farrington, whose head for spirits is harder even than Papa's, would drink himself insensible. Or that Basil, who makes such a scene about going to London, should turn up at the Dessing's party five days later—and the party half over. Really, Mama, what a ninnyhammer you must think me."

Lady Deverell looked up from her book with a blank little smile. "Why, my dear, now you mention it, it is rather odd, is it not?" She shrugged philosophically. "Still, there's no accounting for the strange starts men will take. Don't trouble yourself about it, dear. Pray do not. I daresay there is a perfectly reasonable explanation for everything."

"Oh, I daresay there is," Isabella muttered, sarcastically. "Oh, indeed, there must be. But I'm not about to find it out from you, am I? No, of course not. Why should you condescend to tell your daughter anything?"

The viscountess only chuckled while Lady Hartleigh, feeling much inclined to shake her aggravating parent until her teeth rattled, told off the Fifth Commandment to herself and exited from the room.

Though she was in the company of her godmother when the news was told, Miss Ashmore could not keep her voice steady. "Gone after Mr. Trevelyan? But why on earth should he do that?"

"Will claims he wasn't foxed at all," Lady Hartleigh explained. "He insists that the little he did drink was adulterated with something else, and that it was Basil did the mixing."

Alexandra was very surprised to hear her godmother explode with laughter, as was Lady Hartleigh. The two stared at the older woman.

What on earth, Alexandra wondered, was so funny? Basil was in danger. He could be dead—even now—at Lord Arden's hands. It was horrible, and Aunt Clem was laughing!

"Now, now Alexandra. Don't take on so. Why, child, you look as if you'd seen a ghost. You too, Isabella. Why, of course it's nothing. They are always at each other, those two. Have been since they were children. Oh, but it is monstrous amusing." Lady Bertram wiped away the tears, chuckling as she did so.

"Yes," Isabella seconded, though with less assurance. "That is what Edward says. So you needn't worry about Will. He'll come to no harm, I'm sure."

It had not occurred to Miss Ashmore to worry about Will, but she didn't mind having this convenient excuse for her too-obvious agitation. She got through the rest of the conversation with as much poise as she could muster, which was little enough, though no one seemed to notice.

She managed to muster a bit more that evening when they dined with the Osbornes and some others, though the visit was ghastly. Those dreadful girls carried on so about the gentlemen's absence and dropped such thinly disguised hints about her devoted marquess's desertion that Alexandra wanted to throttle them. The Mama was even worse with a horrid smile pasted on her fat face as she asked two hundred times where all the young gentlemen had gone, and why and how.

The evening dragged on interminably. Between worrying about Basil, hating the Osbornes, and pretending all the while to be perfectly at her ease, Miss Ashmore was nearly dead with exhaustion when she climbed into the carriage to return to Hartleigh Hall.

Finally she could retreat to her bedroom, where the cumulative effects of not sleeping or eating properly and being consumed by anxiety resulted, quite logically, in hysteria.

The others were not unduly alarmed about either Basil or Will—but then, they didn't know what had actually happened last night. Though, when you came right down to it, neither did she. Obviously, Basil had had a hand in Randolph's disappearance; and given what he'd done to Will, Alexandra was afraid to imagine the criminal means employed in her other fiancé's case. She was afraid that even if Will didn't get to dispense his own justice, others would.

Basil lying cold and lifeless on the ground. Basil dangling from the end of a gibbet. Such visions were not conducive to rest. She lay awake, frightened and sick at heart and, yes, angry as well. It was bad enough to have fallen in love with a libertine. To be besotted with a villain—a criminal—well, that was the very acme and pitch of stupidity.

It cannot be expected that even one of so philosophical a turn as Miss Alexandra Ashmore could wait placidly for the denouement. She wept a great deal more than she liked when she was private, though she was able to behave rationally enough in company. She was used to pretending, after all. The past three months, it seemed, had been spent in one performance after another. It was only in the loneliness of her bedroom that she let herself give way. So it went: a performance by day and misery by night, as the days and nights passed and there was no word.

16

"Mr. Latham, I will not have it!" Mrs. Pamela Latham pushed the startled housemaid back into the hall, shut the door, and advanced upon her husband.

"Have what, my dear?" the gentleman asked mildly, removing his spectacles.

"That horrid creature is back again, and I'm sick of the sight of him. Wherever he goes trouble follows." Mrs. Latham collapsed into a chair, her ample bosom heaving. "Was it not he who came with that wicked man in the first place? Was it not he, back again just a few days ago? Now Marianne is *ruined*. Ruined! And the beast dares to show his face again, smiling and preening himself like a sneaky tomcat."

Her husband, who'd been thoughtfully polishing his spectacles during this tirade, now put them back on again. "But my dear, he's not the tomcat who made off with your daughter. So hadn't you better have him shown in?"

There were ominous signs that his calm assessment of the situation would drive his wife into one of her hysterical fits. Happily, he was able to forestall this dangerous prospect by means of quiet but firm words. In another five minutes, Mrs. Latham was herself again. She haughtily bade Mary show the gentleman in to Mr. Latham's study and then see speedily about some refreshment.

"Well then, Basil, it is just as we thought." Mr. Latham spread out a pile of papers before his guest.

"Actually, it's as Randolph thought. He was certain that Sir Charles's travel accounts had been well received though in a quiet way. My own experience with them showed that the baronet is a frugal traveller. Yes, his so-called patron had ample return on his small investment."

"Well, your aunt suspected as much, you know."

There was a brief silence—hardly more than a few seconds—before Basil answered, easily enough, "Did she now?"

"Or did I neglect to mention that she'd written to me after George returned her bank draft? Yes, it troubled me from the first," he went on, running his eyes over the sheet he held in his hand. "Until you got Randolph talking, I was stymied. George keeps his affairs mighty close. Fortunately, Randolph made a few accurate guesses about his father's business associates, and once I tracked them down it was a simple matter. Their records did not match with what George reported to Ashmore. He'd kept two sets of ledgers, you see. Such a pity, when Ashmore never bothered to examine the accounts."

"Our irascible baronet cares only about the work itself, difficult as that is to believe. He wants a better keeper, Henry." Basil lounged back in his chair and smiled. "At any rate, between Randolph's defection and our evidence, I doubt Mr. George Burnham will care to give any more trouble."

"If he thought to, I expect he'll think again when he gets my letter. Marianne and Randolph will be enjoying their honeymoon by then, no doubt."

"Oh, yes. They had less than two full days' journey to Gretna Green."

"Good." Mr. Latham nodded with satisfaction. "My wife is still a tad overset. She wanted titles for all the girls, you know. Wants them all to do the same as Alicia."

"Still, she has two more unwed daughters."

"If they make matches one half as satisfactory as their older sisters', I shall count myself the most fortunate of Papas. Randolph is a good, honest man, and we must make shift to tolerate his family's frailties. If Marianne is content, that's all that counts." The genial businessman looked over his spectacles at his companion. "And what of you, sir? All this hard work and trouble—and no reward in it for you?

Perhaps you'd have done better to have stayed in India or Greece. Certainly there'd have been more profit in it, eh?''

Mr. Trevelyan's smile faded. ''I wish to heaven I'd never gone to Greece,'' he muttered, half to himself. Noting his friend's uplifted eyebrow, he went on quickly, ''But then, I'd never have stumbled upon this Burnham business, and Randolph would never have come here—''

''—and fallen in love with my daughter. Well, how fortunate you did stumble upon this Burnham business, as you put it. Come,'' the older man said briskly, ''let us give you a proper meal. May we offer you a bed this night?''

Basil accepted the offer of sustenance but declared his determination to go back to Hartleigh Hall. ''I can get there sooner than a letter can and will enjoy breaking the news myself.''

''The news. Ah, yes, so you will. So you will.''

''But first, Henry, I believe there is some information you wish to share with me.''

Mr. Latham looked over his spectacles at his guest. ''Is there, sir?''

''My aunt, Henry. What exactly has my aunt to do with all this?''

For all that he hadn't had more than one night's sleep in three, and for all his eagerness to be back at Hartleigh Hall, Basil did have some consideration for his beast. He stopped several times to rest his horse. Hunger had finally caught up with him, if weariness had not, when he reached the Dancing Pig.

While the hostler saw about his mount, Basil made his way into the tiny inn and ordered a little light refreshment from his hostess, the plump owner of the place.

He was just swallowing his last morsels of bread and cheese when the door to the snuggery opened and Lord Arden burst in.

''You—you bastard!'' the marquess shouted, as he launched himself upon his startled victim. His attack was so unexpected and immediate that Basil had no time to react. As

Will's fingers closed around his throat, Basil tumbled backwards helplessly in his chair onto the floor.

It was not the first time, however, that an irate gentleman had attempted to throttle him. Basil's survival instincts quickly taking over, his knee shot up. In an instant Lord Arden had rolled off him onto the floor and was curled up in a fetal position, gasping in agony as he clutched at certain parts of his aristocratic anatomy.

"Good heavens, Will," Basil told the writhing form of his childhood playmate. "What a turn you gave me." He picked himself up, dusted himself off, and straightened his cravat. He'd just restored the chair to an upright position when the hostler came stomping through the door with the hostess behind him, brandishing a broom.

"Here now," the man growled. "We won't have any brawling here. This is a respectable place."

"Why so it is," Mr. Trevelyan calmly agreed. "And as you can see, there's no brawl. Only that his lordship has been suddenly taken ill."

His lordship groaned.

"Now," Basil continued, "if you'd be so kind as to bring in a bottle of your best brandy, perhaps we can help restore the gentleman to rights."

The phrase "his lordship" had a magical effect, and the coins Mr. Trevelyan dropped into a plump, feminine hand an even more miraculous one. The two respectable persons took themselves off, bowing and curtseying as they went. A few moments later, the required bottle of brandy was carried in by the beaming hostess.

"Now, Will," said Basil, as he helped his companion to his feet. "Come sit down and have a glass with me. Tell me what on earth you were thinking of to pounce on me in that savage way."

If the marquess thought of pouncing again, the sight of the golden beverage being poured into a glass must have distracted him, for he did sit down dazedly and take the drink offered him.

It was not the first time he and Basil had scuffled, nor was it the first time that hostilities had been followed up by olive branches in liquid form. At any rate, he knew—and if he didn't, Basil was prompt to call it to his attention—that murder had a rather unwholesome effect upon one's reputation. The murder, moreover, of one of the ton could very easily lead to more unwholesome effects upon one's health. A noose, for instance, was prodigious unhealthy.

Still, the provocation had been very great. "What in blazes did you mean by interfering in the business, Trev? We were on our way to Gretna Green."

"I was only trying to help you, Will."

The marquess shook his head in dazed incredulity. "Help me?"

"Yes. Good heavens, man. How could I stand idly by, knowing the sort of fate that awaited you?"

Lord Arden had any number of "hows" in reply, as well as the very cold assertion that he hadn't asked for any help. But Basil bade him drink and be calm, and the marquess wanted the drink badly. His head throbbed, and he was exhausted after four days spent scouring the countryside. Also, at the moment, certain more vital areas of his anatomy were throbbing as well. He gave a resigned sigh and brought his glass to his lips.

"I myself," Basil informed him, with a pitying look, "have not once, but several times, nearly tripped the parson's mousetrap on her account."

"Oh, come, Trev. Tell me another one."

"It's the truth. Why, she very nearly had me in Albania. Why do you think I kept away from my aunt's house after my return? The fact is, upon discovering that I couldn't keep my hands off your prospective bride if she was within reaching distance, I was obliged to keep myself out of reach."

Basil went on to assert that he would have stayed away had he not been alarmed on his friend's account. He knew he couldn't warn his friend as it was bound to be taken ill. Still, Basil had felt obligated to come and keep an eye on things.

"Oh, really, Trev. You expect me to believe that was all out of concern for me?"

"Well, perhaps not entirely. Knowing you're a wise fellow, on to every trick, I was naturally curious how long it would take you to understand precisely what you were up against." To forestall any hasty defences of Miss Ashmore's honour—and Will was showing signs of rather homicidal hastiness—Basil refilled his companion's glass.

"I'm not trying to slander your Intended," he placated. "But think, Will, for once. Just think what a merry dance she's led you already. Think, too, of the hundreds of Eligibles your Mama has paraded before you, and ask yourself which one of them could have kept you so long a-wooing and driven you to such desperation. Ask yourself how it came to be that you, the future Duke of Thorne, must drag your intended bride off to Scotland in the dead of night in order to be sure of her. And ask yourself, while you're at it, just how sure of her you'd ever be. Ask yourself what pleasure you could take in your mistresses with your mind always on your wife, wondering what she was up to—and with whom."

Lord Arden asked himself these questions and must have found the answers unnerving, for his hand shook a little as he carried the glass to his mouth. He took a very long swallow while he studied his companion's face.

"You don't mean to say, Trev, that you think she'd play me false?"

"I mean to say," was the composed reply, "that the British male population would give you reason to worry. Which, I daresay, is nearly worse. How could you leave her out of your sight knowing there were hundreds like myself, quite unable to keep their hands off her? Of course, you could leave her in the country—but even the country is not so secure a place for unattended wives, as any number of unhappy husbands might tell you. You see the problem, of course. If she could put even *you* into a fever to be shackled, then what effect do you think she'll have on lesser men? The fact is, Will, the woman's a menace to the national peace. Do you know what they called her in Albania? The English Witch. Because even the Albanian men—who think women a species of cattle—were obsessed with her."

As Basil went on to describe the extremities to which Dhimitri had been driven, Lord Arden found himself, for perhaps the first time in his self-indulgent life, thinking twice about something he'd set his mind on having. It confused him. He wanted Alexandra Ashmore as his wife mainly because it was unthinkable that so splendid a creature should grace any other home, carry any other name, bear any other children than his. However, it was also unthinkable that the future Duke of Thorne must submit to the indignity of living in his wife's pocket for fear of being cuckolded. What time would he have for women and gaming and drinking and all the other pleasures his vast wealth practically demanded if he must be forever fending off jackals like Trev?

Like Trev. Will's eyes narrowed. "You want her for yourself, Trev. That's why you warn me off."

"Of course I want her for myself," was the amiable reply. "Didn't I just say so? And I promise you, Will, if you marry her I'll be there in my hunting pinks with the rest, after your lovely fox. I tell you, I can't wait for her to be wed, because until she is I must keep to the sidelines. As you told me once, Auntie is standing guard. One false move and I'd be the nervous, horn-sprouting husband. Though I'm not nearly as possessive as you are and needn't worry about the family honour—after all, that's Edward's lookout, isn't it—still, it's bound to be an irritating sort of existence, don't you think? All these duels, for one thing. So tiresome."

The poison was taking its effect along with the brandy. In another couple of hours, as Basil went on to paint increasingly grim pictures of what the future held for any man rash enough to marry Miss Ashmore, Lord Arden was brought to heel.

He was, in fact, sick of the whole business. True, she was a priceless ornament to add to the Farrington possessions. But she was also, he was forced to admit to himself, incomprehensibly unresponsive to him. It would be pleasant to get back to his far less taxing twins in London. Relieved to have a face-saving excuse for abandoning the tiresome chase and more than a little foxed, he confessed aloud that Lust had blinded him to Consequences, went on to recite some sentimental poetry, and was soon admitting maudlinly that Basil was the very best of fellows, the very best indeed. A man couldn't ask for a better friend and couldn't deserve him if he did.

If Mr. Trevelyan had a conscience, it must have been moved by these expressions of brotherly feeling; but as he hadn't, it wasn't. Besides, he'd done no more than tell the truth, only tinted and arranged it to suit his purposes. After all, Basil silently replied to the thing muttering at the back of his mind that was not a conscience, it could all turn out as he'd predicted. Alexandra didn't love Will, and Will didn't really love her. If he did, he'd have been willing to risk all—the devil with his future peace of mind, his mistresses, and all his other trivial occupations.

Having in this wise quieted the troubling inner voice and having divided the remnants of the brandy bottle, Basil proposed a final toast, "to friendship." Thereafter he suggested that they find themselves beds for the night.

"A bed. Yes," his lordship agreed thickly. "Another lonely bed. Nearly a month of it, Trev. Though that's over, eh?" But as he was rather inelegantly rising from his chair, a thought struck him forcibly enough to make him fall back into it again. "Trev, it isn't over. The girl . . . I proposed. Half a dozen times at least."

"There were no witnesses."

"No." The marquess shook his head and blinked several times, trying to focus and looking amazingly like Freddie. "But still. Honour. Obliged, you know." He stared owlishly at Basil.

"Not at all. You disgraced yourself. Remember? Thanks to me. And though Miss Ashmore knows the truth, she can hardly admit it. With this cloud over you, no one would expect you to have the audacity to offer for her. Nor would my formidable aunt allow her to accept you if you did. No, don't worry about it, Will. Now let us go get some rest."

17

Lord Hartleigh's family and friends were gathered in the sunny breakfast room, peacefully attending to their morning meal, when Basil and Will came sauntering in just as cavalier and careless as you please.

It took all of Alexandra's self-control, amid the ensuing pandemonium of questions and exclamations, to keep from leaping out of her chair and throwing her arms around Basil's neck. Though by now her body should have used up its supply of saltwater, tears of relief filled her eyes, and his face swam before her . . . for a moment. Then it wanted only another moment before the tears dried up of their own accord.

He never even looked at her. True, the others were raising a terrific clamour, and he was kept busy making clever retorts. Still, he might spare her a glance instead of dropping so coolly into the chair next to Jess—at the other end of the table. Will, the faithless fribble, couldn't spare his Intended a glance either. He only stood by the door, smiling appreciatively at the witticisms of his erstwhile rival. Gone after Basil, indeed. To carouse with him no doubt. To share some unspeakable dissipation or other. As disagreeable visions of buxom barmaids and chambermaids paraded through her head, her feminine flutterings of concern and relief precipitously gave way to rather unfeminine heavings of fury. Oh, she wished they *had* killed each other, the selfish beasts.

Miss Ashmore was so busy working herself into a rage that she barely heard the conversation. It was not until she heard the gasps of surprise and Jess's "Oh, Lud!" that Alexandra called herself to attention.

"Eloped!" Lady Hartleigh exclaimed.

Alexandra's head jerked up, and her whole body began to tremble. But no one was looking at her or Will. They were all fixed on Basil, who answered with a little smile, "That's what I said. Randolph has run away with Miss Marianne Latham to Gretna Green. Actually, they're not running any more. By now they must be wed."

Lord Tuttlehope blinked uncomprehendingly at his wife, who blinked back.

"Marianne?" Alicia gasped. "Run away with Marianne?"

"Why, yes," said Basil. "Why do you think she was so obsessed with Athens and Sparta? You yourself remarked it. Not once but many times have I heard you complaining about those tiresome Penelope Wars. You see, when Mr. Burnham and Sir Charles visited, the two young people took a liking to each other. That much even I dimly noticed. I did not, however, imagine it was as serious as it turned out to be."

"But if it was so serious, why elope?" Jess asked.

"One assumes that they believed their respective families would object. Mrs. Latham, you see, wanted Marianne to have a London comeout with Alicia as chaperone."

"Oh, dear," said Alicia in sudden comprehension. "Mama and her titles."

"So, obviously, she wouldn't look kindly upon a wool merchant's son. Moreover, it appears that Randolph's parents also had other plans for him." This was communicated with nary a glance at Sir Charles, who sat speechless, gazing at Basil as though he were Lord Elgin's caryatid suddenly come to life.

Miss Ashmore stared at her plate.

"At any rate," Basil continued, "our two young lovers must have decided it was futile to attempt to bring their respective parents around. Randolph leaves Westford in despair. Then letters are secretly exchanged. The plot is hatched . . . and the two took the only course open to them."

At this point, several at table recollected Randolph's misery upon his arrival and how his spirits had miraculously undergone improvement.

"I thought it was because he'd taken a fancy to Hetty," Alicia admitted ruefully. "They were so cheerful together at that picnic."

While the others carried on noisily about this startling news, Miss Ashmore occupied herself with the story between the lines. No wonder Basil had been so friendly with Randolph. Having wormed his way into the young scholar's confidence, thereby learning of the hapless romance, Basil must have persuaded Randolph to elope. Certainly it wasn't the sort of notion Randolph would conceive on his own.

Now all made sense. The Blue Swan—the nearest mail coach stop on the road north—the night of the gala when, in the great crush of people, the disappearance of a guest or two was less likely to be remarked. And Basil, helpful as always, at the inn to see that everything went according to plan. Randolph had only to board the coach, meet Marianne, and travel on with her to Scotland. Yes, Basil must even have arranged how the young woman was to meet her lover without arousing suspicion. No wonder he'd been so adamant about getting the other elopers back to Hartleigh Hall. Only one wedding was required to scotch George Burnham's scheme.

She stared unseeing at the eggs congealing on her plate. For her, he'd said. He'd done it all for her. He could have let her go off with Will if he didn't care . . . but no. Her disappearance would cause more of an uproar than Randolph's. She and Will might easily have been caught and stopped, for Will's disguises had only made them more conspicuous. She, Will, Randolph, and Marianne, all on the same coach. Good heavens, what a farce. Everything would have been ruined, just as Basil had said.

Yet he could have told her. He could have taken her into his confidence instead of leaving her to make herself miserable over him for five whole days.

Fortunately for her fraying temper, the group broke up at last. While the others were filing out of the room, Basil took Sir Charles aside. "Mr. Latham asked me to put this into your hands," Mr. Trevelyan explained *sotto voce* as he slipped the baronet a letter. "You'll want to read it in private, I daresay."

Alexandra, who'd been hovering nearby, overheard the exchange and saw the envelope. Consumed with curiosity, she followed her father to the library. He sat down at the small study table where Mr. Hobhouse's *Travels in Albania* lay open awaiting his perusal. She sat down across from him and watched as he unfolded the paper and read, apparently oblivious to her presence.

When he got to the end, he gave a faint whistle in surprise and then began at the beginning again. This made Alexandra very impatient indeed. When he'd finished for the second time, she burst out, "For heaven's sake, Papa, what is it? What does it say?"

As the baronet returned from someplace apparently far away, she saw the familiar furrows settling into his forehead. "What does it say? What does it say? Only that I've been played for a fool these ten years and more. George Burnham has been cheating me. *Cheating* me, Alexandra. I can scarcely credit it. Yet the evidence is there, Mr. Latham says. He's talked to those with whom George dealt and seen their records for himself."

His daughter snatched the letter from his hands and read it. "Good grief!" she exclaimed softly. When she was done, she dropped the letter onto the table and looked at her father. Her eyes were filled with compassion—though what beat in her breast was great relief. "Oh, Papa. How disappointing for you. You trusted him—with everything."

"The more fool I," her father muttered. "Who'd have thought there could be so much deceit in this world?"

Her conscience pricked her. "Why you know there is, Papa, as there has always been, because men are greedy for money and power. Without greed, very likely there would have been no Peloponnesian War. No wars at all, probably. No civilisations toppled and rebuilt. All history an open book. No mysteries. Then think how bored you'd be."

He mustered up a wan smile. He was not, after all, entirely without a sense of humour, though it had been cruelly tried in recent months. "Still, it is not pleasant to contemplate how I've been taken in," he growled.

The accusing look he bent upon Alexandra made her a tad uncomfortable. Hastily she replied, "You must look on the bright side. I know you think highly of Mr. Latham. Didn't you once tell me you wished it was he had the care of your troublesome finances? And doesn't he say in his letter that he took the liberty of looking into these matters in the hopes of discovering some means by which he might act as your partner in future? Does he not offer to do so now in the kindest and most gentlemanly way? And his reputation is of the highest. Why, half the peerage has dealings with him."

It took some time. The baronet persisted in grumbling about deceit and trickery. Mr. Trevelyan's name was mentioned more than once with doubt and suspicion. Alexandra's own lack of forthrightness was remarked upon, but at length Sir Charles grumbled himself into a state of weary resignation. Consequently, when she mentioned Lady Bertram's wish to take her to London for the Little Season and the generous offer to take charge of her until a suitable husband was found, the baronet offered no objection.

He would be glad, he told his daughter bluntly, to have her off his hands now that he was free of his obligations. Yes, she might go with Clementina for as long as she liked. He was tired of keeping track of her suitors and fiancés. He wanted to go back to Albania where a man might do his work in peace. Dead civilisations and the dead who'd belonged to them were not nearly so troublesome as one unmanageable daughter aided and abetted by an interfering, overbearing old woman and her unspeakable nephew.

Alexandra listened patiently to his complaints, and when he was bored with them at last she took herself away. Putting aside Henry Latham's letter, he turned to Mr. Hobhouse's work, and in a very little while the furrows erased themselves from his brow.

"Eloped, did they?" Lady Jess said to her brother. She'd followed him to the billiard room where she was in the unladylike process of soundly trouncing him. "Just like that. And I suppose Basil never had a hand in it."

"If he had, he hasn't confided it to me."

"Hasn't he? And you two suddenly the best of friends." One more stroke was sufficient to dispatch her brother. She stood back, surveying the domain of her triumph while absently rubbing the tip of her billiard cue against her temple, smudging it with chalk. "What happened, Will? One minute you can't bear to have her out of your sight for an instant. Today you can't get far enough away from her. What happened when you met up with him?"

Lord Arden only shrugged and put his own cue away.

"You've given up, haven't you?" she persisted.

"You know, Jess," he said, taking her cue from her and putting it away as well, "you really oughtn't to play billiards at all. But if you must, you certainly should not win against a gentleman."

"Then there's no problem beating *you*, is there? Come, tell me. Have you given up or what?"

Her brother gazed down disapprovingly at her. Really, such a hoyden she was. All of twenty-three, and still unmarried. Well, that wasn't surprising was it? What chap wanted a wife who acted like another chap?

"I have decided," he said coldly, "that we shouldn't suit."

"Oh, you have, have you? Well, who do you think will suit you, you inestimable treasure? One of your ballet dancers? Or perhaps one isn't enough. Perhaps you want a matching pair like those redheaded sisters—"

"Your mouth wants washing out with soap, sister dear."

"Will all great Neptune's ocean wash *you* clean of your sins? Come now, Will. After you'd got all my hopes up, you might as well tell me why I'm to be disappointed. Besides, I've beat you fair and square, and you owe me a forfeit."

The marquess bent a withering look upon his sister which she met with perfect equanimity, being immune to the devastating force of his personality. Knowing that she'd plague him until she was satisfied and fully aware that fabrications would be a waste of breath, he gave in and told her. Not everything, but enough to make her understand. When he was done, she gave a little whistle of surprise that made him wince. Plague take her! When would she ever learn to behave like a lady?

"Egad, Will," she cried. "You gave up because you thought she was too much for you to handle?"

"I thought the effort required was excessive," he replied dampeningly. "I don't want a wife who requires so much managing."

"Or one who might manage *you* is more like it. Lud, you're a greater fool even than I thought, to give up such a jewel for so paltry a reason. But it's just as well, I suppose. It's obvious you never intended to mend your ways on her account, and that would leave me to comfort her while you were out leaping from one poxy bed to the next. Well then, I suppose I should be thankful Basil opened up your eyes, if he spared me that unpleasant duty. Obliging of him, wasn't it?"

Her brother made no reply. He found his sister exceedingly tiresome today. He gave her one last cold, haughty stare and exited from the room.

"Yes, very obliging," Jess muttered to herself as she played absently with a billiard ball. "And what, I wonder, makes him such a philanthropist all of a sudden? Wretched, interfering beast."

"Egad, Maria," said Harry Deverell, as he strolled with his wife along the very same sheltered path two couples had trod several days before. "You haven't any scruples, have you? Half the servants spying for you, the other half spying for Clementina—and then to wring family secrets from Jess after using her brother so unconscionably. Really, my lady."

"But my love, when I saw her out in the garden stomping back and forth in such a temper, I was so afraid she'd catch her gown against the rose bushes and shred it to pieces. I only asked her if she was feeling poorly from the heat when immediately she launched into a perfectly exhausting catalog of her brother's flaws of character. Then, quite on her own— for really, I never prodded her in the least—she told me what Will had told her."

"So Basil frightened him off, did he? Well, I must say

your confidence in the wretch proves to have been very well placed. Randolph, Will, even the great debt—all dispatched in less than a week. Amazingly efficient, isn't he, once he sets his mind to something? No wonder Henry Latham speaks so highly of him.''

''Yes, dear. But it's the setting his mind in the first place that's so fatiguing. So obstinate, you know.''

''Ah, well. He's used to doing just as he pleases. When you think what a way he has with the ladies—why, they're mere clay in his hands—it's no surprise he can't bring himself to settle on one.''

Lady Deverell sighed in sorrowful agreement. ''Ah, yes. You charming wretches. It is such great sport for you to play fast and loose with our tender feminine hearts''

''Yes, madam. Great sport indeed. Speaking of which, is this the romantic site you told me of? The scene of stolen interludes, jealous hearts, tears, and I don't know what else?''

They had, in fact, reached the site of recent highly charged events—the place, in short, where Lord Arden had attempted to compromise his Intended. Lord Deverell, having been obliquely accused of certain sporting instincts and furthermore seeing that the place was altogether satisfactory in every respect, determined to live up to the accusation and swept his wife into his arms. That vulnerable creature being, as she'd hinted, no proof against such wicked masculine wiles, gave herself with a low chuckle over to the conqueror.

18

If anyone deserved a good night's sleep, it was himself. Yet Mr. Trevelyan was strangely reluctant to take himself to bed. He took another turn in the garden, and then another, but the cool fragrance of the country night did not soothe him. It had, after an hour's aimless pacing, only brought back vividly another garden far away and another night many weeks ago . . . and a pair of startled green eyes, searching his face.

He'd felt those eyes reproachfully upon him today and had been quite unable to meet them. He should have told her. It had been unkind—at the least—to leave her in the dark. But to see her arrive at that inn on Will's arm . . . well, in a matter of minutes, Basil had gone from jealous rage to guilt and back again. Yet, he'd been very high-handed with her— the more so because he knew he was to blame. Had he confided in her before he left, she could easily have found a way to put Will off.

But no. He'd been all in a dither then, too—because she'd proved, once and for all, how helplessly besotted he was, and because she'd laughed at him just when he was on the brink of confessing it.

He turned and made his way back to the house. Another long, lonely night then. Only this time he'd better think, and to the point. He'd have to speak to her tomorrow. "And say what, you great ass?" queried a mocking voice in the back of his head. "What do you think she'll believe *now?*"

Alexandra sat up and pounded her pillow, though her anger was hardly the pillow's fault. It was, however, an inanimate object upon which she might vent her frustrations with impunity—though it would have been ever so much more satisfactory to be pounding upon Mr. Trevelyan's head and tearing out his tawny hair by the clumpfuls.

For the tenth or twentieth time since she'd retired for the night, she flung herself back down upon the bed and closed her eyes. And for the tenth or twentieth time she cursed the day she'd met him.

The fact was that, like a great many other people whose prayers the gods have answered, Miss Ashmore was wishing she'd worded her orisons more carefully. True, being in love with the man, she must be overjoyed that he'd returned safe and sound. The problem was that, in returning not only unscathed but unchanged and therefore unimproved, he made her feel like an idiot. Virtually everything she'd thought and done from the minute she'd met him had been wrong. She'd driven herself distracted, trying to manipulate her father and Will by turns and had succeeded only in twisting herself deeper into a quagmire. From which Basil had, with hardly a second's thought, extricated her. A snap of his fingers and Randolph, Papa, George Burnham, and Will were all disposed of simultaneously.

There she'd been, plotting and worrying by day, worrying and weeping by night—a prodigious waste of energy. She was a fool. Her brains must have rotted away in the sultry Mediterranean climate.

Look at her prowling about the house and grounds all day today by herself, hoping like a sentimental goose that he'd come to her. Then what? Fall to his knees declaring that he did it all because he loved her? And in some treacly way straight out of a fairy tale, swear always to be faithful because now he'd found his one, his only, his *true* love at last.

Faithful, indeed. It was all a game to him, to play with others' lives. Hadn't Aunt Clem said it? It was a matter of pride with him to succeed completely in whatever he undertook, "particularly if it is something devious." All of this meant no more to him than what he'd done when he was abroad. Why confide in her? Why bother even to talk to her? She was only another of his pawns. Now he'd tied up all the loose ends he'd be gone again. Back to London and his usual dissipations.

If only he could go out of her life as well. But she was going to London herself in another two days, where she'd have to endure a Little Season, catching glimpses of him now and then at some party or other, watching him dance and flirt and reduce other ladies to inbecility. Doubtless she'd hear as well of much worse, for the gossips of London were indefatigable. No matter was too small for their prying eyes and malicious tongues.

That sort of thing she didn't need to witness or be told of. She was already jealous of the hundreds of young women she imagined in his arms because, fool that she was, she wanted him all to herself. How she'd missed him! But when she felt the tears starting in her eyes, she quickly took herself in hand. She would not weep another instant over him.

The clock in the hall struck one. Good grief! Nearly two hours she'd lain here making herself mad. Enough. If she couldn't sleep, at least she could read. There was always the interminable *Clarissa*, and she had finally got to the last volume. As she was getting up, about to light the candle on her bedstand, she remembered that she'd left the book downstairs in the library last evening. Well, no help for it then. She must either go down and get it or stay here and madden herself all night.

She crawled out of bed, pulled on her dressing gown, stubbed her toe on a footstool, and stumbled against the bedpost, but eventually got out of the room. Quietly and very cautiously—not wanting any more bruises—she made her way downstairs and groped along the hall. Having narrowly missed collision with the heavy table that stood by the library door, she found the door handle and opened the door.

Light. There was light in the room, and it was occupied. A single candle burned in a silver holder upon an elegant mahogany table. The soft candlelight bathed the room in a dreamlike, golden glow, and lounging at his ease on the great leather sofa was Mr. Trevelyan.

He was fully dressed except for his coat, which was draped over a nearby chair. His neckcloth dangled carelessly, and his tawny hair, glinting gold like new-minted coins under the soft light, was tousled—the result, no doubt, of being raked with his fingers. Even now he ran his hand through it as though bedevilled by something.

He looked up from the letter he'd been reading and stared at her for a moment as though disbelieving the evidence of his own eyes. Then a slow smile lit his handsome face.

Really, it was most unfair, she thought crossly. He had no right to be so beautiful, draped upon the sofa like some sly Apollo come down among mortal women to destroy their peace. It was positively cruel what that smile did to her. It made her want to do things a lady must not—like hurl herself at him or, at the very least, run her fingers through that tousled, sun-bleached mane. No. A lady, certainly, had better make a dignified—and speedy—exit.

Grasping the door handle, she turned to leave.

"Why, you've only just come, Alexandra. 'They flee from me,' " he quoted. "But no, that's not right, is it? For you never 'did me seek,' did you? More's the pity."

"Do be quiet," she whispered. "Do you want everyone to hear you?"

"Why, they're all sound asleep, their consciences clear. Unlike yours and mine. But yes, my guardian angel," he went on, dropping his voice to a low timbre that sent a chill running down the back of her neck. "I take your meaning. And if I promise to be very quiet, will you stay a minute and talk to me?"

Oh, how she wanted to stay, how she'd missed him. For all that he made her uncomfortable physically—and that was mainly the discomfort of trying to bring her desires into harmony with her morals—there was no one else with whom she could talk so easily. Because he knew her better than anyone else did . . . though she rather wished he didn't know her quite so well.

She looked down at her scanty attire and told herself to be sensible. "No. I only came for my book. I-I couldn't sleep." She glanced around the room, seeking the wayward volume.

"This one?" he asked, taking a familiar tome from the table near his head. "*Clarissa?* The interminable seduction?

You are nearly at the end of it, I see." Idly he turned the pages. "Perhaps, as we're both wakeful, you might read to me."

"Don't be absurd." She was not sure what to do. She could not bring herself to go and take the book from him, nor did she think it advisable that he bring it to her. Nor did she wish to leave the room without it.

"Ah, I see the problem," he said, his eyes scanning her face. "What a thoughtless creature I am, to be sure. For here it is"—he consulted his pocket watch—"nearly half past one in the morning, and there are you in your dishabille, alone in a dim library with an arrant rogue. But see how simple it is? At this hour there's no one to notice the breach of decorum. There is my coat to protect your modesty. As to the rogue part—well, what dreadful thing do you think I'd dare attempt with the circumstances so very incriminating and my family only a shriek away?"

Putting the book down, he rose from the sofa. He took his coat from the chair, and held it up with a beckoning gesture.

She hesitated.

"Come, Miss Ashmore. Or are you afraid?"

Yes, actually, she was afraid. His effect on her was always unnerving, always dangerous. Still, he'd admitted that the risks were too great even for *him*. She put up her chin, crossed the room, and allowed him to help her on with his coat. He gestured towards the sofa, and she sat down gingerly.

She could not, however, suppress a gasp of shock when she saw him go to the door and turn the key in the lock. Grinning at her obvious alarm, he tossed the key to her. She caught it with trembling hands.

"That's in case there happen to be other insomniacs," he explained, as he pulled up a chair opposite her. "If we hear anyone coming, I shall crawl out the window while you take your time about going to the door. You would, of course, have locked it for fear of being disturbed by naughty gentlemen."

If she was uneasy at first, she forgot that as soon as he began talking, because immediately he set to telling her the true story of Randolph's elopement. Her surmises, she learned, had been correct. "But why," she asked, when he'd finished describing the elopement arrangements, "did you insist on going looking for him?"

"I couldn't rest easy until I was certain they were both in the coach and on their way. If the smallest thing went wrong, Randolph would have been helpless. Also, I was obliged to keep Henry Latham informed. We'd agreed, you see, that he'd handle the business end while I saw to the romance part of it."

"You mean he knew about the scheme all along?"

"He knew, thanks to my aunt, about your father's debt to George. He guessed about the romance sooner even than I did and must have dropped a hint to Aunt Clem when he wrote to her, for she dropped hints to me. None of which I picked up, I'm ashamed to admit. But when your Papa spoke that day about Randolph's breaking heart . . . well, to make a long story short, by the day of the picnic I'd not only got the truth out of Randolph, but also, in exchange for devising a workable elopement scheme, some important details regarding his father's practises. So off I dashed to Westford. Henry saw right off that mine was the best solution. It would have taken ages to reconcile his wife, and meanwhile George could have finally torn himself away from Yorkshire to force your marriage to his son. There was no time to be lost."

"So you had everything in hand before you left." There was a note of reproach in her voice.

Basil stared at the carpet. "I know. I should have told you. But the one time we were private—well, it all got driven out of my head. Then I made you hate me . . . and it was getting late. I should have been on my way hours before . . . and, well, I didn't tell you. I'm sorry. Truly I am. Because it would have spared you a deal of aggravation. If you'd known, you could have kept Will out of your hair easily enough, I'm sure."

She played with the key as she considered this. "I'd like to think so," she began slowly. "But it looks as though you've taken care of that, too, haven't you?" The green eyes fixed on him. "I should very much like to know what happened when you met up with him."

Mr. Trevelyan was evasive. He even looked uncomfortable, as he gave a highly edited account of his meeting with Lord Arden.

"What did you say to him?" she pressed. "Why did he avoid me all day?"

"I wish you wouldn't look at me that way. It turns my blood quite cold. I only had a serious discussion with him about the responsibilities of marriage, and he finally admitted he wasn't ready for them."

This, considering Will's impetuosity, she found a trifle hard to swallow. But then, was it so important? Basil had solved all her problems, disposed of all her fiancés. It was churlish to cavil at the means. "Never mind," she said with a small gesture of impatience. "It doesn't matter what you said. So long as I'm free of him."

"Ah, yes." Basil leaned forward a bit in his chair. "So that you may have your Season."

"Yes." She dropped her gaze to the key she held.

There was silence, and then his hand reached out to cover hers. "Then perhaps," he said softly, "we'll meet up with each other from time to time. Perhaps you'll be kind enough to dance with me now and again."

How easily he held her, his long fingers so lightly folded over her own, and how weak it made her feel. Her voice was brittle as she answered, "Why, yes, of course. I owe it all to you, don't I? And I've sat here all this time and never thanked you. I do thank you—"

He shook his head. "No. None of that. Not when I was only doing the little I know best."

She slipped her hand out from under his and stood up. "Well, I'm grateful all the same. Deeply grateful. I've never been free, not in six years at least. Now I am. I can't forget it. And so," she went on rather nervously, when he didn't respond, "I'll be bound to thank you from time to time, and you must endure it."

When she started to remove the coat, he seemed to collect himself from a daydream. He rose, too, moving to assist her. His hands touched her arms as the coat slipped from her shoulders, and she trembled slightly.

"Alexandra."

The sound was like a sigh, and she turned to look at him. The coat fell to the floor as he folded her in his arms. He kissed her, gently and briefly, and he drew away again before it occurred to her to *make* him do so.

He did not draw away entirely, however. His arms still held her, not so very close, but close enough so that she could feel the softness of his lawn shirt through the fragile barrier of her own flimsy garments. Close enough so that she was acutely conscious of the scent of him: clean and masculine and so comfortingly familiar. So comforting after all this time apart that it was quite impossible to break free. She felt so safe, so sheltered, so . . . *right* to be there, that any other possibility seemed quite wrong. That thought in itself was wrong, of course. It was only the spell he cast over her, and yet, to remain so . . . just another moment.

"I suppose," he said, rather sadly, "I'd better let you go."

"Yes, I think so," she answered just as sadly as she stared at the ruffles of his shirt front.

"Otherwise, I couldn't answer for the consequences." He did not release her.

"Yes." She didn't move.

"In another minute it would be too late." He sounded rather short of breath, and this for some reason irritated her.

"You always," she accused, "leave it up to *me*. But only after you make it—" She bit her lip.

He held her a little tighter. "Make it what?"

"So very difficult, Basil." Her green eyes met his.

Perhaps it was because she was breathless now as well, and because her heart beat so furiously, and because these conditions made it very difficult to think clearly. Whatever the reason, her hand strayed to his shirt, played with the ruffles briefly, then came to rest over his heart. It was thumping and that was somehow frustrating. Still, her hand remained where it was, and she went on, confusedly, "It's wicked of you . . . and—and unfair."

"Is it?" His lips brushed her forehead.

"Yes. And I don't see why I must always be the one to put

173

a stop to—to everything. To get you out of the—the difficulties you get yourself into.''

''Because I always get you out of yours. Because we've somehow got into the habit of looking out for each other. I wonder why,'' he murmured, drawing her closer still.

''Well, I'm not getting you out of this one,'' she answered with admirable severity, considering that she was talking into his neckcloth while he continued to drop light kisses in her hair. ''You can just turn around and take yourself away.''

''Can't,'' he whispered. ''You have the key.''

She was never sure afterward exactly how it happened, but one minute he was kissing her—*everywhere,* it seemed—and the next they had tumbled onto the great leather sofa. By that time, the notion of escaping was making less and less sense to her. How could one think of getting away from such caresses, when one's body with every passing moment desperately needed more of them? How could one wish to break free of that lean, muscular, beautiful body that claimed one so possessively? She covered his hand with hers. Fear and longing were mingled in the green eyes that searched his face.

''I won't hurt you,'' he whispered.

''No.'' Reason was fighting, desperately, to reassert itself. ''No. I can't do this. No—I didn't mean—oh, Basil, please—have a little pity at least.''

He had bent to kiss the hand clasping his, but now raised his head to look at her. His face was flushed, and his eyes, so softly golden before, were now so very bright. ''Pity?'' he repeated.

''I'm no m-match for you,'' she stammered. ''You know that. It isn't fair.''

He continued to gaze at her for the longest time, as though trying to interpret this rather inarticulate explanation. Then, very softly indeed, he said, ''Ah, yes. My vast experience.'' His fingers slipped from her nerveless grasp and moved to push a tumbled curl away from her eye. ''But about *you,* my love . . . when it comes to you, it seems I know nothing. I suppose,'' he added, with a wry smile, ''we'll have to *deduce* everything.'' His head bent again, this time to the base of her throat, which he kissed very tenderly, sending tremors through her.

"Please."

She felt rather than heard his long, shuddering sigh as he moved away from her.

"Please," he muttered as he rose from the sofa. "To stop on a mere 'please.' How art the mighty fallen. Oh, Alexandra, you kill me with a word. No, don't look at me like that with those great, drowned eyes, or I shall wrestle my conscience down in an instant and we'll both be undone."

Afraid of what he might have seen in her face, she looked away quickly and struggled up to a sitting position. Only her mind had wanted him to stop. Her heart would have followed willingly, eagerly, wherever he'd led. All she'd offered up in defence of her virtue was "a mere please." For once—and to her shame—*he* had saved her from himself. No, not even that. "Both," he'd said. He'd saved himself as well.

"You'd better go," he was saying now. "I can't be a gentleman and help you up because I don't dare touch you again."

She was up and halfway to the door when she remembered it was locked. "The key," she said, turning back to him in embarrassment and dismay. She was even more dismayed when she noticed the expression on his face. A few moments ago he had appeared . . . well, troubled. Now his eyes gleamed in a too-familiar, wicked way, and his mouth wore that mocking smile. In the next instant, however, he had dropped to his knees to retrieve the key from under the sofa. In another minute the door was unlocked, and she was being propelled through it.

19

Alexandra winced as Emmy pulled the drapes open, and bright sunlight flooded the room. Morning already? But this was her assigned bed, and there was Emmy, pattering about the room, and a cup of steaming coffee on a tray on the bedstand. It all seemed perfectly normal . . . until, in a great, tumultuous flood, all that had happened—was it only a few hours ago?—came rushing into her consciousness vividly enough to set her face aflame. Quickly she turned to take the tray in her lap, but Emmy beat her to it.

"There, Miss," said the abigail, briskly. "Only do drink it up quicklike. Your Papa's waiting in his lordship's study to talk to you. And oh, Miss—he's dreadful cross."

Cross? She flushed again with guilt this time. But he could know nothing of *that*. It must be about Randolph. Perhaps he'd found out the truth somehow.

Hastily, Alexandra swallowed the coffee. She was no sooner out of bed than Emmy had hauled her to the washstand. In another minute the abigail was upon her again, pulling shift and dress over her head and fastening buttons and hooks with lightning speed.

The whole business of washing and dressing was accomplished so rapidly that Alexandra had barely, it seemed, opened her eyes before she was downstairs tapping on the study door. When she entered, she woke up quickly enough, for it was not just Papa standing there but Basil as well.

Her breath caught in her throat as she looked at him. He'd seemed so different last evening, for a time at least. She remembered him, dishevelled and flushed, covering her with

176

kisses and even laughing happily as he'd fallen onto the sofa with her. He'd seemed rather like an eager boy then.

Now, even casually dressed in his buckskins, he was so smart and elegant, his cat eyes cool and mocking, his lips pressed into a faint, amused smile. He looked what he was: a sophisticated man of the world who might have any woman he liked. Could any woman, regardless how sensible or intelligent, resist him for long? His gaze met hers then, and the intimate, knowing expression in those glowing amber eyes made her face burn. She looked away, moving towards the fireplace.

"Deuce take it," the baronet muttered, eyeing his daughter with vexation. "So that's how it is, is it?"

"How what is, Papa?" the daughter asked innocently. She had, however, to fold her hands very tightly to keep them from shaking.

"You. Him. Oh, damnation. Why can't a man ever get a little warning?"

Scrupulously avoiding Mr. Trevelyan's face, Alexandra asked her father what he meant.

"As if you didn't know. But *I* didn't, I admit. And when this—this—"

"Villain?" Basil offered, helpfully.

"When this villain saunters in and tells me he wants to marry you—"

Marry?

Considering the events of recent weeks, Miss Ashmore believed herself entirely immune to shock. She was not. She could not have been more stunned if Papa had hit her over the head with the poker she was now studying in numb fascination. Offered. He'd even gone right to Papa. Her mind was just beginning to resume operation as her father launched into a tirade.

"Of course, as you confide nothing to your poor Papa, how am I to know? So, once again I'm made a fool of. I say, No, of course you won't have him. He insists that you will, and I tell him you won't. Not *my* daughter," the baronet went on sarcastically. "Not *my* Alexandra. She's much too clever to give herself over to the likes of him. And what happens but my brilliant offspring—too clever by half for her ignorant

Papa—walks in and blushes like a green schoolgirl at the sight of him. Great Zeus, woman, haven't you any sense at all?''

In the rush of relief—of exaltation, even—sense had been on the point of deserting her. But her father's words, for once in her life, made an impression. Give herself over to him. Oh, yes . . . easily, because she loved him so. To be his wife . . . *No,* she rebuked herself. Look how jealous and miserable she'd been yesterday, only imagining him flirting with other women. What she could imagine now was excruciating.

"Yes, of course I have sense, Papa," she answered steadily. "And I was not blushing like a schoolgirl—only flushed from running down to you in such a hurry. Of course the answer, as you said, is no." She turned briefly from the grate to throw Mr. Trevelyan a defiant look, but his expression made her turn away hastily.

The baronet's features relaxed. "No?"

"No."

"Well, then." Sir Charles turned to Basil. "There it is."

"No, it isn't." Mr. Trevelyan had moved nearer the door as this exchange was taking place. He now leaned back against it, his arms folded across his chest. "No is the wrong answer."

"I daresay you think it is," Sir Charles retorted with some impatience. "But she won't have you, and I certainly wouldn't consent unless she insisted—and that only to spare myself any more of her infernal wheedling. And so—"

"And so I'm afraid I shall have to tell you the truth," said Basil, quite calmly.

Panic swept through her. "Papa," she pleaded, "he's going to tell some lie. Make him go away."

"What truth? What lie?" the baronet demanded, glaring from one to the other.

"Nothing!" Alexandra shrieked.

"She's ruined," the calm voice went on. "I ruined her. Last night. In the li—"

"No!"

"Ruined her!" the baronet roared. His face contorted, turning nearly purple, as he launched himself at Mr. Trevel

178

yan. "I'll kill you!" he screamed. But he found he couldn't kill the wretch because his exasperating daughter had thrown herself in the way.

"No, Papa. Stop please!" She stood in front of Basil, shielding him. "The servants will hear you. Of course it's not true. You mustn't let him provoke you. He's only made this up to blackmail me, Papa." She went on babbling protestations, which was monstrous difficult when Mr. Trevelyan's finger was tracing a lazy path down her back. She sprang away when she felt a slight pressure at the base of her spine. "Stop it!" she hissed.

Luckily, Sir Charles was no longer looking at them. He was glowering at the carpet, shaking his head. "If it is a lie," he growled, "I shall call him out."

"I see your point, sir. Perhaps, then, I was exaggerating. Perhaps she isn't ruined. Still, the circumstances were exceedingly compromising—"

"Basil!"

Sir Charles considered for a moment. He looked from his daughter whose cheeks were very pink to Clementina's dreadful nephew whose colour had also deepened.

"I see," he said slowly. "I am not such a fool as all that. Why," he demanded, "would any rakehell in his senses tell your father such a thing, truth or not? Only," he answered himself, "if he was set on marrying you. If that's the case, you'd better have him, Alexandra. Either way he'll make your life a misery, but married to him you can return the favour. I wish you joy of each other, indeed I do. It's just as you deserve."

He nodded to himself with grim satisfaction, deaf to his daughter's continued pleadings and protestations.

"No, madam," he said as he absently patted the hand clutching his sleeve. "I don't want to hear any more of it. You have tired me half to death for the past six years. Now you have my leave to tire *him* for the next sixty. Let *him* worry about your admirers and infatuations from now on." He shook off his daughter's hand and marched to the door.

When Basil stepped aside to let him pass, she attempted to slip out as well.

"No," said the baronet. "You had better remain and reconcile yourself to your affianced husband. You will marry him, Alexandra—and so I shall inform your godmother. I daresay it's no news to her, the interfering jade. When you join us—both of you—I expect you to conduct yourselves with some decorum for once. I've had enough scenes for this millenium, I think." With surprising dignity, Sir Charles took himself out of the room.

When the door had closed on her Papa, Miss Ashmore turned on her latest fiancé, her green eyes blazing. "I hate you," she said. "I shall always hate you. And I will never—*never*, do you hear me?—marry you."

"No, you don't, and yes, you will," he answered composedly. "Now come, Alexandra, say something kind to me, for you've hurt my feelings dreadfully." He moved to take her in his arms, but she spun away out of his reach.

"How dare you say such things to Papa?"

"At this point, I'd dare anything. Do you think I mean to let my aunt take you back to London, where you can acquire another set of beaux for me to dispose of? I should think not. Even I would like a bit of rest now and then. I should vastly prefer resting with you in my arms," he added, very tenderly.

This brought forcibly to mind some rather delicious moments when she'd been nestled in his arms. As she felt herself weakening, she grew correspondingly cross. She moved away to take up her post before the fireplace again and frowned into the grate. "That's the worst way of offering for a woman I've ever heard," she told the grate.

"If I'd asked in the normal way, would you have accepted me?"

Yes, she thought, because I'm a fool. "No," she answered. "I couldn't. I can't."

"Why? I mean, besides the fact that you solemnly promised ages ago to jilt me."

She shot him an exasperated glance, but his horrid self-assurance was replaced by a bleak look that knocked all her angry retorts out of her. "It doesn't matter," she said.

In a few steps he crossed the room to stand at her shoulder. "It does matter. Tell me why. And tell me the truth, for once."

She was silent for a moment. There was an ache in her throat, a terrible ache. Really, it should not be so very painful, this process of sparing oneself future pain. Nonetheless, the tears welled up and trembled on her lashes as though to keep the ache company.

"Why?" he asked again. "You might do me the courtesy of telling me why you're so determined to make me wretched."

"You? It's you who'll make *me* wretched," she blurted out past the ache and the tears. "Because there'll always be one temptation or another you can't resist. Oh, Basil, maybe now you think you want me, but in time you'll be bored. How am I to bear that?"

"I see. You're fully convinced that I should make a thoroughly unreliable, unfaithful, neglectful husband."

She nodded miserably.

"Whereas you, on the other hand, would be the ideal wife. Sweet and biddable, never thinking of manipulating her besotted spouse to get her own way. The very soul of honesty who'd scorn to tell her husband even the smallest fib. Certainly he need never worry about all the eager gentlemen clustered about his wife. Your spouse would never have to live in your pocket, for fear of other gentlemen's dishonourable intentions."

Her eyes, still fixed on the grate, opened very wide.

"No, really," he continued, "there's nothing at all daunting in the prospect of marrying the most desirable woman in England, not even though she happens to be dreadfully clever and manipulative besides. Not at all. I'm certain Napoleon's Grand Army might have managed such a business if, that is, they kept well together."

"What," she asked fiercely as she turned to him, "are you implying?"

"I wasn't implying anything. I was telling you straight out. The idea of marrying you frightens me out of my wits. Unfortunately, I'm so desperately in love with you that I must or shoot myself."

Love. He'd spoken tender words last night, the sweet words that came so easily to him, but he'd never uttered a syllable about love.

He was still speaking. "I offer you my very small, very vulnerable, fragile, nearly breaking heart. You trample on it, and remind me that I'm a villain. Well, so what if I am? I'm the villain who's compromised you—not once but several times—and I'm the one who loves you." He pulled her to him. "And I'm the one you're stuck with, because your Papa says so. I wish you'd stop quarrelling with me and kiss me." He must have thought better of it, because he kissed *her* instead.

Recognising that the odds were against her, Miss Ashmore very sensibly yielded to her opponent. In the true British spirit of good sportsmanship, she returned his kiss with enthusiasm. The victor generously returned hers, so she was obviously obliged to return his. So it continued for some minutes until the two found themselves in danger of committing a great impropriety. To her credit, Miss Ashmore became conscious of the peril in time and pulled away from him.

He swore under his breath. "What a curst business this is," he muttered. "Why did I have to fall in love with a proper young lady and be doomed to these furtive escapades in other people's houses? Halls. Libraries. Studies. What next? Shall we rendezvous in the kitchens after midnight? Or will you meet me in the stables?"

"The stables?" she repeated, greatly indignant.

"Sorry. I wasn't thinking. Or I wasn't thinking what I ought. The trouble is, I paced the library all night, and it was cold and lonely without you. I missed you horribly. Then I had to wait ages before your Papa was up. The waiting was horrible. I nearly hung myself."

She'd been about to read him a lecture about his fiancé not being a common lightskirt to be tumbled about in hayracks. The lecture flew out of her head as she gazed up wonderingly into those beautifully wicked amber eyes. "Were you lonely for me, Basil? Really?"

"Good God. For such an intelligent woman you can be remarkably stupid, my love. Did you think I wanted you to leave?"

"You were very abrupt, Basil, and you did push me out the door."

"The only way I know to resist temptation is to remove it.

That should have been obvious. If it wasn't—well, I take back what I said earlier. You *are* stupid. You're the stupidest woman it's ever been my misfortune to fall in love with.'' To emphasise the point, he kissed her once more very lingeringly. As this promised to bring them both into difficulties again, she pushed him away.

"We can't stay here all day," she warned, as she stooped to gather up her wayward hairpins. "Papa's expecting us to join him and Aunt Clem.''

Basil relieved his feelings with a few more quiet oaths as he helped her find her hairpins and restore herself to a semblance of respectability. Finally, the two went forth to face his aunt.

Whatever story was told to Lady Bertram and Sir Charles must have been satisfactory. In another hour, host, hostess, and guests were gathered in the drawing room, listening as Sir Charles—with fiendish relish—informed one and all that his daughter and Clementina's nephew were to be shackled for the rest of their natural, or unnatural was more like it, lives.

Lord Tuttlehope was so astonished that he forgot to blink. *"Marry* her?" he said to his wife. "Is that what he says?"

"Yes, dear," Alicia answered with a giggle. "Isn't it delicious?"

Evidently her husband didn't think so, for when he later offered his congratulations to his friend, Lord Tuttlehope's speech had the lugubrious ring of condolences.

"You might look a little more cheerful when you wish me happy, Freddie," said Basil biting back a grin. "I'm not going to be hung, you know—only married.''

Lord Tuttlehope appeared to think it was quite the same thing. He manufactured an awful smile. "But Trev. You? Can't believe it. Sorry." Distractedly he put out his hand. "Happy. And all that.''

Mr. Trevelyan returned the handshake with all due solemnity.

"But Trev. Thought you hated her.''

"Well, I don't. That wouldn't be a very promising way to commence wedded life, would it? Come, Freddie, don't look so tragic. You're married and happy, aren't you?''

"Course I'm happy. But you're different, Trev," Lord Tuttlehope noted mournfully.

"Yes," Basil agreed. "So is *she.*"

Lord Arden, for other reasons, looked equally pitying.

"Poor fellow," he said, clapping Basil on the shoulder. "You should have heeded your own advice, I think." He glanced past his erstwhile rival towards Miss Ashmore who was surrounded by a group of happy ladies, including his irritating sister. "Still, it's a beautiful trap for all that. Indeed, I do wish you the best of luck, Trev." His gaze turned back to Basil, looking, he thought, rather feral. "You'll need it, you know. Just as you said. Do not be surprised if you see me in my hunting pinks." With that and a brief, mocking bow the marquess left to offer his best wishes to the bride-to-be.

Mr. Trevelyan smiled easily enough as he turned to his cousin who had joined him, champagne bottle in hand. "What a troublesome business this marriage business is, Edward. I'm not even wed yet, and the gentlemen are already announcing their designs on my wife."

"Very gracious of them it is, I must say," was the dry reply. "Will takes his defeat philosophically enough. I'd have thought he'd rather put a bullet through your scheming brain. But tell me," the earl went on, dropping his voice as he refilled his and his cousin's glasses, "what did happen when you met up with him? Did you treat him to one of your gypsy fortune-teller performances like the one you used on my wife? One of your twisted tragic tales?"

"Cuz, you cut me to the quick. I simply told the man the Truth, plain and unvarnished."

"Did you now? Well, it was what he wanted after all. He didn't need even to wring it out of you, did he? Still, I do wonder how you managed to convince that lovely, intelligent girl to trust her future to you. But why do I ask? 'Thou hast damnable iteration, and art indeed able to corrupt a saint.' "

"How you flatter me, my lord."

"For the first and I hope the last time. Well then, cuz," said Lord Hartleigh, raising his glass, "here's to your damnable iteration or the Truth or whatever it is. And though you don't deserve it a bit, I do wish you happy."

20

A month later a newlywed couple sat in a large bed in the most luxurious bedroom of a select, outrageously expensive inn some miles from London. The groom, still partially dressed, leaned back against the pillows inspecting the ring on his wife's finger. She sat watching him, her chestnut curls all unpinned and tumbling in gay abandon about her face.

"I have a wife," Basil said at last, softly and wonderingly. "How very odd."

She looked a little anxious as she asked, "Is it, dear? I know you never meant to have one."

"Didn't I? Well, how stupid of me, to be sure. When I think what might have happened if you hadn't managed to seduce me that night in the library—"

"I did not," she interrupted indignantly, "seduce you."

"You would have, if I hadn't such a scrupulous regard for my virtue. You knew I was exhausted, and therefore in a vulnerable condition, and you attempted to take selfish advantage of my weakness."

"Oh, I see. And which weakness was that? You have so many it's hard to tell."

"A weakness," he said, bringing the hand he held to his lips, "for naughty chestnut curls that will not stay properly pinned. A weakness for green eyes." He kissed each fingertip in turn.

"What a shallow fellow you are, sir. Any woman might have seduced you—and no doubt will, in future."

"Oh, ye of little faith. To speak so, after you've done everything possible to enslave me utterly." Abruptly he dropped her hand, got off the bed, and picked up his coat from the floor.

"What are you doing, Basil? You're not leaving—"

"Hardly." He fished out a much-creased letter from the coat pocket and carried it back to the bed with him. As his wife watched with growing impatience, he settled himself comfortably again.

"Well?"

"Well." He dangled the folded letter before her eyes. "Do you know what that is?"

"Whatever it is, it appears to have been rather knocked about. What is it, Basil? A love letter from one of your high flyers?"

"You might say that."

As he slowly unfolded the sheets, she gasped. "That's my writing," she cried. "What is it?"

" 'My dearest Aunt Clem,' " he began, " 'I am so sorry to trouble you with this absurdity, but matters here have, I think, got out of hand—' " He broke off as his wife tried to snatch the letter from him. "Oh, no," he told her, holding it out of her reach, "I haven't kept it so safely and tenderly all this time that you might tear it to pieces, my darling. Besides, I know it by heart."

"Where did you get that?"

"It was sent me. By my dearest Auntie."

"Aunt Clem sent it to you? When?"

"When I was in Greece."

Though she was a married lady of some hours, Alexandra could still blush. Recalling some of the comments in that letter, she did so now. "In Greece," she echoed faintly.

"Yes. Aunt Clem is monstrous underhanded, you know. Anyhow," he went on, allowing the letter to drop gently to the floor, "I read it and was lost utterly. Your brutally comic description of Randolph and his odious family. As you listed everything that you'd tried and failed with your Papa—well, I felt rather a kinship with you, you know. And then I saw you, dirty and bedraggled in that crowded room. You were so beautiful in spite of it. You knew immediately what I was about and played your part so well. You acted to admiration,

186

my love. I very nearly believed my own lie. Naturally, when I kissed you, I sealed my fate. What could be more romantic?"

His beloved was staring at the bedpost. "You don't mean to say that Aunt Clem deliberately—but no, how could she? How could she possibly guess—"

"Oh, she didn't guess, my love. She knew we were meant for each other. Aunt Clem sees all, knows all. And knowing her, she had Maria in it as well. My precious," he cried as he flung himself back upon the pillows, his hand clutched to his breast, "we're the victims of a conspiracy. You and I— as wicked a set of connivers as ever walked this great island— the innocent victims of an unscrupulous pair of matchmakers. *Matchmakers*, Alexandra. How lowering."

The bride transferred her gaze from the bedpost to her groom. "Lowering? I should say so. I never had the trace of a suspicion. Good grief. And your aunt let me go through all that horrendous business."

"Hasn't a conscience, dear. Runs in the family."

"Is that so?" The green eyes narrowed. "Just how long have you known about this?"

"If you keep on looking at me like that I shall scream. It makes my blood curdle. Really it does." He manoeuvred himself into more comfortable proximity to his lovely wife. "I assure you I feel as stupid as you do. It never occurred to me. In all my frenzy of jealousy and scurrying hither and yon and plotting, there was no room in my brain for my aunt. Once again she has triumphed over me. I suppose I shall have to endure it, just as I endured my gloomy exile." In proof of this stoic determination, he dropped several lingering kisses upon his wife's creamy shoulder.

"Poor Basil. It was none of your doing, was it? But all these wicked females taking advantage."

He murmured an unintelligible reply from the nape of her neck.

"It was I who trapped you, was it? Caught you in my wicked toils? Compromised you?"

"Well, I helped," he admitted. "Because I'm so gallant, you know."

"Oh yes, poor dear."

"At any rate, thanks to Aunt Clem, I've had a month to become reconciled to my fate. We could have had a perfectly acceptable ceremony the next day. Edward had only to use his influence for a special licence. But no. A big wedding, says my aunt, is the only recompence for not giving you a proper comeout."

"It has been a very long time," said his wife. "I've nearly forgotten what it was like exactly. Compromising you, I mean."

"What a shocking poor memory you've got, madam. You've even forgotten that you never did accomplish my ruination. I suppose," he breathed, as he pulled her face down to his, "I shall have to spend the rest of my life helping you remember these . . . matters."

She sighed, and in a very bored and weary sort of way, agreed, "Yes, my love, and how very tiresome for you—"

She was permitted to say no more . . . and very soon thereafter was so agreeably occupied that she forgot what she'd intended to say.